For Better, For Worse

For Better, For Worse

Carole Matthews

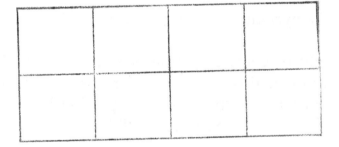

W F HOWES LTD

This large print edition published in 2006 by
W F Howes Ltd
Unit 4, Rearsby Business Park, Gaddesby Lane,
Rearsby, Leicester LE7 4YH

1 3 5 7 9 10 8 6 4 2

First published in the United Kingdom in 2000
by Headline

A CIP catalogue record for this book is available
from the British Library

ISBN 1 84632 330 4

Typeset by Palimpsest Book Production Limited,
Polmont, Stirlingshire
Printed and bound in Great Britain
by Antony Rowe Ltd, Chippenham, Wilts.

To Kevin

For coming into my life and showing me the love I always hoped existed . . .

CHAPTER 1

'I still think about you.' There was a pause in which Josie presumed she was supposed to say something. 'A lot,' Damien added when she didn't.

Josie closed her eyes, marvelling at the red splotches inside the lids, and sighed at the telephone. 'I think about you a lot too, Damien. But it mainly involves dreaming up ways of inflicting pain on you.' Axe through the head, winning the lottery, and Ewan McGregor falling desperately in love with her were the ones which currently featured most. 'Funnily enough, rather like you did to me.'

She twisted a strand of her boring brown hair through her fingers and considered, not for the first time, getting it dyed one of those vibrant, fashionable colours much vaunted in make-over programmes. Would she look good as a Fiery Chestnut? Possibly. But it might be better with a more radical haircut than a neat bob that was more conservative than William Hague. Did they do a Brunette Bombshell? Would it transform her life to switch to Brazen Ebony? Whichever way,

1

the hair she'd currently got needed washing. Another chore to add to the growing list of things she had to do tonight, and none of them involved wasting time talking to Damien. She wriggled her toes and eased the dead weight of her cat from her foot before he made it completely numb. The Cat Formerly Known As Prince gave her a look that would have turned ten blackbirds to stone. Josie blew him a kiss as he strutted into the kitchen, outraged tail flicking the air.

'I never meant to hurt you,' Damien continued, intent, it seemed, on having his say.

'Coming out with "I'm in love with someone else, goodbye" generally does.'

'We should have talked things through.'

'Damien, the first I knew about it was when you came down with a packed suitcase. I thought you were off to a computer conference in Margate or somewhere. I didn't expect you to end our marriage at nine o'clock on a Monday morning.' Particularly not after we'd made love the night before and reached simultaneous orgasm – both of which were very unusual for a Sunday. 'You wouldn't talk about anything. Not even who would get custody of the cat. You breezed out as if you were going to buy a loaf.'

'I don't know what came over me,' her husband said. 'One minute I was happy, the next I wasn't.'

'"Thing" came over you,' Josie said. 'Thing and her double-D cleavage and Lycra leopardskin-effect thongs.' (Yes, I have been to her house and peered over her garden wall. I know she has a rusting whirligig with two bits of wire missing and pegs that don't match, showing a carelessness in the laundry department that you would never have tolerated from me!)

'It wasn't simply about Melanie.'

Melanie, Josie mimicked, pulling a face fit to sour milk down the phone.

'Although, I admit, she was the catalyst.'

Catalyst? Home-wrecker!

'I feel as if I have made an awful mistake,' Damien said. 'A really awful mistake.'

'And how's that supposed to make me feel? I'm just getting my life back together. I no longer need a ton of Kleenex just to watch *EastEnders*. I am no longer emaciated and blotchy and look like I have some deadly disease. Strangers no longer shy away from me in the street. Friends have stopped telling me that I really should see the doctor. I'm happy.'

'Are you?'

'Yes.' It came across as a little too defiant to ring true.

'I'm not.'

There was another uncomfortable pause.

'How's The Cat Formerly Known As Prince?' he said more brightly.

'He's delirious. Eating his Kit-e-Kat like there's no tomorrow. He's coping very well with being a single-parent feline.'

'Good.' Damien didn't sound as if he thought it was good.

3

'What's it like being a substitute daddy?'

Damien exhaled slowly. 'Tougher than I thought.'

Josie smirked to herself.

'The kids put Lego in unspeakable places, I've just had to spend an inordinate amount of money getting Farley's Rusks extracted from my laptop, and they leave toast crumbs in the bed. Most nights, it feels like I'm sleeping in Prince's litter tray.'

I bet that curtails the wild sex sessions that were much vaunted in the early days!

'Does Thing know you phone me?'

She heard Damien bite his nails. Something he always did when he was contemplating lying. 'No.'

'So where is she now?'

'At Tesco's. Late-night shopping.'

Whoop-de-doo! And I thought my life was boring!

'Did you tell her the divorce papers have come through?'

More nail-nibbling. 'No.'

'You haven't sent them back yet?'

'No.'

The Cat Formerly Known As Prince started a hearty wail at the kitchen door. Josie put her hand over the mouthpiece. 'I'll be two minutes,' she whispered. 'You won't starve.'

The Cat Formerly Known As Prince gave her a look that said, If-I-could-use-a-tin-opener-I'd-be-out-of-here.

'Is it really what we want?' Damien was using his best cajoling voice. The one he used to reserve for getting her out of bed at the weekends to make him bacon sandwiches. 'Really and truly?'

'Even as we speak, mine are languishing with Live It Up, Live It Down and Live With It – or something like that – solicitors to the terminally impoverished. Just sign them, Damien.'

'I don't think we should rush into this.'

'You already did.'

'I don't deserve this, Josie. You can't throw five years of marriage down the drain.'

You did. I can.

'Can't I come round to see you?'

'I won't be here.'

'Where are you going?'

'That's nothing to do with you.'

'I'm still your husband.'

'Only due to a minor technicality.' Josie sat up and made shushing noises at the cat, who was whimpering, producing puddles of drool on the floor and looking like he was about to start foaming at the mouth. 'Look, I have to go.'

'Why?'

'I have my own life now, Damien.'

'Is there someone else?'

Josie examined the tart red nail varnish on her toes with the bravado of someone feigning disinterest. It needed redoing before tomorrow. Tart red and the lilac chiffon that was looming on the agenda were not *Looking Good*'s idea of trendy. The Cat Formerly Known As Prince had hurled himself to the floor in desperation.

'Yes.'

'Is it serious?'

'We spend a lot of time together.'

'Oh.'

'Is he handsome?'

'Yes.'

'Oh.'

'I have to go. I'm having dinner with him tonight.'

'Oh.' There was an unhappy little gap. 'Do you love him?'

'I don't want to be having this conversation, Damien.' It was making an already leaden heart feel heavier.

'Is he rich?'

'Damien, I think it would be better if you didn't keep ringing me.'

'I don't want you out of my life.'

The corners of her mouth turned down and she bit her lip, pushing down the emotions that threatened to sneak back up whenever she wasn't looking. 'I already am.'

She put down the receiver and hugged a cushion. Cushions were a luxury she was allowed now that she made all her own choices regarding domestic soft furnishings. Damien had deemed them banned substances along with hanging baskets, wicker laundry hampers and cardigans. They all smacked of being middle-aged, he insisted, and that was something he intended to avoid at all costs. Consequently, she had endured an uncosy sofa for too long, and now it was piled high with the beggars.

The phone rang again, shrill and persistent. The Cat Formerly Known As Prince was turning himself inside out on the lounge carpet, doing his starving-animal impersonation to Oscar-winning proportions. If only Kenneth Branagh had been here to see it, he would have feared for his livelihood. The phone continued to ring and Josie chewed the end of her cushion, settling into a frown of indecision. She'd had enough of Damien. He was comparable to eating an elephant these days, only manageable in bite-sized chunks. The Cat Formerly Known As Prince gave her a look that said, Oh-for-fornication's-sake-answer-it! Josie snatched up the receiver.

'Da—'

'Why did you take so long to answer the phone?'

Josie let go of her death grip on the hapless cushion and fell back on to the sofa. This was a conversation which could only be attempted while horizontal and preferably with a large gin at her fingertips. 'Hello, Mum.'

'You haven't been talking to that low-life scheming toad again?'

'My bank manager?'

'No, that miserable excuse of an ex-husband.'

'Mum—'

'You were engaged for a very long time.'

'We were married for five years.'

'You know what I'm talking about.' Her mother

harrumphed down the phone. 'I know what you're like. Three little words from him and you'll be running back to him with your skirt round your waist and your knickers round your ankles. If you're wearing any.'

'Mum!'

'He was never good enough for you.'

'Mum! No one was. You hated all of my boyfriends.'

There was a hurt silence at the other end of the phone. 'I liked Clive.'

'Clive?'

'Clive was very nice. In an unassuming way.'

'I never went out with anyone called Clive!'

'Yes you did,' her mother tutted. 'He was lovely. Always wore a scarf.'

'I never, ever went out with anyone called Clive.'

'He drove an Austin Allegro. Orange. His father's.'

'You must be thinking about someone else.'

'Perhaps you should have married Clive. He didn't look like the sort who would have abandoned you for a whiff of knicker elastic.'

There was no Clive. No scarf. No Austin Allegro.

'Mind you, your father was the same. Sex, sex, sex. Morning, noon and night. It was all he ever thought of.'

Her father had never ventured further than his potting shed for thirty years and always seemed rather more preoccupied with his pelargoniums than carnal pleasures. He had, however, in his quiet way managed to curb her mother's worst excesses, which had run riot since he was no longer with them.

'I blame all those women who burnt their bras; he was never the same man after that.'

Josie counted to four – ten was asking just too much. 'I was cooking dinner.'

'What?'

'When you rang. I was cooking dinner. The microwave pinger's just gone off. I'd better go or it'll burn, or melt, or disintegrate.'

'You're not having chicken ping again, are you?'

'No, I've pushed the boat out and have gone for Italian ping.'

'I do worry about you, darling.'

'I know.' But then you worry about the western hemisphere and nine tenths of its occupants in general.

'Are you all set for tomorrow?'

Josie eyed the packed suitcase in the corner nervously. There was no way she would want her mother to know that she was having second thoughts about this. It was the first time she had travelled alone in her new nearly divorced state, and her stomach registered a mixture of fear and excitement. She would get to look after the tickets, passports and money all by herself, instead of it being Damien's job. And she wondered how she would manage her luggage by herself before deciding it would be easier to control an airport trolley with a mind of its own rather than a man with one.

'I think so.'

'Now you won't forget anything, will you?'

'I shall do my very best not to.'

'There's no need to be facetious. You know I had to tie your gloves to your school mac with elastic because you were always leaving them behind. If I had a pound for every pair of woollen mittens you'd lost, I'd be living next door to Barbra Streisand now.'

'Yes, Mum.'

The Cat Formerly Known As Prince was looking as though he regretted telling her to answer the phone. She gave him an I-told-you-so stare.

'I have to go. The cat wants his dinner.'

'You spoil that animal.'

'I have no one else to lavish my love on.'

'You've got me.'

'Apart from you.'

'I do hope you find someone soon. I'd make a lovely grandmother.'

'Mum! That is the least of my worries at the moment. There's no way I'm ready for a committed relationship.'

'Even some casual sex would be a start—'

'Mum!'

'I know all about condoms. Mrs Kirby at the chemist told me about them when I was waiting for my Preparation H. Never go out with a man who buys small ones.'

'I have to go, my dinner's about to spontaneously combust.'

'I wish I was coming with you.'

'It's too late for that now, Mum.'

'I should be there. I don't know why Martha had to arrange her wedding in such a rush.'

'Well, that's Martha for you. Maybe she thought he'd change his mind if she didn't dash up the aisle.'

'She has been on the shelf for a very long time,' her mother conceded.

'I don't think Martha needed to worry about getting dusty.'

'Maybe if she's waited all this time, she might get the right man first time round.'

Touché, Mother!

'I'll tell you all about it when I get back.'

'Don't agree to carry anything for anyone else. Particularly if it looks like talcum powder. It might be Class A heroin and you could end up bellydancing in a Turkish prison. I read about it all the time in *Women's Realm*. You young girls don't realise how vulnerable you are.'

'I'm not a young girl. I'm thirty-two years old. I'm a pillar of the community and have been sensible and level-headed since I was twelve. What did it always say on my school reports?'

'That you were very sensible and level-headed,' her mother conceded.

'I rest my case.'

'And don't talk to any strange men on the plane. If you're sitting next to someone who looks a bit funny, ask them to move you. They're obliged to. It's in the rules.'

'I have to go.' Conversation Termination Sequence commenced. Let countdown begin. Five. Josie edged the phone back towards its receiver.

'Give my love to everyone.'

'I will.' Four. Lower.

'Phone me when you get there, then I won't worry.'

'I will.' Three. Lower still. Looking good.

'Promise.'

'Promise.' Two.

'I love you, Josephine Ellen.'

'I love you too, Mum.' One. Made it. Handset to base. Docking completed.

Conversation Terminations successfully accomplished, Josie looked at the clock. Not bad. Approaching a world record, in fact. Pushing herself off the sofa, she noticed the cat, who was reclining weakly by the kitchen door. 'Well, you may have started out as a fake starving animal, but I'm sure your stomach thinks your throat has been cut by now.'

His pitiful meow said it did.

The phone rang again and the cat swooned. 'I knew it was too good to be true.' It rang again. 'I didn't have the run-down of all the neighbours' ailments or the latest update on the window-cleaner's love life.' It continued to ring and the cat continued to plead silently. 'I have to answer. She knows I'm here,' Josie said. It rang and rang and rang. 'I'll be *one* minute!'

Josie picked up the phone. 'Mum.'

'What sort of car does he drive?'

'Damien!'

'Is it a company car? Or is it something sporty?'

'Damien, leave me alone!'

'You've been on the phone a long time. Was it him?'

'It was my mother. Not that I have to answer to you.'

'Is he more important to you than I am?'

'Damien, flossing my teeth is more important to me than you are.'

'Oh.' She heard her ex-husband sigh heavily. 'Josie, I—'

'I'm going now, Damien. Goodbye.'

'Josie—'

Josie slammed down the receiver. The cat looked relieved. 'You and I,' she informed him, 'are going to get slaughtered.'

Josie lit the candles on the table. They were the red ones she had bought for last Valentine's Day, but they had never been used because Damien had phoned to say he was working late on a difficult project. Getting that tiny leopardskin thong off Thing's big fat bottom must have been hell. He eventually rolled up at two o'clock in the morning, pissed and reeking of perfume. (The team had been forced to go for a sociable drink in a hotel afterwards, he apologised through his hangover the next morning.) And she had eaten her lovingly prepared dinner alone.

Tonight, she put her reduced-fat, reduced-taste frozen lasagne for one on the table. The microwave had singed the corners to an appetising shade of black, rendering them as edible as paving slabs, while the middle was still white, wet and luke-warm. The lettuce was limp and two days past its sell-by date, but she wanted to clear out the fridge before she went away and had a pathological hatred of wasting food.

'Here you are, munch-machine,' she said fondly, and placed a tin of Supreme Meaty Chunks on a Royal Doulton plate on the table. It sported a bride and groom in the middle surrounded by ornate gold hearts and more flowers than you could shake a stick at. 'Time for din-dins.'

The Cat Formerly Known As Prince rubbed lovingly round her ankles, covering her black trousers with fur.

'Cupboard love,' Josie chided, sticking her fork into her lasagne with as much enthusiasm as she could muster for something that looked as tasty as wet wallpaper. It was a good sign that her appetite was coming back and she was getting tired of convenience food. Her next step in getting on with her life was to start cooking real, edible food again. Maybe even her vanished breasts might make a timely reappearance at some point.

She hated it when Damien phoned. It churned everything up that was just starting to settle down, like a riptide tugging away under the surface of a seemingly calm sea. He always managed to make her feel defensive, even though he was the one who had chosen to walk out of their marriage and it was none of his business whether she was seeing someone else or not. She could be shagging the entire England football team – and thoroughly enjoying it – and it would be nothing whatsoever to do with Damien Flynn. She took a slug of her red wine and it tasted dry and bitter. Even getting through one measly glass was going to be a struggle. There was very little fun to be had in drinking alone.

The Cat Formerly Known As Prince jumped up on to the chair and put his paws on the table. Josie sighed wistfully. The only man in her life gave an appreciative purr to show he knew which side his bread, or his Kit-e-Kat, was buttered on and buried his head in his plate, eating, as always, as if it was his last meal.

Josie flicked the CD player on. George Michael crooned out. She could listen to all manner of soppy love songs dry-eyed now, which was surely another good sign. 'Careless Whisper'. '*Guilty feet have got no rhythm . . .*' She and Damien had always danced well together, guilty feet or not.

Grief, she was exhausted. Talking to both her virtual ex-husband and her mother had used up her emergency reserves of energy. Still, she could sleep through the flight tomorrow instead of watching the cheesy films that were always out of date enough so that you'd only just seen them anyway. Pulling the chair out and arranging her napkin with an unnecessary flourish, she sat down. The cat glanced up from his meal.

'So?' she said. 'You *are* important to me. Did I lie to him?'

The Cat Formerly Known As Prince gave her a look that said he thought she probably had.

CHAPTER 2

'You're in my seat.' Josie checked the number on her boarding pass and the overhead locker again.

Man-in-her-seat was wearing a personal minidisc player, nodding vigorously and, presumably, in time to the music. Or he could have been having a fit. Either way, it made him look like the suedette Labrador her father used to have on the back shelf of his Ford Cortina which used to bob its strangely detached head erratically every time they turned a corner or hit a bump. Watching it had given her motion sickness for years. And here he was again, reincarnated in her seat. A suedette Labrador with scruffy blond hair. She wondered whether this was what her mother would class as 'funny'-looking.

'Could you sit down as soon as possible please, madam? Captain is preparing for take-off and you're blocking the aisle.'

'But . . .'

The flight attendant tutted and pushed past. Charming. She wasn't in the mood for this. Damien's call had left her unsettled and distinctly out-of-sorts. Her sleep had been restless, punctuated by dreams

17

of Damien doing cruel things to her. The final sequence had involved him pinning her to the bed, sharp claws scratching at her hair. She awoke face down in the pillow to find The Cat Formerly Known As Prince sitting on her neck and padding the back of her head to remind her that breakfast was but a hair's-breadth away. All men were the same, selfish to the end.

Josie tapped man-in-her-seat on the head with the sharp edge of her boarding pass. He looked up at that. 'Seat. Mine,' she said, pointing meaningfully. *Move.*

He pulled out one of his earplugs and examined it. 'Do you mind?' he said. 'I like watching the take-off.'

'Well . . .'

'We can swap halfway.' His mouth broke into a curling smile, which said, 'Play with me, throw my ball and I'll let you tickle my tummy.' A graduate of the Barbara Woodhouse school of charm – that was all she needed.

'Well . . .' Josie hesitated. She wanted to sit by the window. Take-off and landing were the most dangerous parts of a flight and it was always comforting to know quite how far one had to fall to one's death in the event of 'technical difficulties'. 'Okay.' She paused to let him know she was reluctant.

'Thanks. You're a pal.'

I'm not a pal. I'm a disgruntled traveller with more luggage than Joan naffing Collins, because

I'm laden with stupid wedding presents for my cousin Martha's forthcoming nuptials in New York. This is because the majority of my relatives are too tight to pay for the ticket to attend themselves and have, instead, laden me down with cut-glass fruit bowls, monogrammed towels and other sundry marital accoutrements that will lie untouched in the deep recesses of Martha's cupboards for the next twenty years. Because if there's one girl who has everything in life that she could possibly ever need, it's Martha.

Also, because I am about to be divorced, I am *off* weddings!

Man-in-her-seat plugged his mini-disc player back into his ear and resumed nodding. Charming II – the sequel. She'd only seen Madonna 'get into the groove' more than this one. Any minute now, he could whip out his air guitar for a few twangs. It was going to be a very long flight if he insisted on bobbing around like one of the Muppets all the way.

Josie huffed as she hoisted her luggage to her shoulder. And at least Joan Collins would have some minion, lackey, toy-boy-type person in tow to give her a hand. While she, Josie Flynn, thirty-two years old and soon-to-be-spinster of the parish of Camden, had no one. No one. It was worth repeating. Now that she had become a divorce statistic she, *alone*, had to cope with getting Auntie Connie's matching sheets and pillowcases to their intended destination unscathed. They were from

British Home Stores – because, as Constance pointed out, Americans like anything with the word British in it. And Josie knew in her heart of hearts that sunshine-yellow daffodils reclining on a background of cerise swirls were just not Martha's thing. At all.

Mind you, at least she hadn't had to cope with her mother as well. Josie struggled her holdall into the overhead locker, hoping she wouldn't smash the myriad ornaments with Royal Doulton stickers on them, and flopped into the vacant seat. She hoped too that she had thoroughly washed all traces of The Cat Formerly Known As Prince's Kit-e-Kat from Auntie Freda's commemorative wedding plate.

Her travelling companion seemed to pay cursory attention to the take-off he had made such a fuss about, but his eyes brightened considerably when Grumpy the air hostess rattled into view with the drinks trolley.

'Double whisky,' he said, after Josie had been handed her warm plastic bottle of Glacial Valley Naturally Carbonated Spring Water. What's Naturally Carbonated when it's at home? Did someone fart in it? Why couldn't she have a double whisky too? Because she didn't want to arrive in New York dehydrated and with hippo's feet, that's why. Josie opened the bottle and swigged from it tentatively. Glacial spring water! Gnat's pee more like. Man-in-her-seat abandoned his mini-disc and downed the whisky in one.

Josie looked sideways at him. 'Nervous flyer?'

'Terrible.' He licked the edge of his glass. 'I hope they never offer me Alan Whicker's job. The reason for this, though,' he toasted the air, 'is that I'm an unhappy and reluctant divorcee.' He smiled sadly and she noticed that he really was rather cute without the wires running into his ears. 'The decree absolute – and the solicitor's bill – hit the mat just as I left for the airport.'

'I'm sorry.'

'So am I,' he said. 'It's been ages. I thought I'd got used to the idea. Why does it still hurt?'

'Rejection always does. And letting go.' Josie reluctantly sipped the water again. 'It gets better with time.'

'I take it you speak from experience.'

'Oh yes. Been there, done that, bought the T-shirt, traded in the four-bedroom executive detached house in the suburbs for a squalid flat in Camden.'

A frown crossed his face. 'It doesn't sound like you've moved on.'

'I have,' she said, and realised that in a very small way she had. Her conversation with Damien last night had proved that she was no longer twisting and turning with the tide of his emotion. She had emotions of her own to twist and turn her. That had to be classed as an improvement.

'Well, fellow divorcee,' he raised his empty glass to her plastic bottle, 'I'm Matt Jarvis. Here's to us!'

'Josie Flynn.' She donked her bottle against it.

'So what takes you to the good old US of A, Josie Flynn?'

'Martha's wedding,' she replied. 'My cousin. Thirty-four, first time, eternal optimist.'

'Naïve.'

'No. Just convinced she's met The One.'

'Lucky girl.'

Josie shrugged. 'I'm going to be a bridesmaid.'

Matt smirked.

'Don't smirk. I thought I was too old ever to be considered bridesmaid material again. The last time, I was seven and wore lemon chiffon. I got smacked because I went playing in the mud in the churchyard while the photos were being taken and turned my new silk pumps into sow's ears.'

'What are you wearing this time?'

Josie's mouth curled down. 'Lilac chiffon.'

Matt bit his lip. 'How times change in the heady world of bridesmaid's fashions.'

'It's very nice,' she protested. 'It's just a shame it happens to be February. And it doesn't have any sleeves. Or straps. Or back.'

'Sounds very nice . . .'

Josie glared at him. 'What about you?'

'Work. I'm a music journalist for *Sax 'n' Drums and Rock 'n' Roll* magazine. It's twenty years since John Lennon died and we're doing a bumper tribute issue. I'm going out to interview the "new" Beatles for a double-page spread.' He raised his eyebrows cynically.

'Imagine,' Josie said.

'Yes, imagine. How can a bunch of uncouth, talentless youths with baseball caps and co-ordinated dance routines compare themselves with the man who single-handedly changed the face of rock and roll?'

'Didn't Paul help?'

Matt frowned at her in disgust.

'Not even a bit? Or Elvis? Didn't he have a hand in it? I believe he was quite popular at the time.'

'None of them had the sheer genius of John.'

'Oh.' She feigned interest in the Glacial Valley. 'I take it you're a fan.'

He nodded and looked round for the flight attendant. 'I take it you're not.'

'Davids always did it for me,' Josie confessed. 'Mainly Essex and Cassidy. Although I did cast many a longing glance at David Soul.'

'David Soul?'

'I know.' Josie grimaced. 'I was a teenager. I'd had a taste by-pass. It was a difficult phase in my life. I did move on to David Bowie when I grew up a bit and thought I'd become desperately sophisticated. If it had been John, Paul, George, Ringo and David, my life could have been completely different.'

Maybe if she'd married a David, rather than a Damien, her life could have been completely different too. She should have taken much more notice of *The Omen* instead of snogging in the back row with some spotty youth whose name had now been lost in the mists of time – who quite possibly could have been Clive with the scarf and the Allegro and her mother's vote, for all she knew. Yes, if she'd run a mile when she first met Damien, maybe she would be happily ensconced in the Home Counties with two cherubic children, instead of being on the very brink of divorce and scratching a meagre living teaching Information Technology and Business Studies to bored teenagers in a crumbling Camden sixth-form college. Maybe. Life could have had a fairy-tale ending with a David. Instead, Damien the Handsome Prince was found kissing someone else and in a flash of blinding light turned into Damien the Fucking Ugly Frog.

'When did yours come through?'

'What?'

'Your divorce.'

'Technically, it hasn't. I'm in the process of being unmarried at the moment. I've recently sent the papers back. Although it seems pointless paying solicitors when I never intend to enter that particular unholy state again.'

'My wife's getting married again next week. And in the same church!'

They both turned down their mouths at that.

'It hardly seems like a sufficient mourning period,' he muttered. 'She can't wait.'

'Some people like saying "forever".'

'I think it's a bit more pertinent than that.' He swallowed some more whisky. 'She's pregnant.'

Josie grimaced.

'With twins.'

'Wow.'

They both took another drink.

'At least she won't be wearing the same dress.'

They risked a smile.

Josie rested her head back on her seat. 'Love's supposed to taste sweeter second time around.'

'Do you believe that?'

'I have yet to be convinced,' she said. 'Maybe the idea is that you learn from your mistakes and choose a different type of person. Preferably one eminently more suitable than the last.'

Matt shrugged. 'Maybe we'll both be lucky enough to meet someone special someday and it'll be worth risking all that pain again.'

'Maybe.'

They looked at each other doubtfully.

'Another whisky?'

Matt nodded miserably.

'I'll join you,' Josie said.

CHAPTER 3

Josie had left London in grey drizzle and sober. Now it was hot and sunny and she was pissed. New York in February and sixty-five degrees. The red neon temperature indicator was blinking lazily at her, encouraging her eyelids to do the same. The intensity of the sun was making her feel nauseous and she was really, really glad she'd worn her big winter coat. And brought a scarf and gloves. She should never have listened to her mother regaling her with tales of predicted blizzards and temperatures of minus eight she'd inadvertently found while surfing the worldwide web for knitting patterns. Still, the bridesmaid's dress might not give her rampant hypothermia if it stayed like this. And she would be pleased for Martha if it didn't rain on her parade.

Outside John F. Kennedy airport, the queue for a yellow cab snaked interminably along the terminal building. Matt was at her elbow, weaving slightly.

'Shall we share a cab?' he suggested, struggling a little thickly over the esses.

Josie nodded, unsure that her own tongue could cope with the rigours of a 'yes'.

'What are you doing this afternoon?'

Josie intended to shrug, but she wasn't certain the movement made it to her shoulders. 'Shop. Phone my mother. Phone Martha. Let them both know I'm here in one piece. Shop.'

'We should do something together,' Matt said as they fell into their dilapidated, incense-laden cab after a thousand more whistle peeps from the Fat Cab Controller.

The driver swung out into the traffic, ignoring the obligatory blare of horns.

'Like what?'

'Liberty. While it's sunny. She looks lovely with a glint in her eye.' There was one in Matt's too.

Josie smiled her consent, although she wasn't sure her lips were in the right place. 'Why not?'

They relaxed into their fur-lined seats as the cab bounced over the concrete expansion joints in the Van Wyck Expressway and into Manhattan, where the morning sun warmed the faces of the buildings as they stretched up to reach the sky.

She loved New York. There was such a buzz to the place it felt like the pavements were charged with electricity and static crackled in the air. It was the most vibrant city on earth. She'd been here a dozen times before with Damien and with Martha – one of the bonuses of having transatlantic family – but she never tired of it. There was always something new and exciting to do – a melting pot of people and experiences. Everything here was bigger, faster, taller, louder, flashier and more technicolour than anywhere else in the world.

Matt's head was nodding sleepily in time with the bumps in the road, oblivious to the dizzying pace of life being played out around him. The cab driver wound his way through the congested streets, deeper into the heart of the city, where walking was infinitely quicker than driving. This was the first time she'd been in Manhattan alone, but she didn't feel the knot of fear she'd expected. Maybe that was because she'd found Matt – not that he was doing a great deal to help, but it was nice just having someone else there. Looking across at Matt's dozing body, she wondered if he was a seasoned traveller or whether he was just very, very drunk. Despite what he'd said about his ex-wife, he didn't seem to have a care in the world. She'd found him to be a very relaxed person and he was probably the sort who'd drive you mad if you were trying to get somewhere in a hurry or wanted a shelf put up yesterday. Josie felt very easy with him in a coupley sort of way, and she had to stop herself from thinking whether he was potential shelf-putter-upper material. She couldn't believe how long it was taking her to get used to being single again, and wondered how much longer it would be before it felt entirely natural.

Matt roused himself, staring bleary-eyed out of the window at the landmarks made familiar by too many American cop shows. The traffic had ground to a halt. 'My hotel's somewhere near here, on the next block,' he informed her. 'Why don't you drop me off now and I'll meet you down at Battery Park to catch the ferry to Liberty.' He glanced at his watch. 'In, say, an hour and a half?'

Josie regarded her watch, which wasn't much use as she was still running on time from the wrong side of the pond. 'Fine.'

Matt leaned forward. 'I'll get out here, mate,' he said and, reluctantly, the driver pulled the cab fractionally out of the traffic to give him time to make a dash for the pavement.

'I'll see you later,' Matt said.

He waved and stumbled as he staggered out of the taxi, leaving her sprawled on the back seat and with the bill.

Josie's hotel was an anonymous establishment catering for equally anonymous businessmen, who marched purposefully through the lobby in navy blue suits, clearly heading to important appointments. It reminded her of Damien. He was a navy-blue-suit man, smart to the point of catalogue model, and she'd always wished he'd let himself go a bit, occasionally have some designer stubble or a whisper of a goatee. But Damien had never been knowingly under-hair-gelled – until, of course, he ran off with Thing, who was a younger model, and saw the error of his ways and invested heavily in Tommy Hilfiger sweatshirts, Timberland boots and Caesar cropped hair. And Josie had found out his important appointments had all been not so much in local hotels as local hotel rooms. She no longer huffed at the memory. Well, not much.

Dutifully, she followed the bellboy to her room, which was big and boxy with two double beds and was scuffed round the edges as functional, work-a-day hotels are. She wandered to her window and swished back the faded net curtain, feeling the sun beat against the glass. With the entire Manhattan skyline to choose from, her view was of the air-conditioning vents of the office block opposite.

Josie closed the curtain again. It looked better mistier. The view of Manhattan was always spectacular, particularly if you were down on the ground or up in the air. Seeing it from a distance you could appreciate its full glory. Here, slap bang in the middle, it was just row after row of oppressively tall, squashed-in buildings.

She tipped effusively due to her lack of small change, and the minute the bellboy had closed the door fell gratefully on to the nearest bed. It would take nothing for her to close her eyes and slip effortlessly into the land of nod, despite the fact that the most charged city on earth crackled expectantly below her. But she had promised to ring her mother the minute she arrived. Why had she said she'd do that? Probably because it was nice to know that someone was worrying about you even if it was your mother and that was the main part of her *raison d'être*. Mother or Martha first? Pain or pleasure? Get the pain out of the way – Martha could wait.

In this modern era of technology, the phone still took an age to connect. She could imagine her mother scurrying around tidying away all trace of her early supper from the dining-room table, where she always sat to eat even though she was now alone.

'Hello?'

'Hi, Mum. Just thought I'd let you know that I've arrived safely.'

'Oh, darling! I was just beginning to worry about you.'

Josie smiled indulgently. 'Well, no need to. I'm fine.'

'What's the weather like? Is there a blizzard?'

'It's hot and sunny.'

'In February? Never!'

''Fraid so.'

'Never marry a weatherman, sweetheart. You can't believe a word they say. How was the flight? You didn't talk to any strange men?'

'One axe-murderer, two psychopaths and someone who said his hobby was eating small children.'

'You have a very cruel mouth, Josephine Flynn. You are not your mother's daughter.'

'I sat next to a very nice man.'

'How nice?'

'He wasn't a barrister, you would have hated him.'

'Barristers are very useful people to have in the family now that litigation is a fact of life.'

'I'll try to remember that.'

'I was reading the *Daily Mail* while I had my Special K this morning. Wait, I have it here . . .' Josie heard the newspaper rustle. 'Do you know a man called Bill Gates?'

'Yeeeess . . .'

'Why don't you give him a ring while you're in America?'

'I meant I know *of* him. I don't know him personally. We haven't ever been in the same room – or the same country, as far as I'm aware. I certainly haven't shared a bag of crisps with him.'

'Does that matter?'

'Potentially.'

'He's single.'

'He's married.'

'Not according to the *Mail*.'

'He's the head of Microsoft.'

'Then he'll know a lot about computers. That could be very useful in a husband too. My PC still has the flu.'

'A virus.'

'I keep getting a topless Pamela Anderson screensaver. Mind you, Kevin, the young man next door, is always very keen to pop round and see if he can help.'

'Funny, that . . .'

'So will you ring him?'

'Bill Gates? I think it's extremely unlikely. I don't even know if he lives in New York.'

'They have a phone book, don't they? Look him up.'

'Mother, he's the richest man on the planet.'

'And what's so wrong with that? You may see fit to have a Greenpeace sticker on your fridge now, but there was a time when you weren't averse to a little luxury.'

'Well, that all changed and I have to cut my cloth accordingly. I just think Bill Gates is a bit out of my league.'

'I don't know why you have such a low opinion of yourself, Josie.'

'Me neither.' It could be something to do with having my husband walk out on me for another woman, though.

'You were always the best in your ballet class.'

'I gave it up when I was five.'

'Perhaps you shouldn't have,' her mother said enigmatically.

'Well, this little call to Lavinia's Dating Agency and Counselling Service is costing me a small fortune, so I'm going to go now and enjoy myself in Manhattan.' Activate Conversation Termination Sequence. Five.

'You do that, darling,' her mother cooed. 'What are your plans?'

'Sightseeing, er, shopping . . . er, sightseeing, shopping. Shopping, definitely shopping.' There was no way she wanted her mother to get wind of Matt Jarvis. Four.

'Sightseeing or shopping?'

'A bit of both,' she said sheepishly. Three.

'How nice. I do wish I was there.'

And I'm very glad you're not. Two.

'Give Martha my love. And don't forget, Bill might be glad of a call . . .'

One. Josie hung up. Was it a severe case of disorientation brought on by jet lag, or was her mother really trying to fix her up with Bill Gates?

Josie ran her fingers through her hair and closed her eyes, stifling a yawn. She needed to sleep more than ever, but she had agreed to meet Matt and the hour was looming fast. Why? Why had she agreed to change her plans to suit someone she had merely shared a few convivial beverages with when she had vowed never to let a man rule her life again? Whether it was Bill Gates or Billy Bunter, Bill Bailey, Wild Bill Hickock or any bloody Bill. Why? Because her own plans had been lonely-little-wandering-around-on-her-own plans and thinking for one was never really what it was cracked up to be.

If singledom shopping meant that you had no one to tell you whether you looked Gwyneth Paltrow gorgeous or fat enough to need your own postcode, then singledom sightseeing was worse. How could you oooh and aaah at splendid architecture or breathtaking scenery on your own? Making furtive guttural noises on the street was likely to get you locked up, even though Benny Hill had made a career of it. Where was the joy in travelling the world if you had no one with you who cared? They'd soon get fed up of you in the staff room if you said 'Manhattan' every other word.

So Liberty it was. Did it count as a date if it took place in the afternoon, rather than over dinner? It didn't feel very datey. She had been on her own nearly six months now and it wasn't getting any easier to play the ritualised mating game that she had never previously been a part of. Since the age of fourteen, she had slipped seamlessly from one relationship straight into another. As one departed, another came along. More regularly than Virgin trains. There had been none of this delving into the chocolate box of delights, tasting as many as you liked before discarding them heartlessly in the bin of life if they didn't live up to the promise of the picture on the lid of the box. She had never been a Dairy Box sort of dater; she always liked her chocolate plain and in substantial chunks. Serial monogamist was a term invented just for her.

It was difficult to change the habit of a lifetime overnight. As her confidence in her work had grown, she seemed to have amassed a plethora of insecurities about herself in the ensuing years. Where had they come from? Was it because Damien, despite his debonair good looks, was really deeply inadequate and had taken every opportunity to discreetly undermine her? She had come to rely on him for so much that finding her own feet again was proving more difficult than she'd thought.

It wasn't that she was unattractive. On the contrary, given a bit of lip-liner, some judicious back-combing and a jagged parting in her hair, she could give any television breakfast-show presenter a run for their money. To prove it, there had been a few outings with colleagues from work that could loosely be classed as dates, and a few more 'old friends' who had appeared out of the woodwork when the glad tidings of her divorce had reached their ears, but nothing that had reached the dizzy heights of 'going back to his place for coffee' or, heaven forbid, waking up in bed entangled with a man and an unintentional jagged parting.

It was scary to be single again – in a curiously liberating way. But there had been no one that she remotely fancied – if that was a term that could still be applied when you were over the hill of thirty. So there hadn't been the angst involved in hoping that the person you'd fallen in love with would fall in love with you back. She wouldn't have most men with a bow tied round them. You only had to look round the staff room at work; all the single blokes had bald pates, and pot bellies that would look cute on Vietnamese pigs but not on school teachers of a certain age. There were just no decent-looking men left any more. It was official: the new millennium was a crumpet-free zone. Apart from Damien, who was just too damn handsome for his own good and knew it. And Matt Jarvis, who was handsome in a scruffy, unkempt way and was totally unaware of it. Perhaps that was why she was attracted to him.

Josie forced her eyelids open against the pressing weight of jet lag. She'd have to go and have a quick run round a cold shower. There was no time to do anything to tart herself up, and besides, Matt was pissed and probably wouldn't notice anyway. And she wondered, with an unhappy little lurch, whether he would even remember that he had invited her at all.

CHAPTER 4

Damien did not do drunk well. He did not turn into one of those singing, happy people who wanted to be everyone's friend. Damien did maudlin drunk, and he was currently doing it at Alison Williams' leaving do.

The lovely but rather inebriated Alison had, until today, worked in the Human Resources department at PowerConnect, where Damien was Marketing Manager. From the start of the evening, she had made it abundantly clear to Damien that human resources were at the very forefront of her mind. Alison's low-cut leanings had let him know she was available to satisfy his every whim, and her forehead had 'doormat' stamped slap-bang in the middle. Damien had done 'interested' and 'available' and look where that had got him. Now he wanted 'completely uninterested' and 'out of reach', very badly.

Alison was weaving in front of him, bottle of Budweiser clutched in each hand, looking desperate, and Damien realised with something approaching alarm that it was the first time a nineteen-year-old had thrown herself at him and he hadn't the slightest inclination to throw himself back.

It had been the same when he was a child. Everyone had a Tonka truck before he did, and he had craved a sleek black number with a slavering desire that took him on frequent detours on his way home from school past Frimley's toy shop to stare greedily at it, until, at long last, he had been bought one for his birthday. The truck entertained him royally for two weeks and then the sight of its over-engineered gleaming paintwork started to pall. And no matter how hard he tried, he couldn't get rid of it. It was indestructible – that was the appeal and the whole focus of Tonka's marketing campaign. An Action Man could be obliterated in seconds with a strategically placed banger, but this damnably robust little monster just kept coming back for more. How could he move on to the next bigger and better thing when there was absolutely nothing wrong with the one he had? And what on earth was the point in having a toy that you couldn't destroy?

Things hadn't changed much in adult life. The grass always started off very much greener on the other side, but invariably it developed tenacious weeds, first one, then a whole bunch, and then promptly died before your very eyes if you didn't give it due care and attention.

'Cheer up, mate.' Mike slapped him on the back. 'It might never happen.'

Damien tipped his bottle of beer into his mouth. 'That's what worries me.'

Mike was Manager of Operations. Damien's colleague, his squash partner, his affair alibi – which had been reciprocated on more than one occasion – and as close a friend as Damien ever allowed anyone to be.

Mike jumped on to the bar stool next to Damien. 'Where's the beautiful pouting Melanie tonight?'

'She had to go straight home. No babysitter.'

'What a dastardly turn of events,' Mike commiserated. 'That means you'll have to go to Alison's foam party alone.'

'Foam party?' Damien curled his lip. 'Why the fuck would I want to go to a foam party?'

'Have you been to one before?'

'No.'

'Then you must go, my sad and lonely friend, because it is there to be experienced.'

'I haven't jumped off a cliff before and I wasn't planning to just because it's there "to be experienced".'

'Ah, but at a foam party nothing will get broken.'

'It will if Melanie finds out I went without her.'

Mike shook his head. 'This young lady keeps you on a very short leash. How would you ever have become entangled with her if your wife had kept you so confined?'

'I don't know, mate, but I'm beginning to wish she had.' Why was he sitting in this sticky-carpeted bar pining for evenings spent lying quietly on the sofa with Josie? Why now? When he could have done that every night, he had hated the prospect of enforced intimacy and had spent all his time and energy trying to avoid it. Oh perversity, thy name is man!

'I hear a pipe and matching slippers are very inexpensive these days, Damien old man. Perhaps you should consider a suitable purchase in the not too distant future. Tartan is rather fetching, I believe.'

Damien sneered. 'I think that particular state of affairs will be a long time coming.'

'Time has a nasty habit of creeping up on all of us. A few short years ago I was a man with money to spend on mere fripperies, now I spend it all on school uniforms and Reebok trainers, Playstations and mountain bikes with active suspension. How I wish I could go for a pint on a Sunday lunchtime! Instead I mow the car and wash the grass and the only screwing that ever gets done at the weekend is the type that B&Q approve of.' Mike tipped his empty beer bottle upside down and let the remaining drips splash on to the bar towel. 'Let's go to the foam party, if only for my sanity's sake. I need to know what street cred feels like if you're over five.'

'All right,' Damien relented unhappily, wondering if Josie's new bloke would be the type to go to foam parties. 'But I have to go and make a telephone call. Apparently, there's an urgent presentation I suddenly have to get ready for tomorrow or my job's on the line.'

Mike winked encouragingly. 'That's the spirit!'

'And don't wink at me,' Damien moaned. 'I don't want Available Alison spreading the rumour that I'm gay just because I don't fancy going to bed with her.'

The music was loud enough to make your ears bleed. It was that awful house or garage or some other bloody residential building stuff that knocked your brain against your skull from the inside out. There were some half-naked women gyrating on podiums suspended above the dance floor, which lifted the appeal of the otherwise sleazy hellhole. At least he could distract himself by looking up their skirts. Weren't women permanently cold these days? Damien wished he'd brought some ear plugs – he'd got millions of those rigid yellow things they gave away free on planes that he'd never used. He looked at his watch. It was a platinum Rolex, obtained by outstripping all sales targets with last year's punchy PowerConnect marketing campaign. It was during the aftermath of the celebrations of said promotion that Damien first exchanged longing looks and, subsequently, tongues with Melanie, who had been in the realms of day-dream until then. When the champagne had been drunk and the party-poppers popped, it had seemed the inevitable thing to do. Damien liked looking at his watch a lot – it reminded him he was a young, thrusting executive – but not when it moved round this slowly. Mike, who had probably grown a beard since he went to the bar, appeared and pushed two bottles of Becks into his hand.

'Thought it would save queuing again.'

Damien nodded and put a bottle to his mouth. The beer was warm and flat and he could taste dust round the rim of the neck. The platinum Rolex was showing 11.30 p.m. He was far too old to be going out at this time of night and should by rights be climbing up the stairs to Bedfordshire ready to enjoy carnal knowledge with a warm, soft body. But he had gone off the warm, soft body presently waiting for him and hoped she would be sound asleep when he eventually got home.

Where was Josie now? He hoped she wasn't sharing another convivial dinner with Mystery Man and preparing to slip between cool, crisp sheets with him. Damien glared at his beer; it tasted like shit. How could he ever have imagined he was better off without her? Would it be too sad to go and sit outside her house just to be close to her and possibly see any shadows bouncing round the bedroom? Yes, Damien decided. Far too sad.

'Let's dance!' Mike shouted. 'Alison's waiting!'

Alison was indeed waiting. She was wiggling her small, youthful bottom about seductively. It depressed Damien intensely. The music pounded louder, making his veins ache, and fluffy white bubbles of foam started to pump vigorously out of unseen orifices around the dance floor, enveloping the legs of those who were careless enough to stand before it. The flashing lights changed its colour to pink and green and yellow, making the foam look like a puddle of technicolour vomit.

Peter from Purchasing was smearing handfuls of foam over Alison's jutting breasts while she still stared hopefully and directly at Damien. His feet were leaden and nothing, it seemed, would coerce them into moving. Not even the potential of a commitment-free fondle. Mike dived into the foam, waving his beer above his head and jumping happily around, oblivious to the fact that he was the only person in the place dancing like Cliff Richard.

There were girls with very little clothing on, and lots of drunk, scruffy men smoking spliffs. Damien looked down at his designer shoes and his designer socks and his designer suit and his designer watch. It was just past midnight. Misery rushed down on him like a landslide. He didn't know where he wanted to be any more, but he was bloody sure it wasn't up to his knees in foam.

CHAPTER 5

Journeys on the New York subway were always fraught with tension. It seemed to be home to more lunatics per square inch than most self-respecting asylums could ever dream of. Clearly Care in the Community American-style. Josie was lurking nervously with her Metrocard, trying to work out exactly what she should do with it, primarily because her hotel was on the corner of Fifty-first and Lexington, and trying to take a cab through the log-jammed traffic at this time of day was the action of the certifiably insane. There was no way that she could meet up with Matt at the allotted time otherwise – and it suddenly seemed very important that she did.

The worst thing about the subway, apart from the copious nutters, was that Josie never quite knew whether she was going uptown or down-town or whether she would get off at the wrong place, i.e. somewhere positively dangerous where even seasoned tourists weren't supposed to be. If you waved your subway map around, you might as well be standing there shouting, 'MUG ME!' On previous visits she'd always had Damien or

Martha's arm to cling on to. This was the first time she'd done it alone and it had suddenly become a snarling, grinding, clanking mess of metalwork that made the London Underground look like something that had chugged in from Toytown.

It was with some relief that she finally arrived at Bowling Green station, nursing her handbag and a growing headache, but still in one piece. As her next pang of anxiety focused on the fact that Matt might not have kept his side of the bargain and could at this moment very well be passed out in a drunken stupor on his hotel bed, she pushed out of the turnstiles into the fresh winter air. Liberty alone would be fine.

There was a hardy sprinkling of T-shirt vendors who hadn't fled to Florida in the fall, lining the paths in Battery Park beneath the skeletal trees, and an optimistic steel band playing, 'Meet Me In St Louis, Louis', too fast to be considered skilful.

Matt, as promised, was waiting in front of the ticket office, kicking nervously at the ground vaguely in time with the music. Josie hadn't realised quite how relieved she would be to see him standing there. Reliability – becoming increasingly rare in men, as it is in dishwashers. He was wearing a long, army-type coat that smacked of rock journalist, with a scarf slung loosely round his neck. His hands were pushed deep into his pockets and he looked like he wished he had something to lean on. She noted that his face lit up when he saw her.

'You came,' he said with an uncertain smile.

'So did you.'

'I thought you might have changed your mind.'

'I did. Four hundred times.'

He laughed.

'I thought you might have passed out.'

'God, was I so drunk?' Matt cringed. 'I'm sorry. I'm not a great drinker.'

'You seemed to be making a fine job of it. I thought if you hadn't passed out you might have forgotten.'

'I never forget. Even under the influence of extreme alcohol, I have the memory of an er . . . er . . . an er . . .'

'Elephant?'

'That's the one.'

'I bet you have a headache.'

'A shocker,' Matt agreed. The last few stragglers boarded the boat to Liberty. 'The ferry's about to go. I didn't dare buy tickets in case it was a jinx and you might not show up. Still want to go?'

'Yes.' Josie nodded.

He grabbed her hand and gave it a quick squeeze. 'Come on. We need to run.'

Matt bought their ferry tickets hurriedly, just in time to catch the current sailing, and they ran breathlessly across the courtyard still hand in hand as the captain began to hoist up the gangway. He waited, smiling indulgently at them.

'Come on, love birds,' he urged them. 'Time and tide wait for no man, not even young guys like you!'

Matt led Josie to the back of the ferry and held her waist as it lurched inelegantly out into the choppy grey waters of the bay. The noise of the rushing wind made it impossible to talk without shouting, so they stood in silence on the deserted deck, watching Battery Park bob rhythmically out of view and the Manhattan skyline shrink to a less neck-aching size.

Matt looked like his hangover had seriously started to set in. The cold wind on the ferry whipped spitefully at them, pinching his pale cheeks to pink and ruffling his spiky hair, which already looked in need of a good comb. His eyes were twinkly blue, the colour of the unreal sky above them, if a little dulled and red-rimmed by the long flight and an adequate sufficiency of neat whisky. He was tall, slim – too slim to be considered athletic, but not skinny – and slightly awkward in his stance. Perhaps he had been taller than his school friends and conscious of it.

Josie wondered what she must look like herself and shuddered to think. She was normally pale-skinned, but a quick glance in the hotel mirror had told her that she had taken on the unearthly pallor of Morticia Addams – more than likely due to the equally unearthly hour of her departure. Despite a pound of hastily applied moisturiser, her skin felt a size too small and her ankles – as predicted – the size of a hippo's. Her short bobbed hair was being whipped by frenzied gusts around her eyes, which would at least disguise the fact that it was hanging as lank as last week's lettuce. Her nose was probably turning red with cold. Attractive. Not.

Somehow it didn't seem to matter that they both looked as well groomed as Björk on a bad-hair day. She looked at Matt and smiled and he gave her a red-nosed cheeky puppy grin back. They'd formed a cosy little unit standing alone at the back of the ferry, a tiny bubble isolated from the real world. They stood apart but something joined them, a crackle of static maybe, like the feeling you get when you rub a balloon up and down a woolly jumper and it sort of stays there. And even when you remove the balloon, there's a pull there that makes all the fibres of your clothes stand on end for ages afterwards. Everything about her was gravitating towards Matt of its own volition, and she was pretty sure he was gravitating back. It was spooky in an exciting way and she didn't think she'd ever felt like that with anyone else.

She pointlessly pushed her hair away from her face for the millionth time and looked around the half-empty boat. The main joy of New York at this time of year was the fact that there were no tourists to speak of, save the odd huddle of snap-happy Japanese. And what capital city was complete without them, whatever the temperature or time of year? An unruly sprinkling of schoolchildren escaped for the afternoon from the Bronx played havoc with their harassed-looking teacher. Josie knew how she felt. That was about it.

Shielding her eyes against the low winter sun, Josie looked out across the water. Despite the lack of crowds to appreciate her beauty, Liberty was no less magnificent than usual. The lurid copper-green robes shone vibrantly against an impossibly deep blue sky, her awesome foot poised beneath her hem to score a goal for freedom into an unseen net. Once before, in the height of summer, Josie had tried to visit the Amazonian statue – the queue for the ferry was two hours long, and then there was a three-hour wait in searing heat to enter the good lady herself, as it were. She had given it up as a bad job, mainly because she couldn't bear to listen to Damien complaining for so long. Today would be much more fun.

The moment the boat docked, Matt tugged her arm. 'Let's race them to the top,' he said, already breathless in the wind, and they raced ahead of the Japanese, who spoiled their game and headed straight for the gift shop. They hit the monument, still running and giggling, alone. Together, alone. Josie looked at Matt. His coat flapped open in the breeze and he grinned his cheeky, pet Labrador grin and led her inside. Together alone felt good.

The lifts to the first level were out of order. Of course. There was a sign at the bottom of the stairs that warned them, with typical American overkill: 'DO NOT ATTEMPT TO CLIMB IF YOU

SUFFER FROM VERTIGO, CLAUSTRO-
PHOBIA OR HAVE A MENTAL ILLNESS.'
Reassuring.

'Are you sure you want to do this?' Matt asked.

'I don't have a mental illness, if that's what you're
worried about.' Though her mother still frequently
questioned her rationale in marrying Damien,
particularly when it seemed everyone else in the
civilised world had deemed him no good for her.

'I'm very pleased to hear it.'

They both looked up at the stairs, which seemed
to stretch to infinity and beyond.

'I think it might help if we did.'

They looked up again.

'I'm ready if you are?'

Josie nodded. 'Let's do it.'

Despite the odd twinge of misgiving, they started
to climb steadily. Josie was completely knackered
before they were even anywhere near Liberty's
gargantuan toes. 'All those nights of painful step
aerobics have done me absolutely no good at all,'
she puffed.

It was heartening to see that Matt didn't seem
to be faring too much better; another few flights
and there was more heavy breathing coming from
him than the unprofitable end of an 0898 number.

As they flirted with the hem of Liberty's robes,
the stairs petered out into a lighthouse corkscrew
of triangular steps, each one seemingly more precar-
ious than the last. Josie's heart was pounding with
a dull, thudding, heavy-metal beat.

'You okay?' Matt asked breathlessly, concern creasing his brow.

Josie nodded grimly. 'I did not serve five years' hard labour in the Girl Guides to wimp out now.'

It had taken blood, sweat, tears and ten attempts with a Mr Perfect Bake cake mix to gain her Hostess badge – was that the sort of person who gave up easily in the face of a little adversity and sheer, treacherous steps that curled skywards into oblivion? No. Particularly not with Matt watching. Pioneering spirit. Girl power. Josie looked up. She paused for a second, heart banging against her rib cage. 'Oh Lord.'

It was a sod of a long way up or down. They pushed onwards and upwards.

She seemed to have developed an enforced devil-may-care attitude since her split with Damien. It was almost as if the need to prove herself intrepid and fearless had arrived as soon as her mail dropped on her mat addressed to 'Ms J. Flynn'. Her 'new life' involved taking up scubadiving at her local swimming pool (the place where all Elastoplast went to die), joining clubs that she only had the nerve to visit once (such as SPLIT – Single Persons' Leisure Interest Therapy – where she could tell instantly why most of them were divorced), walking into trendy bars unaccompanied *and* brazening out the resulting stares for *at least* one drink. She had got as far as looking up people in the Yellow Pages who did motorbike-riding lessons, and now she was climbing very tall statues when everyone who knew her also knew she had a pathological fear of heights. The one good thing about being married was that you could blame all your inadequacies on your partner. Now she was on her own.

The folds of the robes grew steadily more convoluted, like the inside of someone's brain. The rivets and the strands of scaffolding holding the whole damn thing together looked sinfully insubstantial. There was no handrail, the safety edge of the stairs only came up to her knees, and there seemed to be a lot of fresh air between her and anything else remotely comforting.

She was five foot three on tiptoe, weighed seven stone after eating two Mars bars on the trot, and barely filled a size eight blouse – thanks to the Damien Flynn Pain-Induced Diet – and this was a tight squeeze. How did some of the more hamburgerly challenged Americans cope? Her palms were sweating profusely, and although she was keeping up a constant rhythm of climbing, her knees had set up a counter-knock.

Matt was tucked in snugly behind her, protective, climbing with an unhurried, relaxed step, murmuring encouraging things in between gasps and pants.

'Not much further.' Wheeze. 'This is as steep as it gets.' Huff.

How did he know that?

'Take it nice and easy.' Puff.

Is there any other way?

She had never been more terrified in her life. Her mouth was as dry as her palms were damp, and her chest was starting to burn. Breathing was something that had to be considered carefully, not something that would happen with its usual consummate ease, and she had lost her ability to speak. Even in this petrified state the realisation tiptoed through her brain that Damien would have been racing ahead, proving how manly he was, and pouring scorn on her struggle rather than attempting to comfort and coerce her as Matt was. Not that it made the slightest bit of difference, but it was the thought that counted.

The copper folds of fabric started to swim before her eyes as there was nothing solid to focus on, and a trickle of cold sweat wormed its way down her spine. Her oesophagus was a hard line of constriction that plunged to the churning mass of her stomach and down to the quivering slosh of her intestines. This was a deeply unpleasant experience. It was exactly how she had felt when Damien announced he was leaving her.

'Do you want to stop?' Matt asked when they reached a minuscule break in the otherwise relentless twist of steps.

'No.' Josie forced it out in a squeak.

'Sure?'

'No.' She would never move again if she did. She was certain of it. There was only one way up and only one way down. Such was the organisation of the Americans. Great in theory, but it meant you couldn't turn round and go back. Once you had started upon your chosen path, there was only one way, and that was to see it through to the end.

The Japanese tourists, clearly untroubled by a prolonged purchasing frenzy in the gift shop, were advancing on their heels. There was no way she wanted to end up sandwiched between them and the schoolchildren. A solo ascent was sufficiently stomach-churning without the added danger of a gaggle of knee-high people banging into you. Josie pressed on.

The relief she felt when they burst out into the viewing platform was palpable – if short-lived. The windows which had seemed attractively panoramic when viewed from the ground were about as big as a car windscreen, and smeary. It was clear that no one had troubled them with Windolene for some time. One had been opened to the width of an arrow slit and a puff of chilled air blew seductively into the stiflingly hot cramped space. In the height of summer it would have been tantamount to standing in a tandoori oven in a thermal overcoat.

'This is wonderful,' Matt said, panting attractively.

It was. An uphill struggle, but she'd made it. Like breaking free from Damien. Liberty.

Matt stood behind her and rested his hands on her shoulders. They were warm and soothing. Strong. He kissed the top of her head. 'You were fantastic. I couldn't have kept going without you.'

Now he tells me!

The view back to Manhattan was spectacular. Legoland in human size. It was just a shame her legs were shaking too much to fully appreciate the moment. Josie ran her tongue over her lips. And they still had to get back down.

CHAPTER 6

Matt set the plastic tray bearing tea in paper cups and matching plastic hot dogs gently down in front of her as if she was an invalid. The café was plastic too, in violent pastel shades, and vaguely scruffy in a clinical, run-down-hospital way. They were the only two people inside. The wind had picked up and was tossing handfuls of abandoned burger-joint litter across the deserted terrace. A few tattered gulls pecked their way through it, looking thoroughly pissed off.

'Are you feeling better now?' he asked.

'Yes. Thanks.' Her smile was as weak as the tea. No. Not really.

The hot dogs had been Matt's idea; he thought that she needed some food to settle her stomach. He hadn't explained why hot dogs, and these ones in particular, would qualify as food. He pushed one of the cups of tea towards her. 'It's wet,' he said, eyeing the contents critically.

Josie was quivering all over, inside and out. The hand she held out to grasp the tea looked too tremulous by half and she stuffed it back into her pocket for a few more minutes' respite.

'It was character-building,' Matt said.

'If you mean that it was an experience I would never ever want to repeat in my entire life, even if I lived to be a hundred and ten, then, yes, it was.' Josie shuddered. 'I think having a mental illness should be a necessary requirement before you attempt to climb Liberty.'

Matt laughed.

'I have been on Outward Bound teacher-training courses in the wilds of Wales in November, so I know exactly what being rufty-tufty is all about,' Josie assured him. 'I have abseiled, cargo-netted and canoed along with the best of them. I have crossed Euston Road in the rush hour without the aid of a pelican crossing. Once, and only once, I went on a blind date from one of those seedy personal ads in the newspaper. None of them was even remotely as terrifying,' she confessed. Josie appraised the hot dog and was sure she didn't feel able to subject her stomach to such indignities.

'Aren't you glad you've done it? Don't you feel a sense of achievement?'

'If you mean, aren't you glad it's over, then yes.' Josie smiled. There was a little ripple of excitement starting to appear just beneath the gradually subsiding terror. At least they hadn't had to queue up.

'It's like childbirth,' he assured her. 'Wait until you're telling all your friends back home about it. You'll soon forget all the gore and horror.'

Like the pain of separation, which also receded with time.

'And you know a lot about childbirth, do you?'

'Absolutely nothing whatsoever.' Matt grinned. 'But I know all there is to know about overcoming obstacles and I think getting to the end of this tea could be just as big a challenge.'

'Overcoming obstacles?' Josie mused. She knew a thing or two about that as well. At one point, she'd felt she'd never survive alone; now she often wondered how she'd lived with Damien at all.

Her hands had settled to a fine tremor, barely registering on the Richter scale, rather than the delirium tremens shake they had started out with. Hopefully her knees would soon follow suit. Gradually she was getting back to normal.

She peered into the pale beige liquid in front of her. 'You could be right,' she said.

They wandered round the museum beneath Liberty, arm in arm, marvelling at the American capacity to give even the most banal minutiae overblown celebrity status when it came to filling glass cases, while the gift shop was filled with ten-pence tat with twenty-dollar price tags.

'Let me buy you this as a memento of your momentous achievement,' Matt said, producing the most incredibly tacky green plastic replica of Liberty complete with gold-paint crown.

'Thanks.' It was unbelievably tasteless and she knew instinctively it was something she would treasure forever.

'What about this to match?' He wriggled a large green foam Liberty crown on to her head.

Josie posed obligingly.

'You look beautiful,' he said.

'You're a liar,' she replied. And he laughed and bought it anyway.

Matt held her hand in a non-sexual, matey sort of way as they walked back to the dockside, but it gave her a thrill nevertheless and a rush of warmth under her foam crown.

Dusk was blurring the edges of the towering buildings as they caught the last ferry back. They stood at the rail and watched Manhattan looming up as they bobbed sedately back across Upper New York Bay. The sun had gone in and it was cold. Bone-freezingly cold. Matt pulled her towards him, wrapping his arm around her to keep out the chill. She wanted to go inside and huddle by the warmth of the snack bar, but she didn't want to move for fear that Matt might not see fit to cuddle her again if she did.

'Thanks for a great day,' Matt said into her neck. 'I've enjoyed it.'

This was the horrible bit, the bit she hated. Shuffling around waiting to say goodbye. So long, farewell, *auf wiedersehen, adieu*. It's been great, but I have to go now. Give me a call. No, better still, I'll call you. Sometime. Soon. Bet your life on it. Then there was the worst quandary of all – to kiss or not to kiss? To kiss but not seem too keen? To kiss and not seem desperate?

Whatever it was, she must be doing it wrong, because invariably that was the last she ever heard from them. Why couldn't men just be honest and say, 'Look, it's been great, but you're not my type – I prefer someone taller/shorter/fatter/thinner/blonder/more like my mother – basically, someone that isn't you?' Why did adults feel the need to play more games than kids?

'Josie . . .' Matt sighed.

Oh no, she hoped he wasn't going to say that she wasn't his type. She hoped he was going to give her his mobile phone number and accidentally on purpose get one digit wrong, so that she could blame the vagaries of technology for her bad luck with men and not some inherent flaw in her dating technique. Sometimes it paid to be kind when you were being cruel.

'I feel very . . .' Matt sighed, 'comfortable with you.'

'Comfortable?' Josie frowned. 'As in old slippers?'

'No.' Matt surveyed the horizon. 'As in fine leather gloves.'

'Is that good?'

'Yes.' He turned her towards him. 'That's very good.'

'Oh.'

'Well, it's better than slippers.'

Josie giggled.

'I'd like to see you tonight,' he said against her ear. 'Have you made plans for dinner?'

Oh yes, while I'm in New York I like to look up

a few old chums – Donald Trump, Woody Allen, Sly Stallone, perhaps even Bill Gates. 'Nothing that I can't cancel,' she said.

Matt glanced at his watch. 'I've got to go and catch up with this hormone-ridden boy band.'

'Who go by the name of . . . ?'

'Headstrong.'

'Headstrong?'

A look of dismay settled on his features. 'I know,' he sighed. 'Perhaps I'm getting too old for this. I remember Neil Sedaka. I *like* Neil Sedaka! Even though it makes me shudder with terror to say it.' He shook his head and sighed again. 'The studio's down on the Lower East Side. I might as well face the music while I'm in the area – no pun intended.'

Josie laughed.

'Shall I meet you somewhere later? What do you fancy?'

She was glad the witty rejoinder that went through her brain stayed there. 'Do you like Mexican?' she asked. 'I know a good place called The Alamo on East Forty-eighth street.'

'I love Mexican. Eight o'clock?' Matt searched his pockets. 'I'd better write that down. I think it must be my age. My memory isn't so much like an, er . . .'

'Elephant's?'

'. . . as it used to be.' He produced a pen and a tattered bit of paper and scribbled it down. Tucking the paper back into the depths of his coat, he pulled her to him and tucked her into the depths of his coat too.

Josie's lips were dry. A date. A real night-time, over-dinner date. With someone she hadn't known before. Now, Josie Flynn, spinster of the parish of Camden, that wasn't so difficult. Was it?

Matt smiled down at her and squeezed her against him. A nervous little flutter tiptoed across Josie's stomach, and she knew that this time it had nothing to do with climbing Liberty.

CHAPTER 7

They were four fresh-faced teenagers. There was barely a glimmer of a pimple among them. Which was grossly unfair considering that at fifteen he'd had a face like a deep-pan pizza. Matt settled deeper into the chair, his hangover burgeoning beautifully along with the beat. In the darkened basement of a renovated tenement block, Headstrong were strutting their funky young stuff and singing bland lyrics about love gone wrong in time to an equally bland soundtrack. The new Beatles? Not quite. Where was the tragic lyricism of 'Eleanor Rigby, or 'She's Leaving Home?'

Ooh ooh baby, I want you back, ooh ooh, etc., etc. Synthetic drum beat, clonk, clonk, clonk. *My heart just ain't on track, ooh ooh.*

Right. And what exactly did they know about the tragedies of love at their age? They were hardly beyond the tentative fumbling stage, for goodness' sake. Although if you were a teeny pop idol, there was a good chance you could do your formative courting in better style than the average teenager. In his youth it had been all bike sheds and bus shelters. He'd nearly lost his virginity in a steamed-up late-night laundrette, but the attendant had thrown them out. Just wait until these boys were thirty years old and had been through the mill a few times, then they'd know what it was like to lose in love. Headstrong – weren't we all at that age?

Matt let his eyelids close to block out the discouraging sight of four mop-topped pop heroes prancing round athletically. Hardly ground-breaking stuff. He didn't remember the Beatles needing co-ordinating dance routines to have the fans flocking to ye olde recorde shoppe. Still, it would fill four pages of an otherwise gloomily empty magazine, the deadline for which was looming large in front of him.

He had thought that the fresh air on the ferry had stopped his headache in its tracks, but the fug of illicit substances in the recording studio had made it thump with renewed vigour. Or perhaps it was Josie's company that had made him temporarily oblivious to his pain. For that read both physical and emotional. Headaches you could generally shift with a couple of well-aimed Nurofen and some strong coffee. Heartaches were considerably more tricky to handle.

Why had it hurt so much when his divorce papers had arrived? Was it the fact that it brought back the memory of finding Nicolette romping in their marital bed with someone infinitely fatter, shorter, balder and considerably more boring than he was? Or was it simply because, despite her intended's obvious shortcomings, she was about to scamper down the aisle again with all the enthusiasm of a Labrador puppy, before the ink was even dry, while he had yet to find someone who had managed to raise his eyebrows let alone his pulse rate?

Mind you, Josie Flynn had managed to twitch a few follicles. Now there was a woman who could make you consider eating wedding cake again.

Ooh ooh baby, you do something to me, ooh ooh . . .

Matt opened one eye and glared cynically at the boy band. Indeed. Josie was sexily feminine, in a blokeish, don't-mess-with-me way, with a certain phwoar factor that couldn't quite be defined. There was something about her that said she would never, ever consider sex on a first date – which was appealing because he was heartily sick of bouncing around in bedsits with women he didn't know and didn't really want to know. And she could string two sentences together, which seemed a rare talent today in available women – or at least the ones he had encountered. And she had legs – good ones, ones that went all the way to the top without stopping. And a cute little bottom that jiggled in a perky manner when she climbed a stair, and as he had watched her climb about a million and fourteen stairs and the movement was engraved indelibly on his memory bank, he could consider himself an expert. Altogether, a pretty impressive CV.

To cap it all, he had a date with her, the details of which were lurking smugly in the depths of his coat pocket. He had taken a vow of celibacy, which wasn't necessarily to do with taking the moral high ground, more to do with not having had a sniff of a legover for months. He would, however, consider breaking it for Josie Flynn. Matt folded his arms contentedly across his chest and allowed himself a smirk. All in all a good day, despite being aurally assaulted by this excuse for music.

'Martha? It's Josie. I'm here. The eagle has landed.' Josie held up a multicoloured blouse in front of the hotel bedroom mirror, which was dotted with fingerprints. Too loud for a first date.

'Jo-jo!' Martha's shriek was deafening. 'Did you have a good flight?'

'Excellent. I got drunk with the man sitting next to me. We climbed Liberty together. He's asked me out to dinner.'

'Are you going?'

Josie tenderly fingered the green foam Liberty crown she was still wearing. 'Does the Pope drink pints of crème de menthe? Of course I'm going!'

'Is he a babe?'

'He's gorgeous!' She was grinning stupidly at herself in the mirror.

'I want to know all about it! What time are you coming out here?'

Josie held up a black sweater. Too drab, given the current Morticia pallor. 'When do you need me?'

'We have appointments for facials and French manicures at the beauty parlour at ten thirty, followed at twelve noon by the bridesmaids' lunch at Ginelli's, the wedding rehearsal at six, back to the house for the rehearsal dinner at seven thirty and then off to bed for our beauty sleep at ten o'clock prompt.'

'Are you reading this from a timetable?'

'This wedding has been planned with military precision that would make the Pentagon proud. Nothing, I repeat *nothing*, is being left to chance.'

'Did you get my shoes?'

'I have your shoes. Did you remember to bring the dress?'

'I have the dress.' Seventeen yards of insubstantial lilac chiffon squashed into her suitcase.

'Did you hang it up?'

'I hung it up.' Josie looked guiltily at the crushed mess. I will hang it up the minute I hang up.

'How's it been going?'

'Like hell.'

'How's your father coping?'

'Badly.'

'And you?'

'I can't wait until you get here, Josie.' It sounded suspiciously as though Martha's voice was cracking.

'Hey,' Josie said softly, 'I'll be there before you know it.'

She heard Martha sniff.

'I'll see you in the morning then. Bright and early.'

'You make sure you stick to that, Josephine Flynn. I don't want you spending all night being ravished in a New York hotel room and arriving here bleary-eyed with bruises, love bites and stubble rash all over you. Beauty parlours can only do so much.'

'I promise.' She held up her pink cashmere. 'I will only spend half the night being ravished.' Perfect. Girlish power-dressing. Expensive yet accessible. Soft but sophisticated. With an over-indulgence of blusher, she could look half human yet.

'Don't be late.'

'I won't.'

'Have fun.'

'I intend to.'

'I want to hear *all* about it!'

Josie smirked at herself in the mirror and wondered whether she should risk shredding her shins and shave her aching legs again.

The PR girl was skinny, with boobs like Kylie Minogue, hipster pants and a cropped top. She jutted her flat stomach at him. 'Hi,' she said above the noise – sorry, music. 'Holly Brinkman.'

'Matt Jarvis.' He stood up and shook her hand, which she seemed to find amusing.

'They're cool, aren't they?'

'Er, yes. Cool.' He mustered as much enthusiasm as possible for the less-than-fab four. Maybe he needed to change his job.

'I have a press pack and copies of their CDs for you.'

'Great.' It would join his growing collection of four hundred other promotional CDs he'd never listened to. Perhaps one day he would sell them all and use the proceeds to travel round the world in a catamaran. Except that three hundred and ninety-nine of them were by bands no one had ever heard of – not even really sad people. Slight flaw in brilliant plan.

'When's the feature going to appear?'

'Fairly soon. In each issue we're doing some retro pieces on the Beatles in the run-up to John Lennon's anniversary . . .' She was trying desperately to look interested, while her eyes were saying, *John who?* 'We're comparing them with the new wave of influential musicians.' He looked up at Headstrong. And this lot.

'Cool.' She gave herself a satisfied hug, PR task completed. 'Paul McCartney's a – what do you call them? – an old-age pensioner now. Right?'

'Nearly,' Matt agreed reluctantly. It was too tragic a marking of time to think of the legends of music collecting their bus passes and giving way to this motley crew.

'I hope I get to be that old,' Holly giggled.

'I'd just like to be that good at writing songs,' Matt countered.

'It's good to have a talent.'

It was, and he wondered whether he would ever discover what his particular one was.

Thankfully, Holly interrupted his thoughts before he could sink into depression. 'Have you been in New York before?' she asked.

'Many times.'

'So you don't need a friendly guide.'

'Not really.'

'I'm going to take the guys to eat and then to a club. You wanna join us?'

It's the last thing in the world I'd want to do. 'I've already made plans for tonight.' I have a date that is hot, hot, hot!

'Oh.' She looked disappointed.

He smiled softly at her. She was sweet and young and only trying to do her job, and he was being churlish. 'Thank you for asking,' Matt said. 'Maybe another time.'

'Wanna drink?' Holly waved a bottle at him. 'Jack Daniels.'

'No thanks.'

'A small one?'

'No, really.'

'The guys are going to run through their new single. Stay and listen.'

'I've got to be going soon.'

'One for the road?' Holly looked at him with pleading eyes.

'Just a small one.'

She sloshed the whisky into a tumbler and passed it to him. It gave Matt a headache just looking at it, but it tasted good nevertheless. Hair of the dog and all that.

Two hours later, two more tumblers of Jack Daniels and twenty-two run-throughs of 'I Want You For My Lover, Baby' and Matt knew that he was seriously pissed and should have left a long time ago.

'I have to be going,' he slurred.

'Here's my number.' Holly handed him a card, giving him a direct stare that attempted to be coy. 'Call me. Any time.'

'I've probably got all I need here,' he said, patting the press pack and deliberately misunderstanding despite distinct inebriation. 'I'm coming back tomorrow to interview the guys.'

'I'll try to be here.'

'So will I,' he said, stumbling towards the street.

The Alamo was packed with young, trendy New Yorkers. Men in striped shirts with braces, women in short skirts who screeched and cackled across the tables at each other. There was a celebration of some sort in full flow across the aisle from her, with a winsomely attractive female swathed in party-poppers commanding centre stage. Josie hated her already. A few tables further down, a couple sat gazing deeply into each other's eyes and playing seductively with entwined fingers. They were oblivious to the mayhem around them and the fact that the waiter was at their table doing a party trick which involved pouring a stream of flaming alcohol from a bottle on to their dessert. Very impressive. Did they care? Not a jot. The poor man was flogging a dead horse. When he had finished, Josie gave him a mute round of applause and he acknowledged it with an appreciative raising of his eyebrow.

At her table, right in the middle of the restaurant for everyone to see, Josie was still alone. Matt was an hour late. She knew this because she looked at her watch every minute and had now done it sixty times. Her third strawberry margarita was on its way down and they had gone from tasting like heaven in a glass to being swallowed with all the joy of drinking battery acid. She had toyed nonchalantly with her stripy straw and her watch and her earrings and her hair, but you could only do nonchalant successfully for ten minutes max and then it just became fiddling uncomfortably. Where the hell was he? She'd been so sure that he'd come. Hadn't they had a wonderful time together today? All those stairs, the plastic hot dogs, the insipid tea, the green foam crown. Didn't that add up to a great date? He'd compared her to slippers and gloves – both, in their own way, desirable things. He had said he felt comfortable with her. Very comfortable.

Comfortable enough to leave her sitting alone here like a lonely little petunia in a bloody onion patch, to coin a phrase.

The waiter wafted by with a tray laden with delicious spicy food and looked pityingly at her. Josie sipped the mineral water she had ordered to balance out the trio of margaritas. It had gone flat and warm; not even one little joyous bubble perked to the surface. God, she hated men. All of them. When she got home she was going to become a lesbian. Her friend Catherine had been married four times and now *she* was a lesbian, so there must be something in it. If Catherine 'three times a night' Trewin could make the transition, anyone could. Just think of the advantages – there'd be someone to iron your blouses, water the plants and remember to pay the Barclaycard bill while you went off and played sport. The more she thought about it, the more she could see the sense in it. It was a wife she needed, not a husband.

She wondered whether she should phone Matt to see if he was still at his hotel. She wondered whether she could remember which hotel it was. Perhaps he had gone back there after seeing this band and had passed out in an alcohol-cum-jet-lag-induced coma and was oblivious to the passing of time and the fact that he was standing up someone who was potentially more fun to be with than Denise Van Outen. Perhaps he had been mugged and was lying in an alley bleeding some-where – it happened all the time here; she'd watched *New York One*. Josie downed the flat mineral water. Or perhaps he was just a bastard.

She'd give him just fifteen more minutes and that was his limit.

After half an hour, the waiter walked by again. 'Do you think your friend is coming, ma'am?'

'I don't think so.' They probably needed the table

for some other happy, lovey-dovey couple, not some sad, stood-up divorcee.

'Would you like to order?'

She couldn't eat a thing. Her stomach had shut down and she would probably choke to death if she tried to force an enchilada between her lips. 'No thank you.'

'Another margarita?'

She wouldn't be able to stand up if she had any more to drink, and she had Martha's wedding preparations to be fresh and smiling for tomorrow. 'No, I'd better go now. He could be trying to ring me at my hotel.'

The waiter looked as though he doubted it. And so did she.

The wind was howling down Canal Street when Matt emerged from the recording studio. It was a clear, starry night and the air was sharp and stinging, which went some way to rousing him from his reverie. He should have been having dinner with Josie by now – what had possessed him to stay and get so drunk? He would have some pretty tricky explaining to do. Whatever his particular talent was, it certainly wasn't with women. Grief, what an idiot he was! The first girl in ages to have reached parts that other girls failed to reach, and he was in the process of blowing it big-time.

A cab, a cab, a cab, he needed a cab. And was there one around when he needed one? Of course, dear reader, there was not. They were like police-men, curiously invisible when they could come in most handy.

Matt rummaged in his pocket for the name and address of the restaurant. At some point in the proceedings the scrappy piece of paper had been screwed into a ball. As he started to uncurl it, the wind, spiteful with its perfect timing, whipped it from the tentative grip of his fingers and whizzed it playfully across the road.

'No!' Matt shrieked as it skittered happily between the traffic. He jumped off the pavement, ready to give hot pursuit, but there was a steady stream of cars, several of which tooted their horns in a parti-cularly nasty fashion. 'Come back!' he shouted. The paper clearly wasn't keen to be caught. He could almost hear it shouting, *I'm free, I'm free!*

Matt clamped his hands to his head, running his fingers through his hair. He wanted to weep or kick something inanimate. A cab stopped in front of him. Bemused but grateful, Matt clambered in.

'I want to go to . . . to . . .' Where did he want to go to? 'To . . . to a Mexican restaurant.'

'Me-ki-kan?' the driver said.

'You're Mexican!'

'*Qué?*'

'Mexican?'

'*Sí.*'

'I want to go to a Mexican restaurant!'

'*Qué?*'

'*Sí! Sí!*'

'*Qué?*'

'Where would you go to eat?'

'Eat? Big Mac?'

'No. No.' Shout. Slowly. 'Where – would – you – go – to – eat – Mexican?'

'Me-ki-kan?'

Think, Matt. Think. Beneath this river of Jack Daniels there is a brain. 'It's something to do with a battle. The Little Big Horn, Custer's last stand, the Texas Chainsaw Massacre . . .'

'*Quién?*'

'No, Custer!' Matt flopped back in the seat. 'Oh, for heaven's sake, you're a fucking Mexican, you must know where the decent restaurants are!'

'Big Mac?'

Matt put his head in his hands and pressed hard. Think. Think. Think. But no enlightening thoughts came.

The driver looked at him expectantly. '*Quién?*'

Matt's shoulders sagged. 'Just take me back to my hotel,' he sighed.

'*Qué?*'

'Oh, don't start that again.' Matt gave the driver the address of his hotel.

The appeased driver swung into the traffic and Matt rested his head back on the seat. Fool. Fool. Fool. There was a beautiful woman sitting waiting patiently (or probably very impatiently by now) for him somewhere in this impersonal city, and he was too drunk and too stupid to remember where. It would be a gross insult to sieves to compare his brain to one. He didn't know her number, he didn't know which hotel she was in, it would be like trying to find a needle in a haystack. He was in the city that never sleeps and he was about to go to bed. Alone. And tomorrow night he would have finished with Headstrong and would be out of here on a plane back to Blighty and a golden opportunity would have slipped through his fingers. Nice one, Matthew.

The cab pulled up at some traffic lights and Matt closed his eyes, blotting out the blink of neon light on the dark streets and letting the noise of the city trickle over him and the wail of the ever-present police sirens wash through his brain. His eyes snapped open and he shot forward in his seat.

'The Alamo!' he shouted. 'The fucking Alamo!'

'Ah, *sí señor*, the Alamo!'

'I've remembered. I've remembered.' He felt weak with relief.

'The Alamo.'

Matt clasped his hands in supplication. 'There *is* a God!'

'*Sí.*'

'Quick, quick. Turn round. Take me there. *Pronto. Pronto. Arriba!*'

The pink cashmere was a mistake. A big mistake. It was damp under Josie's arms and itching all over. How could she have read Matt so wrong? She was convinced he had *honesty* stamped all over him. Her judgement was proving as reliable as Hughie

78

Green's clapometer used to be on *Opportunity Knocks*. Here she was, let loose on her own for five minutes, and she was already falling for The Wrong Man. Again. How was she ever going to find a nice man when the wiring in her brain seemed to be all mixed up and couldn't differentiate between decent and dastardly? It had never occurred to her that Matt might not show, and she didn't know whether to be angry or worried.

On balance, angry felt good.

There was no way she should have cancelled her imaginary dinner with Donald Trump to see Matt Jarvis. She should have taken her mother's advice and phoned Bill Gates. He was probably sitting in some Manhattan pad just around the corner being a sad bastard with a pizza and a can of beer, watching crap telly and waiting for someone to ring and ask him out. Contrary to popular belief, being a millionaire probably wasn't all it was cracked up to be. She left a tip for the waiter and pushed her way through the jolly, laughing crowd until she stood on the sidewalk alone.

The air outside was cold – real cold, rather than the artificial cold of air-conditioning that blasted out in the restaurants even though it was winter. Should she try to stop a cab or walk the few blocks back to the hotel and risk being stalked, mugged and shot? She opted for the stalking and shooting. Despite the wild stories of crime in New York, it actually felt safer than London these days. And with that thought cheering her slightly, she set off,

79

berating Matt Jarvis and the fact that he was a complete bastard of the first order.

The yellow cab screeched to a halt outside the Alamo a few feet behind her and Josie turned round to stare at it. It was tempting.

Matt peered out of the steamed-up cab window. There was no mistaking it. Its quasi-Mexican frontage stood out in the otherwise drab street. 'Yes, yes, yes,' Matt chanted.

Josie wavered. Should she wait and nab the taxi from its departing occupant? Indecision. Indecision. No, her mind was made up, she would walk. It would do her good to burn off all those calories she hadn't eaten. She turned and strode briskly up the street.

Matt leapt out of the taxi, paid the driver and then in a rush of affection kissed him on the mouth. 'I love you,' he said deep into the eyes of the bemused man, and rushed headlong into the restaurant.

CHAPTER 8

'Lavinia? How are you?'

'I'm wonderful. Who's that?'

Damien bent a paper clip in half. 'It's Damien.'

'I shall resist the urge to say Damien who.'

Damien leaned back in his chair and put his feet on his desk. God, he had always hated Josie's mother. But then she had started it by hating him first. From the minute she clapped eyes on him, she had taken it upon herself to detest him. Which meant that he and Josie had endured some difficult times during the 'courting' phase, and the wedding wasn't a bundle of laughs either. She made it obvious from day one that she thought he wasn't good enough for her precious daughter – but then she probably would have struggled with any suitor. Even the world's most eligible bachelors would have failed to cut the mustard with Lavinia. Prince Charming himself, no doubt, would have been found to lack a certain charm.

Damien had always been very popular at school, at university, at work – it was a novelty being loathed. But, like most novelties, it soon wore off, and he and Lavinia had given each other as wide a berth as possible, only meeting up when family duty, or Josie, dictated it. Weddings, funerals, christenings, Christmas and Mother's Day. Although Halloween was definitely a day he could associate with Lavinia. Even then, when duty crooked its nasty little finger, he'd managed to work late on most occasions. Except Christmas Day, when try as he might, turkey Lavinia-style had always been endured. His son-in-law hat was pressed into service as surely as the tasteless paper ones from the equally tasteless crackers that were, without fail, produced. He'd always wanted to spend Christmas in the Maldives, but Josie would never hear of it. To Josie, Christmas involved tinsel, turkey, bacon wrapped round sausages, and suffering.

Last year was worse – if that was possible. With Melanie it had also involved two children, getting up at the crack of dawn, pretending that Santa Claus really did exist and generally being even more neglected than he had been in the past. Huge quantities of cash had been poured into the black hole marked 'XMAS' to buy the latest in pointless plastic novelties. The Maldives was a rapidly disappearing dream.

'You sounded like a double-glazing salesman,' Lavinia said.

'Lavinia, I'm trying to find Josie.'

'Perhaps she doesn't want to be found.'

Damien wound an elastic band very tightly

round the neck of a gonk on his desk. A present from Melanie's children – shortly before they decided they hated him too.

'Lavinia,' he made no attempt to hide the weariness in his voice, 'we're thinking of getting back together.'

'Over my dead body!'

It was tempting.

'She's just signed the divorce papers,' his mother-in-law reminded him.

Damien cringed – that had been one of the problems in their relationship: Josie had told her mother everything. Not just exaggerated everything, but real everything. Even when he had that teeny-weeny problem with work-related premature ejaculation, she had been straight on the phone to her mother. And Lavinia revelled in it, not only because she hated him and loved the idea of his tackle being up the creek, but because she thought she was Clare Fucking Rayner.

'And now I think she's regretting it,' Damien replied coolly.

'She will regret it, if I get my hands on her!'

'I've been trying to call her all day, but she's not there. The school said it's half-term and she's on holiday.'

'They should know.'

'So. Where is she?'

'I don't think that's anything to do with you.'

'Has she gone away?'

There was a stony silence. Les Dawson had the

right idea about mother-in-laws. Damien swung his feet off his desk and leaned forward purposefully. 'Lavinia, I need to speak to her urgently. Do you realise that your daughter's future happiness could depend on this?'

'My daughter's future happiness depends on her staying exactly where she is. A long, long way away from you!'

'So she *is* on holiday.' Damien smirked at his ingenuity, before a terrifying thought went through his brain. 'Who has she gone with?'

He could imagine Lavinia's lips pinched white. She had clearly regretted her slip. Picking up his paper knife, he prodded the half-strangled gonk with it. 'Has she gone with this new man?'

'What new man?' His mother-in-law's voice was tight with concern.

Damien smiled with satisfaction and knocked the gonk on to the floor. Take that, Lavinia!

'I will find her, Lavinia, and when I do, I'll bring her back.'

He hung up before his mother-in-law could have the last word, which she invariably did. She would be incandescent with rage. He smirked the sneaky smirk of the terminally self-satisfied.

Damien bit the end of his paper knife and let it play between his teeth. So Josie was on holiday with this new mystery man. And her mother had no idea who he was. The sneaky smirk had vanished from his lips and he drummed the top of his desk with his fingers. This was bad news, this was very bad news indeed. Because if Josie hadn't confided in her mother about him, it meant that the relationship was serious. Very serious. *Extremely* very serious. Which also meant that it needed to be stopped. Now.

CHAPTER 9

Josie, in her Hertz rent-a-car and sunglasses, eased her way on to the Henry Hudson Parkway, leaving the Manhattan skyline and Matt Jarvis somewhere behind her. She had not slept well. The room was noisy, the bed was hard and her temper was frayed. She had finally dozed off when it was time to get up and snarled to herself about her ignoble desertion by Matt as she scrubbed vigorously at her teeth with Sensodyne.

Now she was feeling considerably better, thanks to a cup of strong, black coffee and a blueberry muffin in a greasy diner round the corner from Bloomingdale's, and the perky sounds of 'Jammin' 101' coming from the car radio. The sky was cloudless and the colour of washed-out denim and the sun was still unseasonably strong. And she had remembered to pack the lilac chiffon number, which would make Martha very happy. All in her world was currently well.

She was looking forward to seeing her cousin again. They normally met up at least once a year, taking turns to host the reunion on home turf, and they regularly ran up horrendous transatlantic phone bills whenever crises struck. And there had been a few in recent years. Martha's tortured quest to find true love had never taken the smoothest of paths, and Josie had grown used to early-morning and late-night phone calls as Martha, in the depths of her misery, had forgotten the five-hour time difference. Josie's messy separation from Damien had added considerably to British Telecom's profits, and then suddenly, unexpectedly, the call that announced the death of Martha's mother last summer had stopped everyone in their tracks.

Josie's and Martha's mothers were identical twins. Lavinia and Jeannie. The terrible twosome. Jeannie had waved goodbye to their hometown Liver Birds in the early sixties and, when everyone else was backpacking to India, turning on, tuning in and dropping out, had become a nanny for a wealthy family of New Yorkers. She had worked sixteen hours a day looking after a brood of unruly offspring and had never looked back. She married third-generation Sicilian money and produced the sole heir, Martha Rossani. Lavinia moved only as far as the Home Counties, married moderately and gave birth to Josie. And, despite a physical difference of three thousand five hundred miles, there was never a closer bond between two sisters.

They were both bright, beautiful and bubbly, and now Jeannie was gone. She'd died of heart failure while hitting a tennis ball during a doubles match at her club. And she would have been really pissed off, because they were winning. The whole family was devastated, naturally, but Lavinia took it harder than most, and part of Josie's mother died on that tennis court too. She hadn't attended the funeral and neither had she been able to face coming to Martha's wedding, knowing that her other half wouldn't be there. Which left Josie as the sole representative of the British contingent. Hence half the contents of British Home Stores, Marks & Spencer and Debenhams clanking around in her tote bag.

Josie cruised along the Saw Mill River Parkway, tapping her feet in time to the music, past the now familiar signposts to places with the made-up-sounding names of Tarrytown, Pleasantville, Chappaqua and Mount Kisco, until she finally turned off the road and swept down the hill into Katonah.

Katonah was Peyton Place. A real-life movie set without litter. There was a cutesy old-fashioned railway to transport commuters into Grand Central Station, the core of the Big Apple, and a cluster of clapboard houses skirting a main street of antiques emporia, soft-furnishing stores and delicatessens – even the tiny, white-painted banks were pretty.

Martha lived on the outskirts of town in an imposing sugared-almond-pink house set in acres of land that faded into the surrounding woods. It was all shutters and wood floors and smelled of maple syrup. Josie loved being there and was sorry that the distance was so great between them. As a child it had felt like a second home to her and she had frequently spent entire school holidays there with her mother.

She saw her cousin as soon as she turned the corner into the wide straight road. Martha was sitting on the front porch, legs curled under her on the swing, hunched into herself. She looked tiny and uncertain until she saw Josie's car come into view and launched herself with a flurry of arms and legs down the sweeping driveway to ambush her with the sort of high-pitched screeching that was often favoured by high-school girls in American teen movies. Martha was pulling the car door open, before she had the chance to stop.

Josie got out and they hugged each other warmly.

'You brought the dress?' Martha had dark shadows under her eyes.

'I brought the dress.' Josie held her cousin away from her. 'Where have you gone to? You're all skin and bone.'

'Bride's prerogative. Believe me, I have been living on junk.'

Josie did believe her. At the best of times, Martha's diet was generally eclectic. She breakfasted on a sort of liquefied swamp mud purporting to be green algae, that was all the rage this side of the pond and would probably hit Camden sometime early next spring. It was packed full of vitamins and other 'wonderful' things that would remain nameless. She usually followed it with double chocolate chip muffins or bagels with cinnamon cream cheese, or both. She deserved to be zit-ridden and fat, but such is the fickleness of nature, she wasn't. Martha would have looked perfectly at home bouncing along the beach in Baywatch – she was tall, inexcusably thin, with sickeningly firm breasts and legs like a race-horse. She had long, chemically enhanced natural blonde hair, eyes the colour of fresh spring leaves and a full, permanently smiling mouth with perfect teeth. Damien always said she had the most kiss-able mouth he had ever seen, but then he would. The most annoying thing about Martha, was that she was really, really nice. If she hadn't been her favourite cousin, Josie would no doubt have loathed her.

'I'm so glad you could come, Jo-jo. You don't know what this means to me.'

'Don't start that, Martha. We'll both ruin our mascara.'

'You haven't got any on,' Martha admonished. In Martha's book it was a heinous crime to appear in public without at least one layer of make-up. 'You're looking decidedly peaky.'

'I didn't sleep.'

'Josie, you promised!'

'I was not swinging from the chandeliers.' Unfortunately. 'I didn't sleep for very boring reasons.'

'Your hot date turned out to be lukewarm?'

Josie hauled her bags out of the car. 'My hot date didn't turn up at all.'

'You were stood up?'

'Yep.'

'I've never had that happen to me. Not even in high school!'

'That is not a comforting thought, Martha.'

'Bastard!'

'Double bastard.'

'Let's get these inside and you can tell me more.' Martha swung the holdall over her shoulder, clanging all her wedding presents together alarmingly. She pushed through the door into the breeze way and through to the kitchen, slinging Josie's bag under the table and making the collection of Royal Doulton rattle again.

Martha scoured the giant fridge. 'Do you want some green algae? It's very energising.'

'I'll take your word for it.'

'You need something to perk you up. This is going to be a seriously kick-ass wedding!'

'I think a cup of tea will do nicely.'

Martha flicked on the kettle. 'PG Tips? Lavinia sent us more supplies at Christmas.'

'Good old Mum.'

'How is she?'

Josie plonked herself down at the kitchen table. 'Same as ever.'

'I'm sorry she won't be here.'

'So am I. I think.'

Martha poured out her swamp mud and swallowed it with a shudder. She warmed the teapot as Jeannie and Lavinia always insisted. 'She still misses Mom?'

'Ferociously. She seems to get worse, not better.'

Martha sat down and pushed a cup of tea towards Josie. Perhaps Americans had an innate inability to make tea, even when given the ultimate in ingredients. Her PG Tips looked as insipid as the tea Josie had shared with Matt at the Statue of Liberty diner. Don't you dare give him brain space, Josie Flynn! That way is danger! Martha poured herself a cup of thick, black coffee from a pot on the hot plate.

'I need to stock up on caffeine,' she said as she sat down opposite Josie.

'Won't that negate the effects of your swamp water?'

'I'll leave them to fight it out in my intestines.'

Josie sipped her tea, which hit the spot despite being a pale imitation of a real British hairy-chested brew. 'And you? How are you coping without Jeannie?'

'Try organising a wedding alone.' Martha pulled a face. 'It sucks.'

'Organising a wedding with a mother around isn't a picnic either. I rowed with Mum about the dress, the veil, the cake, the flowers, the church, the seating plan, the choice of bridesmaids and, ultimately, the choice of groom – which I have to say she was right about. The whole thing was nearly off because Damien wanted to wear a leery waistcoat under his morning suit.'

Martha smiled sadly. 'I would have loved to have been rowing with Jeannie.'

'I know.' Josie clutched her hand. 'Everything will be fine, I'm sure.'

'We are going to have fun, girl,' Martha assured her. 'F.U.N.! Anyway, tell me all about this hunky man who dumped you.'

'I couldn't believe it. Why do I always seem to fall for the wrong man? He left me sitting alone in a restaurant for an hour and a half, looking like a prize prat. He seemed so sensitive and caring. How could he do that?'

'The only sensitive and caring men in New York already have boyfriends.'

'He's English. I met him on the plane.'

'But English guys are such gentlemen.'

Josie sighed. 'They might have been when Rex Harrison was treading the boards, but not any more. They all snore and wear nasty underpants and smelly socks.'

'You're kidding me!'

Josie was warming to her theme. 'I wish I was. Most of them are lower down the evolutionary scale than the amoeba when it comes to emotions.'

'So he's no great loss.'

Josie slumped. 'I thought he was a bit different. Well, maybe a *lot* different.'

'Nah, they're all the same.'

'He was nice, funny, kind, scruffy. As unlike Damien as you could get, basically.'

'Kind enough to stand you up,' Martha snorted.

'I really liked him, Martha and I haven't *really* liked anyone for a long time.'

'Like is good. Stick to like. If you'd said you loved him, I'd be very worried.'

Josie felt her cheeks flush. 'Love is a very big word.'

Martha shook her head. 'It's four little letters . . .'

'Yes, like bonk, pooh and bugger.'

'Bugger has six.'

'Commitment has ten – a much, much bigger word.'

'Don't I know it.'

Josie sighed. 'Anyway, it all amounts to English men are complete gits. I hope you've got yourself a good all-American boy.'

Martha gulped down her coffee. 'We have to go.' She waved a piece of paper in front of Josie. 'Wedding Preparation Itinerary. Deviate from it at your peril. And the clock is currently ticking at Beatrice's Beauty Parlour. We're meeting the other girls down there. Paris facials and French manicures. And I'm thinking of having my pubic hair depilated into a heart shape for the honeymoon.'

There was one thing you needed to know about Martha: having an English mother from Liverpool and a Sicilian father had given her a very weird sense of humour.

CHAPTER 10

Headstrong were smashing their amplifiers up with their guitars and clearly enjoying it immensely. The record company lackeys stood by and smiled indulgently. Matt wished that someone would tell them that The Who had done it all before and in considerably better style. At the end of the day, they were only posing for photographs with the blessed things; not one of them could hope to coax a note out of any of the instruments. A snare drum rolled across the floor in front of his feet. God, this was tedious. All he wanted to do was interview them and fuck off home.

Holly Brinkman appeared at his elbow. 'Hi.'

She clearly was. As high as Matt was low.

He would have liked to claim that he had spent the night awake, tossing and turning, pining for Josie and ruing the mess he had made of their arrangements. But he couldn't. The truth was, he had staggered back to his hotel, crushed by the fact that Josie hadn't seen fit to wait a measly hour and a half for him, and was in the dead zone the second his head hit the pillow.

He was woken only by the maid bursting into his room at noon with the vacuum cleaner at full warp speed. Only when he had stood scraping his razor gingerly over the bloated, bearded face that peered wanly back at him did he seriously admonish himself for his mistake.

He was known as Mr Reliable. It was one of the many things his ex-wife hated about him: she viewed the fact that he generally did exactly what he said he would do as a failing and labelled it a lack of spontaneity. He rang when he said he would, he came home at the prearranged time, and remembered to send cards on every occasion that required this commercial show of solidarity. 'Good old Matt,' his friends would say with a jocular lilt while clapping him heartily on the back. 'He'll never let you down!' And yet he had let down the only person who had mattered in months. The only time he had been persuaded into unhindered spontaneity, and it had cost him dearly. Even now Josie was probably filing a complaint to the Bureau of Bastards. And quite justifiably.

Matt turned his attention back to Headstrong and the wanton destruction taking place around him. Holly was smiling vacantly. He had to get out of here.

'The interview isn't going to happen today, is it?' It was more of a resigned statement than a question.

'I guess not. Wanna reschedule for tomorrow?'

Not particularly. 'Yes, that's fine.'

'Want some?' She held her joint out to him.

'I don't smoke.'

'Wanna go for a beer?'

'I have some things to do.' Matt was certain in his heart that he didn't wanna do anything that involved booze, drugs or music. He wanted to go back to his hotel, make another attempt at turning himself into a human being and do something, anything, that would bring Josie Flynn back into his life. 'I'll see you tomorrow,' he said, and escaped into the New York sunshine.

Deciding to walk back to his hotel, Matt wound a route through to Broadway, ambling past the discount electric shops and delis with a lack of purpose that would have been nice to share with someone. With Josie. He took a refuelling stop at Bigi's Diner, a place of chrome and plastic seats with the stuffing coming out. Bigi produced wonderfully exotic Italian subs. And, working on the theory that a surfeit of calories might soak up some of last night's excesses, he followed his pastrami and dill pickle on rye with some warm pecan pie with ice cream and a frothing mug of hot chocolate. Human race, here I come!

What would Josie be doing now, he wondered? She was here for her cousin's wedding, she'd said. What was her name? Maria? Maureen? Marian? Maude? Martha! That was it. Martha's wedding. She was here for Martha's wedding. Matt grinned to himself. If she hadn't been so fat and toothless, and with a moustache better than Des Lynam's, he could have vaulted with joy over the counter and kissed the Italian mama who was serving. It was clear that the hot chocolate or something had mobilised his brain cells, for now he had a cunning plan. All he had to do was find somewhere in New York that was holding a wedding for someone called Martha. How difficult could that be?

There were four bridesmaids in all. Felicia, Betty-Jo, Kathleen and Josie. Which made them sound like the Teletubbies, she thought. They had been chosen, it seemed, to give Martha's wedding a United Colours of Benetton feel. Felicia was black, Betty-Jo of Italian parentage, Kathleen Chinese and Josie, it appeared, the token English rose.

Felicia had been Martha's best friend at high school and was now working as a radio producer in the Midwest. She was unsure whether she was gay or just so radically feminist that she couldn't tolerate the myriad inadequacies that most men she had so far met possessed. She had tried both sexes and found neither satisfactory, so had bought a dog instead and was now blissfully happy.

Betty-Jo worked in real estate in Arizona, making a fortune by selling retirement homes to jaded, pasty New Yorkers and anyone else who wanted to spend their twilight years in snow-free zones hacking round golf courses and sipping mint juleps in airy condominiums on meticulously manicured developments that had the good sense to ban children under sixteen. To redress the balance she took toy-boy lovers who, in her own words, she changed with the regularity of her pantyhose.

Kathleen was gorgeous and had married well to a handsome, jock-style computer something. She worked as a financial adviser in Boston and week-ended at their home in Martha's Vineyard, filling in time until their bright, pretty, well-behaved family came along, as no doubt it would.

Josie had tried, and failed, to make teaching in Camden sound romantic. It was, however, patent for all to see that she wasn't an It girl. She was more a Would-Like-To-Be-It-If-Only-I-Had-More-Time-Money-Confidence-Etc. girl. She could tell that they were deeply unimpressed by her life, even though they tried to sound interested. They did, however, coo ecstatically over her accent and make her say 'actually' several times.

They were all lying in a row in a room as pink as a baby's bottom in Beatrice's beauty parlour, tipped back on reclining couches, their bodies swathed in towels, their faces covered with some strange-smelling gloop that was supposed to exfoliate their dead skin cells and regenerate the superficial layers of the epidermis. Or something. Josie could hardly wait. As long as it made her look ten years younger and more like Sharon Stone she was prepared to endure it as a primitive form of torture. It certainly didn't seem to have done Martha any harm. At all.

'So what's this hunky man you're marrying like?'
'Jack?'

'Unless you've got another one lined up. You've said very little about him, and that's not like you.'

'Jack . . .' There was a vaguely discontented snorty noise from Martha's nose. 'He's . . . er . . . he's great.'

Josie lifted a cotton wool pad from one of her eyes and angled herself towards Martha. '*Great*.' She mimicked Martha's flat tone.

Martha's cotton wool stayed in place. 'Uh huh.'

Josie lowered her voice. 'Can we do this one more time with a little conviction?'

As Tammy Wynette warbled 'Stand By Your Man' over the sound system, Martha remained strangely silent. Josie whipped off her other eye pad and wriggled to face her cousin. Even beneath the layer of rapidly hardening face mask, she could tell Martha's lip was trembling querulously.

'You don't sound like a woman in a desperate hurry to scamper down the aisle and vow to be shackled to this person for the rest of your life.'

'Leave it, Josie.'

'There's something wrong, Martha.'

'There's not. Jack's nice, he's kind . . .'

'He's great.'

'Yes.'

'So why are you talking about him in the same tone as you'd discuss the latest thrush cream you've tried?'

Martha whipped off her own eye pads and sat up. 'Because I'm nervous, Josie. Tomorrow I'm going to do something I've never done before. I'm nervous in case my dress doesn't look right. I'm nervous I'll say my vows wrong. I'm nervous that the shrimp served at the reception will be off and will give the whole wedding party food poisoning . . .'

'But you're not nervous because of the whole marriage deal, are you?'

The door opened and four identical beauticians stood there, armed with bowls of water and implements that looked as though they were intended to inflict serious damage on those neglectful of their beauty routines.

'Martha?'

'Be quiet, Josie, and prepare to be exfoliated.'

Her face was raw from being scrubbed by rough sponges by the bitch queen beautician from hell. Her cheeks were pink and glowing, but Martha seemed to think this was the desired effect for a bridesmaid. All four of them were sitting in a row, having had their nails filed, buffed and varnished in a variety of toning pastel shades, as chosen by the discerning eye of Beatrice, who had clearly wielded her fair share of nail polish in her time. Josie thought her fingers looked like those of a person who also had a tag round their big toe, but then she wasn't naturally a nail varnish sort of person. She was glad she'd been wise enough to obliterate all evidence of the tart red she had briefly flirted with as the sort of thing she ought to do now she was single.

The drying process was now taking place, and

she and Martha were sharing some kind of ultra-violet gadget that was supposed to speed things and seemed to be doing nothing but make soporific whirring noises. The other United Colours of Benetton bridesmaids were reading magazines and giggling over the problem pages, and it suddenly made Josie feel as old as time itself.

Martha was looking pensive. She glanced up from studying her perfect pearlised silk wraps. 'Were you worried before you married Damien?'

'Not as worried as I should have been, given the gift of hindsight.'

'You know what I mean.'

Josie sighed. 'You haven't known Jack very long, have you?'

'Do you think that makes a difference?'

'I don't honestly know. I thought I knew Damien inside out, but in the end, I didn't. I thought that might be what was making you feel uneasy.'

'I'm not uneasy.'

'I am your favourite cousin, Martha Rossani, don't lie to me. We have no secrets. Remember? I was the first person who knew you had lost your virginity – apart from your good self and the gentleman involved.'

'Curtis Neill was no gentleman!'

'And I seem to remember that you were no lady!'

They both narf-narfed into their newly painted nails.

'Were things a lot easier then, Jo-jo? It feels like a million years ago.'

'You're sounding very melancholy for a bride-to-be.'

'Maybe it's just a severe case of wedding nerves, or maybe I'm just missing Jeannie. She'd know what to say. She'd know whether Jack was the right person for me.'

'No more than you should, Martha.'

'I feel I need her approval.'

'What does your dad think?'

'He thinks it was time I was married. *I* think it's time I was married. But he's become very bitter since Jeannie died. He seems to think that no one deserves happiness because he's in the depths of despair and can't see a way out of it. They were very happy. For over thirty-five years.'

'That's a hard act to follow.'

Beatrice was moving along the line of drying nails, checking for their suitability to be let out into the big wide world and remain unscathed. If only it took just half an hour in a drier to protect delicate humans in the same way.

'Do you love Jack?'

'Is that all there is to it?'

'It sort of helps.'

'He's kind. He's considerate. He makes great pasta sauce.'

'The bedrock for a wonderful marriage, I'm sure.'

'It is if you're of Sicilian descent.' Martha sighed. 'I want big family dinners round my own kitchen table. I've had enough of calorie-counted dinners for one.'

'There are worse things than frozen lasagne, Martha.' Josie paused. 'Actually, there aren't.'

Martha laughed.

'Laugh you might,' Josie said. 'But you still haven't answered my question.'

Beatrice came and switched off their drier. 'I think you're both cooked there, honeys.' She looked admiringly at Martha. 'You are sure going to make one heck of a beautiful bride. I bet you can't wait until tomorrow.'

Josie knew Martha's dazzling smile was forced and she stayed her cousin with a hand on her arm as she made to settle her bill and tick off another completed task on her military-style Wedding Preparation Itinerary.

'I read something once – probably in *Marie Claire*. It said if you were nervous about committing yourself to marriage and it was because you doubted yourself and whether you would make a good partner, then that was only natural and you should go ahead. It also said that if you doubted that the other person was right for you, then you should stop it.' She stared at her cousin earnestly and spoke slowly, like you do to French people or Belgians, or people who you think don't know their own mind. 'Whatever stage you're at, you should stop it.'

Martha stood up. Her jaw was set, her fresh green eyes as cool as summer grass after a rain storm. She strode to the salon desk on her long, racehorse legs with a determined air. She paid Beatrice, smiling beatifically, tipped expansively. The other bridesmaids were gathering their belongings – magazines, handbags, sunglasses – and heading towards them.

'We'll see you in the morning, bright and breezy,' Beatrice trilled.

'Six a.m.?'

'You bet your booty.'

What was the collective name for a group of bridesmaids? A bossiness? A bubbliness? A bouquet of bridesmaids? Josie had no idea, but the other three scoured and painted companions were bearing down on them chattering girlishly, pushing, shoving and organising each other, and the sand was trickling too quickly through the hour glass for her to say what she needed to.

'Martha, please . . .'

'I can't stop it, Josie.' Martha met her cousin's eyes, her expression unreadable. 'Not even if I wanted to. Everything's booked.'

CHAPTER 11

There were four million, one hundred and twenty-seven hotels in New York City – or so it seemed. Matt sank on to the bed, the New York version of the Yellow Pages spread in front of him. Suddenly, his cunning plan had receded to a million-to-one shot. It was said that a thirty-five-year-old-man had more chance of having a heart attack directly after purchasing a ticket than winning the Big One on the National Lottery. His chances of finding Josie in this city full of hotels could probably be ranked about the same. He looked at the A's – pages and pages of them, stretching ahead of him like a life prison sentence. He lay back and massaged his eyes. Cunning plan number two!

Making a pyramid over his temples with his fingers as he'd seen Ewan McGregor do in *Star Wars Episode One: The Phantom Menace*, he tried to transmit telepathic thoughts to Josie. *Ring me! Ring me! Ring me!* He stared at the phone and did it again. *Ring me! Ring me! Ring me!* Nothing.

So much for his skills as a Jedi Knight. Old Ben ObiWan Kenobi wouldn't need to worry about his job just yet. Matt gnashed his teeth in frustration.

Well, no one said it was a good plan.

Revert to Plan A. He was a journalist, for goodness' sake. Wasn't the mere name synonymous with investigative skills? No matter that he had never been called upon to investigate anything more taxing than his navel fluff; surely it must be inbred in him somewhere? Did faint heart ever win fair lady? I think not. Matt picked up the Yellow Pages again. A for Aardvark. More specifically, The Aardvark Comfortable Inn. Oh, please! Some people would resort to anything in the name of commercialism, and the Americans were worse than anyone.

Matt punched in the number. He could have fathered several children in the time it took them to answer.

'Aardvark Comfortable Inn.'

'Hi. Do you have any weddings taking place tomorrow?'

'Weddings?'

'You know, bride, groom, cake.'

'Yes, sir, we do.'

'Is there someone called Martha getting married?'

'Do you have another name, sir?'

'No, just Martha.'

He could hear the desk clerk sighing silently. Now he was The Phantom Menace. By the time she came back to him, the children were just about to leave home and go to university.

'No, sir. There's no Martha getting married here.'

'Are you sure?'

'Positive.'

'Thank you for looking.'

'You're welcome.'

She didn't say, 'So long, loser,' but he could feel it.

Did he let it daunt him? Well, yes, slightly. Matt flicked the pages – two inches of hotels. At least. Oh god, he could die before he got to P. And supposing Martha's wedding was at Zigfield's Wedding Lodge? Martha could be on honeymoon and Josie on a plane back to Heathrow long before he bowled up at the front door. This was a nightmare. He should just forget about it. Mark it down to experience. He was in New York. He had an unexpected buckshee day. The sun was splitting the pavement in two despite it being February. There were places to go, sights to see, shops to bend plastic in. And he was sitting in his hotel room planning to phone every hotel number in the Yellow Pages. Get real, Matthew!

Matt looked disdainfully at the directory in front of him. A is for Abbie's Luxury Inn.

Two hours later, when he had come to a complete dead end with Albie's Amish Inn and was about to dial Alicia's All-American Motel, the telephone rang. He stared at it unbelieving. Was he really a distant relative of Doris Stokes and had reached

108

Josie through the mysterious and all-powerful communication of the mind? He snatched at it hopefully.

'Yes?'

'Matt? Hi, this is Holly.'

Holly? Who the hell's Holly?

'Holly Brinkman,' she supplied into the uncomfortable pause. 'Headstrong's publicist.'

'Oh, hello,' Matt said when the cent finally dropped. He hoped he didn't sound as disappointed as he felt.

'I was ringing to confirm that the guys will be available for an in-depth interview tomorrow morning.'

How in-depth could four cerebrally challenged teenagers get? What did they want to discuss? Quantum physics, the theory of relativity, the big bang? Or did they want to mull over the fact that England could no longer play tennis, football or cricket despite inventing them all. Mind you, he had interviewed enough boy bands by now to realise that they all viewed themselves as world experts on almost any subject you cared to mention. Perhaps that was what being adored by the entire population of fourteen-year-old girls did for you. Was he just getting old and sour? Even when he had been fourteen, fourteen-year-old girls hadn't been interested in him.

'Right. Right.'

'Can you come down to the studio around eleven in the morning?'

'Yes, that's fine.' I can't wait.

There was another pause, during which they both missed their cue to hang up.

'I was wondering whether you'd want to do dinner tonight?'

'With the band?' Oh, very sharp, Matt!

'No.' Holly Brinkman let out an exasperated little sigh into the telephone. 'Just with me. I know a nice place in Greenwich Village.'

'Well . . .' Matt chewed his nail and tried to think why he shouldn't. Okay, she was pushy. PR was certainly the right job for her. But she was pretty too, in an underfed sort of way. And what else had he to do? Apart from work his way through every listed hotel in the entire Manhattan area? 'Can I get back to you, Holly? I'm following up another project at the moment.' Journo-speak for going on a wild-goose chase.

'You have my cell phone number?'

'I think so.'

She gave it to him again so that he really did have no excuse. Matt obligingly scribbled it on the corner of the hotel courtesy notepad. Little did she know that he couldn't be trusted with bits of paper no matter how important they were to him.

'I hope you call me, Matt,' she said.

He hoped she didn't hope too much. 'If I can, I will.' Was that noncommittal enough? How did you let someone down lightly these days? 'See you round.'

He hung up. God, that sounded so hick. *See you round?* Staring at the wall, Matt surveyed the screw holes where a picture should have hung. Why couldn't he have just said yes? This was why. Picking up the Yellow Pages with a weary little huff, he plunged back in.

By the end of the afternoon he had reached Aylene's Homely Lodge and the conclusion that he was completely insane.

This was bolstered by the fact that every single hotel receptionist he had spoken to so far had also decided he was completely insane. But then surely they were used to that in New York?

'You are an idiot, Matthew James Jarvis,' he said into the blandness of his poky hotel room.

He was down to the last A. Oh good, only half a day wasted and a mere twenty-five letters left to go.

'I know,' he answered himself above the whirr of the air-conditioning. Perhaps there weren't many hotels starting with X or Y. He flicked to the relevant pages and was down-hearted (i.e. totally pissed off) to see there seemed to be more than an adequate sufficiency to worry his dialling finger.

Azekal's Manhattan Motel seemed, somehow, to have the ring of a place not ideally suited to wedding celebrations. Matt forced himself to punch out the number, his fingers performing a pedantic plod over the buttons. When the perky receptionist answered the phone, it was with a certain lack of conviction that he began to deliver his well-practised script.

'Hi. Do you have any weddings taking place tomorrow?'

'We certainly do, sir. How may I help?'

'Is there someone called Martha getting married?'

'Let me check our wedding register for you.'

He walked his fingers patiently across his duvet while there was the sound of fingernails clicking against a computer keyboard.

'Do you have the last name for me, sir?'

'No.'

'Do you know what time the wedding is taking place?'

'No.'

More clicking. Matt flung himself flat on the bed. God, why was he doing this to himself? There are plenty more fish in the sea, Matt Jarvis. Yes, but you've already decided that most of the ones you've met are old trouts.

'The reception starts at twelve noon, sir.'

Matt sat bolt upright. 'What?'

This was unbelievable. What was it Humphrey Bogart said? In all the hotels in all the world . . .

'It starts at twelve noon.'

'Are you sure?'

'We only have one Martha getting married here, sir.'

'At twelve noon.'

It couldn't be. Could it?

He wanted to rush over to Azekal's Manhattan Motel and kiss the lovely lady at the other end of the phone for bringing him such good tidings of great joy. For the second time in two days he had fallen in love with a stranger. Three times if you counted Josie.

'When are the wedding party arriving?'

'Not until tomorrow, sir.'

'Do you have a contact number for Martha?'

'I'm afraid I'm unable to divulge that information. But I can leave a message to say you've called.'

Matt gave his hotel name and his room number. 'It's very important.'

'Are you on the guest list, sir?'

'Not yet,' Matt said with a smile. 'Not yet.'

Matt put the phone back on the receiver. He'd found her. My God, he'd found her. Only five short hours of continual phone-calling and he'd found her. How should he celebrate? Matt prepared to salsa round the limited space his hotel room provided. He wanted to dance, sing, shout Josie's name from the top of the Empire State Building. He was feeling at one with the world and a divine benevolence to all fellow mankind.

Contrary to popular mythology, he had, courtesy of Azekal's Manhattan Motel and the wonders of modern communication, been given a second chance to make a first impression.

Matt jiggled round his room, da-da-ing the tune for the conga out loud. He stopped in his tracks. Had he really just said he loved Josie? He was afraid he had. This was a much more serious state of affairs than he had realised. Love at first sight? Didn't that only happen in soppy songs? And

certainly not to a thirty-two-year-old rock journalist who, although temporarily feeling a little
emotionally overwrought, was generally a sane and
reliable human being. *Ooh ooh baby, all it took was
one look, to read my heart like the pages of a book.
Ooh ooh . . .*

My, my, wouldn't Headstrong be proud of him?

CHAPTER 12

The church was a gothic monstrosity, and cold. Colder than hell if it ever froze over. Which was fine if you were wearing moon boots and thermal underwear, but Josie wondered just how lilac chiffon was going to be a match for the job. She sat huddled in a pew at the back, taking in the solemnity of the building, the smell of incense and damp. It was no wonder priests were celibate. Martha was skittering around, flirting with the clergy and generally looking a bit happier about being an impending bride than she had been a few hours earlier, which Josie was more than a smidgen relieved about.

Perhaps with the prophecy of doom from the divorce statistics these days it was more reasonable to be unsure of the validity of the marriage vows. Forever was a very long time in anyone's book. How many people really understood or meant what they were saying when they uttered the words 'till death us do part?' Wouldn't it be better as part of the general dumbing-down in life to redraft marriage to a ten-year renewable contract subject to the agreement of both parties? At least people's expectations might be more realistic. Could couples still stand before God and say that they would forsake all others for the rest of their lives and honestly believe it? Forever had been five years for her and Damien. Quite a short forever, all things considered.

Martha came striding towards her. 'Josie, don't sit all scrunched up at the back. Come and meet everyone.'

She tugged Josie into the aisle. 'This is Peggy. Her two daughters are going to be flower girls.'

'Hi.'

'Hello, pleased to meet you.' Josie shook the woman's hand.

'Oh, you must be the English bridesmaid!'

'Yes.'

'Lovely accent.'

'Thank you.'

'Martha's been so looking forward to you coming.'

'I've been looking forward to it too.'

Martha shot off and reappeared pulling a man behind her. 'Josie you remember Glen?'

'Glen.' Her eyes widened. '*Glen?*'

The Glen in question was tall and blond, built like a brick outhouse. He was wearing some sort of varsity sweatshirt and jeans and looked as if he would have been more comfortable carrying an American football rather than the flower posy that was currently getting squashed beneath his arm.

'Hi, Josie. Long time no see.'

'Yes.' Had a word come out?

'Glen's going to be Jack's best man,' her cousin informed her.

Glen had been a lot of things in his time. High-school heart throb, fitness fanatic, fashion model and now a successful marketing manager for an international sports company. He had also been Martha's boyfriend for at least three years, if Josie remembered correctly. And she was horribly sure that she did. Her cousin's first true love too, if she wasn't mistaken. Now, it appeared, he was to be her fiancé's best man. Curiouser and curiouser. Had she suddenly slipped into an episode of *Neighbours*?

'Glen is one of Jack's students at the martial arts academy he owns,' Martha tossed into the air before she flounced off. 'I'll leave you two to become reacquainted.'

Martial arts academy?

Glen proffered the flowers from under his arm. 'Practice bouquet,' he said. 'Martha wants to make sure everything goes right.'

'Nothing left to chance,' Josie muttered, taking it from him.

'So how's married life suiting you?' Glen asked.

'It isn't. I'm separated.' She tried a laugh, but it sounded pathetic.

'Gee, I'm sorry.'

'So was I, but it happens.' Josie smiled. What a thing to be talking about in a church the night before a wedding. 'I'm revelling in being single.'

And it's a good job my nose isn't made of wood, otherwise it might have grown six inches.

'Me too.'

'You never took the plunge?'

'No.' Glen laughed uneasily. 'The words aisle, altar, hymn kinda put me off.' He glanced after her cousin, who was holding court with high-pitched chatter and flicking her mane of blonde hair about like a skittish colt. 'Maybe I should have asked Martha.'

'Well, you know what they say about the one that got away . . .'

'Is that the same as the one about the early worm catching the bird?'

'Something like that.'

'Are you staying over at Martha's place?'

'Just for tonight. I've got a hotel in Manhattan.'

'I should have checked with Martha. I was in town last night. I could have taken you to dinner, shown you the sights.'

'That would have been nice.'

'Did you have plans?'

'No.' Matt Jarvis? Who's Matt Jarvis? 'I had a quiet night.'

'In New York?'

'Martha's instructions. She said I wasn't to have my usual drugs and booze orgy.'

'Right.' Glen looked uncertain.

'I was joking,' she said, remembering that irony was a peculiarly British thing.

'Have you met Jack yet?' Glen clearly thought it wise to change the subject.

'No,' Josie admitted. 'I'm looking forward to it. How do you know him?'

'He's my ju-jitsu teacher. I train with him when I'm home at the weekends.'

Hence the rippling biceps. 'And you've known him a long time?'

'Five years. But it's only recently that I found out he and Martha were . . .' Glen cleared his throat. 'I bet Martha talks about him all the time.'

'Er . . . yes.' John Noakes was a more current topic of conversation than the future bridegroom. 'Constantly.'

'They're really in love then?' Glen looked at Martha wistfully.

'I hope so.'

'Here's the man himself,' Glen said, his face breaking into a smile.

Josie turned to watch the man coming through the church doors. The expression froze on her face. Martha rushed forward.

'You're late.'

He squeezed her indifferently. 'Important business.'

'Well, no matter. We can start now you're here. Kiss me and then come and meet my cousin all the way from Britain.'

Jack pursed his lips and kissed her, making a sound like a horse chomping an apple.

'Josie, this is Jack.' Martha beamed with pride.

'So you're the English bridesmaid.' Jack took her hand and it was clammy, just as she had expected.

'Yes,' she answered, auto-pilot kicking in.

The moment was frozen, extending her discomfort interminably. Glen was beaming amiably, Martha for once seemed to glow with happiness and Jack held her fingers with all the charm of a dead fish. It was one of those times when you would be unable to recall anything else that was going on around. The roof could fall in, the organist could be rogering one of the choirboys behind the pulpit, you wouldn't notice the ice-cold wind that had turned your body to stone.

She stared at them both, her beautiful cousin and her future intended, and, swallowing the lump that was in her throat, wondered if Martha had completely lost her mind.

CHAPTER 13

Damien sat drinking tea from a delicate bone-china cup in Mrs Bentham's front room. The handle was far too small for his fingers and he clutched it precariously, sipping at the warm, milky Darjeeling. It was like the sitting room time forgot – stuffed with floral this and floral that, china whatsits and frilly thingies. A stark contrast to Josie's flat upstairs, which was Ikea minimalist. He had only been allowed in once. To the lounge. Nowhere else. It was stark and chic, with no itsy-bits of memorabilia to remind her of their life together. No wedding photographs – not even one for old times' sake. He was probably still languishing in the bottom of a packing case in her loft. He had never seen the bedroom of his former loved one and he wondered if the mystery man had. He'd always loved the smell of their bedroom. It smelled of Josie, a sort of sweet, fluffy, stuffy aroma, the floral fragrance of the duvet cover mingling with the musky scent of sleep – pear drops meets Brut 33. Melanie's bedroom smelled like a busy night at a brothel, pungent with the unmistakable whiff of raw sex. Not that it mattered whose

121

bedroom smelled of what. Damien had been told, in no uncertain terms, never to darken Josie's door again. And Josie could be very stubborn when she wanted.

The arms of Mrs Bentham's chairs all had crocheted protectors on them, and there was a walnut display cabinet filled with ornate glasses and teapots and fragile glass posies. The gas fire was burning off the North Sea reserves all by itself, and Damien, used to climate-controlled offices and cars, was sweating profusely. The Cat Formerly Known As Prince was not similarly troubled. He lay on the brown shag-pile rug, offering his white belly to the heat, wearing an expression denoting ecstatic trance.

Mrs Bentham's bird-like hands flitted over her hair. 'She went yesterday,' Josie's neighbour informed him, sipping at her tea. 'I'm looking after baby until Monday morning.'

The Cat Formerly Known As Prince opened one eye and gave Damien a look that said he knew when he was on to a good thing. If only Damien had been blessed with that bloody cat's intuition before he legged it for the lovely Melanie. Once the sex had subsided to sub-Olympic levels there was nothing very much left. Melanie didn't have Josie's brains, integrity, culinary ability or earning capacity – although, on the plus side, she did have a fairly amazing range of PVC lingerie.

'She told me she was going on holiday.' Damien laughed at his own forgetfulness. 'It had *completely* slipped my mind.' He tutted and Mrs Bentham giggled at him. He rolled his eyes to reinforce what a complete idiot he was. Her sympathy was touching. You only had to look at her to see that she was clearly at the age where she needed to write lists to remind her to eat breakfast every morning. 'I can't even remember where she said she was going.'

'Silly boy,' Mrs Bentham admonished. 'She's gone to Martha's wedding.'

Oh, but this was so easy! He'd known watching all those episodes of *Jonathan Creek* would come in useful one day. All you had to do was turn on the charm, quiz the batty old neighbour, who'd guilelessly spill the beans, and Robert is your uncle and Frances is your aunt. Damien sat back in the moquette sofa and allowed himself a slow smile. 'Martha's wedding.'

The Cat Formerly Known As Prince gave Mrs Bentham a look that said Traitor and one to Damien that said Lucky Bastard! Damien narrowed his eyes at the cat. You will be back on Tesco's cheap and nasty fishy chunks if I get my way, mate! And lobbed off the bed at night. I've had enough clawed balls to last me a lifetime! I will very soon be regaining prime position of affection in Josephine Flynn's life, and you and Mystery Man can both take a running jump! Be afraid. Be very afraid!

The Cat Formerly Known As Prince looked unconcerned and slipped back into his hypnotic state with a smirk on his face.

Damien downed the rest of his Darjeeling, resisting the urge to shudder. 'Well, I'll leave you alone,' he said.

'Do you want to leave a message for Josie?'

'No, I'll catch up with her soon.'

'Stay and have some date and walnut loaf. I baked it myself,' Mrs Bentham cried. 'There's no need to dash off.'

'I must be going.' Damien stood and brushed the cat hairs from his navy-blue trousers with a loaded scowl towards The Cat Formerly Known As Prince. He kissed the back of Mrs Bentham's hand and she tittered girlishly. 'It has been so nice meeting you.' And so useful!

'Stay a little longer.'

'I would love to,' Damien assured her, 'but I have things to do.'

Catching a plane to New York being one of them.

Mrs Bentham stood up, smoothing the pleats of her skirt, and walked him to the door. 'Josie told me she was getting divorced,' she said. 'But you're nothing like I imagined her ex-husband to be.' She lowered her pince-nez. 'You're a very nice man.'

Damien straightened his tie and gave her a winning smile.

'It's very strange.' Mrs Bentham smiled back. 'Josie said she'd been married to a complete bastard.'

CHAPTER 14

The trouble with feeling at one with the world and a divine benevolence to all fellow mankind, Matt concluded, was that he had decided to include Holly Brinkman in it. Which was why he was standing in a dingy nightclub with the sweat of a thousand bodies ripe in his nostrils, clutching a lurid-coloured drink of dubious description and listening to music that had all the poetic appeal of twenty synchronised pneumatic drills.

Psychedelic patterns swirled across the walls and the mirrored ceiling, and Matt reflected that the last time he had felt quite so queasy had been in the Fun House on a school outing to Blackpool when he was nine. Holly was shrieking loudly about something to do with goodness knows what, and spraying the inside of his ear with foam from her extortionately priced bottled beer. He wondered if there was a nice quiet job for him on Radio Two. Squeezed in somewhere between Ed 'Stewpot' Stewart and Terry Wogan. Did they play tracks by the Beatles these days? Did anyone?

If only he had lost the slip of paper bearing

Holly's mobile phone number instead of the one which had linked him so tenuously to Josie Flynn, then he wouldn't have had to be here at all. But that was being unkind. Holly was young, trying very hard to impress him and definitely up for some fun.

'Dance?'

'What?'

She put her mouth to his ear. 'Dance?'

'What?'

'Dance?' Holly wriggled herself in front of him.

How? He'd always been a two-left-feet merchant, only briefly coming into a blaze of glory in the last throes of the pogoing era of punk. After all, any fool could jump up and down on the same spot without too much trouble. All you had to do was remember not to land on your neighbour, who was no doubt sporting a Mohican haircut and a nose ring and would thus probably give you a good kicking despite his knees being tied together by bondage trousers. Dancing. Matt always hated this point in a relationship. You could spend weeks trying to appear as chill as Mr Ice Cool to someone. You could wine them, dine them and be getting along just nicely – then in one small moment it could all go horribly wrong when she found out that your dancing style was closely based on Scott Tracey's walk (pilot of *Thunderbird 1*). Would Holly suddenly realise how much older he was than her when he slid on to the floor with all the grace of an unhinged marionette?

'Okay,' Matt said with a degree of reluctance that he hoped indicated dancing was not his thing. He may not have wanted to knock Holly's eyes out with his Travoltaesque skill, but neither did he want to look a total wanker. At least it gave him a chance to abandon the multicoloured cocktail.

Holly slid her hand into his and led him on to the dance floor, which was so crowded that, to his infinite relief, it was impossible to move. The music slowed and changed to something with a vague rhythm. Matt stood there and shook himself a bit while Holly raised her arms above her head and sort of rubbed her body against him. It wasn't an entirely unpleasant experience.

'You're a great mover,' she said above the noise.

'Thanks.' I bet no one's ever said that to Scott Tracey! 'You're not too bad yourself,' he shouted back. Oh, very sophisticated, Matt. Taken from the *Men Behaving Badly* book of chat-up lines, perhaps?

It was a long time since he'd had a woman rub her body up and down his on a dance floor, or in any context for that matter. He was buying condoms in packets of three and then throwing them away months later unopened for fear of rubber fatigue, or some such, setting in. He had no intention of practising safe sex and then ruining it all because he had a puncture. Perhaps it was listening to all those soppy love songs, or perhaps it was the fact that his hormones suddenly seemed to have become supercharged after meeting Josie, but all this rubbing up and down seemed to be having a long-forgotten effect. Matt decided to rub back a bit. What harm could it do?

Tomorrow he would interview Headstrong faster than you could say One-Hit Wonder and be out of there and on his way to Azekal's Manhattan Motel to gatecrash Martha's wedding and make peace with the best-dressed bridesmaid in the west. Or the east.

The tempo slowed right down again and the songs became positively tuneful. Give them a few more minutes and they'd be playing Headstrong, heaven forbid. A new wave of dancers surged on to the floor and crushed him against Holly. She made no attempt to move and slid her arms round his waist. What could he do with his? He was jammed up against her with no place to go. He slid his hands down her back, which was bare due to the ridiculously skimpy nature of her top. Her skin was warm and damp and suddenly his top lip was too. Holly pressed against him and rested her head on his shoulder. He felt the gulp travel down his throat. So now what, Matthew?

CHAPTER 15

Imagine, if you will, one of those dogs with a thousand wrinkles and a skin ten sizes too big for it. You know the ones. A Sharpei. Cute in a very ugly sort of way. Imagine it wearing a technicolour ethnic hand-knitted sweater down to its chubby little knees, and a long Chinese-style plait hanging down its back. Oh, and a head otherwise as bald and shiny as Buster Bloodvessel's.

That was exactly what Martha's intended looked like, and Josie had been unable to fully close her mouth since she first saw him. The beautiful, lean and long-legged Martha was marrying a man who made Danny DeVito look like Mr Universe. The fact that he was nearly as old as Martha's father also bore some relation to the open-mouthed status of her cousin.

They were back at Martha's house, which was now crammed full of caterers, old codgers and Sicilian cousins who had also flown in specially for the wedding. The rehearsal had gone according to plan and now the rehearsal dinner was in full swing – a chance for previously unacquainted families to size each other up.

Three brothers argued violently over the authenticity of the lasagne, a slender, pale-faced girl painted her nails next to the pasta salad and two slicked-back teenage boys from Palermo were teaching an elderly uncle, who had never previously ventured out of his home town, useful sayings from an English phrasebook. Beneath them the flower girls were rolling round on the floor pulling each other's hair and trying to tear the limbs from a Barbie doll. Josie took it as a good sign. If they got it out of the way now, there was a fair to middling chance they might behave themselves tomorrow.

The house had been decorated with flowers, previewing the theme of the wedding. Unopened presents adorned every conceivable surface, and that was without adding the British Home Stores sheets. People wandered from room to room with plates piled high with canapés, cannelloni and ripe cantaloupe melon.

Martha and Jack were at opposite ends of the room. Her cousin's arm was linked through her soon-to-be mother-in-law's, they were talking to her father and the tension was palpable. At the rehearsal, Martha's father, Joe, had objected to everything – the priest, the music, the money it was costing. It looked like he was having a rerun now.

The elderly uncle sidled up to her, a warm smile radiating from the thin white lips in his wrapping-paper face. 'Hello. Who are you today?'

'Josie,' she said. 'Martha's cousin. The English bridesmaid.'

Putting his hand on his heart, he gave her a little bow. 'I have been Uncle Nunzio.'

'Pleased to meet you.'

He pursed his lips and blew her a kiss. '*Bella. Bella*. Have a good shag, it'll make you feel much better.'

'Thank you,' Josie replied. 'I'll remember that.'

The slicked-backed boys giggled from the corner, hiding their phrasebook behind their backs. Very funny. Josie gave them her best schoolteacher look. Though she had to admit, Uncle Nunzio was probably right.

Glen came towards her bearing a bottle of wine. 'Looks like you need a refill.'

Feels like I need a vat full. Josie held out her glass. 'Thanks.'

'I thought the rehearsal went well.'

'Mmm. So did I.'

'It's nice that we're partnered together.' Glen sipped his wine. 'It means that I get to look after you all day.'

If men fluttered their eyelashes, then there was definitely a flutter. She couldn't think of anything nicer. A perfect panacea for forgetting Matt Jarvis.

'So do you currently have any men in your life?'

'No.' Josie sighed. 'And there's not much life in any of the men I know.'

Glen gave her an All-American gee-I'm-a-nice-guy grin. 'Maybe that'll change. You could be living on the wrong side of the pond.'

Out of the corner of her eye, she could see Jack peeling himself away from the Sicilian cousins and making his way in her direction. His Chinese plait was draped over his shoulder.

'Perhaps.'

'Hi.' Jack shook her hand again. 'We haven't had a chance to talk yet. Martha's told me a lot about you.'

'Did she?' Why did she feel she sounded just like Mary Poppins? 'I don't know whether to be delighted or worried.'

'You guys go back a long way, right?'

'Our mothers were twin sisters.'

'Cool.'

Did men approaching their late fifties have a licence to say 'Cool?' No one over fifteen would be caught saying it in Camden without losing street credibility.

'Excuse me.' Glen gave her a look that she hadn't a hope in hell of interpreting and disappeared into the depths of the lasagne-eaters before she had a chance to protest. She looked back at Jack with dismay. His face was pasty, he had eyebrows like Groucho Marx and there was something unidentifiable lurking in the corner of his moustache.

'I guess you're glad someone's going to be finally taking Martha in hand.'

Josie felt the hackles rise on her neck, exactly like The Cat Formerly Known As Prince's did when he saw next door's Rottweiler, Gerald. 'I'm not entirely sure Martha needs taking in hand.'

Jack nodded knowingly. 'I think that's why the universe brought us together.'

'Oh, right.' Josie took a slug of wine. 'And where did you two meet?'

'Wal-Mart.'

'Oh, so the universe has a sense of humour.'

'Excuse me?'

'It's probably the only time Martha's ever shopped at Wal-Mart, so it must have been down to the fickle hand of fate.'

'I think I've been brought to Martha to show her how to live her life.'

'Really?' Where was Glen with that bloody bottle? 'I think Martha does pretty well with life already. I just hope you have sufficient money in your bank account to fund a small South American revolution; that would be enough to keep Martha deliriously happy.'

'I believe she'll relinquish her addiction to material goods after we're married.'

'I hope you're right.' Josie tried not to laugh, as Jack really did look quite serious about what he was saying. 'I feel it inappropriate to tell a little tale about King Canute and waves.'

'You may snigger, Josie, but inside Martha there is a deeply spiritual person yearning to get out.'

And inside me there's a murderer yearning to strangle you!

'I want Martha to become a vegan after we marry, to cleanse her body and prepare her for my child.'

'How romantic,' Josie said, watching Martha select a sticky spare rib from the tray that wafted by her.

'It's for her own good.'

Did he realise that this girl had been brought up on McDonald's, Kentucky Fried Chicken and Dunkin' Donuts? 'I wish you luck.'

'I hope you mean that, Josie. I'm going to take good care of her.'

'I hope you mean that too, Jack.'

They both surveyed the crush of well-wishers. Unfortunately for Josie, there seemed to be no one in the immediate vicinity who needed rescuing or was likely to rescue her.

'Drink?'

He gave her a superior smile. 'I don't poison my body with alcohol.'

What a shame you don't poison it with strychnine.

'Martha may have mentioned that I'm well versed in the mystic arts of the East.'

Martha has mentioned nothing about you and now I know why! 'Well, Jack, I'm about to become well versed in the less mystic art of alcohol abuse.'

His expression screamed disapproval.

'You don't mind if I do?'

'Go ahead, it's your life.'

Which Josie interpreted as, I hope your liver falls out during the speeches. 'Thank you.'

'Josie, I can understand your concern, particularly after your failed relationship, but please don't worry about Martha. I love her.'

Her cousin looked over from the other side of the room, beamed one of her beautiful toothsome smiles and mouthed, 'Help.' Josie decided it was her call. Either that, or she could stay here and stick a garlic breadstick up this arrogant bastard's nose.

'I hope to bring her enlightenment.'

She downed the remains of her wine and stared directly at the man next to her. 'So do I, Jack. So do I.'

Josie pushed through the crowd, grabbing another glass of wine on the way. What on earth was Martha thinking of? It was true that beauty was only skin deep, but beneath his rather old and craggy exterior lurked a man who believed he was more saintly than Mother Theresa. Martha had dated men who made Brad Pitt look plain. Take Glen, for instance. Not shabby at all in the looks department. Charming, successful, presumably not gay. Why had it gone wrong? Martha had broken up with so many men, it wasn't easy to remember why Glen hadn't stayed the distance. Had she chucked him or did he chuck her?

It was rather nice to think that he was going to be giving Josie his full attention tomorrow. She grinned to herself. Strike while the bridesmaid's posy is hot. She was going to free Martha from her father and her outlaws, and then find Glen and get her claws sunk steadfastly into him before anyone else did. It would be just her luck for Felicia to decide to give men another go. Oh yes,

135

she'd had enough of being the virgin incarnate; she was going to transform herself with the aid of lilac chiffon into a red-hot mama and grab herself a man. See what Matt Jarvis would think to that!

CHAPTER 16

Holly Brinkman was inexhaustible. She looked like the sort of person who, along with all the drugs she took, would take lots of vitamins too. Someone should take one or both of them away from her. It was late, very late, and she was still bouncing off the walls. Her lipstick was smeared and her mascara was forming Alice Cooper circles under her eyes.

The club had taken on a furtive, low-life feel. The fug of smoke from dope and cigarettes furled in front of the strobe lights. The music and the people were getting sleazier. Matt had never done this scene very well, despite it being a hazard of the job. Perhaps his ex-wife had been right, he was essentially a boring fart at heart.

Holly lunged at Matt with her lips and missed.

'Come on, twinkle toes,' Matt said. 'I think it's time we went to bed.'

Holly swayed in front of him. 'Are all you English guys so forward?'

'That was what we British quaintly call a "royal we". I meant you should go to bed. Alone.'

Holly swayed some more. 'Are all you English guys such spoilsports?'

'You need coffee. Lots of it. Black.'

'I don't do caffeine.'

It was probably just as well, Matt thought.

'Come back to my place.'

'I don't think that's a good idea.'

'I do.'

'I think we should keep our relationship on a professional basis.'

'We may never see each other again after this weekend. Can't we enjoy a little fun while you're here?'

'I've always found that a little fun leads to an awful lot of complications.'

Would he be saying this if he hadn't met Josie? Why was he feeling the necessity to remain faithful to someone he had stood up on their first and probably their last date? Perhaps Cupid's arrow, straight and true, had not only pierced his heart, but had gone straight through one of his testicles too.

Matt glanced at his watch. 'Let's have breakfast together. Sharing some cinnamon toast can be just as much fun as romping around the bed with a total stranger.'

Holly looked dubious.

'Trust me.'

'Well,' she whined, 'I am hungry.'

She actually looked like she was going to vomit majestically. God, he hoped that she didn't, as he always had this incredible urge to join in.

'You don't look very well.'

'It's you talking about food. I haven't eaten all day.'

Oh great!

Matt took her face in his hands. 'If I promise to get you something to eat, will you promise to keep it all inside your stomach and not reproduce it as a Jackson Pollock canvas all over my trousers?'

Holly giggled, which he took as a yes.

'Come on then.'

'I know a great place.'

Matt steered her through the crowd, knowing that at some point in his life he was going to regret this.

The city that never sleeps was looking pretty drowsy to him. There were a few people propped up in the corners of the diner just off Times Square that Holly had chosen, but other than that it was virtually deserted. Which was a shame, because the pancakes and maple syrup he was currently enjoying were like a little bite of heaven, though this could also have been due to the fact that a Beatles compilation was playing softly in the background, 'All You Need Is Love', 'You're Going To Lose That Girl' and 'I Saw Her Standing There' adding a certain nostalgic charm and a not un-noticed hint of irony to the ambience.

Outside the window, the dawn was grey and wintry. The clear night sky had given the air sharp teeth and it nipped at the down-and-outs who shuffled joylessly by, their entire wardrobes wrapped

139

around their street-wasted bodies and making them look like replicas of the scarecrow from *The Wizard of Oz*. Other than these poor unfortunates, there was very little sign of life. The odd taxi bounced by and the street cleaners were mobilising themselves, but that was about it.

Holly shovelled scrambled eggs and bacon so crisp that you could snap it in half into her pretty pink mouth. For someone who looked as though a stiff wind would blow her over, she had a fairly hearty appetite. An unruly mob of blonde corkscrew curls swamped her pointy little face and Matt found himself wondering if Holly's drugs habit was as out of control as her hair. He glanced at her over his pancakes. She was sobering up nicely, a flush of colour had returned to her peaky cheeks and she no longer looked like a candidate for a sick bag – which was a mighty relief.

Matt tried to guess how old she was. Twenty-three? Twenty-four? Maybe a little older. It was hard to tell these days. He had a thirteen-year-old niece who looked twenty-eight if she was a day. Maybe that was why he felt more protective towards Holly than predatory. Who knows? He just hoped it wasn't all down to JFS – Josie Flynn Syndrome. He hoped he wasn't going to go through life comparing every woman he met with Josie. How could you harbour the furtive and unthinkable thought that you'd found your soulmate one minute and then lost her through a stupid act of carelessness the next?

'A penny for them,' Holly said, crunching her bacon.

She had tomato sauce on her chin and looked very sweet. Matt picked up a serviette and wiped it away.

'It'd be a waste of money,' he said. 'Just coasting.'

'You had a very deep frown.'

'I was contemplating the meaning of life.'

'Wow.' Holly grinned. 'I thought I was the one who did drugs.'

'Too much maple syrup always has this effect on me,' Matt said.

'You don't seem to fit too well into the music scene.'

'Maybe I did once.'

'I thought London was a hip-hop-happening place.'

'It is. Perhaps I've just seen the same thing hipping, hopping and happening too many times.'

'How long have you been a rock hack?'

'Several lifetimes.' Matt sipped his hot sweet tea. 'Or at least it feels like it some days.'

'Can I ask you something?'

Matt nodded.

'What did you really think of Headstrong?'

'Really?' Matt pushed the last bit of pancake on to his fork.

'I would like to know. Really.'

He placed his cutlery on his plate and sat back, listening to John Lennon crooning from the overhead speaker. *I've got something to say that might cause you pain . . .*

141

Matt folded his hands in front of him. 'I thought they were really, really terrible.'

'How terrible?'

'Extremely terrible.'

'More terrible than . . . ?'

Matt swallowed his pancake and twirled his fork. He had lived through the Bay City Rollers, the Wombles, the Nolan Sisters and songs by yodelling hamsters, and compared to Headstrong they were all truly, truly terrible in their own way. 'More terrible than . . . than Marie Osmond singing "Paper Roses".'

'That terrible?'

''Fraid so.'

'Oh.'

Holly snapped another piece of bacon with her fingers and crunched it. 'Guess what?'

Matt waited.

'I think so too.' A slow smile spread across her mouth, lighting up her face. She lowered her eyes and started to chuckle.

Matt laughed too, deep and hearty, drowning out John Lennon and making the other occupants of the sparsely populated diner pull their attention away from their breakfasts.

'You'll give them a great review anyway.'

'I could be persuaded.'

'They're nice guys,' she said. 'When they're not trying to rule the world. But their music stinks.'

'Doesn't that make your job a little difficult?'

'I'm a great liar.'

'Well, you had me fooled.'

Her face was suddenly serious. 'I don't think you'd be easy to fool at all, Matt.'

'I'm not good at playing games, Holly.'

'You don't even know what games I have in mind.'

'It's late,' he said gently. 'Or is it early?'

Matt went to pick up the bill.

'My treat.' Holly slid it from beneath his fingers. 'Expenses.'

'Thank you.'

'You were right,' she said. 'Breakfast was a lot of fun. But maybe not quite as much fun as commitment-free sex.'

'There's no such thing.'

Holly pulled on her jacket. 'My place isn't far from here.'

'I'll hail you a cab.'

'We could walk back. The air will do us good. You could maybe put your arm around me.' She stared at him, her eyes daring him. 'You never know, you might enjoy it.'

'Do you never give up, Holly Brinkman?'

She stood up and took his hand. 'Only when I've got what I want.'

CHAPTER 17

The Wedding Preparation Itinerary had been abandoned. Temporarily. The ten o'clock beauty sleep deadline had long since passed. The guests had departed and even the other bridesmaids had faded away soon after midnight, but Martha was showing no signs of wanting to go to bed.

Martha and Josie were sitting on her windowsill, legs dangling on to the sloping tiled roof below them. The eaves of the house merged into the inky blackness of the clear sky and the pinpricked holes of the stars were as sharp as the night air. It wouldn't be too long before the dawn eased them away.

Martha had found them both fleecy pyjamas and fluffy socks and they were wrapped in blankets against the chill. Her cousin dragged on the joint they were sharing. 'I haven't done this since I was seventeen,' she said.

Josie took it from her as she blew the smoke in a steady, melancholy stream from her nose. 'Me neither.'

'Doing drugs isn't fashionable these days,'

Martha said. 'Neither is drink or casual sex. All the little pleasures in life are gradually being eroded, aren't they?'

'Before long they'll probably discover that watching television gives you eye cancer, and then where will we be?'

They chuckled together.

'I'm so pleased you're here, Jo-jo.' Martha reached out and squeezed her hand.

'Me too.'

'It's been hell without Jeannie.' Martha's eyes were glittering in the starlight. 'She was a great mom.'

'You fought like cat and dog.'

'It's funny how those things don't matter any more when it's too late.'

'You'll miss her tomorrow.'

Martha nodded. 'Jack and I will stop by to see her when we're done at the church. Just for a few minutes. I'm going to leave her my bridal bouquet.'

'That's nice.'

'It's funny how things turn out, isn't it?' Martha gazed at the sky. 'That's Orion.' She pointed at the constellation with the spliff. 'The handsome hunter. I used to think that somewhere in the world my hero was looking up at him too and one day he would appear and we would know that some-how we were connected and were meant to be together forever.' Martha giggled the giggle of a stoned person. 'Romantic, hey?'

'And did you find your hero?'

'I thought I had once. I think he came pretty close. Maybe the timing was just wrong.'

'There's not a lot of them about. You should have hung on to him.'

'You're preaching to the converted. I thought the world was full of nice men. All you had to do was sit back and take your choice. The older I get, the more I realise all the good ones are snapped up and I've got to pick through the leftovers.'

'What happened between you and Glen?'

Martha glanced sideways and snorted. 'What makes you ask about Glen?'

'Curiosity.'

Martha raised her eyebrow.

'Okay then, being nosy. I was a little surprised to see him here.'

'More than a cursory interest?'

'Perhaps.'

'He's cute.'

'I've noticed.'

'He thinks you're cute too.'

'Even better.'

Martha leaned her head on the window frame. 'I thought he was The One. We went all through high school together. He was everything I wanted. I adored him. And I thought he adored me.' She watched the smoke curl into the air.

'And . . . ?'

'And. When we graduated and had the whole of

our lives ahead of us, I fell pregnant.' She pursed her mouth at Josie.

'Shit.'

'I didn't tell anyone,' she continued, hugging her knees to her chest. 'Not you. Not even Jeannie. No one. I didn't tell anyone but Glen. And he totally freaked. He said he couldn't cope with the responsibility. He felt it would ruin our lives. He'd just been offered a great job in Europe and wanted to take it. In short, he didn't want our baby and he didn't want me.'

Josie took a deep breath. 'Shit.'

'I had an abortion. Which Glen chivalrously paid for. He took the job in Europe and that was the last I saw of him.'

'Bastard.'

'He wrote to me every year until two years ago. Each time he said he regretted his actions, he still loved me and would do anything to make it right.'

Martha took a last deep pull on the dwindling joint and crushed it out on the windowsill. She tilted her face to the stars and breathed out heavily. 'I tore all the letters up.'

'Shit,' Josie breathed. They both looked out in silence at Orion. 'Do you regret it?'

'The abortion or breaking up with Glen?'

Josie shrugged.

'I took both hard. They seemed like the right decisions at the time. I can't change them now. I'd handle it differently given the chance again.'

'Ah, that old sop. Turning back the clock.'

'We all suffer from that, Josie.'

'Don't I know.' Where would she turn the clock back to? Pre-Damien? Certainly pre the Matt Jarvis stand-up routine. Conversation rewind.

Would you like to meet me tonight for dinner, Josie?

No, get lost. (Flounce out, head held high.)

Martha grinned, breaking into her thoughts. 'So you don't know everything about me, Josie Flynn.'

'So it seems.' It was lucky she hadn't fallen out of the window in shock. 'And now he's Jack's best man?'

Her cousin laughed. 'Strange, hey?'

'Nooo,' Josie breathed, 'not at all!'

'Jack and I, we got engaged a month after we met.'

'At Wal-Mart . . .'

'You heard about that?' Martha rubbed her face. 'It's a long story. You would not believe it!'

'I think I'd believe anything now.'

'Anyway, Jack told me he knew this great guy. Jack was his sort of guru at the martial arts academy. This great guy had been having personal problems and Jack had helped him through. It turned out to be Glen.'

'Does Jack know about you and him?'

'He knows we had a fling. He doesn't know about the baby.'

'And how do they feel about it?'

'Do you mean the fact that they both know I give great blow-jobs?' Martha cackled.

'Martha Rossani, you are outrageous! Take this seriously.'

'They're cool.' She pulled down the corners of her mouth. 'Although I haven't really talked to Glen. I guess there are some things that are better left unsaid.' Martha shifted on the windowsill and pulled her blanket round her. 'He had his faults – don't they all? – but no one has come close to equalling the good times.'

'Not even your future intended?'

'I've spent the last ten years looking for someone who would match up to Glen.'

'And Jack does?'

'Jack's different.'

You're telling me!

'So,' her cousin turned to her and twitched her eyebrows mischievously, 'are you going to hit on Glen?'

'Not after what you've told me.'

'He's a very sexual person,' Martha said. 'And he has great buns.'

'I'm looking for rather more in a man,' Josie replied loftily.

'Is there any more?'

'Damien had great buns too. The trouble was, he liked to share them with other women.'

'Do you still think about him?'

Josie picked at her nails. 'Less and less.'

'The only way to get over someone is to replace them. That's not terribly PC, is it?'

'It's probably true, though.'

'I like being in a relationship. I don't feel whole without a man. Is that pathetic?'

'Very.'

'Felicia terrifies me, she is so at one with herself. She loves being alone. I can't do that. I need someone to need me. With Jeannie gone, I feel as if I've been set adrift. I've lost my anchor, Josie.' Martha struggled with the last sentence and hugged herself silently for a moment before crossing her eyes and saying: 'Too heavy!'

Josie laughed.

'Look at this guy you met in New York. He ditches you after one date, crushes your self-esteem, moves on to the next kill and leaves you wondering what you did wrong. Why do we let them do that?'

'Hormones,' Josie said. 'I blame them for everything.'

'I think Glen would suit you.'

'I am so scared of falling for the wrong man again.'

'You're thinking about this guy you met a lot, right?'

Josie nodded. 'More than I want to admit.'

'Then maybe you've fallen for the wrong man already.'

'I can't go down that route again, Martha. My confidence won't stand it.'

'Then think about having some fun with Glen. He's changed, Josie. Jack says he has a lot of integrity. It's been a long time, things move on, people move on.'

'And you believe what Jack says?'

'I respect his opinion.'

'He has a lot of them.'

'I'm not even going to ask what you think of Jack.'

'And I'm not going to say anything.'

'You don't have to. It's written all over your face.' Martha tugged her blanket tighter round her.

'Martha,' Josie said patiently, 'you are the most gorgeous creature on this planet. Catherine Zeta Jones or Douglas or whatever-she-calls-herself now excepted. And he is . . . well, possibly a creature from *another* planet.'

'Looks aren't everything. You've just said so yourself.'

'They are if you look like Quasimodo after a heavy night's drinking.'

'That's unfair.'

'He looks like a Sharpei.'

'I like dogs.'

'But you wouldn't marry one.'

'Josie,' Martha sighed, 'I have done hunks. I have done punks. I have done sophisticated. I've done artistic. I've done new money. I've done old money. I've done no money at all.'

'So now you're doing bald, ugly and obnoxious.'

'None of them have made me happy.'

'And Jack does?'

'I met him the week after Jeannie died. He has been so fantastic. He has held me, counselled me and encouraged me to open up my inner self.'

'Since when has your inner self been closed?'

'I am more in touch with myself and my emotions since I have known Jack.'

'Is that any reason to marry him?'

'I want a baby, Josie. I have a big baby-shaped hole in my life. I want to push a buggy. I want to know all about disposable diapers. I *want* to be a mommy.'

'Is this more about putting the past right than being in love with Jack?'

'That's something else that happened since Jeannie died, I've realised that nothing else matters. Not money, not looks, not eating at fancy restaurants, not having the latest style of handbag. I want a child before it's too late, and Jack is ready for that commitment too.'

'He's ready? Martha, he's pushing sixty from just about the right side.'

'He's forty-eight. He just doesn't believe in moisturiser.'

'If that's what martial arts does for you, then give me an excess of Fry's Turkish Delight any day.'

'I'm not getting any younger, Josie. What if all my eggs are mutated due to drinking too much diet cola or something?'

'You are thirty-four years old. There's plenty of time.'

'You never truly know that.'

'Supposing his sperm aren't up to the swim any more? Suppose all they can do is paddle about in the shallow end? Would you still marry him then?'

Martha pouted unhappily.

'You can do this without marriage. A baby can be conceived with a jam jar and a turkey baster. For heaven's sake, you celebrate Thanksgiving, you must have one lying around somewhere!'

'This is a ridiculous conversation. I want a child conceived out of love.'

'Love! That is the key word here, Martha.'

'He loves me. He adores me. He cherishes me. He is the only person who has ever asked me to marry him. Everyone else has just wanted to take from me.'

'But do you love him, Martha?'

'It is far too late to be asking this kind of question, Jo-jo.'

'No, Martha, if there is any doubt in your mind, it's exactly the right time to be asking.'

'Have you ever started on a route that you don't feel you can deviate from? Have you never felt that destiny is pulling you along, despite your own misgivings?'

'Is this about destiny or is this about having caterers booked?'

'I need to hit the sack.'

'Martha, do you love him?'

'This is the right thing for me to do, Josie. It fulfils my needs.'

'Do you love him?'

Martha took a long, lingering look at Orion. 'I love him,' she said. 'Now let's get some sleep.'

CHAPTER 18

'Yes!' Damien replaced the receiver and punched the air. He rubbed his hands together with delight, giving them a final, affirmative clap. One business class ticket with Virgin Atlantic Airlines to New York had cost him an arm and both of his legs, but it was worth it. At seven a.m. precisely, with an executive degree of comfort, flight VA 100 would take him straight to John F. Kennedy airport and, soon after, into the arms of one Josephine Flynn. He was all set to go.

'What are you doing?'

Damien spun round.

Melanie was leaning on the door frame of his study. Her hair had been messed up by the sleep gorillas and it stuck out from her head at unattractive angles. She wore a short silk dressing gown and a surly expression.

Damien sighed.

'It's three o'clock in the morning,' she pointed out. 'Are you coming to bed?'

The dressing gown fell open at the neck, exposing the full swell of her breasts, which heaved with indignation. They were firm and soft all at once and had been one of the reasons he'd fallen in love with her.

Damien sighed louder. This was hard. He was hard!

'No,' he said. 'I'm not coming to bed.'

Melanie glanced at the holdall he had hastily packed while she was watching *Coronation Street*. Natalie, the landlady of the Rovers, was having an affair with yet another younger man, and the nation, including Melanie, was riveted.

'What's this all about?'

'I can't do this any more,' Damien said.

'What?'

'This!' Damien spread his hands and gestured at the house.

The normally suntanned Melanie had turned pale. 'Why?'

'I can't do this any more,' he put his head in his hands, 'because I think I still love Josie.'

'You bastard!' Melanie turned on her heel and slammed into the kitchen. He winced as he heard the kitchen cupboards whang on their hinges, the kettle crash against the taps and two china mugs clang against each other.

He sighed the biggest sigh in the world. 'Oh, fuck,' he muttered, pushing himself wearily away from his cheap make-do MFI desk and following the sounds of domestic appliances being slammed down.

Melanie was leaning against the worktop, crying.

Her face was red and blotchy, contorted with anger or pain or both.

'Melanie . . .'

'Does she love you?'

Er, tricky that one . . . 'Yes.'

'You've still been seeing her?'

'No.'

'Liar!'

'I am trying to be honest,' Damien said, and went to put his arm round her.

'Damien, you wouldn't know honest if it bit you on the arse.'

'I resent that remark!'

'And I resent you coming into my life, messing it up, messing my kids up because you think you still love your ex-wife!'

'She's still my wife.'

'Damien, you have been living here for six months. You were shagging me over your office desk for six months before that! You're not exactly the epitome of a devoted husband.'

'I knew you'd take this badly.'

'Badly!' Melanie's face turned a thunderous shade of black. 'I haven't even *begun* to take this badly!'

'I want you to know that this hurts me as much as it hurts you.'

'No it doesn't Damien. Nothing hurts you. You are the one who causes hurt. But here's something that might give you some idea of just how badly I'm taking this!'

Melanie picked up the sugar bowl and hurled it across the room. It hit the wall above Damien's head, shattering into a thousand pieces and showering him with Tate & Lyle granulated white sugar.

'Melanie!' Damien hid behind his hands.

She picked up the two china mugs and launched them after the sugar bowl. One gave Damien a glancing blow on the head before smashing against the door frame.

'You're going to do something you'll regret,' Damien warned.

'No. You are,' Melanie said, opening the cupboard. Her face took on a determined air as she pulled out a stack of plates and grabbed hold of the top one. 'I will make sure you regret this, Damien.' She aimed the plate at his head and threw it like a Frisbee. It whistled through the air, shattering against the Hotpoint frost-free fridge-freezer. 'I will make sure you regret this for the rest of your days!'

CHAPTER 19

'Make me look really tarty,' Josie said. 'Natural is good, Beatrice,' Martha instructed as she meticulously massaged vanilla-scented hand cream into her slender fingers.

'Natural, but breathtakingly gorgeous in a tarty sort of way,' Josie corrected.

'You don't want to be more beautiful than the bride, do you?' Beatrice fluffed at her with a blusher brush.

'Of course I do,' Josie said. 'But I think that would probably involve major cosmetic surgery and growth hormones. Just do your best with eye shadow, Beatrice.'

It was six o'clock in the morning, still dark, and there was a hard frost sugaring the trees outside and making them look magical. If it hadn't been minus five and falling, it would have been a perfect day for a wedding. The assembled party were sitting in Martha's kitchen drinking coffee and being painted and coiffured by Beatrice the beautician and her lovely assistant Christina. The way they were flicking their make-up-laden brushes about made Rolf Harris look like an amateur. Which was just as well, because Josie's eyes were so red and swollen she looked like she'd cried her way through *The Bridges of Madison County* a thousand times.

Shortly before she and Martha had retired to bed at some ungodly hour, Josie had discovered she was to lead the bridal procession down the aisle, followed by Martha and her not inconsiderable train. She was also to read a lesson, start the dancing and probably perform a one-woman stand-up act at the wedding breakfast to entertain the guests. It seemed there was to be no skulking at the back getting pissed as bridesmaids did at English weddings.

Josie eyed the line of lilac dresses waiting patiently on coat-hangers having been ironed to within an inch of their lives. 'Couldn't we have had sleeves, Martha?'

'Stop whining, you'll look fabulous, and this is going to be one HOT wedding! Wait until tonight and you will be steaming!'

The photographer and his lovely assistant were also buzzing round them like bees, as was the video man and his distinctly less than lovely assistant. Josie was unsure that she wanted this image of her in Martha's spare pyjamas, half made-up, with rollers in her hair, recorded for posterity, but recorded it was going to be.

'I fancy the photographer,' she hissed across the divide of their two chairs.

'He's gay,' Martha said, downing her swamp algae so that Beatrice could apply her lipstick, despite the earliness of the hour. 'The man holding his light meter is his boyfriend.' Martha peered round Beatrice. 'What is wrong with you, girl?'

'I think this brief encounter with the English hunk-bastard, Matt Jarvis, has made my hormones all start knocking together or something. Uncle Nunzio said I need a good shag.'

'Uncle Nunzio said that?'

'In a round about way.'

'Then shag you must. Uncle Nunzio is one who must be obeyed.'

'Really? He looks like his next cigarette could possibly be his last.'

'Looks are sometimes deceptive, Josephine. You of all people should know that by now.' Martha regarded her cousin whilst holding her fingernails out for admiration. 'Uncle Nunzio is one tough old cookie. He's the titular head of our family and very respected in his home town. No one messes with Nunzio Rossani.'

'Then who am I to question his advice?'

They both laughed.

'Felicia,' Martha shouted at a vaguely inert form in pyjamas, 'could you phone the florist and check that I have a throw bouquet as well as a bridal bouquet?'

'It's six thirty, Martha.' Felicia continued to stuff bagels and sour cream as if her life depended on it.

'They have a message service. I may forget. And it could be your big chance.'

Felicia shuffled to the phone. 'If my future happiness depends on catching your damn wedding bouquet, then I'm going to slit my wrists now.'

The rollers came out and the curling tongs went in, followed by a flurry of back-combing and enough hairspray to make the ozone layer flinch.

Felicia hung up. 'You are now the proud owner of a throw bouquet.' She went back to her breakfast.

The phone rang. Felicia hauled herself back over to the breakfast counter to answer it. Holding the receiver away from her, she shouted, 'Aunt Lavinia. Who wants first shot?'

Martha waved away her cloud of hairspray and took the phone. 'Hi Lavinia. Yes, we're just about there. Yes, Josie's behaving herself.'

Josie growled with irritation and Martha stifled a giggle.

'Yes, I'm wearing something old, new, borrowed and blue. Yes, I wish you were here. Yes, Daddy's fine. Yes, I miss Momma too.' Martha bit her lip. 'Yes, I know you're thinking of me. I have to go now, Lavinia, thank you for calling, I'll talk to you real soon. Here's Jo.'

Josie took the receiver. 'Yes, I got here fine. Yes, I'm behaving. Yes, I will continue to behave. Yes, she's looking good. Yes, I will give everyone your love. Yes, I wish you were here too. What?'

Josie paused.

'No, I am not thinking of getting back with Damien. Whatever put that in your mind? Yes, I'm sure we'll have a nice day. Mum, why did you ask about Damien? Mum . . . Mum . . .'

Josie held the receiver away from her ear, frowning. 'She hung up without me going through the Conversation Termination Sequence. That's a first.'

She flopped down again next to Martha. 'My mother just asked me if I was thinking of getting back with Damien.'

'I heard.'

'We are currently at home to Mr Divorce. What is she thinking of?'

'Your mother can be a little weird sometimes.'

'You're telling me.'

Martha's father, Joe, wandered in. He was wearing a vest and unzipped pants, and his shirt flapped round him like a sail. 'I can't get this freaking penguin suit done up!'

Felicia came to the rescue. 'Here, Mr Rossani, have a bagel while I do up your shirt.'

'Jeez,' he moaned, 'I'm glad I only got one daughter. I coulda bought a row of condos for what this little show is costin'.'

'Stop complaining, Daddy. Momma would have wanted this.'

'Your mother would have loved every minute.' He tugged at his bow tie. 'Me, I can't wait to get this goddamn thing off. Why'd I gotta get dressed at this hour? It's still the middle of the night.'

'We don't want to be late at the church.'

'We ain't due there for hours yet.'

'There's lots to do.'

'You girls sure make hard work of lookin' good.'

'Daddy!'

He held up his hand. 'I'm outta here. I'll be in the den watching *Win Ben Stein's Money*. Yell when it's time to get this party moving.'

Martha watched him go, chewing her lip. 'He loves it really,' she said uncertainly.

'Of course he loves it,' Josie assured her. 'Your father's like my mother. They both love to complain. He'll have a great day and talk about nothing else for years.'

Martha and Josie vacated the beauty hot seats. Felicia and Betty-Jo moved in.

'Martha, do you want breakfast?'

'I'll smudge my lipstick.'

'You've already gnawed half of it off. Beatrice can put some more on for you later. You have to eat.'

'My stomach has shut down.'

'Eat.' Josie pushed a bagel towards her, and they both nibbled tentatively.

'Did you think about what I said last night?'

'I spent the entire night suffering from anxiety insomnia.'

'And?'

'This is the right thing to do.'

'Are you sure?'

'I'm sure.'

'Really sure?'

'How many more times do I have to tell you?'

'Just once, but sound happy about it.'

'I'll be a lot happier when I don't feel so nervous.'

'Relax and enjoy it. The day will go by so quickly you'll hardly remember it.'

Martha's hands were trembling. 'I want it to be a perfect day, Jo. I want everyone to remember it for the rest of their lives and say hey, wasn't Martha's wedding something else?'

'Don't worry.' Josie took both of her cousin's hands and pressed them together. 'They will. I'm sure they will.'

Suddenly, there was a loud crunching sound outside of the house and the windows were blacked out.

'The cars are here,' Martha said.

Sure enough, three of the largest, whitest limousines ever built had pulled up outside Martha's house, obliterating the sun that had nudged over the horizon.

'It's time for us to get dressed, baby cousin,' Martha announced.

'Oh my God,' Josie said, and sat back on Martha's bed. She bit her lip, ruining the last traces of Beatrice's lipstick.

'Don't cry, don't cry, don't cry, your face will run.'

'I'm not crying, I'm just snivelling a bit.'

Martha twirled round. 'You like it?'

'You are the most beautiful bride there ever was.'

'So that's a yes?' Martha admired herself in the mirror.

The gown was princess satin, tight-fitting, with a pearl-encrusted bodice and, Josie noted with a faint twitch of pique, long sleeves.

'Do you remember when we were kids and we used to use your mum's nightdresses to play at being princesses? Well, you look just like a princess now.'

'This is what every woman should feel like on her wedding day.' Martha twirled again and the gossamer train floated over the floor, billowing as the air caught it and lifted it.

'Jeannie would have loved it.'

'She would, wouldn't she?' Martha's eyes filled up with tears. 'Don't say anything else, you'll make me cry.'

'She would have been so proud of you.'

'Jack wanted to get married in Fiji, just the two of us. I'm glad I stuck out for the whole show.'

'I hope he's worth the effort.'

'I think the princess will live happily ever after.' Martha swayed in front of the mirror. 'Don't they always?'

'No,' Josie said. 'Not always.'

'I'm sorry,' Martha said, letting her arms drop. 'Are you thinking of Damien?'

Josie nodded. 'I was so sure. So sure. It was perfect. We were perfect. How did it all go wrong?' She wasn't even sure when it had started to crumble. Was it after their first row? Neither of them had been good at saying sorry. Was it because they could never agree on wallpaper? Was it because Damien liked Bon Jovi while she thought Will Smith was the funkiest dude on the face of the earth? They had even argued over naming the cat. Josie had thought Prince was a feisty little bundle of pop fun and an appropriate role model for a cute and perky kitten. Whereas Damien had thought he was merely an arrogant, undersized prick. And a ponce. And hadn't wanted any cat of his to be named after such a short-arsed wanker. Damien preferred Tiddles or Fluffy or Puss-Puss with the singular lack of imagination that typified his life. They had tossed a coin and Prince reigned.

'I was standing there, just like you, Martha, five short years ago. Dressed like a princess and hoping for everlasting happiness. What happened between then and now?'

'Damien shagged someone else.'

'Yes, thank you for that concise assessment of the situation,' Josie huffed. 'But what made him do that? Was it me? Was it something I said? Was it something I did? Or didn't do? He never told me, Martha. He never told me what I did wrong.'

'You shouldn't get all screwed up and insecure just because your ex-husband is an asshole.'

'That's why I'm worried about you, Martha. I don't want you to make the same mistakes as I did. And I don't even know what those mistakes are.'

'I'll be fine.'

'I read something once – it said you shouldn't

marry someone you thought you could live with, you should marry someone you thought you couldn't live without.'

'Josie, you read a lot of shit.'

Her cousin laughed. 'It comes with being divorced and spending too many nights in alone.'

'I've done my fair share of that too,' Martha said. 'Now I want to know what married feels like.'

'I hope you do it better than me, cousin Martha.'

'So do I.'

They both giggled.

'Come here,' Martha said, and they threw their arms round each other.

'Follow your heart, Martha, whatever that means.' Josie held her away. 'Be happy, promise me that.'

'I will.'

'Martha,' Felicia shouted from the bottom of the stairs, 'the photographer's waiting. Are you ready yet?'

'Coming!'

'Josie, you need to get your dress on too!'

Oh, joy! The moment she had been waiting for. Lilac chiffon, here I come . . .

CHAPTER 20

Heathrow Airport at the crack of dawn was not a happening place. The few armed policemen on duty ambled around looking bored. They all appeared the type who wouldn't know what to do if they were ever called upon to shoot someone or wrestle a terrorist to the ground. The cleaners were buffing up the floors to lethal proportions and the shop staff were thinking about ruining their peace and opening up for the day, subjecting themselves to the iniquities of the great unwashed general public.

Given the fact that he had very little leeway in his schedule, Damien was pleased to note that all flights were departing on time. He heaved his holdall on to his shoulder and trudged through the concourse. He was feeling rather self-satisfied with the way the plans for Mission Win Josie Back were shaping up. What woman, faced with this overt display of testosterone, could fail to fall into his arms? It wasn't many men who would travel transatlantically at the drop of a hat just to prove a point. Let Mr Mystery Man compete with that!

However, all was not tickety-boo. As Damien

passed Tie Rack, he examined his face in the window. It was not a pretty sight, bearing as it did the scars of Mad Melanie's plate-throwing act. But on the other hand, if Josie was feeling hard-hearted towards him, as she was inclined to do on occasions, being criss-crossed with crockery scratches might win him the sympathy vote. He had suffered the slings and arrows of outrageous treatment to woo her again and he hoped she bloody well appreciated it. Damien smoothed his fingers across his skin. It smarted. That Melanie had a deadly aim. It was a good job she hadn't gone for the knife drawer or he would be talking in a much higher voice.

He couldn't understand what he'd seen in her – aside from the obvious attractions of big breasts, bouncy bottom and not too many brain cells. But perhaps there wasn't any need for explanation. It was just a man thing. Everyone at the office was at it these days – it was surprising that any work ever got done. He blamed e-mail; the whole system was a hot bed of love notes. Human Resources were considering making it a disciplinary offence to conduct a relationship with a colleague while using company property. If that ever saw the light of day, half the work force would be sacked! Including the Managing Director and his secretary.

Damien checked his watch. He had hours to kill yet. He wandered down the row of shops, looking idly at the aged leather briefcases, handmade silk shirts and Panama hats on display. That was what he would be like when he was older. Stylish to the point of suave. Let's face it, if you were still going to be a serious contender in the floosie magnet stakes in your fifties, you couldn't be content with shopping at Next.

That was when he saw it, and he was captivated. It sparkled in the harsh spotlight in the window, sending out twinkles of blue, pink and green. He had to have it. It was the biggest, flashiest, fuck-offiest diamond ring he had ever seen. This, in the way that nothing else could, would win back the heart of his estranged love. Diamonds, in this case, were a man's best friend. It was pure, clear, set in the shape of a tear-drop (how apt!). Damien could not believe just how romantic he was. A re-engagement ring. He would fall to his knees and beg Josie to have him back. Show-stopper!

The jeweller must have thought all his Christmases had come at once, Damien thought bleakly. He was grinning with uncontained glee as Damien tucked the velvet box deep inside his top pocket, patting it to make sure that it was nestling comfortably. Even his Amex card, which was well accustomed to extravagant purchasing frenzies, had winced in pain when it had been run through the credit-card machine. It may well have been a fuck-off showy diamond, but it had a very fuck-off showy price tag to match. He was sure, however, that he would more than recoup the expense. What he had paid for this little sparkler amounted to an extraordinarily large slice of humble pie.

She was worth it, though. A woman like Josie was one in a million, whereas the Melanies in life were ten a penny – why hadn't he discovered this earlier and saved himself a lot of pain and solicitor's fees? No one would ever support him like Josie had. And what had he got from his relationship with Melanie? The dubious honour of being the world expert on how to get fucking Weetabix out of the video recorder slot. It had been a hard lesson. And expensive. Damien patted his pocket again. But now he was a reformed character. No matter how many times he was unfaithful in the future, he would never, ever be tempted to leave Josie again.

All he needed to do now was find out where the big event was taking place. He dialled Martha's number on his mobile phone, tapping his foot as he waited for the call to connect through the ether.

'Hi,' a distant female voice said.

Damien put his finger to his ear. 'Martha?'

'No, this is Felicia. Martha's kinda busy right now. She's getting ready to leave for the church.'

'I'm due at the wedding, but I've misplaced my invitation. Can you remind me where the reception is?'

'Sure.' Felicia reeled off the name of the hotel while Damien scribbled it down on the back of an envelope he'd fished out of his pocket.

'Thanks, that's great. Is Josie there?'

'Yeah, but she's kinda tied up too. Is it urgent?'

'No.' He had the rest of their future together to deal with this.

'Can I tell her who called?'

'No. Don't bother her.' He wanted this to be the surprise of her life.

'I guess we'll see you later then?' Felicia said before hanging up.

Without a shadow of a doubt, Damien thought with a smile.

CHAPTER 21

Holly looked absolutely dreadful and was very subdued. She was dragging deeply on a cigarette and drinking something that looked suspiciously like full-hit coffee despite her insistence that she was a caffeine-free zone.

Matt felt like something the cat had considered dragging in and then, considering it a health hazard, had left outside. Headstrong, surprisingly, had turned up at the studio, not at the allotted time, of course, but they were there, which in Boy Band Land was something of a minor miracle. They were entertaining themselves with Nintendo Game Boys while they waited for what would loosely pass as an interview to start. The engineers in the mixing studio were working away soundlessly at the tracks they had recorded yesterday. *Ooh ooh baby, how was I to know, you'd mean so much to me when I let you go. Ooh ooh baby . . .*

Matt wondered where Josie was now. She would be donning the lilac frock and doing bridesmaid-type duties and in a few short hours he would burst forth into Martha's wedding celebrations and give her the surprise or shock of her life.

Matt sat down beside Holly, who smiled wanly. 'Did you sleep well?'

Holly wrapped her hands round her cup and nursed it to her. 'If you'd have stayed, as invited, you would know the answer to that question.'

'You know it wasn't a good idea.'

'I thought it was a great idea.'

Matt had left Holly at the door to her apartment block. They had kissed goodnight. Not passionately, but with a bit of tongues, nibbling and sucking noises involved. And very pleasant it was too. But Holly had been decidedly miffed when he made it clear he didn't want it to go any further. She had whined, even begged a bit, and had generally been very persuasive – in fact, one iota more of persuasion could have clinched the deal. It wasn't that he was taking his vow of enforced celibacy too seriously – he was as weak-willed as the next man – but it seemed important these days that if you were going to have sex/make love/do the horizontal tango with someone you, at least, were enthusiastic about the whole thing, wanted to spend time with them and not rush off before the bacon and eggs hit the frying pan. It also sort of helped the whole process if you actually knew them. He had tried to explain all this before abandoning Holly and hailing a cab back to his hotel. Holly, it seemed, did not share his views.

'Maybe another time,' Matt said now, hoping it didn't sound too dismissive.

'Your loss, English boy.' She sounded cool and he hoped he hadn't hurt her. 'Want to know these guys' thoughts on matters of world importance?'

'I can't think of anything I'd rather do.'

Their eyes met and Holly winked. 'I can.'

Headstrong were not, as Matt had believed, native New Yorkers. Justin, the cutesy one, was from Basildon; Tyrone hailed from Barnsley and probably went through hell at school with a name like that; Bobbie was from Accrington; and Stig had spent his formative years in Maidstone, no doubt a charming slice of rural England in its own way, but not exactly the hippest place on the planet. But then was Liverpool, pre-Beatles?

So why had he come all this way to interview them instead of meeting them in Lewisham or Camden? They were flying in the face of tradition, Holly explained in PR-speak, and were going to crack America first. World domination would follow naturally, it appeared. Good and luck were the first words that came to mind. They were going to need it.

Matt felt like a school teacher with an unruly class. Headstrong sat before him, playfully slapping each other round the head and kicking each other's ankles. They had three GCSEs between them and, until they had been plucked from obscurity by Beeline Management Company, none of them had travelled further than Ibiza. Their schedule of partying and travelling was obviously catching up with them. A six-inch layer of tangerine-coloured make-up or fake tan covered their faces, hiding what it could of burgeoning acne and bum-fluff shaving rash brought on by neglect that spoke of being far too busy having a good time to be bothered to wash. Their teeth, however, still shone with an unnatural whiteness that could only have been attained by severe Colgate abuse. Perfect smiles, it seemed, were the most important asset in the promotional stakes. They all wore trousers big enough to hide small troupes of girl guides in. No wonder female teenagers adored them and the male of the species loathed them with abiding hatred. What was it Matt's editor said? When you are tired of interviewing boy bands, you are tired of life. This lot were rapidly making him lose the will to live.

Stifling a heart-weary sigh, Matt flicked his tape recorder on again.

Matt: Who would you say were the major influences in your music?

Justin: What?

Matt: Which bands do you like the best?

Bobbie: Out of what?

Matt: Out of all the bands in the whole wide world.

Stig: Does Fatboy Slim count as a band?

Matt: What about the more established bands, say the Beatles?

Bobbie: My nan likes them. And that Jane MacDonald woman off the telly.

Stig: Didn't they do 'My Generation'?

Tyrone: That was Jim Davidson.

Matt: That's *The Generation Game*. 'My Generation' is a song.

Tyrone: Oh.

Matt: It was by The Who.

Bobbie: Who?

Matt: Precisely.

Tyrone: I've heard some stuff by Frankie Goes To Hollywood, they were well wicked.

Matt: They were all gay.

Stig: (Huffily) There's nothing wrong with that.

Justin: Didn't the Beatles have that nerdy bloke with the glasses?

Matt: John Lennon.

Justin: What a tosser!

Bobbie: My nan likes them.

Matt: So did a few other people. The Beatles are the most successful band of the twentieth century. To date the total worldwide sales of their albums amounts to one hundred and six million. A touch more than Headstrong, I think.

Justin: Wasn't he giving some fat Chinese bird one?

Matt: He was married to Yoko Ono.

Justin: I bet we end up bigger than them.

Matt: *Sergeant Pepper's Lonely Hearts Club Band* was number one in the album charts for a hundred and forty-eight weeks. They released five blockbusting feature films – way ahead of their time.

Justin: So did the Spice Girls.

Tyrone: They're a bit old-fashioned now, aren't they?

Justin: Four-eyed git! Wanted world peace!

Matt: And what are you going to be remembered for? Services to hair gel?

Justin: What sort of a name is the Beatles, anyway?

Matt: What sort of a fucking name is Headstrong? Perhaps you ought to think about changing it to Headcase!

Justin: What's your problem, mate?

Matt: You. What's your problem?

Matt forgot to flick his tape-recorder off before the scuffle ensued. He pushed Justin in the chest, and Justin pushed him back with a surprising amount of force for one who danced so puffily. Matt lurched for Justin's throat in a frenzy of blind rage.

There were defining moments in one's life. The

first was usually when you realised all the policemen were younger than you – and this, Matt felt, he had borne with stoic good nature. The second was when you woke up one morning and all your mates were married except you. Then began the desperate rush to find anyone you went out with deeply attractive in an attempt to get someone veiled before the year was out. This could go some way to explaining why he'd proposed to Eileen Fisher (known widely as Fisherman's Friend – something to do with sucking) after only six weeks of casual dating. Fortunately, she'd turned him down. Unfortunately, six months later, his wife hadn't. The third defining moment was when spotty boy bands said that your pop idols were also favoured by their grandmothers, compared them to cabaret singers from *The Cruise* and singularly failed to respect one of the foremost musicians of our time. Had they no idea what the word 'icon' meant? James Dean? Janis Joplin? John Lennon? They probably thought that Marilyn Monroe was the woman who worked behind the counter at their local Blockbusters video shop. It was all too much to ask a man, particularly a divorced, down-hearted, jaded rock journalist, to bear.

CHAPTER 22

Josie was at the back of the church clutching her posy of white roses in blue hands while a gale-force wind whistled round her knees, which were already knocking. It was not warm. Martha had given them fingerless lace gloves which matched hers, to keep out the cold she said. It was an eternally optimistic gesture.

The bride's car arrived and moments later Joe and Martha came in through the double door of the church. Joe's lip was trembling and Josie was sure it wasn't because Ben Stein had kept his money once again.

Glen and Jack were already in the church. Jack kept his gaze straight ahead, while Glen turned round nervously, fiddling with the rose on his lapel, every ten seconds. They both wore black tuxedos, and Josie had to admit that Jack had scrubbed up very well. Glen looked absolutely gorgeous – wide shoulders, slim hips, dazzling smile – if a little like a nightclub bouncer. There were three other groomsmen to accompany the bridesmaids, but the only one Josie knew was Martha's cousin Albert. The other two were both

Jack's brothers, who were complete hunks. It was clear that Jack must have got the brains.

The music struck up, the familiar strains of 'Here Comes the Bride' reverberating round the vast, echoing space of the church. Josie took her place at the head of the bridal procession and forced a deep breath into her lungs. All heads swivelled to face her. It looked a very long way to the altar. Why couldn't she stomp sullenly down the aisle at the back of everyone else? Her goose pimples were on full show. Perhaps Glen would think she was very pleased to see him.

'Hey, Josie,' Felicia whispered loudly, 'some guy called for you just before we left, but you were having pictures taken.'

'Who was it?'

'He didn't leave a name. Said he'd catch you later. Had an English accent.'

Who knew that she was at Martha's wedding? Josie's heart lurched. There was only one man that she could think of. Matt Jarvis! She was aware that the palms of her hands in her gloves had gone clammy.

How on earth had he tracked her down?

'You look pale,' Martha said. 'You okay, cous?'

'It's you that should be pale!' Josie smiled at Martha. She had never looked more radiant. 'All set?'

Her cousin flicked her train into position.

'Let's go kick some ass,' Martha said.

★　★　★

182

There wasn't a dry eye in the house, including Josie's own, when Martha entered the church. A reverent hush fell over the congregation, broken only by the odd escaped sniffle. Her cousin glided down the aisle, shining, regal, a woman in love. Martha's father wept openly all the way to where Jack stood waiting at the altar, clinging to her as if he was never going to let go. The unspoken thought was that Jeannie would have revelled in it.

Jack and Martha moved to the altar. He held Martha's hand tenderly and his eyes shone openly with adoration. Perhaps Josie was wrong about him. It was one of her worst failings, making black-and-white judgements about people. She did it all the time and then it took a monumental effort to change her opinion. Or a monumental let-down. Matt Jarvis, case in point.

Martha handed Josie her bouquet.

The priest began reciting his lines. 'We are gathered here today to join the lives of these two people, Martha and Jack . . .'

He droned on incessantly and Josie's gaze wandered round the church. Why did people still favour this outmoded institution? How many of this congregation had happy marriages? How many wished they had married other people? How many of them were getting jiggy with other people's wives? How many of them would think up all sorts of just impediments to prevent themselves from tying the knot again? Were there people here finding love sweeter the second time around, or was it beginning to taste bitter in the mouth, just like the first? Who were the brave souls on second or third marriages? Experiencing the joy of juggling stepchildren and ex-spouses, trying to keep everyone happy and, ultimately, pleasing no one. Each liaison entered into more optimistically than the last – surely they must have learnt something from their mistakes? Surely?

It was something she was having to face in life post-divorce. Nearly everyone she encountered had baggage of some sort and huge maintenance payments to meet. Damien had never wanted children, yet had run off with someone who had two. What could you make of that? She imagined it would be difficult enough to manage life with your own baby, let alone cope with someone else's.

There was cold in her bones, her teeth were keen to set up a chattering movement and her feet were numb. If you got frostbite in your toes, how long was it before you had to have them amputated? Martha and Jack were mooning, dewy-eyed, at each other. Hankies were being whipped out all round. Glen looked solemn and stood like a stone statue, carrying out his duties as Best Man with a capital B and a capital M. The priest was speaking to Martha.

'. . . do you promise to love, honour and obey . . .'

They were ridiculous promises to make, Josie thought. How could she ever have stood there and thought that she had a chance of keeping them?

Damien had broken his vows first, and there was a certain smugness in knowing that she was the wronged party. But how long would it have been before her head was turned by someone else – not that there seemed to be many head-turners in the glamorous, champagne-fuelled world of teaching. Would she have grown tired of loving, honouring and obeying Damien? There didn't seem to be an awful lot to honour about him, looking back.

'. . . for better, for worse, for richer, for poorer, in sickness and in health . . .'

Most men went to pieces if they needed an Elastoplast put on. What were the chances of them running up and down the stairs with soft-boiled eggs and hot home-made soup to tempt the appetite of sick wives? They were all straight down the pub at the first mention of a period pain. How could women possibly agree to all this with a straight face? What made thousands of people day after day throughout the world, throughout time, make these rash commitments? Mother Nature and exotic holiday brochures had a lot to answer for.

'. . . and, failing all else, keep you only unto him as long as you both shall live?'

There was a hushed pause in the church. Then Martha's voice rang out clear and strong.

'I will.' She turned to Jack. 'This is my solemn vow.'

There was one consoling thing, Josie thought. Despite the long talk into the night and her cousin's last-minute nerves, resulting in Josie staying awake all night worrying about her, Martha sounded very sure.

It was snowing when they came out of the church. The flakes hit the lilac chiffon with wet blots and stayed there. Even Josie's goose pimples had goose pimples and her nipples could have poked someone's eyes out. Glen's arm was linked through hers.

'You look great, Josie,' he said sincerely.

'You obviously have a thing for blue people.'

'Pardon?'

'Thanks, Glen. You look pretty spruce yourself.'

He moved her down the steps and kept his arm lightly round her.

'Snow on your wedding day is such bad luck!' Martha complained. 'How come I didn't order better weather?'

Some serious shivering was starting to set in.

'You are freezing,' Glen said.

'Very,' Josie agreed.

'Just a few shots,' the photographer shouted.

'Don't any of you dare look cold!' Martha said. 'I will not have any purple lips in my wedding pictures!'

'At least they'll match the frocks,' Josie muttered.

The photographer arranged them on the church steps and snapped away.

'Here.' Glen whipped off his tuxedo jacket. 'Put this round you, it might just stop you catching your death of cold.'

The limos pulled up outside the church. A flurry of damp confetti was hurled over Martha to land in forlorn little clods at her feet, and without further dallying, they all hurried down the steps. Martha and Jack went in the front car. The bridesmaids and groomsmen followed in the next one.

Josie flopped into the leather seat and slid along to make room for the others. Glen followed her. The CD player was turning out transatlantic smooch music and the myriad tiny disco lights set into the ceiling of the limo pulsated in time. Glen produced a bottle of champagne, popped the cork without spilling any – which was a major feat as the car was already whizzing along the freeway towards the wedding reception – and poured them all a glass.

He held up his glass to hers. 'A toast to the most beautiful bridesmaid,' he said.

Josie clinked her glass against his. 'And to the most handsome best man.'

Glen's eyes twinkled in the disco lights. Josie slipped his jacket from her shoulders, taking the strap of the lilac chiffon with it. Suddenly, despite the snow pelting against the windows, it was an awful lot warmer in here. Josie was so glad that her cousin hadn't acquiesced to a quiet little do in Fiji. She was beginning to enjoy Martha's wedding rather a lot. She allowed herself a little self-satisfied smile and the strap of her dress to slip some more. Matt Jarvis might have made one measly phone call of apology, but he might have made it just too late.

CHAPTER 23

'Trying to punch four people at once is not something even Sugar Ray Leonard would have attempted,' Holly said, dabbing enthusiastically at Matt's face with a tissue dipped in Jack Daniels. Her face was white with worry and her fingers brushed his hair.

Matt was stretched out over three chairs in the recording studio, some crushed ice in a plastic bag held to the cut on his cheek. 'It's only a flesh wound,' he muttered through clenched teeth. 'I think it's my pride that's more injured.'

She was right, though, it was a pretty dumb thing to do. Why had he got so riled over a couple of misguided wisecracks by some spotty teenagers who would be returning to oblivion in a few short weeks? They were barely more than children. Stroppy ones, though. Headstrong, it seemed, was a rather fitting name. Matt was known for his patience in the face of adversity. Even when he'd caught his wife having bouncy cuddles with a Bernard Manning look-alike, had he followed his first instinct and pushed the guy's teeth down his throat as he'd wanted to? No. He hadn't even caused a scene. He'd gone quietly to the Cock and Bull, drunk eleven pints of something alcoholic and passed out unnoticed in the corner until someone tidied him up with the empties at closing time. So what had happened to shorten his fuse to explosive proportions? Mr Sane and Reliable seemed to have gone on a short vacation and had been replaced by Mr Totally Irrational who had an unhealthy penchant for cocking things up. Was it just frustration that he couldn't seem to get anything right these days? Good old Matt Jarvis, *Sax 'n' Drugs and Rock 'n' Roll*'s answer to Mr Bean.

Holly handed him two Tylenol and a tumbler of Jack Daniels. He swallowed the tablets with a grimace. 'What time is it?' He was aware of the taste of blood in his mouth.

'They gave you quite a roughing-up. You've been flaked out for over an hour. I thought you'd died. I nearly called 911.'

'Another boy band?'

'They share their name with our emergency services.'

'Oh.' At least someone nearly cared for him. 'Thanks.' He struggled to a more upright position and glanced at his watch. The glass was smashed.

'It's two thirty,' Holly said. 'The guys have gone. They felt really bad about it. They hope it won't affect what you write about them.'

'Of course not,' Matt said with a scowl, glad that the pen was mightier than a right hook any day of the week.

'I told them John Lennon was your half-brother and that's why you were so pissed by their wise cracks.'

'And they believed you?'

'Hey, Matt. They ain't rocket scientists. They're singers – and even that's doubtful.'

Matt laughed through lips that felt like a pair of pork sausages. 'Do you have an answer for everything?'

'Mostly,' Holly said. 'Do you have all the information you need for your article?'

'Plenty.'

'Then it's playtime. Wanna go eat?'

'No. Thanks.' Matt touched his mouth gingerly. 'I don't think I could even if I wanted to. Besides,' he said, 'I've got someone to look up while I'm in New York.'

'You always have other stuff to do, Matt Jarvis.'

'Busy life,' he agreed apologetically.

'Maybe later? I have an invitation to a party. An old friend. It should be a blast. I've arranged for the guys to play a few numbers. Maybe you could come along?'

'Maybe not.' How could he tell her that he was hoping to spend the night smooching away with a rather sexy bridesmaid at Martha's wedding.

'Another club?'

Matt grinned. 'I don't think my constitution could stand it.'

'You know, Burt Reynolds didn't get to where he is today by playing hard to get.'

'I'm not playing hard to get. Last night was fun. But I'm probably going to be busy tonight and I fly out tomorrow afternoon.'

'Maybe you'll look me up next time you're in town?'

'I will. Definitely.'

'Liar.'

'Really. I will.'

'Maybe we'll meet up when Headstrong do their Conquer the World tour.'

Matt grinned. 'Maybe.' He pushed himself up tentatively from his bed of chairs. Nothing felt broken, but plenty of it felt bruised. 'I have to go.'

'So long, Matt,' Holly said. 'It could have been a lot of fun.'

It was snowing when he came out of the depths of the recording studio, so Matt took a cab to Azekal's Manhattan Motel. It was a spruced-up brownstone building in the Flat Iron district and looked like a pretty funky place to hold a wedding even if it did have a naff name.

He paid the cab and sprinted into the lobby of the hotel shaking a sprinkling of snow from his hair on to the plush red carpet. The foyer was filled with the type of over-the-top flower arrangements totally suited to a wedding. Cream flowers spilled out of Grecian urns, bowers or whatever you called them (floristry had never been his forte), hung in swathes from the rafters and the receptionist was almost completely obliterated by greenery.

Matt sidled up to the desk, plastering his damp hair against his forehead.

'I'm here for Martha's wedding,' he said hoping he sounded sufficiently assertive and not at all like a gatecrasher.

'Martha's wedding?'

'I believe I'm in the right place.'

The receptionist tapped at her computer. She smiled up at Matt, looking vaguely nervous. 'I'm sorry, I just took over from lunch. Martha's wedding is in the Great Room.' She leant past her flower arrangement and pointed. 'Up the stairs, turn left. It's straight ahead of you, sir.'

'Thank you.'

'And the men's room is to your left.' She gave him a look that said *Visit it*!

Matt fingered his cheek gently. He could be bleeding.

'Thanks.'

'You're welcome.'

Matt dashed up the stairs to the washroom. This too was decked out with cream floral arrangements – fairly unusual for a men's loo, even at a wedding. This Martha must have one hell of a flower budget.

Looking in the mirror was not a great idea. He was bleeding. Not a lot, but enough to make him look more like an armed robber than your average wedding guest. He shrugged off his topcoat and hung it on the rack. Was this tie going to be too leery? South Park was all the rage in the UK – well, it used to be when he bought this whimsical tie – but what would people think of it here? At least he *had* a tie. He hoped it would make up for the absence of a jacket. He had packed to interview boy bands, not attend weddings.

Hopefully, Josie would be suitably swept away by his ingenuity in finding her to forgive him a little roughness round the edges. Matt dabbed at his cut cheek with some dampened loo roll. Headstrong might be made up of nothing more than irritating children, but one of them could certainly pack a punch.

Matt straightened himself up, puffed out his chest and turned his good side to the mirror. Then he sagged. Not convincing. He hoped the lights were dim in this place.

'This is not good' he said, and began pacing in front of the mirror. 'I'm turning up unexpectedly, I look like day-old shit and I am wearing the standard uniform of a slob. The fair Josephine may not be impressed by this.'

Deep breath, Matthew. You didn't come this far to falter now!

'On the other hand, I have tracked her down to apologise for my heinous crime in deserting her. I will bombard her with adoration vibes and she will realise instantly what a top bloke I really am.'

This sounds too easy. She could cause a scene, have me thrown out, push wedding cake up my nose. Get everyone else to push wedding cake up my nose!

'Pull yourself together, Matt,' he snarled at the mirror. 'Are you a man or a mouse? What is the worst she can do? Tell you to get stuffed? At least, you'll be able to hold your head high and say that you tried.'

Matt bounced round the floor, limbering up. He aimed a few psych-up punches at the mirror. Pity he hadn't done that before wading into Headstrong; he might have thought better of it. Shrugging his shoulders, he pushed out a few calming breaths.

'I am as ready as I will ever be,' he announced to the mirror.

The cubicle door behind him opened. 'That's good,' the emerging man said. 'If you want my opinion, you look okay.'

'Thanks,' Matt said sheepishly. 'Sorry, I thought I was alone.'

'Ah, so what.' The man pulled on his cigar. 'You made taking a crap a lot more entertaining.'

The man headed towards the door.

'Wait,' Matt said. 'You aren't by any chance a guest at Martha's wedding?'

'Sure am.'

'Do you think I might accompany you?'

The man shrugged. 'Sure.'

'Thank you. Thank you.'

'No problem.'

'I don't know anyone, you see.'

'Apart from Martha . . .'

'Oh, yeah, right.' Matt shook his hand. 'I'm Matt Jarvis, by the way.'

'And I'm Uncle Hymi.'

'Pleased to meet you.'

'You ain't missed nothing yet,' Uncle Hymi assured him. 'The party's just startin'.'

'Great.'

They walked towards the door together.

'This woman you want to impress,' Uncle Hymi said.

'Josie?'

'Josie. You should take her flowers.'

'Flowers?'

'Knocks 'em dead every time. Flowers.'

'Flowers.'

Matt scanned the room and grabbed an arrangement from a vase next to the washbasins. He tugged the oasis from the bottom and shook off the drips of water. Pulling two paper towels from the dispenser, he wrapped them round the bottom of the flowers. He just hoped Josie wouldn't want to use them to knock *him* dead.

'Flowers,' Uncle Hymi said approvingly.

'Flowers,' Matt agreed.

'Let's go knock her dead!'

'Yes,' Matt said uncertainly. And they set off together to celebrate Martha's wedding.

CHAPTER 24

The peacocks looked half dead with cold, Josie thought. They were shivering their feathers with an enthusiasm she'd never seen from peacocks before, and their noise was even more dreadful than normal. She wondered whether they came from warm climates and she also wondered who had wrestled them into submission to force cream silk wedding bows round their long, shimmering necks. She was just glad it wasn't another bridesmaid's duty. Did bridesmaids in Britain realise just how lightly they got off?

The entire battery of wedding guests was standing outside on the terrace, flanking Martha and Jack, champagne in hand. Josie curled her fingers round her glass, hoping for reflected warmth, but it was even colder than her bottom – which was pretty damn cold at the moment. What a shame they weren't drinking hot, beefy Bovril, she mused. Most of the women had already abandoned their hats and were shivering gracefully in the sub-zero temperatures. Despite the cold, the snow had stopped, which was something to be grateful for, even though it gave a new slant on a white wedding. They were all gazing skywards and had been for ten minutes.

Glen was being very attentive. She was wearing his jacket again, while he stood manfully by in shirt sleeves, a protective hand on her waist. God, it felt so good to be found attractive again. Perhaps that was why she'd had such an unnecessarily positive reaction to Matt Jarvis. Was she so desperate for a man in her life that she'd gone overboard on the first one who had shown her any attention? She had read *Bridget Jones's Diary* – had she learned nothing?

Mind you, he had seemed very sweet. In an unreliable sort of way. It was a shame he hadn't turned up. But then that was life these days. Everything was disposable. Milk bottles. Razors. Nappies. People.

She wondered if he would try to call her again. Perhaps she would be otherwise engaged. Once bitten, twice very wary. Turning to Glen, she was gratified to feel him give her a friendly squeeze. He towered over her and she stepped nearer into the warmth of his arms. Onwards and upwards, Josie Flynn!

'Not long now,' he said.

And, on cue, a small aeroplane appeared in the white winter sky that bore the faint grey tinge of an overwashed shirt. It circled the grounds of the hotel, the engine making wet, spluttering farty noises as it swooped round towards them.

Suddenly, clouds of white smoke started to pour out of the back of the plane and it ducked and dived, tumbling somersaults across the bare expanse of sky. The crowd oohed nervously. It wheeled back, turning on itself like a mad seagull before plunging weightlessly towards the ground. The peacocks shrieked loudly.

Slowly letters emerged until the smoke spelled MARTHA across the bleak New York skyline. The plane's engine droned alarmingly and the smoke turned to blue, spelling JACK alongside his bride's name. Another swoop and whirl and the smoke streamed out in a red plume, the plane twisting and turning until it had circled both names with a red heart.

To the cheers of the crowd, the plane shot vertically heavenwards, rotating in a victory roll and finally flew above its creation unfurling a banner which read IN LOVE FOREVER! The wedding guests whooped and hollered to a man, clapping until their palms were red.

The plane, job done, disappeared into the wide blue yonder whence it came, and the crowd started to peel away, following Martha into the hotel so that the wedding feast could begin.

Glen turned her to follow the others. 'What did you think of that?'

'Different,' Josie said.

'That sort of stuff goes down big in England too?'

'Not awfully.'

'No?'

'We're more low-key about things.'

'This is a very high-show wedding.'

'We consider ourselves lucky to get a warm sausage roll and a curled-up sandwich these days.'

'You should see the food in there. Someone pushed the boat out big time. That Jack's one hell of a lucky guy. I hope he knows it.'

'Glen.' She cleared her throat. 'You know Jack better than I do. *Much* better. Do you think he and Martha are well suited?'

'Hell, who am I to say? Martha looks like she thinks so.'

'She does, doesn't she?' Josie kicked at the paving stones with her silk shoes which were pinching her toes. 'Is he a nice guy?'

Glen turned back to stare at the sky. 'Hey, would you catch a look at that!'

Josie followed his eyes. The smoke of the message was drifting, curling away on the breeze. The letters were growing faint, shifting, merging. Glen started to laugh. JACK was melting into the sky, fading away, leaving the legend JERK in its place. MARTHA and JERK. The man beside her was chuckling heartily, tears filling his eyes. But for some reason, Josie couldn't find it within her to laugh at all.

'Thank the Lord that is over!' Martha said as she flopped on to the chintzy sofa. 'Now the fun can begin.'

The hotel had thoughtfully provided the bridal party with a courtesy room in which to freshen up before the marathon photography session took place. The guests, meanwhile, were enjoying cocktail hour – a finger buffet stacked high enough to feed the five thousand should they care to drop by, and enough free booze to float the *Titanic*. This was before the real eating and drinking started, and Josie could now understand why Martha's father had been complaining about the cost.

Two waitresses came in bearing trays of scallops wrapped in bacon and the largest shrimps she'd ever seen.

'Champagne, ma'am?'

Martha held out her glass eagerly. 'I am going to get *so* wasted!'

'Do you think you should drink alcohol on your wedding day, sweetie?' Jack asked, covering his glass of orange juice with his hand.

'What better day?' She tugged at her veil and failed to move it. Beatrice appeared to have spot-welded it to her scalp. 'I think after all the organising I've done, I deserve it!'

'Perhaps a little won't hurt.'

'If I have a lot,' Martha said, kicking off her shoes and reclining, 'I won't feel any pain at all.'

Felicia picked at a shrimp, dipping it in tomato sauce. 'Great shrimp, Martha!'

Jack wandered over to the trays of delicious food. 'Didn't I specify no bacon products for the cocktail buffet?'

'Lighten up, Jack,' Glen said. 'It's your wedding day. Best day of your life and all that. What difference does a little dead pig make? Let your hair down.'

'I don't have any hair,' Jack answered.

'Have some shrimp then,' Martha suggested, picking one from the tray Felicia offered her.

'They're bottom-feeders.'

Martha made a rude gesture with her shrimp.

'Have some bubbles,' Glen urged. 'It may help you to unwind.'

'I think I'll go somewhere quiet and do some rainbow chi kung.'

'Jack!' Martha pouted. 'We have pictures to do and our guests are waiting.'

'I have to be in the right frame of mind,' he said, and left the room, shutting the door firmly behind him.

'Jack!' Martha cried.

'Leave him,' Glen said. 'Give him a few minutes and then I'll go after him. He's been very nervous about all this. It's a big step.'

'It is for me too!' Martha's lip looked as if it was about to start trembling.

Glen slipped his arm round her shoulders. 'You know what he's like.'

'Do I?' Martha said, slumping against him.

'Champagne?' The waitress proffered the half-empty bottle into the tense silence.

'Could you perhaps bring us some tea?' Josie suggested.

'Oh, how bloody British, Jo-jo! When the going gets tough, the tough put the kettle on and have a nice cup of tea?' Martha held out her glass again. 'I need more champagne,' she said.

Glen stood up and gave Josie a worried look. 'I'll go after Jack.'

Martha was sipping her tea placidly while Josie reapplied her eyeshadow for her. Not that it needed it. It would take a trip through a car wash to get this lot off tonight. Beatrice must have been a plasterer before she took up beauty work. She would have to give herself a good scrub-down with a Brillo pad the minute she got back to the hotel.

Felicia and the other bridesmaids were flaked out on the sofa behind them. The photographer had last been seen tapping his foot impatiently.

Her cousin was looking distinctly subdued.

'You okay?' Josie asked, as she daubed her brush into the make-up.

Martha nodded.

'Sure?'

Martha failed to answer.

'If it's any consolation, Damien and I had a row on our wedding day.'

'Don't you think that might have been an omen?'

'You're probably right,' Josie agreed. 'He was pinching the bridesmaid's bums.'

'Mine included.'

'Oh yeah,' she said, remembering.

Martha let out a lingering sigh and lowered her

voice. 'Do you think I've done the right thing, Josie?'

'Of course you have!'

'I'm feeling . . .' Martha gnawed her lip, 'strange.'

'Of course you are! It's your wedding day, you're a bag of nerves, you've been frozen half to death, now it's like a sauna in here, and you've had nothing to eat, unless you count half a bagel and a glass of swamp water. Of course you're feeling unsettled!'

'Supposing I was already starting to have regrets . . .'

'You should never regret the things you've done in life, only the things you haven't done.'

'This is another "they" saying, right?'

'It could be,' Josie said defensively.

'Only I was thinking about what you said last night.'

'Oh, you shouldn't pay any attention to me. If I've got nothing to worry about, I worry about that. I was putting my insecurities on to you.'

'You don't think I've rushed into this? My emotions have been so screwed up since Jeannie died I'm not thinking straight. Should I have waited?'

'We went through all this and you know it was the right choice. You want babies, remember?'

'Supposing he can't have any? You were right. I didn't think of that.'

'You'll have hundreds. Enough to form your own football team.'

'Soccer.'

'Soccer team,' Josie corrected.

Glen came back in. 'Jack'll be here in a few moments.'

'Is he okay?' Martha's face looked pinched.

'He's fine.'

Martha smiled wanly. Glen chucked her under the chin. 'You can do better than that,' he said.

'I'll have to,' Martha agreed. 'We have all the pictures to do.'

Jack came back into the room and dropped to his knees, kissing her hand. 'I'm sorry, honey,' he said. 'I guess this has been stressful for us all. Forgive me.'

Martha twisted her fingers round his plait, examining it as if it wasn't there. 'Is everyone ready?' she said. 'The photographer's waited long enough.'

Jack slid his arms round her waist and held her to him. Martha stared over his shoulder, biting at her lip, and her eyes connected with Glen's, and only Josie seemed to notice the look that passed between them.

CHAPTER 25

'Hava Nagila' was in full swing when Matt and Uncle Hymi opened the doors to the ballroom. Uncle Hymi started to clap and click his fingers instantly, swaying his hips to the music. Matt stood awkwardly with his bunch of flowers wrapped in paper towels and searched the room for any sign of Josie.

'Get into the groove,' Uncle Hymi suggested, and pulled Matt into the circle of dancers – every one of whom seemed to know what they were doing, bar him. Dare he admit it – if it had been 'The Birdie Song' or 'Saturday Night', it would have been a different matter, but somehow the movements to accompany ancient Jewish folk songs had passed him by.

He was standing there clapping his hands against his flowers, craning his neck above the circle, when suddenly he was grabbed by the arm and swung round by a woman who was smaller than R2D2, but had breasts bigger than Dolly Parton. The flowers smashed against a marble pillar, showering petals all over the dance floor. Aunty Dolly smiled encouragingly at him and whizzed him round the other way. His arm was caught by another relative, who twirled him back into the centre of the circle. The other men were performing ritualistic twitching movements while the outer circle clapped and cheered. Men over a certain age really shouldn't attempt to dance, Matt noted. Michael Flatley might just get away with it, but it was a close-run thing. Lesser mortals should stick to bowls or golf. Someone prodded Matt in the back and obediently he lifted his legs mimicking the others, kicking frantically and waving his bouquet in the air. He glanced round to see if Josie was watching him and was relieved to see she wasn't.

'Good grief, woman,' he puffed through gritted teeth, 'you'd better be worth all this humiliation!'

If only he could work his way towards the cake, he might have a chance of spotting a bridesmaid, or even *the* bridesmaid. The music appeared to be slowing down; Matt stopped flailing his legs so wildly and mopped his perspiring brow with his South Park tie. There was some more whooping by the dancers and the music speeded up again. For heaven's sake, what was this? The twelve-inch version? Hadn't they had enough? They obviously made New York pensioners of strong stuff. Aunty Dolly appeared in front of him jiggling her breasts with abandon. Most of the flowers had lost their heads. He aped her movements and was profoundly grateful that he hadn't bunked off all of his country dancing classes at primary school. He'd known that one day they must come in useful.

They were off again. Threading his way through a ribbon of adjoining arms that twisted and twirled him any way but the way he wanted to go. Matt threw what was left of the bouquet of battered flowers to one of the passing waiters and let himself go with the flow.

Just as they were all starting to need hip replacements, the music stopped abruptly and with a cheer all the dancers left the floor as suddenly as they had started. Someone shoved a glass of champagne into Matt's hand, which he downed in one gulp. He was breathing heavily and realised that he wasn't as fit as he once thought he was.

'Come and help yourself to some food.' Aunty Dolly steered him towards the buffet table, which groaned with sumptuous food.

'No, really . . .' Matt protested.

'Don't be shy,' she insisted.

Matt looked round in panic. 'I'm not really—'

'Oh, you're English,' she gasped. 'My oh my! I have visited Stratford-upon-Avon. Have you been there?'

'Yes, I have,' Matt said. A plate was pushed into his hand and he was nudged along the table.

'That William Shakespeare was one hell of a guy.'

'Yes,' Matt said, allowing his plate to be loaded with things he didn't want to eat.

'I've seen all his films. He looks just like Joseph Fiennes.'

'Yes,' Matt agreed.

'And you've come all the way from England for Martha's wedding?'

'Well, no. Well, yes. Well, not exactly.'

'Have you known her for long?'

'Not that long.'

'How do you two know each other?'

'Er . . .'

'I didn't think Martha had ever been to Europe.'

'I . . . er . . . I . . . would you excuse me?' Matt said, and snatched his brimming plate and headed for the nearest pillar that looked big enough to hide behind.

After swiping glass number three and swallowing the chill bubbles gratefully, Matt caught a glimpse of the bride. She was tall, blonde and incredibly beautiful. The dress screamed expensive. Martha was definitely a high-maintenance babe. She was sneaking drags of a cigarette which was hidden behind the towering wedding cake, and she was also knocking back champagne as though it was going out of fashion. It was a huge wedding. Hundreds of guests milled round the vast room and it was clear that Martha's daddy must be worth a bob or two. He scanned their faces hopefully. Where had the bloody bridesmaids got to? Josie must be here somewhere.

Matt leaned against his pillar and tucked into a lamb cutlet.

'Ladies and gentlemen,' a saccharine-sweet voice announced. 'The bridesmaids and their groomsmen will lead us in the next dance.'

Yes! Matt thought, and grabbed another glass of fizz from a passing tray. Yes, yes, yes!

The guests clapped enthusiastically. The band struck up and a path parted in the crowd.

Four women drifted serenely on to the dance floor. Matt's heart was thumping loudly, his mouth dry despite the excess of champagne. They moved into the arms of their waiting partners and wafted effortlessly round the floor like a formation team from Home Counties North on *Come Dancing*.

'Oh, fuck,' Matt said. He looked down at his brimming plate of food and suddenly he had lost his appetite completely.

They all looked beautiful. Shining, radiant. They gazed into the faces of their partners with rapt attention. The dresses were magnificent. Filigree creations in fabric as delicate as spiders' webs.

'Fuck, fuck, fuck,' Matt said. He sank to the floor behind his pillar.

The bridesmaids danced on, oblivious to his suffering. They were so exquisite, tiny, pirouetting princesses. Why did it happen to him? Why did it *always* happen to him?

There was only one thing wrong with the dresses, from Matt's point of view. But it was quite pertinent. They were pink. Sugar-frosty pink. Candy-floss pink. Barbie pink. Extremely pretty but, nevertheless, pink.

Not lilac.

The music came to a close. The bridesmaids smiled beguilingly. They were all adorable and, in their own way, he knew he could potentially have fallen in love with any of them. And he also knew, with a certainty that was heart-breaking, that he had never, ever clapped eyes on any of them before.

Matt banged his head gently against the pillar. 'Fuck.'

Whoever this Martha was, she had nothing whatsoever to do with Josie Flynn.

CHAPTER 26

'Ladies and gentlemen,' the man with the microphone and the Mr Whippy hairdo said, 'please put your hands together to welcome your bride and groom, Mr and Mrs Jack Labati!'

Martha and Jack entered the room to a drum roll, taking the centre of the ballroom floor, Martha twirling like a ballerina, her train depositing a sprinkle of persistent confetti from its folds. The guests stood up and gave them a round of applause.

Josie bit her lacy glove nervously and Glen adjusted his bow tie.

'Ladies and gentlemen, the wedding party! Matron of honour, Ms Josie Flynn, all the way from London, England, and the best man, Mr Glen Donnelly!'

They also strode to the centre of the dance floor, though Josie thought it wise to leave the twirling to Martha. The rest of the bridesmaids and grooms-men were similarly introduced with much fanfare and raucous applause. There was so much more razzmatazz than at an English wedding, where by now they would be sitting down to leathery roast beef and dried-up Yorkshire pudding, due to the seeming inability of any hotel in Britain to serve hot food to more than four people at once. The mothers would still be getting their money's worth out of their hats and everyone else would be moaning about not being able to hear the priest, not knowing any of the hymns, and the slow service at the bar.

Glen took her into his arms.

'*Have I told you lately that I love you . . .*' the wedding singer crooned.

He smiled down at her. 'You can relax now,' he said. 'The worst is over.'

Josie allowed the tension to go out of her shoulders. He ran his hands over her bare arms and she felt a rush of heat go through her.

'Feeling a bit warmer.'

'A lot warmer. Thanks.'

'We'll soon have you thawed out.'

She hoped so; she didn't particularly want to go through life with a heart as frozen as a Popsicle, although that probably wasn't what he'd meant. Josie glanced up at him. There was an unsettled look in his eyes, dark like a troubled sea, dangerous hidden currents in their depths. That was one thing she had liked about Matt: there seemed to be an honesty, a truth in his eyes that was missing from so many men these days. It felt as if he spoke right into her. It was amazing how wrong you could be. God, she must have been more drunk than she thought to trust a stranger.

Still, he was history. Josie looked up at Glen again. No wonder his eyes looked unhappy. This must be so difficult for him, she thought. What would she feel like if she heard Damien was going to get remarried to Thing? Imagine attending the wedding and giving them good wishes. It didn't bear thinking about. And here was Glen having to cope with watching his best friend marry his past love. It couldn't be easy.

She wanted to tell him that she understood what he must be going through, that she knew about the baby, that Martha had loved him more than anyone at that time. What did he feel about Martha now? Was it possible to feel benign indifference to someone you had once loved? It had been such a shock to her that all her love for Damien could have turned to hate in the space of a few ill-timed words. 'I'm in love with someone else' – the sentence to stop a loving heart in its tracks and send it grinding into reverse gear.

How did it happen that someone you had loved and shared your life with for so long was suddenly no longer a part of it, any necessary communication carried out by impersonal solicitor's letters costing two hundred pounds an hour? It was true, there was a very thin line between love and hate. There really should be no such thing as an amicable divorce. If you could handle all that pain civilly, wasn't it less effort to knuckle down and make a relationship work?

Glen bent down and put his mouth to her ear. 'Do you think they look happy?'

She watched Jack and Martha dancing together,

holding each other tightly. Jack looked so proud and Martha, far from the blushing bride, appeared radiant in her self-assured confidence. She knew that she looked great and was milking it for all it was worth. And why not, she deserved it. Her cousin had been through a hell of a time since Jeannie died. She was due a little happiness.

'I do,' Josie said.

'Me too.' Somehow the thought didn't seem to cheer him.

'Do you want to sit down?'

'I think we can sneak away for a few quiet moments, if you'd like that,' Glen said.

Josie nodded towards the French doors. 'Come on then.'

They headed towards the garden, grabbing two glasses and a bottle of champagne from a waiter on the way.

'You're quiet,' Josie said.

'It's been a long day,' Glen replied, and tossed back his champagne.

They were sitting in a boathouse in the grounds, overlooking a small grey lake dotted with chilly-looking ducks. The boathouse was a twee clapboard affair with Georgian windows. It clearly wasn't used too often, as there was a housing estate of undisturbed spiders hanging from the rafters. The doors were open so they could look out over the lake, and Josie had her feet up on the narrow bench, hugging her knees to ward off the cold. She was swathed in the folds of Glen's tuxedo for the third time today, and it still felt good.

'You look a little tired too.'

'I bet that's not the first thing anyone notices about Cameron Diaz,' Josie huffed. 'Hey, Cam, how are the black shadows and the puffy bags doing?' I bet she hasn't been stood up recently.

'It wasn't the first thing I noticed,' Glen protested. 'I was trying to be considerate.'

'Sorry,' Josie said. 'I'm growing unreasonably defensive and suspicious in my old age.'

'You're a very attractive woman.'

'That is not a good thing to be called in England,' she told him. 'It basically means that although you don't quite qualify for a paper bag over your head, you're not considered a raging beauty. It does, however, mean that you can usually be relied upon to buy your round in the pub.'

'Well,' Glen said, 'in New York, it's a compliment.'

His smile was a bit of a knee-trembler, Josie conceded, glad that she wasn't standing up. He moved closer to her and she could smell the faint tang of his aftershave – one of those new-fangled androgynous jobs, sporty and fresh, that showed he was a with-it sort of guy. Probably got it free by the gallon from his company. Josie hankered for the long-gone days of Gingham and Charlie – definite girlie scents that you could nick from your mother's dressing table when she wasn't looking. Why was it all these trendy concoctions always managed to smell like Old Spice on her?

'More champagne?'

Josie nodded. Glen leaned over and held her hand to steady her glass while he poured, which made it wobble even more.

'Enough?'

'Not yet,' she smiled, 'but I'm getting there.' The bubbles had reached her toes from the inside out, making them tingle in the cold air.

They sat back in companionable silence, watching the ducks fidget their bottoms around trying to get comfortable.

Josie stretched back her head, easing the tension from her neck. 'Martha and I spent most of the night talking.'

'That's not unusual for Martha.' He gave a melancholy laugh. 'We sometimes used to sit on the back porch, just shooting the breeze, until the sun came up.'

'That's nice.'

'It was a long time ago.'

'Is this difficult for you?'

'Drinking champagne with a beautiful woman?' Glen laughed. 'Terribly difficult.'

'You know what I mean.'

He poured some more champagne and settled back against the rough boards of the boathouse. 'It's harder than I thought.'

'Why did you agree to do it?'

'I've asked myself that very question several times since.'

Josie watched two ducks nestling down together

at the edge of the water and felt a pang of envy. She wondered if male ducks were all commitment-phobes with roving eyes. 'You two could have made a nice couple.'

'I think I could have made her happy once, but I goofed up.'

'She told me what happened.' Josie studied her glass. 'All of it.'

'Was this what you talked about until the wee small hours?' he teased.

'Some of it.'

Glen let out a long, lingering sigh. 'I treated Martha very badly. I have to live with that.'

'Do you regret it?'

'It's the biggest mistake I ever made, and I've made a few, believe me.'

At that moment, Martha's head popped round the boathouse door. Her cheeks were flushed and her eyes too sparkly. Her head-dress was looking slightly skewwhiff and waves of champagne splashed over the rim of the flute she was clutching in her hand. She swayed slightly, steadying herself against the door before she spoke.

'What was your biggest mistake?'

They jumped apart, feeling unnecessarily guilty. Glen recovered his composure first.

He beamed at Martha. 'Not whisking you up the aisle while I had the chance.'

'Really?'

'You know that as well as I do.'

'Is it time I left?' Josie asked.

'Nonsense.' Martha shook back the tendrils that had fallen round her face. 'We're just teasing. I came to get you because I'm about to throw my bouquet and I wanted you both there. You never know, Glen, you might end up marrying Josie!'

Josie stood. 'No thanks. I've been second best once.'

'That wouldn't be the case. I've moved on,' he said. 'I've had to. She spurned me like you'd spurn a rabid dog!'

'I did not!' Martha protested, tottering on her silk shoes.

Glen held out his hand to steady her. 'Perhaps you'd be the first to give us your blessing if we were to become an item?'

Martha giggled uncertainly. 'Come on, Josie,' she said, 'Let's get this bouquet tossed and see if you're ever going to say "I do" again.'

'I can tell you that without the need for any preliminaries,' Josie warned.

'Come on,' Martha urged petulantly. 'Everyone's waiting. They didn't know where you'd got to.'

'We only came out for some fresh air,' Josie tutted.

'There's no need to explain to me,' her cousin teased.

Glen wagged his finger at her. 'You are priceless, Martha Rossani.'

Martha's smile faded for a moment and she held up her finger with the wedding band on. 'Labati,' she corrected. 'Mrs Martha Labati.'

'Well, *Mrs* Labati,' Glen said, 'let's get you back to your wedding. It's bad manners to keep the groom waiting.'

Martha turned precariously on her heels and marched unsteadily back towards her waiting guests.

The light was fading now, the chill afternoon darkening into a cold, clear night. They stood up and traipsed out of the boathouse after Martha. Glen slipped his arm round Josie's shoulders and they followed silently in her cousin's turbulent wake. His elbow stuck out at an angle, and instead of comforting her, it was tense and bounced on her bony bits, jarring against her rhythm as she walked along the path. This was not a comfortable place to be. There was definitely unresolved business between Martha and her former lover and she wondered if her cousin had really told her everything.

Martha was stomping ahead of them, bashing the tightly bound bouquet against her leg. Petals showered the ground as she walked. At this rate there would be very little left of it to throw.

CHAPTER 27

att had been 'Hava Nagila'-ed to death. He'd done the rounds with several under-fives, Aunty Dolly, Uncle Hymi and Uncle Tom Cobbleigh and all, it would seem. He had performed the Chicken Dance, which appeared to be the American version of 'The Birdy Song', the Electric Slide, which required more slick turns than he was capable of, and some elementary line-dancing steps to something that sounded vaguely like 'Achy Breaky Heart'. He had also shuffled with deepening embarrassment, rather than gyrating suggestively, through 'Hey, Macarena' – something which should never have been allowed out of Ibiza without a health warning. Very happening for a funky rock journalist. Not for the first time this weekend, he questioned his chosen profession.

Now he was dancing with a very nice bridesmaid. Not *the* bridesmaid, he had to concede, but a very nice one anyway. He'd availed himself of Martha II – The Wrong Bride's champagne, and despite being terminally broken-hearted and thwarted in his quest to find Ms Josie Flynn, who

220

was out somewhere in this sprawling city, he was feeling rather fine.

His liver hadn't suffered such abuse since university days, and by the time he got his flight back to Heathrow, it would no doubt be as pickled as a jar of gherkins.

Matt stopped twirling with the bridesmaid. She was a lovely girl, slender as a reed, with brown curls like the Tressy doll his sister used to have. She also thought William Shakespeare made great films. Now she looked up at him, smiling breathlessly, and he had never felt so sad in his life. What was he doing here? He was a gatecrasher among all these aunts, uncles, cousins and friends. He didn't belong here. A nice gatecrasher, a gatecrasher who'd had a wonderful time, but a gatecrasher nevertheless.

He held both of the bridesmaid's hands. 'That was great. Thanks,' he said. 'But I have to go now.'

'So early?' she protested. 'This'll go on for ages yet.'

Somehow he didn't doubt that.

'There's more food, more dancing.'

Matt felt like he'd already eaten the entire contents of a supermarket trolley and had danced more than Lionel Blair on a good day.

'I have to be somewhere.'

'It's been nice,' she said.

'Yes. Great. Thanks . . .' He didn't even know her name.

'Alana.'

'. . . Alana.'

Why couldn't he have met all these accommo-dating women before being mesmerised under Josie Flynn's spell? Well, all two of them.

He said goodbye to Aunt Dolly and Uncle Hymi and they kissed and hugged him like a long-lost son, promising to look him up in London next time they came to see Shakespeare. He said goodbye to Martha II, wished her a happy future and made a mental note to send her a ridiculously generous thank-you present on his return to England.

Matt walked out to the men's room to collect his coat. The vase that he had swiped Josie's flower arrangement out of remained empty and forlorn. Matt looked at the sprinkle of petals that lay beside it and snorted unhappily to himself. So, he had failed miserably in his quest to find Josie Flynn when he thought he had been so close. So near, but yet so far. The story of his life. He shrugged on his coat and found his scarf, wondering if it was still snowing.

There was a doorman out at the front of the hotel hailing cabs, and Matt joined the queue. Where was he going to go? He checked his broken watch and noticed that the shattered glass had disappeared somewhere during the dancing. He also noted that it was midway through the evening, not yet nine o'clock – too early to find a bar and drink alone. The lights on Broadway would be twinkling at their brightest. He shuffled forward, draping his scarf round his neck. It was freezing, the sharp air nipping like little razors, the wind funnelling down the streets finding its way inside your coat when you weren't looking, and there was the threat of more snow in the air. God, this could be a desolate place to live when it was cold and you were alone. Worse than the Lake District.

A little finger of warmth stroked Matt's neck. Wait. There was one place he could go. Someone he knew who would want to see him. Holly. Why hadn't he thought of her before? The doorman blew his whistle. Matt was next in line for a cab. He couldn't keep treating Holly like this, picking her up and putting her down when it suited him like . . . like something you picked up and put down when it suited you.

Before his conscience could prevent him, he punched Holly's number into his mobile phone, clasping it to his frozen ear.

The phone rang until the answering machine clicked and whirred into life.

'Hi. I'm sorry I'm not home. Please leave your number and I'll get right back.'

Message. Message. Message. Think of a message, Matthew!

'I, er . . . Hi, er, Holly. It's, er, Matt, here. Matt Jar—'

There was a screech of answerphone being interrupted down the line. 'Hi,' Holly said, breathing heavily.

A cab pulled up and Matt ushered the man behind him to the head of the queue.

'It's, er, Matt.'

'I hoped you'd call.'

'You sound out of breath.'

'I ran back up the stairs when I heard the phone. I was just going out.'

'Oh. Oh. Okay. Then it doesn't matter.'

'What doesn't matter?'

'I, well . . . I . . .'

'Are you available?'

'I er . . . I, er . . . My plans fell through,' he said limply. 'I, er . . .'

Holly ended his misery for him. 'Come right over.'

'Ohhkaay.' Was she going to make a big deal out of this? Was this an unutterably dreadful idea, similar in magnitude to the one he'd had about finding the slender needle of Josie Flynn in a city that laughed in the faces of mere haystacks?

'If you want to,' she added a little less brashly.

'I don't want to mess you about,' Matt said. 'Maybe you should stick to your original agenda.'

'I'd rather see you.'

'Oh.'

'Do you wanna come over?'

'I do,' he said, and at that moment he really did.

'You remember where it is?'

'I wrote the address down.'

'Where are you now?'

'Just off Sixth Avenue.'

'Then I'll see you in five.'

The phone went dead, leaving Matt staring at it. Another cab pulled up next to him and Matt squeezed a tip into the doorman's hand as he helped him into the back seat. The doorman touched his cap as he closed the door, cocooning Matt in the steaming, incense-laden heat of the cab. Matt settled into one cosy fur-lined corner. There were worse jobs to have than being a rock hack.

'Where to, Mac?'

Matt uncurled Holly's address from a piece of paper in his pocket. Why had this ability to be careful with inconsequential items of stationery suddenly manifested itself? Didn't it know it was three days too late?

He gave the cab driver Holly's address and they bounced their way down Sixth Avenue, the cab driver with a strange sense of direction and a kami-kaze instinct; Matt with a strange sense of elation and foreboding.

CHAPTER 28

Despite having been cunning enough to procure an executive mode of transport for his quest and being several thousand pounds lighter in his wallet than he had been this time yesterday because of it, Damien still felt like shite. The flight had been packed with overweight business executives on expense accounts. The bloke in the seat next to him snored like a rutting pig all the way to New York, in spite of Damien's best attempts to prod him awake. The films had all been romantic crap. And the trolley-dollies had been a bunch of tight-arsed lesbians who had dished out the champagne as though it was coming out of their own cellars. It had been a supreme struggle of will and patience to get even remotely mellow. And there was nothing worse than turning up at a wedding when everyone else was as pissed as parrots and you were the only one more sober than a missionary on mass day. He might as well have been squashed in with the plebs at the back. Except that the plebs had all planned their trips months in advance and there were no plebby seats left for men who couldn't help acting on impulse.

It had taken aeons to clear customs, and now Damien stood and tapped his feet impatiently as he waited for his baggage to appear. He could die of old age before it trundled past on this carousel, and he was fed up of the jostling; he had paid too much to be jostled. Why hadn't he thought about sending Josie a fax? Sometimes he was just too reckless for his own good.

Running his fingers through his dishevelled hair, he dislodged a shower of Tate & Lyle which from a distance looked suspiciously like dandruff. He brushed it from his shoulders with a disdainful mutter. He felt crumpled and unkempt and wished he had time for a shower and a shave. Josie always liked her men to look smart; that was why she fancied Jeremy Irons and Pierce Brosnan, not these scruffy, lived-in Ewan McGregor types. He glanced at his watch. She would have to take him unwashed, with a bit of hope that it would appeal to the mothering instinct in her. God knows, she'd lavished enough of it on that wretched spoilt brat of a cat of theirs. Damien checked the time again. This really was cutting things fine.

Melanie, on the other hand, liked her men rough and ready. Ready at any time of night or day preferably. He'd been knackered after the first few weeks of illicit meetings and had been forced to tell Josie that he'd been playing squash straight after work to explain why he was arriving home late, red-faced and sweaty. They probably burnt off the same amount of calories between them, so it wasn't strictly a lie.

He wondered what Melanie was doing now. Probably hacking one sleeve off all his Armani suit jackets and shortening the trousers by six inches with the Sabatier bread knife, or filling his Rockports with ripe camembert. He should have thought to bring all his important clothing with him. She might be a hell-cat between the sheets, but unfortunately the less attractive part of that characteristic extended well beyond the bedroom walls. Melanie would not go down without a fight. Metaphorically speaking.

By contrast Josie had been compliant in her devastation when he'd walked out on her. There hadn't been a pot hurled in anger, no unnecessary bending of the golf clubs, no denting of the BMW, no weeping, wailing or generally over-the-top behaviour that could be classed as histrionics. She had stood there pale-faced, dry-eyed and accepting. No, Josie had handled everything with dignified silence. In fact, he wished there had been a bit more unfettered emotion; he might have felt a bit more as though she cared.

Her mother, on the other hand, had invented a whole new stream of invective to hurl at him, some of which even Channel 4 would blanch at.

He did, however, hope that his wife would be as compliant about their inevitable reunion and not rub it in too much that he was having to do more back-pedalling than Gerald Ratner.

At the thought of Mr Ratner, Damien tapped his pocket with proprietorial pride. No one could call this little baby crap. This little rock was the mother of all insurance policies.

He was so sure that he would be sharing Josie's bed tonight, he hadn't seen the necessity to book a room. See what matey-boy thought of that! Wondering if it was turning into a nervous tic, Damien checked his watch yet again, a tiny shiver of excitement running through him. With a bit of luck, a following wind and a string of taxis waiting outside JFK, he would be making his entrance within the hour just as the proceedings were coming to a close. Now that's what you call perfect timing! Weddings were always such bloody boring affairs, it was a wonder people continued to endure them. Finally, his suitcase deigned to trundle into view. Damien smiled to himself as he snatched it from the rickety carousel. Hopefully his entrance would add a little extra spice to Martha's wedding.

CHAPTER 29

'One!'

Martha was on the stage, heading the group of single girls who had rushed enthusiastically from their seats to form an unruly gaggle behind her. Josie had been dragged unceremoniously by her cousin to the very front row. This was not her scene, but she had painted a smile on her face to please Martha. She might as well have been given a banner saying DESPERATE – I HAVE NO BLOKE!

Felicia, she noted, had also been pressed into reluctant service, and Josie wished with a little pang of regret that her co-bridesmaid had taken down a number for Matt, or an address or something, when he'd called earlier. She might never want to see him again, but it would feel better never wanting to see him again if she knew she could if she wanted to. Josie frowned to herself.

Martha was grinning maniacally at her and Josie felt herself tense. God, she hated standing at the front making a twonk of herself – it was a wonder she'd gone into teaching really. Her cousin teased the single girls, looking over her shoulder to offer them a glimpse of the battered bouquet. The guests whooped and whistled.

'Two!' the wedding singer shouted into the microphone.

Martha warmed up the bouquet with a few practice throws, whizzing it through the air like a missile without letting it go. The girls jostled against each other like eager shoppers preparing to rush the shop doors at the start of the summer sales. The crowd cheered some more. Martha smirked mischievously and wobbled on her heels.

'Three!'

She launched the bouquet, flinging it high into the air. It sailed over her head with a flurry of falling petals before hitting the spangly ball that hung from the ceiling above the dance floor and dropping straight into Josie's waiting hands. She stared at it with a mixture of amazement and terror, wanting to drop it like the hot potato it was. The wedding guests went wild, shouting and whistling.

'Give a round of applause to the English bridesmaid, Ms Josie Flynn!' the wedding singer cried.

The crowd obliged. Josie could feel her cheeks flaming. She gritted her teeth into a smile, held the bouquet aloft and headed straight to the bar as fast as her legs would carry her. What was this? By now, at an English wedding, she'd probably be pissed and lying in an alcoholic coma somewhere under one of the tables.

'Ladies and gentlemen,' the wedding singer shouted, 'let's find out who gets the girl!'

The single guys were considerably more reluctant to engage in a ritual likely to bring ridicule upon them. They had to be cajoled on to the dance floor by burly Sicilian men in black suits and then stood shuffling around with no apparent purpose. Glen lurked uncomfortably at the back. He looked over at Josie and winced his embarrassment; she gave him an encouraging smile back. Jack had joined Martha on the stage and, to the accompanying strains of 'The Stripper', was peeling a pale blue lacy garter from her thigh with lascivious leers at the raucous guests.

Josie took a swig from her champagne. She wondered if she would ever grow to love the man her cousin had married. His hands didn't look right on Martha's thighs. They were chubby, white and wrinkled like some nasty garden grub against Martha's smooth tanned skin. There were some people you just couldn't imagine making love – your mum and dad, Prince Charles and anyone, Martha and Jack. Imagining herself with Matt Jarvis or even Glen was a different story altogether. Imagining Damien and Thing wasn't hard either – in fact it was a frequent and recurring nightmare.

Task completed, Jack flicked the garter into the air with a flourish. The guests yelled their encouragement. He went through the same routine as Martha, but with infinitely less drama.

'One! Two! Three!'

He threw the garter behind him. It floated on the air, soaring above the heads of the men who grabbed at it with fumbling, futile hands. Glen launched himself forward, jumping high and catching the lace frippery on the fly. The wedding guests went wild, cheering his prowess.

Glen bowed magnanimously and held the garter in triumph above his head.

'Ladies and gentlemen, the best man, Mr Glen Donnelly!'

The band played some sort of victory theme and the drummer did an over-the-top drum roll.

'Would the lucky couple please take the floor!' The wedding singer was warming up to belt out a tune.

Lucky couple? Josie downed her champagne.

Martha appeared by her side. 'That's you,' she hissed. 'Go and get him.'

Josie tutted with mock annoyance and hooked the throw bouquet over her wrist. 'Thanks, cous,' she whispered gleefully and headed for the dance floor.

Glen was standing with his arms wide, waiting to embrace her. Well, perhaps it wouldn't be so bad after all, she smiled quietly to herself.

He took her in his arms, again to the cheers of the wedding guests. Martha was back on stage, clapping sedately and holding Jack's arm. She looked pale and Josie realised that she must be feeling pretty exhausted by now.

'*It's just a little crush . . .*' the wedding singer crooned.

Glen twirled Josie into the centre, and a few

more couples joined them as they moved round the floor.

Glen bent to her ear. 'I meant what I said,' he whispered.

Josie looked up, tucking her hair behind her ear in what she hoped was a seductive manner. 'What about?'

'Martha's married now. She's no longer available.' He pouted his lip. 'I am, though.'

'Me, too.'

'I think we could have some fun while you're here.'

'Me too again.'

He pulled her closer. 'Maybe we could go back to Manhattan together tonight. I have an apartment overlooking the park.'

Josie gulped. 'I have a flight tomorrow afternoon.'

'We could spend some time together before then – take in some sights, have lunch. Who knows? Have you any other plans?'

'Not really.' None.

Glen grinned. 'Then it's settled?'

'It's settled.'

He tightened his arms round her and steered her round the floor. People were joining them now, smiling and offering congratulations as if they were the married couple.

Josie let herself relax into Glen's embrace. He was quite a hunk. Perhaps his teeth were a bit too pearly white and his hair just a little too immaculately gelled into place, but hey, she could live with that.

No one's perfect. So what if he didn't have Matt's easy charm and scruffy schoolboy good looks. She could cope with catwalk-model charisma instead, and it seemed as good a time as any to begin Operation Get On With Your Life And Stop Letting Losers Latch On To You. In fact, Josie thought as she snuggled deeper into Glen's arms, this could begin to feel quite comfortable.

Martha marched up to them. Her face was bleach-ed white, her mouth pinched. Her body was tense and moving jerkily. 'Josie, would you mind if I took Glen away from you for just a few moments?'

Josie looked surprised. 'Right now?'

'It won't take long.'

'Is there something wrong?'

'No.' Martha flashed her a warning look. 'Glen?'

Glen was not about to be bullied. 'Martha, let me twirl this lovely lady round the dance floor until the end of the song and then I'll come to find you.'

Martha looked as if she was going to protest, but thought better of it. 'Fine,' she said. 'But don't be long.'

She strode off, pushing her way through the crush of dancers.

'What was all that about?'

'Search me.' Glen looked puzzled. He carried on twirling her just as he'd told Martha he would, but Josie noticed that he twirled a little bit faster.

Josie pressed her lips together and watched the swish of Martha's veil as she headed up the stairs towards the courtesy room where they'd been earlier. Some things about her cousin just never changed. Even as a child Martha had hated anyone else playing with her toys.

CHAPTER 30

Matt paid the driver and watched the cab lurch away into the darkness. He stood hesitantly in front of Holly's apartment, the place where they had shared their goodnight kiss, taking in the neon glow of the sky, then climbed the stairs to the huge front door and trawled the list of residents. A little black scrawled 'HB' shone out bravely from the illuminated Perspex.

As Matt paused with his finger hovering over the buzzer, the intercom crackled into life.

'Hi.' Holly's disembodied voice sounded small and broken with static. 'I'll open the door. Come up.'

The buzzer sounded and the door clicked open a fraction of an inch. Matt pushed inside, pulling his scarf off and stuffing it into his pocket. The hall was hot and too brightly lit. The glare bounced off the faded white walls and showed up patches that were more damp or cracked than was wholesome. The floor was dark scuffed wood that hadn't been polished for a while. An ornate spiral staircase wound up one side and there was an ancient open wrought-iron lift slap bang in the centre. Smoothing his hair down, Matt headed towards it.

Holly's voice came down over the banister rail. 'It doesn't work! You'll have to take the stairs.'

'Right.'

Matt started to climb, bounding up the stairs two at a time. It reminded him of Liberty, without the added attraction of Josie's bottom wiggling up ahead of him. That was the only thing that had kept him going to the top, and he wondered if she'd guessed that beneath his bravado, he was terrified of heights.

By the third turn he was puffing heavily. He was going to give up booze and stop taking cabs and maybe rush out and buy a mountain bike the minute he got home.

'Only two more floors!' Holly shouted encouragement. Her riot of hair flopped across her face and she hung over the rail at a dizzying angle.

Matt stopped, leaning against the curved wooden banister fighting for breath. 'I hope you've got oxygen up there.'

'Even better. I have tequila.'

He started the ascent again. 'No wonder you're so skinny.'

'Come on! Give me a break. You're making me feel bad. Not far now.'

Matt staggered on to Holly's landing. He should have taken his coat off at the halfway stage; he was feeling unpleasantly damp in various orifices. Forcing himself upright, he breathed a heavy sigh of relief. 'Made it!'

'I'm glad.'

He looked up at Holly, who was smiling shyly at him.

'Wow!' Matt said through a swallow.

'You like?' She gave him a twirl.

'Very wow!' Matt reiterated. 'Where did hippy chick go?'

'I give her the night off once in a while.'

'You look great.' Gone were the funky jeans, the sneakers and the belly-button. In their place was a little black number and heels. High ones. Dominatrix ones! The dress was all little stringy bits holding it together that looked woefully inadequate against the rush of testosterone that had charged unbidden from somewhere. There wasn't an awful lot of it, but it looked gorgeous nevertheless.

Holly took his hand before he'd had a chance to wipe it on his jeans. 'Come on in,' she said, pulling him through her front door. 'Welcome to Chez Moi.'

Chez Moi was a cluttered garret with huge windows overlooking the bright lights of the city. It was filled with artist's materials abandoned on every surface – pencils, paints, stub ends of pastels. Large splashy canvases in primary colours adorned the otherwise bare walls.

'Take off your coat.'

'Thanks.' Matt gratefully stripped off his coat and draped it over the back of a battered rattan chair by the door. It was still hot and his shirt was making his neck uncomfortable and itchy.

He swivelled slowly, taking in the bold paintings. He pointed to one. 'Yours?'

Holly shrugged. 'I was at art school.'

'They're good.'

'Not good enough to keep me in the style I'd like to be accustomed to.'

'That's why you work in PR?'

She nodded as she sauntered past into the kitchen. 'For now.'

This was a revelation. Matt loved clutter. Cluttered women were earthy and sexy, unlike his ex-wife, who was a devotee of bin bags, Harpic and Domestos. He'd vowed never to fall in love with a tidy woman ever again and hoped fervently that Josie was a slattern.

There was a pile of discarded clothes in the corner of the room – an eclectic mix of what appeared to be charity-shop bargains and designer gear. On top of it were some running shoes and Lycra shorts. The bookcase held a range of fabulously esoteric books that looked as though they'd been bought from second-hand bookshops or borrowed from libraries and never returned. He picked one up and ran his finger along the dusty, threadbare spine, realising with a sudden jar how little he knew about Josie. There was an untidy collection of photographs round the mirror showing Holly with people Matt assumed were friends and family, and also with a selection of well-known and less well-known pop stars – Headstrong included.

Matt followed Holly through to the kitchen.

This room looked lived in too, but there was an order to the chaos. A subtle organisation of the kitchen implements and pans. There was a bottle of good-quality balsamic vinegar and a jar of succulent olives by the cooker, and a selection of well-thumbed cookery books that made it clear that she wasn't too shabby at knocking together a half-decent meal. To balance it, there was an unhealthy mound of crumbs next to the toaster and a pile of washing-up in the sink.

Holly opened the fridge and grabbed a bottle of tequila, waving it in front of him. 'Small or large?'

'I may as well continue as I started,' Matt said. 'Large.'

The twelve-step detox programme could start on Monday.

Holly poured out a lethal measure and handed it to him. She filled her own glass and then clinked it against his. 'Cheers.'

Matt swirled the ice-cold liquid round his mouth, enjoying the serious afterburn.

'You're looking vaguely stunned.'

'This isn't what I'd expected.' Matt leaned against the cupboards, crossing his legs. 'There's more to you than meets the eye, Holly Brinkman.'

'I'll drink to that.' She held Matt's stare and downed her tequila in one gulp. 'Perhaps this time you'll stay around long enough to find out some more.'

'I intend to,' he said.

'Let's get comfortable,' Holly suggested, pulling him into the lounge and easing him on to the huge shabby cream sofa that dominated the centre of the room. A sofa that bore telltale smudges of paint that had been inexpertly scrubbed off.

Matt flopped back against the cushions. His feet ached and he knew what it must feel like to have bunions – although it didn't seem to have stopped Aunty Dolly flitting about like a demented water-nymph.

Holly reached back, stretching to flick on the CD player, a seemingly practised seduction technique. The soft sounds of acid jazz drifted into the apartment. She kicked off her shoes with more drama than was necessary and curled her legs beneath her, propping herself up on the back of the sofa and feeding her fingers through her thick mane of blonde curly hair. 'So, now I have you all to myself, do you want to tell me your life story? Or shall I tell you mine?'

Matt sipped his tequila and contemplated the bottom of his glass. 'My life story makes a very uninspiring read – unhappy at work, unlucky in love, aspire to live in a beach hut in the Bahamas writing best-selling novels, probably never will. What about you?'

Holly puckered her lip. 'Same, same. Making the best of work to pay the rent, too flaky for commitment so have no idea what true love is, aspire to hit the heights of Manhattan's art circles as the hottest new discovery, probably never will.'

'You deserve to.'

She flounced her hair. 'Ah, you English guys have all the lines.'

They both took a drink and Matt noticed that his glass was emptying rapidly. So did Holly, who topped it up. She slid forward on the sofa so that her mouth was only millimetres away from Matt's. 'Well, now we know all there is to know about each other.'

'I guess so.'

'And they say talk is cheap.'

'That didn't cost us a penny.'

She inched forward again, resting her hand on his thigh and looking at him from beneath her eyelashes. Grief, why had he spent his entire life chasing women who could run faster than he could, when all he had to do was sit back and go with the flow? And, it had to be said, Holly's flow was pretty fast. Her fingers crept up his shirt, toying with the fabric, teasing, easing over his skin. He could hear his heart pounding and his chest felt quivery as if there were thousands of tiny ants crawling all over it. Nice ants. Her mouth found his, and it was soft and warm and tasted like kiwi fruit. She ran her tongue along his top lip and he wanted to gasp, and it was a long time since he'd wanted to gasp. Except when he'd run after a bus on the Embankment last week and then he couldn't help but gasp. And when he was climbing Liberty.

Matt was horrified. Don't you dare spoil this, Josie Flynn! I've never had a woman desperate for my body before! You just clear off and leave me alone! I have tried and I can't find you, so let that be an end to it!

He closed his eyes and, thinking of Tottenham Hotspur winning the Cup and other unlikely but distracting scenarios, surrendered himself to Holly's kiss.

As suddenly as she had started, Holly pulled gently away from him.

'Are you hungry?'

'No.' Why stop now?

'I don't have too much food,' she admitted. 'Just assorted pots of goo and some sushi.'

'I can live without goo,' Matt replied. Just keep doing what you were doing! 'And raw fish.'

'We could go to the deli on the corner,' Holly suggested. 'They do great veal piccata.'

'I've eaten enough today to last me for the rest of the week.' Matt massaged his straining stomach as proof.

'So what happened?' She tucked her hair behind her ear. 'Did your date stand you up?'

Matt thought guiltily of Josie sitting alone in the Mexican restaurant two nights ago. 'No,' he said hesitantly. 'I didn't have a date. As such.'

'I don't mind,' Holly assured him. 'I'm cool.'

'No. I definitely didn't have a date.'

'So, what did you spend your day doing – apart from eating?'

'Er . . .'

'Sightseeing?'

'Well, actually, I did some "Hava Nagila", some line-dancing, some Electric Slide, some Chicken Dance, some "Hey, Macarena" . . .' Matt sang, putting his hands on his hips and giving them a less than enthusiastic thrust.

'Excuse me?'

Matt let his head rest back and closed his eyes. 'I went to a wedding.'

'No way!'

'Oh yes indeed, an all-singing, all-dancing ethnic Jewish-American wedding.'

'I didn't know you were going to a wedding.'

'Neither did I. Well, I sort of did.'

'Did you know the bride or the groom?'

'Well, sort of neither again.' Matt swallowed a slug of his tequila. 'It's a very long story.'

'What a coincidence.'

'What? You didn't know them either?'

Holly was wearing a very strange expression.

A cold trickle of something wormed its way into Matt's psyche. It was just like a horror film, when the door creaks and the lights fail and the music goes DA-DA-DA and you want to grab a cushion and stuff it in your mouth because you know something awful is about to reveal itself to you.

It was then he noticed the wedding present, beautifully wrapped, standing next to an unfinished canvas that looked like half a bowl of fruit. The paper bore silver splashes and 'Good Luck' written in an overly curly hand; bows and ribbons blossomed from the top and cascaded delicately down the sides. He looked back at Holly and tried to keep his mouth from falling open. Please don't let this be!

'I was just on my way to a wedding when you called.'

All the hairs on the back of Matt's neck stood to attention. He was having a *Twilight Zone* moment. 'This was the party you invited me to and I said no?'

Holly shook her head. 'I didn't know you were already going to one. You should have said.'

How many times had that phrase been used in his life? 'You should have said.' You should have said you wanted to go out with my best friend, you should have said you wanted promotion at work and not let snot-face Simpson become the editor, you should have said you loved me more then I wouldn't have left you, etc. etc. How many more twists and turns would his tortured life have taken if he'd said half of the sodding things he should have said? He should have said that out of all the weddings that were potentially happening in New York City today, he was looking for one particular one, one particular woman, one particular bride, one particular bridesmaid. *He should have said.* What a stupid bloody phrase!

Holly moved forward to kiss him again, and instead of saying anything, he let her mouth cover his. He let her tongue find his, tasting it, teasing it, the tip flicking over his teeth.

It couldn't be. It would be just too surreal. It couldn't be. Could it?

His tongue was exploring Holly's lips, but his

eyes were open and his mind was whirring.

Her fingers were unbuttoning his shirt with an expertise that was vaguely alarming. Her hands found their way inside and they were cucumber cool against his hot, fevered skin. Matt's eyes widened. She was starting to moan! Sweet, encouraging little sounds that did nothing to drown out the noise of the question clodding through his brain. There was no way he could continue snogging her without asking. He had to know. Matt stopped her hand as it travelled inside his shirt to his neck.

'Wait a minute,' he said, easing away from her. 'Tell me more about this wedding.'

Holly appeared puzzled, but then that was perfectly reasonable given the circumstances.

'It's important.'

She sat back on the sofa, not looking as annoyed as she might, and spread her hands in a where-do-you-want-me-to-start way. 'An old friend is getting married. I was at art school, she helped out in a gallery in SoHo. She sold a lot of paintings for me to her moneyed friends. She fed me through college. I owe her.'

Matt gestured for more.

Holly gestured back. 'I've arranged for Headstrong to play a few numbers for her at the wedding reception. It would have been a blast. I'm happier to be seeing you.'

Holly indicated that that was it. Sum and total.

Matt dabbed at the cold sweat that had appeared

on his upper lip. 'Won't your friend be mad that you didn't turn up?'

Holly laughed. 'I won't be missed.'

He tried to keep his voice level, when it seemed intent on going up and down uncontrollably. That always happened when he was nervous; it was the reason he had been thrown out of the school choir. 'Maybe we should go along.'

'Two weddings in one day! Can't get enough of a good thing, hey?'

Matt swallowed the lump of anxiety in his throat. 'I'm very sentimental at heart.'

Holly snuggled up next to him and stroked her hand up his inner thigh, leaning into his body.

'So am I . . .'

Matt breathed heavily.

'. . . but I can think of other things we could do.'

'Ha, ha. So can I,' Matt said. 'What time is it?' He tried unsuccessfully to free the arm that Holly had pinned to his side.

'It's getting late.'

'Could we get there before it finishes?'

Holly sat back again. A frown corrugated her forehead. 'You really want to go?'

Matt shrugged nonchalantly, while his heart did the tango. 'It would be a good chance for me to listen to Headstrong again.'

'You hated them.'

'Maybe it was a rash judgement.'

Holly smiled. 'You're doing this for me, aren't you?'

Matt smiled back. Cheesily. He tried cute and raised his eyebrows whimsically. 'Found out!'

'I'll call and explain when she's back from honeymoon. They're having three weeks trekking in the Amazon.' Holly looked impressed.

'Great,' Matt said.

'Don't worry.' Holly gave him a look that conveyed extreme understanding. 'We can stay here and be cosy.' She reached out and poured some more tequila into their glasses. 'Martha'll be cool.'

Matt felt himself shrink to the size of a mouse and a giant scream started inside him. He grabbed Holly by the hand.

'Get your coat,' he barked, trying to do up his shirt buttons.

'What?' He pulled her to her feet. 'Matt!'

She'd spilled her drink down her black number and was trying frantically to brush it off with her hand as he tugged her towards the door.

'What?' she repeated.

'Coat!' he said. He was already hitching his on to his shoulders. 'Hurry up! We're going to a wedding!'

'You are mad!' Holly said, hobbling as she struggled to put her shoes back on.

'Come on. Come on.'

Matt was halfway out of the door when he stopped and turned to Holly. 'Where's this wedding being held?'

'Long Island.'

'Long Island! Whereabouts on Long Island?'

'Zeppe's Wedding Manor.'

'*Zeppe's* Wedding Manor!' Matt repeated, and thought that quite possibly he was going to faint.

CHAPTER 31

Josie twirled the throw bouquet around, feeling stupid. Glen and Martha had been missing for a long time. A very long time. Jack was starting to look pathetic and lost hosting his wedding party on his own. He was dancing with an aged and tiny Sicilian aunt with hair the colour of Quink and he looked as if he was being kind.

Josie wanted to kick something. Hard.

Where had her bloody cousin got to? And more importantly, where had her bloody cousin got to with *her* man! She'd endured that bouquet-tossing fiasco to win him fair and square! Where could they be? And what was so important that she'd had to drag Glen away from her just when they were getting cosy. Martha might be gorgeous and nice and funny, but she was *the* most unreliable person on the planet. Josie searched the crowd for a glimpse of a floating veil or a hunky best man. Nothing. Wherever they were and whatever they were doing, it was the wrong time to be doing it.

'Where's that goddamn daughter of mine got to?' Joe barked as he danced past with the wife of his eldest brother.

'She's popped out for a minute, Uncle Joe. Fresh air.'

'Fresh air, my ass. Jesus, that girl'd be late for her own funeral.' Then he realised what he'd said and his face crumpled.

Bugger. Josie stood forlornly at the edge of the dance floor. Uncle Nunzio appeared beside her. 'Dance, lady?'

'Why not?'

He took her delicately in his ancient wizened arms – arms that looked as though they had ploughed fields and harvested grapes, even though Martha had told her Uncle Nunzio was a multi-millionaire and ran some sort of export empire. Whatever he did, he was a mover, and he weaved her skilfully through the other dancers, as light on his feet as Fred Astaire.

Despite the strains of Celine Dion warbling 'My Heart Will Go On', Josie couldn't shake her concern and scoured the hall over Uncle Nunzio's shoulder for a glimpse of her errant cousin.

'Relatz,' Uncle Nunzio instructed. 'You need a good shag.'

'For heaven's sake, don't start that again. I'm trying,' she said, 'really I am. I met someone the day before yesterday who I would have jumped into bed with at the drop of a hat – and that's not like me at all – but he naffed off into the wide blue yonder. And I've been chasing the best man all day and now he's missing too. I'm about to develop a complex about this, so just give me a break.'

Uncle Nunzio gave her a toothy grin and she laughed back.

'You haven't the foggiest idea what I'm talking about, have you?'

'Bollocks,' he replied.

'Thought not.' Josie smiled at him. 'No different from any of the other men I've been out with, then.'

Jack appeared by their side, negotiating a turn with his toy-sized, blue-rinsed dance partner. 'Josie, have you seen Martha?' he asked.

'Not for a little while. Why?'

'They're about to serve the next course. I didn't want them to start without her.' His brow was creased – or, at least, more creased than normal. 'I'll go and look for her.'

'No, no,' Josie said, unsure why she was panicking. 'I'll go.'

'Maybe Glen knows where she is . . .' Jack searched unsuccessfully for a glimpse of his best man. 'I can't see Glen either.'

'He's around here somewhere,' Josie said confidently.

'Do you think she's okay?'

'I'm sure she's fine.'

'I think she's been gone for some time.'

'Maybe she's got a headache.' Josie tried to be reassuring. 'Long day and all that.'

Maybe Martha *had* got a headache. Who knows? thought Josie.

'I'll look for her, Jack. You stay with your guests.'

'Thanks, Josie.' He smiled, and there was a depth of warmth to it that took her by surprise. He turned to move away from her.

'Jack.' Josie squeezed his arm. 'Congratulations. This has been a lovely wedding.'

'Thank you,' he said with touching sincerity. 'I'm glad you could be here.'

'Me too,' Josie said.

The photographer popped up between them and snapped away. Josie and Jack blinked in unison.

'Caught in the act!' Jack said, and waltzed away, laughing.

Josie turned back to her dance partner. 'Uncle Nunzio, I have to go.' She was shouting at him as if he were deaf.

Uncle Nunzio smiled and carried on dancing.

'I have to go.' She pointed to the door. 'I have a cousin to murder.'

'*Sì, sì,*' he said, nodding enthusiastically. '*Sì.*'

'*Sì,*' she replied, untangling herself. 'Catch you later.'

'My testicles are on fire for you.'

'I can't say many men have voiced that particular emotion.'

'You have a great ass,' he said.

'Thank you,' Josie acknowledged with a smile. 'And you have a dreadful vocabulary.'

Abandoning her partner before she was tempted to wash out his mouth with soap, she made her way towards the staircase. Perhaps Martha had gone up to the courtesy room for a lie-down. Or worse, perhaps she and Glen were ensconced somewhere, reliving their past romance at a time that was entirely inappropriate. She would kill them both if they were chatting about 'old times' – it had waited so long, it could wait a bit longer.

Jack had taken his seat at the wedding table. He looked anxious and alone. A string of well-wishers were straggling by, filling in the guest book with witty quips which, like the photograph albums, would never get looked at again once the wedding was over. Not one of them noticed his discomfort.

Josie increased her pace. Wherever Martha was, she'd better come back double quick.

'Ladies and gentlemen.' The wedding singer tapped his microphone. 'We have been Wedding Belles! We'll be entertaining you through dinner before making way for . . .' he consulted his notes, 'some hot new talent on the New York dance scene – Headstrong!'

Josie stopped. Headstrong?

Waitresses appeared bearing steaming trays laid with slivers of filet mignon.

Headstrong? Where the hell had she heard that name before?

CHAPTER 32

It was snowing and they couldn't find a cab. Anywhere. Holly was hopping about attempting to get her feet comfortable in heels that were definitely not intended for serious walking. Matt was trying to stride out to get out of the cold and the stinging flakes that were splatting against their wet faces.

'This is deeply unpleasant,' Matt complained, pulling Holly along.

'We don't have to go,' Holly pointed out.

'We do,' Matt explained. 'We do. Don't ask me why. We just do.'

'Is this an English thing?' Holly brushed her damp curls from her mouth. Her hair was flat on top and had gone all crinkly and wide at the sides like Crystal Tipps' hair in *Crystal Tipps and Alistair*.

Heaven knows she was cute, and getting more cute by the minute. At any other time he would have rushed her back to her warm, untidy, artistic apartment and ravished her. But not now. Now he was intent on trudging along in a scene from *Ice Station Zebra*, looking for a woman in a lilac chiffon frock who was blissfully ignorant of the fact that she was ruining his love life.

'Is it bad luck not to turn up at a wedding?'

'Terribly,' Matt puffed.

Holly stopped stock still. She offered her hands to the sky. 'I'll risk it,' she said. 'What will happen? Will I break out in hives?'

'Come on. I can't remember. Dreadful things. Really dreadful things.'

'Will I become allergic to alcohol? That's the most dreadful thing I can imagine.'

'Five more minutes,' Matt cajoled. 'Just five teeny-weeny more minutes, and if a cab hasn't come along by then, we can call it a day.'

'I'm going to look horrible. I'm wet and my hair's all frizzy.'

'You look beautiful,' Matt said dismissively.

'Do you mean that?' Holly was twirling her hair round her finger.

He looked at her. Her wet shiny nose. Her wet frizzy hair. Her wet silly shoes. 'Yes,' he said honestly. 'I do.'

'Let's go back to my place, Matt,' she said.

He stopped, snow splashing on his nose, on his coat, plastering his hair to his head. He could hear his breathing even above the constant noise of the traffic. Neon lights flashed round them, blurring at the edges in the white flurries.

Unbidden a taxi stopped right next to them.

Matt stared at it open-mouthed. This was fate. This was the fucking ickle-fickle hand of fate!

'Get in,' he instructed. He held open the door and they both climbed in.

CHAPTER 33

The rowdy sound of the wedding celebration was receding quietly into the background as Josie climbed the stairs towards the courtesy room where they had all freshened up earlier. The carpet was thick plush, haemoglobin red, and dragged her aching feet into its depths. Her toes were throbbing nicely in her tight lilac shoes.

Josie stopped, leaning her weight on the mahogany banister, which curled endlessly ahead of her. It had been made slick with polish and every handprint left a mark on its pristine surface. Keeping it sparkling must be a task equal to painting the Forth Road Bridge. Now she had stopped it was proving inordinately difficult to get moving again. She was absolutely knackered. Her knees begged for her to sit down and she sagged to the stair below her, gratefully.

Was this all worth it? The organisation, the stress, the expense? For what? Who ultimately benefited from this ritual extravagance? Her wedding had been perfect, and yet, five years later – virtually to the day – it was over, ended, kaput, as if the wedding vows had never been uttered. She hadn't gone into marriage with rose-tinted spectacles – it was obvious to her that every couple had to go through difficult times – but she hadn't expected anything so insurmountable as that tenacious little tart from Accounts. Then again, maybe it shouldn't have been too much of a surprise: Damien's libido had always been acutely more active than his IQ.

They'd been so happy, or at least she thought they had. There had been ups and downs – someone who couldn't put up a pair of shelves without recourse to half a ton of Polyfilla and subsequent visits by an electrician, a plumber and the fire brigade was always going to be a major source of domestic irritation – but they'd had so much fun too. Did he and Melanie play shadow-puppet theatre with their feet after making love like they had on the plain magnolia wall that they'd always meant to paint another colour and never had? Did he always insist his 'mating elk' was the outright winner? Did they cry with laughter on the kitchen floor because the cheese sculptures they had made that were supposed to look like each other bore more resemblance to Beavis and Butthead? Possibly not. She didn't think Melanie looked like a cheese sculpture sort of person.

Perhaps she should have reacted differently. Affairs were so commonplace now, should they be the great ender of marriages that they once were? Shouldn't people now be adult and sophisticated about mere infidelity? Did it really matter in the scheme of things? It seemed so at the time; now she wasn't so sure. Damien had been un- repentant. Adamant in his assurances that if she had been a better wife, none of it would have happened. There wasn't much mention of him being a pretty crap husband. It wasn't affairs that did the damage – the worst thing was the destruc- tion of trust and respect. Once they had gone, nothing else remained.

What was Damien going to do now? Now that he was fed up of playing house with Melanie and her brood. He'd made an attempt to wheedle his way round Josie, but it had been a half-hearted effort – a handful of phone calls, usually drunken and at one in the morning; a few bouquets of flowers, never her favourites; some sexy underwear that was far too gross to be serious. Damien in full wheedle mode was unstoppable. Who would be his next unsuspecting victim? she wondered – unlike a vampire, Damien's forte was sucking the self- esteem out of his willing dupe. Although she wasn't sure it was ultimately any less messy than blood.

It was difficult living alone; she missed the cuddles and the company that The Cat Formerly Known As Prince could only go so far in supplying. There were times, mainly three o'clock in the morning, when all rationale departed and she missed Damien so much she could almost feel him in the bed next to her, and she'd put out her hand and pretend to stroke him – even though he'd never actually set foot or any other part of his anatomy in this particular bed. Those were the times she pressed her Oscar the Grouch hot-water bottle into service, and by the morning it had usually passed. But on the whole, she concluded, living alone was infinitely more attractive than living with Damien.

Josie looked up the stairs. She hoped that Martha would fare better than she had. Sounds of laughter drifted up from the hall. Grief, she'd better get a move on or poor Jack would be sitting there all night on his own. Forcing herself upright, Josie began to climb again.

It was so quiet up here, peaceful. Josie tiptoed along the hall, her footsteps being absorbed by the preponderance of Axminster. You could die up here and not a soul would notice.

She turned into the anteroom, no more than a short corridor that led to the courtesy room. Martha's going-away outfit hung in a transparent cover from a gilded hook on the wall. A trouser suit in the faintest whisper of blue. Dark blue ankle boots waited patiently in place. Josie stood admiring it. Martha would look perfect. Just perfect. But then she always did.

The courtesy room was ahead of her and she could hear faint murmurs coming from behind the closed door. It must be Martha. Perhaps she'd come up here to make some phone calls, last-minute arrangements.

Josie tapped quietly on the solid wood with her knuckles. 'Martha?'

There was no answer, but she knew someone was in there. The murmuring grew louder, the voices more familiar, clearer. She strained to hear more, but the door was too thick.

Josie knocked louder. 'Martha!'

She turned the handle and the door opened silently on its well-oiled hinges.

'Ohmigod,' Josie said. Her hand flew to hush her mouth the moment she had spoken, but it was too late. Far too late. Her chin had already dropped to the soft plush carpet.

CHAPTER 34

It was snowing, and Matt was staring out of the taxi window listening to the slap-slap-slap of the windscreen wipers. The traffic was backed up all along the road because, like Londoners, New Yorkers seemed to suddenly forget how to drive the minute the roads had a frosting of snow on them that was about as lethal as the icing sugar on a cake. Not that Matt himself had driven for months. The car had gone, along with his Gustav Klimt prints, his Breville cheese-toastie maker that had prevented him from starving at university, and his half-share of the marital bed.

'Slow going,' he said, making a limp attempt at a smile.

Holly snuggled against him. 'I'm cold.'

'Here.' He unwound his scarf and threaded it under her hair, wrapping her gently in it.

'Thanks,' she said, and snuggled against him some more.

The driver was wearing a leather hat with fur ear muffs and was clearly economising on warmth. You could spend the whole of your time in New

York complaining about the temperature – they didn't seem to understand the concept of ambient temperature, and everywhere was either too cold or far too hot. Matt let a long, confused breath escape slowly from his mouth and watched as it travelled across the cold air of the cab. What on earth was he doing? Why was he racing (ha, joke!) across Manhattan while cuddling an extremely attractive girl – who, if she wasn't desperate for his body, was at least extremely keen – in order to catch a glimpse of an English bridesmaid who would probably tell him in no uncertain terms to naff off? Were these the actions of a sane man? Wouldn't he be better off just forgetting about the Flynn woman and enjoying what pleasure could be salvaged from the situation?

He looked down at Holly. Her eyelids were heavy and she had a drowsy, dreamy look on her face. 'Do you think it will be over by the time we get there?'

'Probably,' she said sleepily, and stifled a yawn.

'Even Headstrong.'

'Probably.'

'This isn't really what you had in mind for this evening, is it?'

Holly raised an eyebrow and a lazy smile travelled across her lips. Well, at least she could still smile about it, Matt thought.

'Not really,' she answered without looking at him.

'In one way and another, I'm making a right royal cock-up of this weekend,' he sighed.

Holly wriggled herself against him, sliding her hand inside the neck of his coat. It was cold and her icy fingertips made him shiver. 'It isn't over yet,' she said.

'No.' Her eyes were still closed, but her mouth had moved miraculously to within kissing distance of his. All it would take was one very slight movement of the head and docking procedure could begin. Indecision was kicking inside him, making his heart beat as erratic and out of time as Headstrong's drummer. Matt glanced up, catching the eye of the driver, who was watching them intently through his rear-view mirror.

Matt shrugged his quandary to the driver. The driver shrugged back. That was all he needed. Matt sank back into the cold plastic seat and pulled the hot, sleepy warmth of Holly with him.

They had been going nowhere for a very long time. Damien clamped his hand over his watch. There was no way he was going to look at his fucking watch again, otherwise it would develop into a serious affliction. There had been a boy at his primary school called Joseph Miller who had made everyone laugh by pretending to stammer, but he'd done it so often that eventually he couldn't stop. Damien had bumped into him at a computer conference in a hotel in Harrogate two years ago, and he was still stammering then. It had taught him that you should never underestimate the power of neuroses or the pull of wanting to be

266

popular. Instead, Damien forced himself to relax back into the chilly, unyielding seat of the cab.

Timing, in life, is everything. Comedians know it, farmers know it, stockbrokers know it, lottery winners know it. So how come naffing taxi drivers were so blissfully unaware of it? His driver had semi-reclined in his bead-covered seat, and despite the fact that he had his hand permanently rested on his car's horn, he looked distinctly half-hearted about it. Even if Damien had told him, he looked the sort who would remain untroubled by the fact that his passenger had seriously battered his Amex card to get here and was packing a ruddy great lump of South Africa's finest in his top pocket in an attempt to rescue his failed marriage.

This was not going well. If they stayed here much longer, he was going to meet Josie coming back.

The snow thickened to Hollywood proportions – like the scene in *Holiday Inn* where, with a certain lack of necessity, Bing Crosby sings, '*I'm dreaming of a White Christmas . . .*' and you can hardly see him for the ton of thick white stuff that's being tipped on him by some demented lackey with a snow machine. Damien tried to stay calm, but calm was generally not his thing. Josie did calm. Josie did calm quite well, but he was more of a short-simmer-and-then-blast-away-like-an-Uzi-eight-millimetre type of person. His short simmer was rapidly approaching boiling point, not helped by the fact that Trini Lopez or someone was blaring forth 'La Bamba' into the cab, loud enough to make the speakers fizz and the door panels vibrate.

Damien leaned forward. 'Can't you contact your control or something to find out what's wrong?'

'I no speak Eengleesh,' the cab driver said.

'Isn't there a traffic report station on the radio? This *is* one of the most technologically advanced cities in the whole fucking world, is it not?'

'*Hablo español,*' the driver said.

Damien slumped back. '*Moi aussi,*' he muttered. '*Dos cervezas, por favor.*'

'Ha, ha,' the driver said. '*Cervezas!*'

The car in the lane next to them inched forward. Damien shot forward in his seat. Why had he inched forward and they hadn't? This was always his luck; every queue he joined, whether it was in the bank, building society or supermarket, the other queue always, always, always moved quicker. Lots quicker. Damien glared out of the window and the man in the next lane inched forward again.

'Right, that's it,' Damien said, launching himself into action. He might not be able to walk to Long Island, but he wasn't about to sit here without knowing exactly what was going on.

'Stay here!' he shouted at the taxi driver, who was jammed in on all sides by Buicks and Lincoln Continentals and yellow cabs and was clearly going nowhere in a hurry.

Damien jumped out of the cab, slithering precariously on the icy road surface. He slammed the door behind him for good measure, and to show that when Damien Flynn meant business, business got done. Pulling his jacket lapels up round his ears, Damien was painfully aware of fat, wet snowflakes flicking him squarely between the eyes. He jammed his hands deeper into his pockets and hunched down against the weather, setting off at a ferocious pace along the line of stationary traffic, whose tail-lights winked facetiously far into the distance. 'Let's see if an Englishman can't get this fucking show on the road again!'

Matt's cab driver had been watching them snogging in the back seat. That much was obvious. He was now sitting looking very apologetic and more than a touch sheepish to boot.

'Are you all right?' Matt asked, removing what appeared to be long-dead hamburger remains from Holly's coat.

'I think so.' She brushed her hair back from her face, looking a little dazed. And who could blame her? One minute they had been enjoying a tender, lingering kiss, the next minute – bang – and they'd both slithered off the back seat and on to the floor. The bang was not a metaphorical or emotional explosion of love, lust or elation. No. It was considerably more earthbound than that. The bang in question had been their taxi driving squarely, and with some considerable force, into the back of the one in front. Followed quickly by another bang as the one behind shunted into them. And, at this moment, none of the drivers looked particularly happy.

A plume of steam or smoke or something that definitely shouldn't have been there wafted its way from under the crumpled bonnet to disperse itself into the ether. The boot of the taxi in front was buckled in the middle and had sprung open, showing its contents to be a muddled mess of jacks, rope, tyres and toolboxes. Some of which might well have come in handy if the driver had retained one iota of good humour about this. It appeared that he hadn't. He came over to their cab, shouting. Loudly.

Matt picked Holly up off the floor. He laughed feebly. 'I bet you're beginning to think I'm more trouble than I'm worth.'

'Yes,' she said.

'Oh.'

She sat on the seat, checking her neck for whiplash. It appeared to be unbroken, unlike the heel of her shoe, which had snapped in half during their ordeal.

'Fuck,' Holly said, and sighed heavily. She looked perilously close to tears. 'There's never a dull moment when you're around, is there, Matt Jarvis?'

'Not often,' he admitted.

Their driver had got out and was arguing fiercely with the driver of the taxi in front. Both men were shouting and waving their arms in a threatening manner. God, he hoped there wasn't going to be a fight. He was crap at fighting, as the regrettable Headstrong incident had proved.

'I'd better nip out and see what's happening.' Matt clambered over Holly and opened the door.

'I don't think we're going to get to Martha's wedding tonight,' she said. 'I'll just have to sit and wait for the hives to start or whatever it was that was going to befall me.'

'I think that only happens if you don't go deliberately. If you've tried your very hardest to do something and have been thwarted at every turn, then I think the universe probably lets you off.' He hoped he sounded reassuring and he prayed that on a small scale he was right.

'Do people still say "thwarted"?' Holly asked as she joined Matt on the snowy road.

He turned to her and made sure his scarf was protecting her from the cold. 'Rock journalists do.'

'Right,' she said.

There was quite a merry gaggle standing on the tarmac – except none of them was merry. The two original taxi drivers had been joined by the third taxi driver and a very irate guy in a flashy business suit who was shouting in an English accent.

As Matt and Holly stood shivering in the snow on the periphery of this heated discussion, their taxi driver turned on them and jerked his thumb at them with what Matt considered an unnecessary amount of venom. It wasn't that he was a coward, but he sincerely hoped he was going to survive this little incident without getting decked.

His cuts had hardly healed from last time.

'It was these two guys,' the driver ranted. 'They was making out in my cab. It was kinda distractin'. That's why I hit you up the rear end.'

'We were not "making out",' Matt protested. 'We were having a tender moment. And anyway, you were the one that encouraged me. I didn't know what to do until you did that funny movement with your shoulders. That's why I kissed her.'

'Is it?' Holly said darkly.

The cab driver spread his hands to show his innocence. 'I did nuttin', lady.'

'I'll explain,' Matt added hastily.

'You will,' Holly agreed.

'That doesn't explain why *you* drove into the back of *him*,' the man in the business suit yelled to his driver. 'I leave you alone for five minutes, *five minutes*, to find out what's happening and why we're in a frigging traffic jam, and I come back to find a mangled cab!' The man put his hands over his face in a supreme effort to control himself. 'Were you watching them making out too?'

'We were *not* making out,' Holly and Matt said in unison.

'The rest of my life hangs in the balance while we are standing here discussing dented fenders.' The man started to tug at his hair. 'I am in a rush like no one has ever used the word rush before. R-U-S-H. Rush! I have travelled three and a half thousand miles across the Atlantic Ocean in the time it has taken me to travel from JFK to here.

Please,' he said weakly, 'can we not just get our *fucking arses* into gear and move?'

They all stood without moving.

'Please?'

Still no one moved.

The man smiled sweetly and made encouraging hurry-along movements with his fingers.

The traffic all around them was free-flowing now, horns blaring at them from all directions as they stood in the middle of the freezing freeway being pelted by snow. Matt huddled into his coat, berating himself under his breath. Bad decision number four hundred and twenty-seven, Matthew. Grief, he should have stayed at Holly's flat, eaten raw fish, got totally pissed on tequila and, hopefully, got laid too.

The driver of the dented cab in front shuffled towards his boot and gave it a tentative slam. It bounced open again and everyone held their breath. He tried again, more firmly and still it bounced open. He looked round blackly and gave it another hefty slam, whereupon the boot lid, wisely, stayed in place.

There was a collective sigh of relief.

Mr Angry in his blue suit marched back towards his cab, barging into Matt as he went. 'You are so lucky I didn't hit you, mate,' he hissed between gritted teeth like a pantomime baddy.

'Me?' Matt said.

'You!' The man stabbed at him with his finger and continued to stride doggedly along the road.

'Why me?' Matt shouted after him, when he was at a safe enough distance not to turn back.

The man's cab driver followed him humbly and they both got into the car, and with a lot of grinding of metal and puffing of steam, the taxi inched out into the traffic and disappeared into the night.

Matt clapped his hands together for warmth. 'Well, I guess it's just us,' he said brightly.

'Get in,' the taxi driver ordered.

Holly slid into the car silently and Matt followed, brushing the snow from his hair.

'You are so lucky *I* didn't hit you too, *mate*,' she said, folding her arms and slinking into the corner.

Matt sat there, speechless with indignity at being so unjustly accused. The traffic was rushing past them, headlights blurring through the snow-splattered windows. The taxi driver made himself comfortable on his bead seat and readjusted his leather flying helmet. The car in front pulled away, taking their front bumper with it, which dragged along the freeway screeching like a parrot being tortured.

The driver looked round open-mouthed.

'Just drive,' Matt instructed coldly.

He was going to get to naffing Martha's wedding this night of our Lord if it was the last bloody thing he ever did.

The driver put the car in gear, let off his handbrake and glanced in his rear-view mirror, presumably to check if it was a safe and snog-free zone.

Matt risked a peep at Holly, who was huddled into the corner, a fierce little scowl on her wet little face – definitely no danger there.

The driver turned the key in the ignition. Click. Nothing. He tried again. Click. Nothing. Again. Click. Nothing. Click. Click. Click. Nothing. Nothing. Nothing. He swivelled round in his seat and looked questioningly at Matt. But what could he say? Other than that he had seen doornails that weren't quite as dead.

CHAPTER 35

Martha's skirt was round her waist and her beautiful gossamer train was draped in the tomato sauce that went with the giant shrimp that her bottom was narrowly missing. Glen's trousers were somewhere round his ankles. And they were both making the sort of noises normally reserved for bad 1960s porn films. Despite the amount of bouncing that was going on, Martha's veil was still very much in place. That Beatrice had done one hell of a job.

Watching, frozen to the spot, Josie's tongue lolled attractively out of her mouth and her eyes popped out on stalks like some demented cartoon character. They were so totally engrossed in each other that they didn't even notice her come in. Supposing it had been Jack? Supposing Jack had walked in and stood watching them fucking each other for all they were worth? How would Martha wriggle out of this one? And wriggling she was.

It was a bizarre experience being an uninvited audience to such frenzied intimacy. Had Damien ever shut out the rest of the world for her? Had she ever enjoyed passion to dizzy heights that excluded all else, especially in circumstances as dubious or as dangerous as these? If she had, she couldn't remember it, which wasn't necessarily a good sign.

The room they'd been in earlier hadn't changed at all; it was still hot and stuffy and getting more so by the minute. The bacon products that Jack had complained about lay long cold in a platter of white grease; Martha's make-up bag sat half open on the dresser; the cushions on the chaise-longue were still crumpled where Felicia had put her feet up for five minutes to stop her toes throbbing. Why weren't they making love on that? Surely it would be more comfortable than sitting in tomato sauce and a shrimp platter?

Martha was coming to orgasm, giving a whole new meaning to 'Here Comes the Bride'. The gasps were getting louder and, to Josie's ears, more theatrical. She sounded like Meg Ryan in the restaurant scene from *When Harry Met Sally* – put on and unconvincing. Damien had always complained that Josie didn't make enough noise. If it was louder, it must be better. Rather like the car stereo. Why did no one appreciate the quiet, understated version of ecstasy? Martha's eyes were closed and she was clinging on to Glen, clutching at his tuxedo, and Josie thought how stupid he looked with his shirt undone and his trousers down and his dinner jacket still on. Clearly they'd been in too much of a hurry to consider undressing properly. Somehow women could get away with wearing random items of clothing and still look seductive; men, however, did not look good half dressed. And Glen was no exception.

Now Martha sounded as though she'd gone into labour, shrieking and crying and tossing her head about like a thing possessed. Then she opened her eyes and looked straight at Josie and the next shriek that came out wasn't of pleasure, Josie was pretty sure of that. But Glen seemed blissfully unaware and started to shriek back. This was unbearable. They could move on to farmyard impressions at any time now. Damien had taken her to Brighton once, supposedly for a romantic weekend. The couple in the adjoining bedroom had gone at it like rabbits all night, which made their paltry twice look distinctly unromantic. The headboard had banged with monotonous regularity against the wall, and added to that, they'd quacked like ducks until twelve, brayed like donkeys until one, baaed like sheep until two, grunted like pigs until three and finally, at four, just before they came to a full 'Old MacDonald' simultaneous orgasm and shut up, Josie had bounced around on the bed and joined in with their cock-a-doodle-doo noises. Damien was furious. He said she'd ruined their romantic weekend. *She* had? He said she was jealous and small-minded, which she was – and tired too. He said they'd have to face them over breakfast, which they may well have done. There were several women in the breakfast room who looked like potential grunters and squawkers, but none of the men looked remotely as if they were capable of lasting that long in the sack. She ought to have been in awe really, but she was fractious and feeling unloved and she and Damien didn't speak all day. So much for romance. Perhaps he would have been happier if she'd spent all night grunting like something out of *Babe*. Another thing she had wondered at the time was if she and Damien could hear so much through the walls, what would it be like to be in the same room as such a couple? Now she had some idea.

Martha was still staring at her, transfixed, her face contorted with a mixture of terror, horror and pleasure. This was too weird. It was time for Josie to leave.

Slamming the door behind her, Josie leaned heavily against it. She felt sick. Sick to her heart and sick to her stomach. It was tempting to open the door once more and take another peek like they do in melodramatic movies to make sure that the bad thing they've seen really is that bad. This was bad. She knew it without needing to take another look. And, to be honest, the last thing she ever wanted to see again was the sight of Martha being soundly shagged by her husband's best man.

Josie's throat had gone dry and her tongue felt like a carpet tile. The lilac chiffon seemed to have shrunk to constrict her ribs and squash her breathing out of her cleavage. Horrid little droplets of sweat had pricked up on her top lip and her palms were hot and clammy as if she had been running for miles. This was bad. Very bad. Only a few hours ago, Martha had promised to love, honour, cherish and all that crap. And she'd sounded so convinced. What had gone wrong? It could be that this is a one-off, Josie thought, her mind racing through possible scenarios. A minor aberration . . . a *minor* aberration! Sneaking upstairs to screw your best man during your wedding reception is not a *minor* aberration, she reminded herself. Clearly, living with Damien for too long had skewed her moral boundaries. But it could be a . . . a . . . Josie closed her eyes, searching her brain files for inspiration. It could be a . . . a . . . Nothing. Try as she might, she couldn't find Martha an excuse for this.

The oohs and the aahs and the oh yes's and the pig noises from the other side of the door had stopped and were being replaced by the rustling of net and the zipping of zips. Josie shot off into the ladies' cloakroom before the dishevelled Martha appeared, to give herself time to think what on earth she was going to say to her cousin that wouldn't somewhere involve the word bitch.

Josie was running her hands under the cold-water tap, letting her fingers play in the stream until they were numb at the tips. In the harshly lit mirror, her face was the colour of wallpaper paste. Lilac was not her colour. Not today.

The door opened hesitantly and Martha edged

her way in. The veil was still anchored to her head, but her lipstick was smeared all round her mouth and the end of her train was pink, with bits of congealed sauce clinging to it.

Josie looked at her in the mirror.

'You've still got your lace gloves on.' Martha motioned to her hands in the water.

'I know what I'm doing,' Josie snapped, pulling her hands and her sodden gloves from under the tap.

Martha leant against the wall and sighed. 'And so do I.'

Josie whirled round. 'Do you?' Martha looked awkward and pathetic, but there was a defiant flash in her usually soft green eyes that now glinted as hard as the filling in Mint Cracknel. 'It doesn't seem five minutes ago to me when you were looking all dreamy-eyed and saying "forever". Remember, Martha? "Forsaking all others", "keeping yourself only unto him", et cetera, et cetera . . . Did you mean any of that rubbish?'

'I did at the time.'

'At the time!' Josie exploded. 'It wasn't a year ago. It wasn't six months ago. It wasn't even six days ago, Martha. It was . . .' Josie counted the time off on her fingers. 'It was barely six hours ago.'

'I know.' Martha's voice was small but determined. 'Things change.'

'Not that bloody quick they don't!'

'They do.'

'They don't.'

'How long did it take Damien to walk out on you?'

'That's below the belt, Martha. They were totally different circumstances. We'd been together five years, not five minutes. You haven't even cut the wedding cake yet!'

'Maybe we could get a refund on it,' Martha muttered.

'You're supposed to keep it for the christening.'

'I think that's a bit optimistic given the circumstances.'

'And I think it's pertinent to mention that I hardly think you're giving it a fair crack of the whip.'

There was a velvet seat in the corner just below the Tampax machine and the free-flow air drier, and Martha sank on to it, yanking her train round her knees. 'He's not right for me.'

'Jack?'

Martha glared at her. 'I was thinking of Brad Pitt.'

'And I was thinking of Glen,' Josie said. 'Be sensible about this.'

'Yes, Jack. I don't think he's right for me.'

'This is the wrong time to be saying this, Martha. Yesterday would have been a much better day to come to this conclusion.'

'You told me he looked like a Sharpei.'

'He does.'

'And you told me he was too old for me.'

'He is.'

'So?'

'And you told me that you loved him. You told *him* that you loved him. You stood up in front of half of Sicily in the church and said that you loved him!'

'I did,' Martha protested.

Josie wished she still had her hands in cold water or was holding Martha's head under it. One of the two. 'But not now.'

'No.'

'Martha.' She spoke to her cousin in a voice she hoped sounded reasonable and considered. It was the voice she used to try to control her more difficult students. 'Jack may look like something grown in a laboratory. He may look as old as time itself. He may be a downright opinionated bastard. He may not be the man I'd choose for you. He may be all of those things and more. But you *did* choose him, Martha, and he doesn't deserve this. Whatever he is and whatever he's done, he doesn't deserve this.'

'He's done nothing. It's me.'

'That may not make him feel any better.'

'I can't help that,' Martha said belligerently.

'You can, Martha. You are the one person that can stop this right now.'

Martha's mouth turned down.

'Your *husband* is downstairs right now waiting for you while you and his best man are getting bouncy with each other. He is dancing with a small Sicilian

283

person with blue hair and a face like a screwed-up paper bag and he's being extraordinarily nice to her.'

'I can't stay with him just because of that, Josie.'

'He's done nothing to hurt you. You said yourself he adores you, he cherishes you. Doesn't that count for something?'

'You did nothing to hurt Damien and he still left.'

Josie's voice of reason was flying in the face of complete lack of logic. It would have driven Mr Spock insane and it wasn't doing much for her. 'So where does Glen fit into this tawdry little picture?'

'I love him.'

'Does he feel the same?'

'Yes. He always has.'

'You're putting a lot of faith in a bloke who ran out on you because he couldn't cope with the responsibility at a time when you needed him most.'

Martha flinched visibly. 'That was years ago.'

'And you haven't seen him since then,' Josie reminded her with a huff. 'What makes you think that once the band has stopped playing and the lights have gone out that he won't be heading for the hills once again? Is he going to stay and help you clear up the mess? How do you know he'll be here for you this time?'

'I think he will.'

'I *think* is a world of difference away from I *know*.'

'I *know* he'll be here for me this time.'

'Would it surprise you to know that about an hour ago he asked me to spend the weekend with him?'

'He thought he'd lost me.'

'Well, I guess as best man at your wedding, he might just get that idea.'

'We can't live without each other.'

'You've been doing pretty well up till now.'

'Not any more.'

'Martha, can I ask you this? Have you been banged on the head recently by anything particularly heavy?'

Martha stood up, pushing herself from her velvet stool with a weariness that looked bone deep. 'We're back to the beginning of this conversation, Jo. I know what I'm doing.'

'And might I ask exactly what that involves?'

'Glen and I are going away together.'

'Now!'

'Now.'

'Don't you have a shrink? All Americans have psychiatrists, don't they?'

'Yes, I do have a "shrink", as a matter of fact.'

'Ring her then. Ring her now. See what she tells you to do about walking out of your wedding.'

'She'd say that I was to do what my feelings dictate.'

'Then she's a crap psychiatrist! Listen to me instead.'

'My feelings are dictating that I leave.'

'You *cannot* do this, Martha.'

'I have to.'

'You don't. Carry on with the rest of your day as if nothing has happened, dance with Jack, smile at your guests, drink champagne – preferably lots of it – and cut the naffing cake. And then give yourself six months, *at least* six months, to think this through properly. You've been apart all this time; what difference will another few months make?'

'I can't wait so long.'

'Another few weeks then.'

Martha stood motionless.

'Another few days . . .'

Martha said nothing.

'Tomorrow?'

Martha fiddled with her train and seemed to notice for the first time that it was rather more tomato-sauce-coloured than it had started out.

'For heaven's sake, Martha! Please, please don't leave Jack with all those guests, all that cake and all that explaining to do, all by himself.'

'I want to be with Glen tonight.' Martha grabbed her hand and Josie noticed her glove was still wet. 'I want you to help me.'

Josie backed away. 'Oh no. Oh no. Oh no, no, no.'

'I want you to tell Jack.'

'No. No. Three times no.'

'You're my cousin. You have to do this for me. Please.'

'This is not in my bridesmaid's contract. No way.'

'You didn't read the small print.'

'No!'

'I can't face him.'

'You have to, Martha. You at least owe him that.'

Martha gave a hearty tug at her veil and tiara and singularly failed to budge it one inch. 'I have to get out of this,' she whined. 'It's killing me.'

'Not as much as it's going to kill Jack,' Josie said.

CHAPTER 36

'I don't think I want to be with you right now,' Holly muttered, kicking at the clumps of snow drifting at the side of the road. Her hair looked as though it had been Brylcreemed flat to her head and she was shivering inside her coat. Trembling fingers lifted a cigarette to her mouth and she tightened her already pinched mouth to drag on it, spitting the smoke out into the falling snow. She held out her hand. 'I feel like you're invading my personal space.'

'I'm trying to give off reflected heat,' Matt said.

'I don't need it.'

'You do. Here, take my coat,' he offered, undoing his buttons.

'You'll catch freakin' hypothermia,' she complained. 'Leave it on. I'll suffer. I just wanted you to know I was suffering.'

'We'll both get hypothermia,' Matt pointed out. 'Let's get back in the car.'

'Hitler won't let me smoke in his cab.' She stabbed the air with her cigarette.

They were standing on the edge of the narrow pavement watching the traffic crawl by and waiting for a replacement cab, which had been requested some time ago by their driver, who was leaning on his bonnet enjoying a cigarette and not looking at them. But then he was wearing a sheepskin coat and a flying helmet.

'Can't you manage without a cigarette?'

'No, Matt,' she snarled, 'I can't. I can manage without a lot of things at the moment, you included, but the one thing I can't manage without is a cigarette. It is helping what is left of my stretched nerves to stay in the arrangement that my DNA intended.'

Matt thought it pertinent to kick the snow too. 'I'm sorry about tonight. It's been a bit of a mess, hasn't it?'

Holly snorted.

'I'll make it up to you,' Matt promised.

'When?' Holly abused the cigarette again. 'You're going home tomorrow.'

'I'll be back.'

She stared at him.

'Sometime,' he said. 'Sometime soon. I'll arrange it.'

Holly snorted some more.

'And then I'll make it up to you. I'll take you out, somewhere nice. Dates with me are usually a lot of fun.'

Holly made the biggest snorty noise in the world and the taxi driver turned round and looked at them. Matt apologised with his eyes and the driver turned his attention back to his own nicotine habit.

'Martha's wedding will cheer you up.' He was tempted to nudge Holly, but thought his jocularity might be best kept to himself. 'We can have a drink, a dance, listen to Headstrong.'

He wiggled his hips encouragingly in front of her. Steam came out of his companion's nose. Holly's mascara was making tracks down her cheeks and she was starting to look like one of the less attractive members of Kiss. But he could hardly blame her, could he? It was his wretched fault they were in this mess.

'The last thing I want to do on this earth is go to Martha's wedding,' she said slowly. 'What I want to do right now is go home, take a nice long hot bath and then fall into bed.'

Matt's eyes brightened. Maybe that was what they should both do. He should give up this search for Josie Flynn, which was beginning to resemble Monty Python's quest for the Holy Grail at this juncture, and settle for the bubble-bath-and-commitment-free-sex option.

'Alone,' she added, dropping her cigarette to the floor and grinding it purposefully into the snow.

Fuck, Matt thought. Or not fuck, as the case may be. Why couldn't he just let this thing with Josie drop? What thing? From where he was standing there was no *thing* at all! He'd read a book once about a man who'd fallen obsessively in love with someone who he didn't even know. It was called De Clerambault's Syndrome and it meant you saw secret messages of love in bushes and clouds and sheep droppings, sent by telepathy or something from your heart's desire. Pop stars suffered from the effects of it all the time – mad, obsessive people who thought they knew everything about them, but didn't know them at all. There was a woman who was convinced every song that John Lennon wrote was penned for her – and not just when you're depressed or have been dumped and you listen to Radio One and think, Ha, that song's just for me! but real, hand on heart, John has written that just for me. Scary. Wonder what she thought when he wrote 'Yellow Submarine'? Or was that little aberration entirely Paul's fault?

Matt looked up at the clouds. The only message coming from his loved one in the elements was that there was a lot more snow still to fall. He had to find her. Goodness knows why, but he had to. Perhaps he didn't have a syndrome or an obsession, perhaps he was just plain old-fashioned lovesick. There was a feeling somewhere deep in him that knew Josie was too good to lose – somewhere just around the second bend of his colon, judging by the nervous stomach it was giving him. He felt she'd reeled him in and he was bound to her, and it was purgatory knowing that she was somewhere in this hell-hole of a city just tantalisingly out of his reach, round the next bend or over the next hurdle or beyond the next broken-down cab.

On cue their replacement taxi pulled up next to

them. Holly bounced into the back before Matt could even move to open the door for her.

'I want to go home,' she said to him as he slid in tentatively beside her, grateful for the sudden blast of heat.

'Would you mind terribly if I went to Martha's wedding without you?' he asked, the warmth making his nose run and his body tingle with pain.

Holly whirled round in her seat. 'You want to go to *my friend's* wedding without *me*?'

'Er, yes,' Matt said. 'If that's all right with you.'

It wasn't pain his body was tingling with, it was pleasure, Matt realised. Excited pleasure itching through his veins with all the torture of a scratchy wool pullover.

'Am I missing something here, Matt?' Holly's eyes searched his.

'I think we both are, Holly.' And he was horrified to find that it had come out sounding all dreamy.

CHAPTER 37

'Josie,' Glen said as she and Martha walked back into the dressing room. He looked like a man in need of a cigarette or strong drink, or maybe a space transporter – anything that would lift him painlessly out of his current predicament and into another world.

Martha flopped down in front of the dressing table; she was quite the most sullen bride Josie had ever seen. Josie treated Glen to one of her mother's most withering glares – the one she reserved for traffic wardens, delivery men and council officials. The look that cut little men to their knees. Glen withered visibly. At least he was fully dressed again, Josie noted. The sight of a fully grown man withering without the aid of his boxer shorts would have been too unpleasant by half. Martha had been right, Glen did have great buns; she only wished she hadn't seen them in these particular circumstances.

'I know what you must be thinking,' Glen offered.

'No, Glen, I don't think you do.'

'You must think I'm a real asshole.'

'The words were fucking and bastard, actually.'

'We never meant this to happen . . .'

'Then why did it?' Josie asked. 'No one forced you to do it.'

'I love her.'

'I expect you love yourself more, otherwise you'd never be able to do this to her. If you'd loved her you'd have stayed away. It's her wedding, for pity's sake! You're her husband's best man! How could you do this?'

'I don't think there's any point in trying to explain.'

'It's not me you should be explaining this to, it's Jack.'

'That wouldn't be fair . . .'

'No? But it's fair to run off with his wife and it's fair to ask me to do your dirty work for you, you spineless—'

'Josie,' Martha said tightly, 'I need to get out of this dress.'

Josie went over to her cousin and started to tug at her zip.

'We haven't got time for that,' Glen snapped. 'We need to get out of here now.'

'I can't go like this!' Martha protested.

'You'll have to.'

'At least let me get this off.' She yanked ineffectively at her veil.

Josie joined in, ferreting under the acres of filigree netting. 'You've got about three hundred hair grips – bobby pins – in here. I can't budge it.' Josie wondered what Beatrice would think when she found out her hairdo had been more enduring than the marriage.

'Leave it, Martha. We can buy you some things tomorrow. Clothes, shoes, I don't know. Whatever you need. Jack could come looking for you at any minute.'

'I don't want to see him,' Martha said tearfully.

'I can't get this off,' Josie said. 'Beatrice has drilled it into your head.' Perhaps that's why your brain's not working properly.

'What am I supposed to do?'

'He's right, Martha.' Josie gave up trying to wrench the veil from Martha's head and let her arms drop. 'If you're going to do this, just go. Just get out of here now. Leave the spilt milk for everyone else to clear up.'

'What about my going-away suit?'

'Leave it,' Josie sighed. 'Just leave it. The less you have to remind you of this, the better.'

Glen put his arm round Martha and helped her up. She was crying now. 'Josie, you will tell Jack, won't you?'

'Yes.'

'Tell him I didn't mean to hurt him.'

'That might have a slightly hollow ring, Martha. You don't do this sort of thing to people that you don't want to hurt.'

'You still love me, don't you, Jo-jo?'

'Right now, Martha, I don't even like you.'

Tears rolled down Martha's face. 'You said I

should follow my heart. Whatever that meant. That's what you said.'

'You shouldn't listen to me. I spend most of my time talking out of my backside. Now I suggest you go before you're missed.'

'Thanks, Josie,' Martha said, and hugged her. And in spite of her resolve to be hard on Martha, Josie started weeping too.

'Be happy, cousin.'

'I will.' They held each other and cried while Glen shuffled uncomfortably in the background.

'Let's go,' he urged.

Martha pulled away from her cousin reluctantly.

'Ring me and let me know where you are,' Josie said. Martha nodded, wiping her tears with the lace sleeve of her wedding dress and adding mascara to the growing list of unsightly stains.

They opened the door, peeping out into the corridor to see if the coast was clear like some bad B movie. The coast, of course, was clear.

'Goodbye, Josie.'

'Ring me.'

'You've said that already.'

'I don't know what else to say.'

'There isn't anything else to say.'

Josie shrugged. 'Goodbye, then.'

'Goodbye, Jo.' Martha kissed her again and edged out of the door, clinging to Glen's hand. It was needless melodrama as there was no one in sight, and Josie suddenly felt like the weariest person in the world.

'Martha,' she called after them, 'you said you wanted people to remember your wedding.'

Martha turned and smiled sadly through her tears.

'I somehow think they'll have trouble forgetting it,' Josie added to herself.

Josie wiped her tears away with the back of her bare arm and plodded listlessly down the plush velvety carpet, watching Martha and Glen, just ahead of her, retreat furtively into the night. Their pace had quickened and they had begun to giggle like newly-weds setting off on their honeymoon.

'Oh God,' Josie said, rubbing her wet-gloved hands over her face.

There was a waiter at the bottom of the stairs, bearing a tray of brimming champagne glasses. Josie grabbed one and downed it. 'I'm not nearly drunk enough to be doing this,' she muttered. Swiping another glass, which followed the last with equal haste, she put a hand over her mouth to stifle a burp and headed, reluctantly, for the ballroom.

She stood at the doorway and surveyed the party. It was in full swing – a great wedding. And the emotion of the unexpected turn of events hit her with the weight of a Jonah Lomu rugby tackle. The band were playing now – four youthful hip-shaking, heartbreaking teenagers doing a sort of rap rendition of an old Beatles number which had the Sicilians twisting for all their worth on the dance floor in a way that would have made Chubby

Checker proud. *'Everybody's green, 'cos I'm the one who won your love . . .'*

Headstrong! Josie knew where she'd heard the name now, but before it had time to sink to her stomach, Jack came over and greeted her with a peck on her cheek. He was wearing a grin as big as Bristol. 'Did you find Martha?' he asked, pulling Josie into the room by the arm.

She'd never believed people really ever said this, except on *EastEnders*. 'Jack,' she lowered her voice, 'we need to talk.'

'I have a surprise for her.'

Her hand covered his. 'I think she has one for you too.'

'Fireworks,' he said, his beam getting wider. 'She loves them! I've set it up in secret. She has no idea about it. They're just about to start.'

'I know,' she said softly, 'but this really can't wait.'

His brow creased with concern. 'Is Martha okay?'

'It depends what you mean by okay.' Josie took him by the hand. The guests were making their way out on to the terrace for the firework display. 'Let's leave them to it; we need to go somewhere quiet.'

'This is not good, is it, Josie?'

'No.'

The beam disappeared and with it most of Josie's courage. 'Come on,' she said.

Guiding Jack through the tables and out towards

the boathouse, she tried not to think of the irony of her last visit there. It was going to be cold outside, and this time she wouldn't have the comforting warmth of Glen's tuxedo jacket to protect her. She couldn't believe this was happening. It was like a bad, bad dream, the ones you wake up from at three in the morning, cold and sweating; and she hoped to God that she was still in bed and would wake up soon, and that she wouldn't have to go through with this. Perhaps the alarm clock would go off in a minute and she'd be all set for another exciting day in the world of Information Technology at ye olde crumbling Camden college. There was no way she should be doing this. Glen Donnelly. What a bastard! He was nothing more than a yellow-bellied, lily-livered, cute-bottomed scumbag! Both he and Matt Jarvis were prime candidates to walk away with first prize on the Bastard of the Year Award Show.

She risked a sideways glance at Jack. His mouth was drooping down like his moustache and the look on his face said worried in the extreme – as well it might. On the way out, she reached across and grabbed a half-empty bottle of fizz from amidst the debris of one of the tables, and two glasses that looked reasonably clean.

'I don't drink,' he reminded her.

'You will,' she said. 'Believe me. You will.'

The yellow cab pulled up outside Zeppe's Wedding Manor with a screech of tyres and a little puff of smoking rubber – Damien finally having managed to impress on the driver what the word 'rush' meant. He wondered if Rhett Butler would have had the same impact if he'd had to catch taxis everywhere.

Damien paid the driver and deliberately didn't tip him. How could you tip a man who had crashed while trying to watch someone else snogging? Still, he was here now, in the nickiest nick of time, and that was all that mattered.

Damien got out of the cab and noticed it had stopped snowing. The sky was clear and the air crisp, tingling with the touch of ice. He rubbed his hands together, a little movement to ward off the cold and his growing excitement. He could hardly contain himself. Whatever being contained meant. Did men who were contained fly all this way, contend with all this hassle and spend all this money just to demonstrate their undying love? He doubted it.

Damien pulled his case out of the cab and slammed the door behind him.

'Hey, buddy,' a man shouted, 'would you hold that cab for us?'

Damien peered in the driver's window. 'Hang on, mate,' he said. 'There's another fare for you.'

Then he looked up. It was Martha. Looking distinctly more pissed and bedraggled than the average bride ought to be.

'Martha?'

Martha noticed Damien for the first time. Her eyes widened and stared straight at him, but they were all fuzzy and red and looked as though they might start to rotate at any moment. The girl must have glugged back one hell of a lot of champagne to get in this state, he thought. But then she was known for it. Martha could mix it with the best of them – a lioness among party animals. He only hoped that this bloke knew what he was taking on.

The eyes came into focus briefly. 'Damien!'

'You look fabulous,' he said.

'What are you doing here?'

'I couldn't miss giving my congratulations to my favourite cousin-in-law!' He dumped his case on the pavement and put his arms round Martha. 'Congratulations!' He kissed her firmly on the mouth. 'Congratulations!'

It had to be said, she was less than enthusiastic. Thank heaven he hadn't flown all this way just to congratulate her! That would have put a real wet blanket over the proceedings.

'We're just leaving,' she said.

'Don't tell me I've flown all this way and have missed the party!'

'No. It's just us . . . me . . . er . . .' Martha lapsed into silence.

'Where's the big send-off, then?'

Martha looked round, anxious. 'There isn't one,' she said.

'Sneaking off quietly, eh? I see. Nudge nudge, wink wink.'

'I guess so.'

'Where are you off to then?' Damien winked.

Martha looked dazed. 'I don't know.'

'Big secret, eh? I hope it's some exotic Caribbean island.'

'Oh, I see what you mean . . .'

The man who had asked Damien to hold the cab came over now, looking threatening.

'Martha, we'd better leave.'

'This must be your husband,' Damien said, grabbing him by the hand and shaking it roughly. The man's hand hung limp in his and he made a grimaced attempt at smiling. Grief, it must have been one humdinger of a wedding if even the bride and groom were so naffing miserable! 'Congratulations, mate.' Damien clapped him on the shoulder and it was like hitting a shed. 'You're a very lucky man.'

'I know.'

Martha looked at the floor.

'You must have something special to bag this one. Never thought she'd go down the aisle without a fight!'

'Martha,' the man said, with a pointed glance towards the taxi.

Martha twisted her fingers through her veil. 'It's a long story, Damien, and I really don't have time to fill you in on the gory details.'

'Oh,' Damien said, feeling more than a tad deflated.

'We have to go.'

'Have a great honeymoon,' he said. 'Don't do anything I wouldn't do!'

The newly-weds exchanged glances.

'See ya, buddy,' the hulk said, and hustled Martha into the waiting cab.

Damien banged on the roof. 'May all your troubles be small ones!'

Martha leaned out of the window. 'Josie's still inside,' she said. 'You need to talk to her.'

That was exactly what he'd come all this flaming way for.

'Sorry about the divorce and all that,' Martha added, as the taxi lurched off into the night, leaving Damien standing alone on the pavement. He couldn't help but feel piqued that Josie's cousin had spoiled his dazzling entrance.

'Watch this space, Martha.' He patted his pocket for reassurance. 'Watch this space.'

A firework exploded against the night sky, accompanied by appreciative ooooo's from the watching guests. The Wedding March played along in time. And it seemed like another lifetime ago since Martha and Jack had walked down the aisle to the same refrain, full of hope and promises at the start of their new lives together. Two new lives in one afternoon. Martha certainly didn't do things by half.

Jack and Josie, sheltered in the boathouse, watched the reflection of the exploding rocket in the still, calm water of the lake. A shower of pink and green and yellow sprinkled itself over the surface, before it faded to inky blackness once again. The ducks floated by, unfazed and unimpressed.

'I love her, Josie.' Jack had his face in his hands.

Josie was swathed in a cobwebby blanket she'd found tucked away on the corner of the bench, and was trying not to think where or how big the cobweb's owner might be. She poured a glass of champagne. 'Here, drink this.'

'No.' He pushed the glass away, took the bottle from her instead and tipped half of the contents down his throat, then wiped his mouth with the back of his hand. 'Not bad,' he said, glancing at the label.

'You okay?' Josie asked.

'No.'

'I can't believe she'd do this to you.'

Jack laughed, but it was bitter and empty and echoed against the wooden walls of the boathouse. 'She's so beautiful, so funny, so loving.' He turned to Josie. 'I couldn't believe it when she agreed to marry me.'

'Well . . .' Josie said.

'You couldn't believe it either, could you?'

'I . . . er . . .'

'You hid it very well.' He laughed again, and this time it was softer.

Whizz. Bang. Oooo. They watched as a shower of white snow floated serenely across the water.

'Martha's been very mixed up since Jeannie died. It's been hard for all of us. I don't know what she wants. *She* doesn't know what she wants.' Josie shook her head. 'My mother would say all she needs is a good clip round the ear.'

'I would have looked after her, Josie. I would have made her a good husband. I adore her.'

'Then she's the loser in this. I'm not sure that Glen will adore her.'

'I had no idea that she and he were . . .'

'They weren't. It was just today.' Today, of all days!

'I don't know if that makes me feel better or worse.' He took another slug at the bottle of champagne and coughed.

'Oh, Jack.' Josie rested her head on his shoulder. 'I'm so sorry.'

Jack put his arm round her. 'There's no need to be. There's nothing you could have done.'

'Maybe I could have done more to make her listen to me. I tried to stop her. Really I did.'

'She's very headstrong,' he said. Josie flinched slightly at the unbidden thought of Matt's boy band with the same name. 'Once she makes her mind up to do something there's no turning back. It was one of the things that attracted me to her.'

'Even though she's my cousin and I love her, I could kill her!'

'Unfocused anger is very damaging,' Jack said.

'It isn't unfocused,' Josie persisted. 'I know exactly who it's focused on!'

'The most important thing now is how I sort this all out.' Jack lifted the bottle to his mouth again, but it was empty. 'What am I going to tell all those people? They'll be so hurt. What about Martha's father? Does he know?'

'Oh, bugger,' Josie said. 'Poor Uncle Joe, I'd forgotten all about him.'

'He needs to know.'

'I think there could well be another display of colourful pyrotechnics. We have to think about this, Jack. The minute you tell him about Martha, it's going to be a case of light blue touch paper and retire.'

'What about all the presents?'

'They can be sent back,' she said. 'A few bath towels are the least of your worries.'

Jack bit his lip. 'Shit, Josie, I'm going to cry.'

Josie pulled his head to her shoulder, holding him tightly and rocking him gently as he sobbed.

Whizz. Bang. Oooo. A spray of gold glitter tipped with red feathers. Beautiful.

'Don't worry, Jack,' she said. 'I'll think of something.'

The spit and crackle of firecrackers and the smell of cordite filled the air as the finale of the fireworks rattled the sky. A shout went up and a rapturous round of applause. At least one set of fireworks was over. An extravagant, pretty, pointless display that had finished as soon as it had started.

Josie leaned her head back against the wall of the boathouse and twirled her champagne glass thoughtfully. Oh-kay, so she'd told Jack she'd think of something. She just wondered what on earth that might be.

CHAPTER 38

There was no one in the reception room when Damien sauntered in; they were all outside, apparently, applauding the end of the spectacular firework display that had been lighting up the Long Island night sky. Pretty impressive. But nowhere near the scale of the little sparkler in his pocket.

He took a glass of champagne from one of the waiters, who were lounging idly around waiting for the festivities to start up again, and wandered towards the door. Four baseball-capped band members sat temporarily redundant on the side of the stage, furtively smoking joints. The room looked like a cross between the *Marie Celeste* and the aftermath of a St Trinian's food fight. There had clearly been some serious partying going on.

Damien sat down at the end of the buffet table and reached over to pick at the canapés piled on silver trays that decorated the corners. He scrutinised the miniature pastries, trying to work out what they might be. This was hardly the arrival he'd envisaged. He'd seen himself walking into a wedding in full swing, being kissed and greeted by

307

the bride and groom like a long-lost and much-loved relative, and finally sweeping a tearfully grateful Josie into his arms, before falling to one knee and announcing their re-engagement to an astounded and enchanted crowd. *That* was the arrival he'd envisaged. Damien spat the caviare he had inadvertently eaten into a napkin – if there was one thing he hated, it was fish eggs – and looked disconsolately at the spent party poppers. Picking up another canapé, which he hoped was better than the last, he stuffed it whole into his mouth, contemplating what the odds must be on getting two duff appetizers in a row.

The crowd had finished applauding and were starting to wander back into the hall, chattering animatedly to each other. Oh well, to the job in hand. Damien helped himself to more champagne. He'd better go and see if he could find the woman he intended to stay as Mrs Flynn.

Holly was sulking. But not as much as she had been, and the corners of her sulk kept curling up into a nearly smile. And her leg had moved towards him along the seat of the cab, in a movement that a student of body language would have taken as definitely encouraging.

Matt leaned towards her and smiled. 'Whatever you do,' he said, 'don't smile back at me.'

Her lips started to tremble and she clamped them down.

Matt grinned wider. 'Don't smile,' he warned.

Her mouth turned up at the corners and her teeth started to show.

'Don't!'

Holly burst out laughing and pummelled him on his arm with her fists.

'Matt Jarvis, you are a pain in the goddamn butt!'

'No one's ever said that to me before.'

'You surprise me.' Holly huffed back against the seat. 'I don't know how you talked me into this.'

He didn't either. One minute she was stamping her feet and saying no. The next they were wending their way to Long Island in an undented cab. Now they were a stone's throw away from Zeppe's Wedding Manor and Matt couldn't wait. Even a tiny bit of gravel would have reached. They had come all the way across to Long Island without event – no crashing cabs, no falling meteorites, no being abducted by aliens – and were turning towards their final destination.

Matt was experiencing a moment of dry-mouthed calm. He knew instinctively that this was the right wedding, the right Martha and not a bogus one with lemon or green bridesmaids. This would be the right Martha with lilac chiffon bridesmaids and Josie Flynn. He could feel it in his heart, his water and in the marrow of his bones.

'I don't even want to be at this wedding now,' Holly complained.

'You do,' Matt said. 'We'll have a great time. I promise you.'

He felt really shitty doing this to Holly. Dragging

her out here so he could chase after another woman. He tried to convince himself he was doing her a favour, and that without him she would have missed her friend's wedding altogether, but the facts didn't really hang in place when he started piecing them together.

What was he going to do when he got there: rush off after the beguiling Josie and just dump Holly? Put her in front of him if Josie decided to take a swing at him? Leave her there with the less-than-fab four and dance off into the night with his fantasy woman? This was the sort of behaviour associated with Warren Beatty or Matt Le Blanc or Johnny Depp – the ones who *Hello!* magazine would have you believe revelled in their bad-boy images. He was not revelling in this. Normally the boot was on the other foot: he was given the run-around by women he adored. It had always been the same since Julia Mulville in the fourth form had broken his heart by running off with Keith Kirkby just because he had a better collection of Jam records. Oh yes, Julia Mulville had set the pattern for all of his future relationships. A future that made him not a heartbreaker but a heartbreakee.

The cab bounced through ornate wrought-iron gates and travelled along a sweeping drive cut through a wintry trellis of towering oak trees. Fountains of rainbow-coloured fireworks lit up the sky. This was clearly bringing out the journalistic instinct in him, because he could tell just from looking at the place that this was one swish joint, and he wished he was wearing something more civilised than his favourite old coat and his South Park tie.

Holly still looked gorgeous, if a bit weather-beaten. She wound her arm through his. 'Tell me we won't stay long, Matt,' she said. Her face looking up at him was soft and gentle and sort of sexy. 'There are other things I'd like to do tonight.'

'Right,' Matt said. And suddenly, just as things seemed to be getting better, he wondered if they might yet get considerably worse.

CHAPTER 39

'How are you feeling, honey?' Glen squeezed Martha's arm.

'A bit strange.' What she was actually feeling was empty, hollow, trapped, liberated, miserable, ecstatic and more than a little bit car sick.

The cab was taking them to a hotel, and she thought of the honeymoon suite standing empty at the Waldorf Astoria, waiting in vain for her and Jack's arrival. The bed would remain neat and tidy, the bubble bath unused and the champagne unopened – which was probably just as well, as she had already drunk quite enough.

Glen loosened his neck tie and stifled a yawn. 'It has been one *hell* of a day, Martha,' he said. 'I never thought it would end like this.'

'No.' Martha stared out of the window and watched the blackness rushing by.

'We could have gone to my apartment.' Glen slid along the seat until she was jammed up next to him. 'I think you'll like it.'

'I wasn't happy doing that straight away, Glen,'

she said. 'Somewhere anonymous seemed better. I need some time to adjust to this.'

'I understand, honey. It's a big step.'

Martha smiled without humour. 'As big a step as getting married.'

'You sure you've done the right thing?'

Martha nodded and fought back her tears. 'I'm sure Jack will think so too. Given time.'

'We'll need somewhere bigger to live,' Glen said, leaning back. 'I'll have to start looking for a new apartment. Maybe one in the same block. It has fantastic views over the park, I'd hate to leave that.'

'Maybe we should look for a house upstate,' Martha suggested. 'New York is no place to raise a family.'

'Sure,' Glen said. And Martha heard the hesitancy in his voice.

The cab stopped for the toll booth and Glen silently handed the fee to the driver.

'Though I'll have to keep an apartment on in the city to live in during the week,' he said as they drove back into Manhattan. 'I do a lot of client hospitality. I can't take a train out to Sunnyville after that.'

'Maybe it's just too early to be talking about this sort of stuff. We need to get to know each other all over again.'

'You're right,' he said. 'Come over here and kiss me, Mrs Labati.'

'Don't call me that, Glen. It's not right. I'm feeling very bad about this.'

'It didn't seem to bother you too much in the courtesy room.' Glen wiggled his eyebrows seductively.

'That wasn't real,' she said. 'This is.'

'It felt real to me.' He pulled her to him, winding his arms round her. 'It'll be fine,' he assured her, kissing the top of her head where her veil was still firmly clamped. It was giving her a headache and she was sure that it was going to have to be surgically removed. 'You won't regret this.'

But she would. She knew she would. In the small hours of the night she would toss and turn and wake up wondering how she could have done this to such a kind and caring man, whose only mistake had been to fall in love with her.

What would Jeannie have said about all this? she wondered. She would have said the same as Josie – stick with it, make the decision when your head isn't full of champagne and emotions knocking round and round in a dizzy random pattern like the little hard silver balls in a pinball machine. If Jeannie had been there, maybe she wouldn't have had the chance to slip away at all. Or perhaps her mother wouldn't have let the wedding happen in the first place.

What would her father say? Grief, he had been lost somewhere in the equation. She hadn't thought to tell him. Maybe because she knew he wouldn't have let her do it either. Their relationship had taken a turn for the worse now that her mother was no longer between them to stop them sparring, but if there was one thing that Sicilians were big on, it was family duty. And he would have made sure that she stayed and did hers. Somehow that loyalty seemed to have skipped a generation, and she knew that she would be a terrible disappointment to him, having humiliated him in front of his friends on what was supposed to be her big day.

He would have to know before too long. She'd ring him from the hotel and tell him that she was okay – providing she knew that he couldn't trace her. Otherwise he would come with Uncle Nunzio and some of the burlier cousins and drag her back. No, it was better, on reflection, that she had slipped out without telling him.

She cuddled down into the crook of Glen's arm, which was warm against the inadequate protection of a lace wedding dress. All that money wasted. All those people who would never speak to her again. This was a very public error to have made and no one would forgive her lightly. Least of all herself.

The hotel was swishy, swanky, the haunt of pop stars, film stars, kings, queens, heads of state, wealthy tourists, Lotto winners and, it would seem, honeymooners. She'd been there before, to a gallery promotion of some radical, minimalist African artist, but she couldn't remember the name – or the name of the artist either, for that matter. But then her brain wasn't running at optimum power right now.

Martha felt awkward, shuffling aimlessly in her tattered wedding dress while Glen booked a room.

'May I congratulate you, ma'am,' the desk clerk said as Glen filled out a check-in form. 'I have upgraded your room for you with the compliments of the management.'

'We're not—' Martha started.

'Leaving for our honeymoon until tomorrow,' Glen interrupted with a beaming smile.

'Yes,' Martha said, tugging self-consciously at her veil. 'Tomorrow.'

'Do you have any bags?'

'Er, no . . .' It was Glen's turn to look embarrassed.

'If there's anything you need, I'm sure room service will be able to help you out, sir.'

'Thank you.'

The desk clerk's smile didn't waver as he handed the key card to Glen. 'I hope you enjoy your short stay with us.'

And Martha wondered what he thought about the lateness of their booking and the less than pristine appearance of the bride, who had a tear-stained face but no toothbrush. Tactfully, he had already turned away to log their details into his computer.

'Why did you pretend we were married?' she asked Glen as he steered her towards the elevator.

'Primarily because you're wearing a wedding dress, darling.' He smiled stiffly at the bellboy. 'Did I do wrong?'

'No,' she said. 'I guess not. I just felt uneasy.'

'This is a whole new ball game for me too, Martha,' he pointed out. 'It's gonna take some adjustment on both of our parts.'

'I know,' she said. 'I'm sorry.'

Glen took her in his arms as they entered the elevator and the doors closed behind them. 'We have the rest of our lives to do it in, honey.'

The elevator lurched upwards and Martha's stomach lurched down. *The rest of our lives*. It was something of a recurring theme.

CHAPTER 40

Josie held Jack's face between her palms and looked at him. He had stopped crying now, but looked pale and tired and like a man who had been dumped at his own wedding.

'Feeling better?'

Jack nodded. 'Maybe I need to sit here a bit longer.'

'Chin up,' Josie said, and gave him a kiss. 'I'll stay here with you for as long as it takes. If you want me to.'

Jack smiled weakly. 'I'd like that.'

'Oh, how cosy!' a voice said at the door to the boathouse. 'How very fucking cosy!'

Josie peered at the silhouette in the darkness. The man leaned on the door frame with an arrogant air that was definitely familiar. It couldn't be. He moved into the small pool of light created by the lanterns round the lakeside.

'Damien!'

'Ah, you do remember me,' he said.

'What on earth are you doing here?'

'Feeling a bit like a spare prick at a wedding at the moment, to coin a phrase.' He jerked his thumb at Jack, who was looking very confused. 'I hadn't expected to see him here.'

'Jack?' Josie and Jack stared at each other. 'Why ever not?'

'If your mother had said *he'd* be with you, I wouldn't have trailed here after you.'

'What's my mother got to do with this?'

'She's the one that's hoping for a reconciliation.'

'Between us?' Josie started to laugh. 'I think she'd rather see me married to someone with all the flair and excitement of Postman Pat than back with you, Damien.'

'And what do you see in *him*?' Damien's face was black as he glared in Jack's direction. 'He's old enough to be your . . . your . . . older brother.'

'What do I *see* in him?' Jack and Josie looked at each other again. Josie wrinkled her nose. 'Damien, if this is a tree you're barking up, it's the wrong one.'

Damien snorted cynically.

'Do you want me to handle this, Josie?' Jack asked. He went to stand up.

Damien pushed him in the chest and Jack sat back down with a surprised *oouf*. 'I think you've handled quite enough, mate. She's still a married woman, you know. I don't suppose she told you that, did she?'

'I'm fully aware of Josie's marital status.' Jack pushed himself up again and stood in what looked to Josie horribly like some sort of kung fu I'm-going-to-deck-you-in-a-minute pose. 'I don't, however, think you fully understand mine.'

'I don't give a toss about yours, mate.' Damien squared up to him. 'Well, actually I do. I do if it involves *my wife*.'

'It doesn't involve your wife at all.' Jack did this funny wiggly movement with his hands that made him look as though he was trying to hang on to his temper.

'And I say it does.' Damien prodded Jack in the chest.

Jack did the funny movement again. A sort of squashing-down of something that didn't exist. 'I think we should all calm down and regroup here.'

'You can think what you fucking like, mate,' Damien said, before drawing back and aiming his fist at Jack's nose.

Josie stood there, amazed. She had blinked and missed it. The whole thing was over in a split second. One minute Damien was about to punch Jack; the next he was lying face down on the boathouse floor.

'Ah, ah, arrgh,' he said.

Jack's foot was on Damien's shoulder, and Damien's arm was stretched backwards, his fingers clamped firmly in Jack's grip. Jack's face was a picture of serene calm. If it had been Josie she would have punched Damien's lights out and enjoyed it. Damien struggled ineffectually.

Josie folded her arms and stood over his frantically wriggling form. 'I think it's about time you were formally introduced, don't you? Jack, this is Damien, my ex-husband.'

'Pleased to meet you, Damien.' Jack nodded, but it was lost on Damien, who was eating carpet – well, floorboards.

'Damien, this is Jack. He's a martial arts expert,' Josie said unnecessarily. 'He's also Martha's husband.'

Matt strolled into the lobby of Zeppe's Wedding Manor trying to stay as cool and casual as possible, given that what was going on inside his head was that noisy bit at the end of 'I Am the Walrus' where everything descends into squeaks and farts and discordant peeps. Out of all the wondrous music Lennon and McCartney had produced, he'd never liked that bit. And he liked it less going on in his brain, his heart and his stomach.

Holly, beside him, was in bare feet. She was carrying her broken shoes in her hand and deposited them without a word in a trough of flowers as they passed. He slipped off his snow-sodden coat, took Holly's as she wriggled out of it and handed them both to the cloakroom atten-dant. Then he smiled at Holly tightly and she grinned back with a light, forgiving laugh – both relieved for different reasons that they were finally here.

His heart was pounding inside his shirt, big heavy thuds that in a man of more mature years would no doubt indicate the onset of a coronary. This was it. The moment of truth. He couldn't believe, after all the trials and the tribulations and the false starts, that he had finally made it. He ran his hand nervously across his mouth and fingered the burgeoning stubble of his beard. He'd have a seven o'clock shadow that would compete with Huckleberry Hound's. Shit, he should have shaved. Somewhere in all this effort he'd forgotten that he looked like a total scruffbag. Would Josie notice? Of course she would. The woman had eyes, didn't she? He would have to blind her with his sparkling repartee instead. Which brought him to a very moot point. What exactly would he say to her? How could he convey what he felt without coming on too heavy? How could he tell her, without sounding like someone currently enjoying Care in the Community, that since the moment he'd met her he'd been sick with longing? Tricky, that one.

Holly linked her arm through his. Without her huge shoes she was tiny, and he felt like the big bad wolf for treating her so meanly. Right at that moment, a bridesmaid walked past. Not *the* bridesmaid, but a bridesmaid. A bridesmaid wearing lilac. It was a backless, sleeveless, floaty piece of nonsense – all those things, just as Josie had described. Matt closed his eyes, wanting to shout with delight.

As they entered the hall, he could see Headstrong playing, and Holly waved to them in acknowledgement.

Matt pointed in amazement. 'They're playing "Got To Get You Into My Life"!'

'I know,' Holly sighed. 'They don't know it's a Beatles number. They think it's by Oasis. Please don't tell them.'

'They're not making a bad job of it, are they?' Matt was pleasantly surprised to find his foot was tapping.

'Want to dance?' Holly said.

'Shouldn't you find Martha?'

'Maybe,' Holly said. 'It shouldn't be hard to spot her. There can't be many people here in big white dresses. Wanna have a look around?'

'I think I'll leave you to it,' Matt said. 'I'd better pop off to the little boys' room. Weak bladder from all the excitement . . .'

'Okay,' she said. 'See you back here soon?'

Matt nodded. 'Won't be long.'

Holly disappeared though the throng of dancers, wiggling her fingers and her rear end at him as she went.

Matt rubbed his hands together, just as all villains do when they're hatching a dastardly plan. Now to find Josie.

Three laps of the dance floor later and he was depressed. He'd searched every nook and cranny, but so far even a passing glimpse of the lovely Josie had eluded him. Matt scratched his head, as all villains do when their dastardly plans are coming unstuck. She must be here somewhere. He was in the right place, at the right time, with the right Martha. All he needed now was Ms Right to put in a timely appearance.

CHAPTER 41

Martha sat on the edge of the bed where, four hundred and twenty-six bobby pins later, Beatrice's firmly attached veil finally parted company with her scalp. The relief was enormous and the blood rushed back to her hair follicles with a vengeance, making her crow with delight.

Glen turned to smile at her. His tuxedo jacket lay across the chair, along with his bow tie. The neck of his shirt was undone and he had rolled up the cuffs to his elbows. His hair had lost that just-gelled look.

'I thought I was never going to get that damn thing off,' Martha said. 'I thought I was going to have to go through life shopping at Target with a wedding veil on.'

'You would have turned more heads than you normally do,' he said.

'Quite possibly,' she replied. Using one of Josie's phrases brought on a sudden rush of longing for her cousin. She wished Josie were here to help her. It had been no fun pulling out all her own bobby pins, and now she didn't know what she wanted to do next either. Josie would have told her. But then when Josie *was* telling her what to do, she hadn't listened. Martha felt a flutter of indecision in her stomach. Maybe she should have.

'Shall I order some champagne?' Glen asked.

'Champagne?'

'To celebrate.'

'To celebrate?' Was this a celebration? Walking out of her marriage and into the arms of another man all in the same day. It didn't really feel like she had anything to toast with champagne.

'I thought you'd want to do something to mark the occasion.'

'I've had enough champagne for today,' Martha said with a sigh. What would Josie do? Have a cup of tea, no doubt. 'I'll be sick if I drink any more.' Martha tugged at her lace dress, which was beginning to itch. 'I need to get out of this.'

'Want me to help you?' he asked, and his grin took on a leery quality that was best reserved for daytime soaps. He came and sat beside her. Pushing the hair back from her face, he feathered light kisses along her hairline. His mouth felt cold and wet, whereas earlier it has been warm and tantalisingly moist. He ran his fingers along the nape of her neck, teasing inside the edge of her wedding dress, and she shivered.

No, she didn't want him to help her out of her dress. No, she didn't want champagne. And no, she didn't know what she did want!

A weariness had crept over her, making her

joints ache and her bones stiff, as if she had worked out for too long. 'I think I need to be alone for a little while, Glen,' she said, rubbing her shoulders. 'I have a lot to think about. Maybe I'll take a bath.'

Glen pulled her closer. 'Want to slip into the tub together?'

'I think maybe alone would be good right now.' She eased away from him a little. 'Glen, I'm finding this very strange.'

'So am I, honey. That's why I'm trying so hard to please you.' Glen kissed her nose. 'And failing miserably!'

Martha kissed him back, the uneasiness between them lifted. 'I'm sorry.'

'That's okay. I guess we're both a little uncertain here. It's been a long time.' He wrapped his arms round her waist. 'I'll make it right for you, Martha. I promise. Just wait and see.'

Martha felt some of the tension release from her neck. 'Why don't you phone room service? Have a little something while I have a soak.'

Glen stood up and massaged his stomach. 'I could not eat another thing. That was one hell of a wedding reception. Your father's going to get a monster check for that party.'

'It's a shame that's all he's going to have to show for it.'

Glen dropped to his knees in front of her, and his gaze held her eyes. 'You've done the right thing,' he said. 'It may not feel like it right now, but you couldn't have gone through with it. People will learn to live with it.'

She thought of Jack living with it. She thought of her father living with it. And she knew her mother would have killed her rather than live with it.

'I need to phone Daddy,' Martha said. 'I should let him know that I'm okay and haven't been abducted against my will. He watches a lot of late-night cable TV shows; he's probably decided you're an alien.'

'He'll send the Sicilians after you,' Glen warned.

'I think maybe they're all too drunk to drive,' Martha laughed. 'But I'll put a block on the phone number just in case.'

'I'll tell you what I'll do,' Glen said. 'I'll go down-stairs to the lobby bar, have a nightcap and leave you in peace for a while. How does that sound?'

'That sounds fine.'

He stood up and stretched. He was looking tired, a faint greyness pinched at his cheeks and the lines round his eyes had settled a little deeper. It must have been a difficult day for him too.

'I don't want to leave you alone,' he said. 'Sure you'll be okay?'

'I'll be fine.'

His eyes searched hers.

'Really,' she said.

Glen grabbed his tuxedo jacket from the chair and threw it over his shoulder. 'I won't be long.'

'There's no need to hurry,' Martha said.

He kissed her full on the mouth and then

winked. 'Miss you already,' he said as he walked out of the bedroom door.

The hot water gushed out of the taps like a waterfall, filling the bathroom with curling steam. Martha carefully poured in a capful of the hotel's complimentary bubble bath, inhaling the sweet artificial scent which wafted into the air. She paused and then tipped in the entire bottle – if you were going to have foam, it might as well be big foam. Was it a vain hope that maybe the bubbles would massage all her cares away? Probably.

Turning to the mirror, she cleared a space in the mist that obscured it with the palm of her hand and stared at the face framed by the droplets of condensation. Her eyes were tired, black-ringed, and that was without the smudges of eyeliner and mascara adding to the effect. Her lipstick was smeared and her blusher long gone. If she was looking this terrible, what effect must it be having on Jack?

Martha lifted her arms and struggled to undo her dress. She needed Josie again. There were a thousand tiny pearl buttons trapping her inside it, each one lovingly hand-stitched, each one tight in the newness of its confines. She was tempted to rip them apart, but knew she wouldn't have the strength and admitted defeat instead.

She sat on the edge of the bath, letting the hot water rush over her hand, soothing her. Glen probably wouldn't be long; she could tell he was keen to get into bed. And why shouldn't he be? She should be too. But all she wanted to do was lie down and sleep, a deep, abiding sleep that would blot out the day's events from her mind.

It was time to call her father. Martha wandered back into the bedroom, nibbling anxiously at her perfectly manicured fingernails. Sitting at the desk by the telephone, she lifted the receiver and dialled for an outside line. What was she going to say? She put the receiver down again and chewed at her nails some more. Where should she call – the hotel or her father's cellphone. Where was he least likely to shriek at her? Heaven knows, she was lucky this hadn't given him a heart attack – or maybe it had and she just didn't know.

Martha took a deep breath and put the phone to her ear. She took another deep breath and put it down again. This was a nightmare. She could quite easily hyperventilate at the thought of it. How could she have left Jack to deal with all this alone? Dear, sweet Jack. Josie had been right all along. He'd done nothing to deserve being treated like this. She hoped that her cousin was looking after him well and that they hadn't both made an effigy of her out of the marzipan from the wedding cake and were currently sticking pins in her.

Outside the hotel, sirens wailed, their plaintive sound echoing in the hollowness inside her. How long would she feel like this? she wondered. Had she really expected that running away with Glen would be easy? She certainly hadn't thought that walking away from Jack without a backward glance would be so hard. She looked at the bed. The bed that she and Glen would soon share. It wasn't quite the wedding night she had envisaged. And Martha laughed out loud to herself in the lavishly furnished but oh so bland bedroom. They had promised themselves that they would make a baby tonight, she and Jack. A wedding-night child to start their future, to seal their happiness and make them a family. Would Glen want that? He was a stranger to her now. An intimate stranger. Would a baby be on his current list of 'must haves'?

Martha abandoned the idea of a phone call and walked to the window. Drawing back the comfort of the velvet drapes, she let the dark night flood the room, taking in the nocturnal view of Fifth Avenue. She leaned her face against the cold of the window, enjoying the chill against her burning-hot cheek. The snow had gone, its intransigent whiteness vanished, leaving nothing to show for itself but gleaming wet roads, a temporary mirror for the streetlamps and the red tail-lights of the cars. Two tracks of water meandered down the outside of the window in slow, steady rivulets, like lonely tears streaking its face, and Martha traced their tortuous route with her fingers, amazed to find that she too was crying.

She had done the wrong thing. She knew that now. Why hadn't she listened to Josie? How could she have made those promises, spoken those vows, and then turned away at the first temptation. What had suddenly made Glen seem so attractive that she could turn her back and hurt all those people, especially Jack? And for what?

How long would it be before the burden of guilt crushed her new relationship? How long before the what ifs became so loud that they caused a constant clamour in her head? How long before they could all pick up the pieces of their lives and carry on as if nothing had happened?

Martha looked at the telephone. There was only one way she could rectify this. Just one thing to do. She trailed her fingers over the window, a wave of melancholy washing through her soul. Her mind was made up. It would be best for them all.

The residents' lounge bar was sumptuous and subdued. Glen lifted his third brandy to his lips with a distinct lack of enthusiasm. The sparsely spread clientele were murmuring to each other in muted tones; there were two ladies with short skirts and high voices who looked as though they might have a professional interest in a group of Japanese businessmen sharing a risqué joke. In the far corner a pianist in a white tuxedo tinkled out some soft jazz, but among the high ceilings, the red velvet sofas and the hard-backed gilded chairs he failed to create the intimate atmosphere he was striving for. Much like Glen's own efforts with Martha, really.

As a last resort he turned to the barman, who was pretending to be busy polishing glasses, but even he avoided making eye contact. Glen wondered if he should return to Martha yet. He wanted neither to go back too early or stay away too long. The atmosphere, much like this bar, was strained and unnatural, and he wanted to do all he could to make it better.

'Paging Mr Glen Donnelly.' The bellhop in his bright red uniform with gold epaulettes strode through purposefully, mouth pinched tight, concentrating on his mission. 'Paging Mr Glen Donnelly.'

'Hey!' Glen lifted his glass in the direction of the bellhop. The young man came over to him.

'Mr Donnelly?'

'Sure is.'

'I have a message for you, sir.'

'Shoot.'

The bellhop lowered his voice. 'We have a slight emergency situation involving your room, sir.'

Glen's brandy froze on his tongue. 'What type of emergency?'

The barman looked up with interest for the first time that night, cloth poised mid-polish.

'I'm not certain, sir. The duty manager is on his way to your room with a key pass, but we'd like you to be there. Could you please accompany me?'

Glen swallowed the rest of his drink without tasting it and jumped down from the bar stool, striding out after the bellhop, who had quickened his pace. They reached the elevator at a half-run and stood silently, both shifting uncomfortably, as they waited for it to clank and grind its way to their floor.

The duty manager was fumbling with the lock as they both raced along the corridor. He was confusing the electronic lock in his haste to open the door, and both the red and green entry lights were flashing at once. He stopped and looked at Glen, giving both it and him a chance to calm down.

'What's the problem?'

'We've had a report from the room below of water seeping through the ceiling.'

Glen could hardly contain his relief. 'Water?'

'It may be from your bath, sir.'

'Is that all?' Glen said. 'You've dragged me up here because the bath's leaking?'

The bellhop and the duty manager exchanged anxious looks. 'Where's your wife, sir?'

'My wife?' Glen frowned. 'Oh, I see. Er, my . . . my . . . my wife's taking a bath, I believe. Maybe there's a leaking faucet.'

'We've tried calling the room, sir, but couldn't get an answer.'

The blood in Glen's veins turned to ice water. 'Give me that.' He snatched the key pass from the duty manager, who looked relieved to be giving up responsibility for it.

They burst through into the room, banging the door handle against the wall and taking a chunk out of the wallpaper. There were no signs of life.

'Martha!' Glen shouted as he made his way to

the bathroom. He flung the door open and was consumed by a swirling fog of steam and the scent of vanilla. 'Martha!'

A mountain of white foam crept over the side of the bath and was oozing its way merrily along the tiled floor. The water was washing an inch deep below it. Glen paddled through and snapped the taps off.

Wherever Martha was, it wasn't in the bath.

He turned to the duty manager, who looked cross, though the colour had at least come back to his face.

'I'm sorry,' Glen said. 'I don't know what's happened.'

'I'll send someone from housekeeping to clear up for you, sir,' the manager said politely.

'Thank you.' Glen walked back into the bedroom, raking his fingers through his hair. 'I'll pay for any damage,' he said absently, wandering over to the window.

'I'll make a note of that, sir,' the duty manager said. 'I wouldn't want this small incident to spoil your wedding night. Would you care to be moved to another room?'

Glen was at the window now. The drapes were open, the windows misted with condensation. He stood stock still. 'I don't think that will be necessary, thank you,' he said. 'Perhaps you'd prepare my account for me. I'll be checking out shortly.'

'Yes, sir,' the duty manager said and retreated

from the room without question, ushering the puzzled bellhop out with him.

Glen turned back to the window and stared at it without seeing. In the mist, Martha had written: 'I thought I loved you, but I can't do this. Forgive me.'

Glen cleared his throat, which had suddenly closed. He pulled the drapes together, shutting out the night and Martha's farewell message. Then he sat on the bed, put his head in his hands and cried as he'd done the last time he'd let Martha slip through his fingers.

CHAPTER 42

'How was I supposed to know he was Martha's husband?' Damien complained.

'Try using your brain before your brawn and engage your mouth before your fists,' Josie advised him. 'It might help.'

'That's not fair. What was I supposed to think? I'd just seen her getting in a taxi with some hairy-arsed Incredible Hulk look-alike.'

'Glen,' Josie said. 'The best man.'

'Fuck,' Damien said.

'Yes, they did.'

'What?'

Josie shook her head. 'It doesn't matter.'

They were walking by the lake, having left Jack in the boathouse wondering what he was going to tell his remaining guests, when he eventually plucked up the courage to go back inside. Josie was still wrapped in her cobwebby shawl against a night that was becoming increasingly cold. A few ducks bobbed bravely over the lake's surface in the deepening gloom, but they looked frozen half to death.

'I wonder if they'll get in the *Guinness Book of Records* for the shortest wedding in history?'

'I think that's possibly the last thing on their minds at the moment.'

They were side by side, close. She could feel the fabric of Damien's suit brushing against the bare part of her arm, and she hoped that wasn't what was giving her goose-bumps. It was a long time since they had been alone like this, and in any other circumstances it could have been considered romantic. The moon was out, fresh-faced, shining hopefully. She took a sidelong glance at her husband. He was very handsome in a hard-edged way, and you couldn't doubt the confidence and belief he had in himself. It was why women continued to fall for him. Josie looked at him with a sad smile. If only there had been some softness in him, a little rounding of the edges. If only he'd cried at *The Sound of Music* or liked Winnie the Pooh or didn't think 'Lady in Red' was a 'steaming heap of crap', unquote. Josie snapped herself back to the present.

'You still haven't said what you're doing here,' she said, scuffing her shoes on the gravel path.

'I would have thought that was obvious.'

'I didn't think you were so fond of Martha,' Josie remarked. 'You never said so.'

'I'm not fond of Martha,' Damien snapped. 'She's a fucking airhead!'

'She is not!' Josie snapped back. Then again, today's events didn't really stand close scrutiny. 'She's confused,' she added thoughtfully.

'As confused as a March hare,' Damien finished. 'And besides, I did tell you why I've come out here.'

Josie looked blank.

'In the words of Tammy Wynette – our D-I-V-O-R-C-E becomes final at any moment.' Damien sighed heavily and spread his hands. 'And I don't want it to.'

Josie started to laugh. 'You can't be serious, Damien!'

'Why are you laughing?' Damien looked mortally offended. 'Of course I'm serious.'

Josie laughed some more. 'You're not?'

'Of course I bloody am!'

'And you've flown all the way here to tell me that?'

'Of course I bloody have!'

Josie stopped and turned to face him. 'Why?'

Damien looked perplexed. 'What do you mean, why?'

'Just that. Why?'

Damien fidgeted about. 'Why?'

'Why?'

Fidget. Fidget. 'Why?'

'Why?'

'Why are you making this so difficult?'

'I'm not. I just want to know why.'

'I've left Melanie for you,' he said.

'You've done what!'

'I've left her.' Damien hung his head. 'Last night.'

'Just like that?'

'What else could I do? It's you I love,' Damien insisted.

'And what does Thing think about your hasty departure?'

'Melanie . . . Thing wasn't a happy bunny at all,' he said. 'She threw plates at me.'

Josie snorted. 'You're lucky to have walked out without a John Bobbitt customisation, I'd say!'

'I know.'

They turned and walked further along the lakeside. Strains of music drifted out from the reception, so it was clear that Jack hadn't yet been in there and told them all to pack up and go home.

'This isn't quite going as I planned it.' Damien puckered his lips. He looked as if he was going to take her hand and then thought better of it. 'I was going to come into Martha's wedding and sweep you off your feet and ask you to marry me again.'

Josie stopped in her tracks, her mouth dropping open.

'I even brought a ring,' Damien said hopefully.

'So you were going to stamp in here in your size elevens and make a big show about something that's intimate between the two of us?'

'Er . . . yes.'

'And spoil Martha's wedding?'

'Now hold on . . .' Damien protested. 'I think she's made a pretty good job of that herself.'

'You are an insensitive bastard, Damien Flynn.'

Damien scowled. 'You say that as if it's a bad thing!'

'It is. Of course it is. I've had enough of your manipulations. I have my own life now, Damien, and you're not in it.'

'I think you're being just a bit hasty here, Josie.'

'This was your choice, Damien. Remember?'

Damien pulled the plush velvet box out of his top pocket. 'It's a very big ring,' he said, opening the lid.

Josie gasped.

Damien let a slow smile spread across his lips.

'My word, Damien. It's beautiful.'

'I knew you'd like it.'

'I don't know a woman that wouldn't.'

Damien eyed the gravel reluctantly and then dropped to one knee. 'I love you, Josie.' He took the ring out of the box and held it up to her. Josie took the ring and gazed at it.

'I've never seen anything quite like this.' The moon glinted on it, illuminating a myriad different colours trapped inside it. It sparkled and danced with a life of its own.

'Let's get engaged, Josie,' Damien said. 'Let's call off the divorce and start again.'

'We can't.'

'We can.'

'Damien, we can't.'

'We can. All we have to do is stop the papers going through.'

Josie looked at the ring and sighed. 'It's not that simple.'

Damien shifted on his knee. 'Why?'

Josie let her hands fall to her sides, hiding the ring from the lure of the moonlight. 'Because I don't love you any more.'

Damien struggled to his feet and snapped the empty ring box shut, stuffing it in his pocket. 'I can't believe this!' He stamped up and down on the path and yanked at his hair in frustration. 'This is about *him*, isn't it?'

'Who?'

Damien pointed somewhere off into the distance. 'Him!'

'Him who?'

'Him who!' Damien sneered. 'This new man in your life. This man you're sharing cosy dinners with. This man that's *important* to you. It must be serious, because you haven't told your mother about him, and you tell your bloody mother *everything*!'

Josie started to laugh. 'That's what this is about, Damien,' she said. 'It's not about you wanting me back. It's about you not wanting me to be happy with anyone else. It's about you proving that you're better than him.'

'Does he buy you diamonds?'

'No, he doesn't.' She hesitated before ploughing on. 'It's not that kind of relationship.' She held up the ring. 'And as a matter of fact, this is a frivolous and pointless gesture. I need reassurance,

341

remorse, security and love, Damien. Not a ring the size of a flaming football.'

Damien's face was as black as the night sky. 'That diamond set me back twenty-thousand notes, I'll have you know. I could have bought an entire farm in the Orkneys for that.'

'I wish you had,' Josie said. 'And had moved there too. Even though the sheep would have good cause to be worried.'

'What's his name?'

'His name?' Josie pulled the blanket round her shoulders. 'Er . . . Matt.'

'As in doormat?'

'As in Matt Jarvis.'

'Do you love him?'

'Yes,' she said defiantly. And then she added quietly: 'Yes, I do.'

'What is he? Some pipe-smoking, anorak-wearing, Labour-voting chemistry teacher you've met in the staff room?'

'I'm glad you have such a high opinion of my taste in men, Damien. After all, I did choose you.'

Damien gloated. 'I bet that is one nail I've hit right on the head.'

Josie put her hands on her hips. 'He's a rock . . . musician,' she said.

'A rock musician! What are you doing with a rock musician?'

'Having a lot of fun,' she said.

Damien pointed at the ring. 'That is a sign of my commitment to you, and all you can do is throw it in my face. How can you not be moved by this? What else do you want? A new car? A new dishwasher? We can go on one of those Thomson's posh and expensive holidays too, if that'll make you happy.'

'You're missing the point entirely, Damien. This is not what I want from a relationship. I can't be bought back with your money.'

'You are an extremely ungrateful person, Josie Flynn.'

'And you are a misguided, opinionated *ex*-husband,' she said. 'And I'm not throwing this in your face . . .' Josie held up the ring, '. . . I'm throwing it in the lake!'

The ring splashed into the water, surprising a duck who was floating along haplessly next to it. And with a cheerful quack, the duck dipped its beak into the water and swallowed it.

Josie and Damien watched with mouths gaping. The world continued in slow motion, until Josie spoke again.

'I'm leaving,' she said. 'I've had enough of men. I've had enough of you, in particular, Damien Flynn. And I've had enough of this naffing wedding!' She turned on her heel and marched off into the night.

Damien watched the ripples in the pond, transfixed, unable to move, unable to do anything to stop Josie as she left his life, eyes firmly glued to the duck which had swallowed his diamond ring. Even in his state of shock, he knew he should do something – wade in after it, throw a stone or at least hurl abuse – but he couldn't make his rigid limbs respond. The duck gave a strangled quack, fluffed its feathers and sailed on serenely. And if Damien hadn't been a rational man, he would have sworn it was smiling.

CHAPTER 43

How had she managed to marry such an . . . an . . . an ARSEHOLE! Josie was quietly fuming. She was standing in reception waiting for the arrival of a yellow cab, and she was tapping her feet and wringing her hands and indulging in all those little gestures that indicate pent-up fury – short of tearing out handfuls of hair and shrieking at the top of her voice. Her cheeks were burning and it was the first time all day that she'd been hot, but she rubbed her bare arms nevertheless.

How could Damien think that by waving that extravagant . . . *bauble* in front of her nose she'd be swooning into his arms? It was typical of his lack of thought and basic understanding of living in the real world. She had struggled so much to make ends meet in London since they'd split up. How dare he flaunt his wealth in front of her! Even the Cat Formerly Known as Prince had been weaned off those expensive tiny tins of gourmet nonsense – delice of prawn and lobster tails in caviare sauce, goujons of John Dory in truffle aspic, soupçons of calamari with crab

mousse – and on to bog-standard meaty chunks
Whiskas. Except for special occasions. And he was
still bearing a grudge. Yet Damien had produced
a present that was worth a year's salary to her.
Maybe if he'd turned up at the building society
and paid her mortgage for six months she might
have been more impressed. But then, she had to
concede, that wasn't generally, in the scheme of
things, considered an overtly romantic gesture.

Knowing Damien, it was complete cobblers
anyway. He'd probably got the ring free in a
Christmas cracker or by collecting Weetabix packet
tops or something like that, and it only looked like
a humdinger of a diamond. There was no way he'd
part with that amount of cash unless he was really,
really desperate. And Damien had never been
desperate for anything. A frown wrinkled her forehead. Maybe she shouldn't have thrown it to the
ducks, though.

Josie looked through the doors, back into the
wedding reception, which was still in full swing
despite the notable absence of a bride. The boy
band, Headstrong, were quite good, and if she'd
been in the mood and this wedding hadn't been the
disaster of the century, she might have been
tempted to go back in there and dance. And she
tried very hard not to think of Matt Jarvis or wonder
what he'd made of his interview with them or
wonder why he hadn't turned up at the Alamo as
arranged.

Josie's lip felt as though it might start to tremble.

There were couples in there who looked happy. Or, if not happy, then not totally miserable with each other. That was all she wanted. Was it too much to ask? Perhaps she should put an advert in the lonely hearts column of her local paper – Nice man wanted for frustrated divorcee. Smokers, skinflints, losers, lardies, lager drinkers, baldies, perverts, estate agents, white van drivers, football supporters, *Sunday Sport* readers and criminally insane need not apply. Mind you, that would narrow it down considerably. Who would be left? What was wrong with men these days? Why couldn't she find someone who'd managed to read past BONK in the dictionary and was at least up to 'C' and, therefore, knew what the word COMMITMENT meant?

Josie's taxi pulled up outside and she shot out into the cold, frosty February night. As she jumped into the cab, she hoped that Damien wouldn't leap out from behind a bush. The last thing she wanted was another confrontation; she'd had enough surprises today to last her a lifetime. All she wanted to do was go back to her hotel, take off these lovely lilac shoes that were currently crippling her, have a steaming hot bath and drink her mini-bar dry.

Matt and Holly were dancing to 'I'm Happy Just To Dance With You', yet another Beatles rendition by Headstrong. The dance floor was busy and he was being jostled by a thousand pointy elbows.

How had people ever managed to glide serenely around when the waltz, the quickstep and the foxtrot were in fashion? Dance floors must have been a lot bigger in those days – now there was barely room to stand upright without treading on your own toes, let alone your partner's. Holly looked blissfully oblivious to his discomfort.

'Seen Martha yet?' Matt asked casually for the fortieth time.

'No.' Holly wrinkled her nose. 'I don't know where she can be. One of the guests said she hadn't left yet, so I guess she must be here somewhere.'

They wiggled a bit more, but Matt's legs wouldn't do what he wanted them to and his arms were starting to wander about of their own volition without rhythm.

'Are all their songs by the Beatles?' Matt asked.

'A lot of them,' Holly admitted. 'The ones with words, anyway.'

'And no one's seen fit to tell them?'

'Well, it isn't very cool, is it?'

'I don't see why not. I wish you'd pointed it out before I put one of my fists down one of their throats yesterday. It could have saved us all a lot of trouble.'

'I don't think they're holding any grudges,' she said.

'I might be!'

'Matt.' She looked at him in a pitying way.

'The scars of this go deeper than a few superficial scratches, I'll have you know.'

'Is there something else on your mind? You're very edgy and it can't just be over a few Beatles songs.'

Matt stopped still. 'I'm not really in the mood for dancing, Holly.' His legs had ground to a halt. It was all that 'Hava Nagila'-ing earlier. It had worn him out. 'Do you mind if I go outside for a few minutes and leave you to it?'

'No,' she said. 'I'll hang out with the guys. They must be due to finish soon.'

'I won't be long,' he said, and turned from the dance floor, heading out, hopefully, to find sanctuary and Josie. Not necessarily in that order.

The door of a yellow cab slammed and it screeched off into the night as Matt sauntered into the cool calm of the reception area. The thump, thump, thump, of 'You've Got to Hide Your Love Away' being slaughtered receded into the background. Thankfully. Still, it didn't seem to be bothering the other wedding guests. But then pissed people would dance to anything – as Boney M had proved on many an occasion.

Now that he'd escaped to sanctuary, he found there was nothing to do there. Matt wished he smoked or something. All this tension was turning him into an exponent of St Vitus's dance and he had nothing useful to do with his hands. He supposed he could take up something useful, like nose-picking or nail-biting or counting his dandruff flakes. This was definitely turning into one of those groundhog days where you wish you could turn back the clock and do it all over again. And this time get it right. Josie must be here somewhere. She couldn't have just vanished in front of his very eyes. Not from her own cousin's wedding.

Damien had taken his shoes off. Two hundred and fifty pounds' worth of Patrick Cox's finest was reason enough not to go paddling in them. He had also taken off his socks and put them neatly inside his shoes. The grass at the edge of the lake was absolutely freezing on his bare feet and he would probably need to have his toes amputated if this took any more than five minutes. Maximum. He was currently in the process of rolling up his trouser legs and trying to stare out the diamond-swallowing duck without falling over.

'Come here, you fucking monstrous animal,' Damien said with a Jack Nicholson grin. 'Come to Daddy.'

'Quack,' the duck said, and stayed perfectly still.

Damien edged towards the water. 'This is going to be a thoroughly unpleasant experience,' he said, gritting his teeth. He had Josie's cobwebby blanket to hand, which she had abandoned on her flight back to the wedding manor. 'Come here, nice little duck,' Damien said sweetly. 'You could make this a lot easier for me.'

'Quack,' said the duck, and floated further out to the centre of the lake.

'Look,' Damien shouted. 'All I want to do is stick my hand down your naffing neck and get my diamond back. Is than an unreasonable request?'

'Quack,' said the duck.

Damien looked at the water, which was as black as that poncey squid-ink stuff they shoved on pasta these days in over-priced trendy restaurants. There was no doubt that it was going to be very, very, very cold. Damien inched forward and let the water lap at his toes. The iciness of it took his breath away, making him gasp out loud, just like he did on the rare occasions when the lovely Melanie deigned to suck them.

'Quack, quack,' said the duck.

'If you move one muscle,' Damien threatened it, 'I'm going to shove my other hand up your little duck's arse just for the sheer fun of it!'

The duck sat up and flapped at the water round its chest. Then it heaved itself up, skimmed over the surface for a few feet and settled back down again.

'Don't you dare,' Damien hissed. 'One awkward bird tonight is *more* than enough!'

Damien stood in the water. His toes sank effortlessly into the squishy, slimy mud. Any feeling below his ankles had already disappeared. 'Fuckitfuckitfuckitfuckitfuckitfuckit,' he muttered to himself as he waded out into the lake.

CHAPTER 44

Josie fell gratefully on to the bed of her hotel room, kicking both shoes off in one wonderfully foot-liberating movement. Her big toes cracked with the pleasure of release and the duvet was warm and welcoming on her frozen limbs. The lights of the city fingered their way through the curtains, accompanied by the incessant whirl of police sirens, and she wondered where Martha was now. Not in the honeymoon suite of the Waldorf Astoria with her husband Jack like she was supposed to be. That much was certain.

She prayed Martha would be all right with Glen, that things would work out well for them, but there were niggling bite-sized worries nipping at her consciousness. Could he be relied on to look after her second time around? She hoped so. However, his eyebrows did meet in the middle, and her mother would have deducted marks straight away for that heinous crime alone. Hirsute men were never to be trusted, according to Lavinia. Seeing as her own criteria for judging men was failing her miserably, perhaps she ought to start listening to her mother in future.

Josie stretched out, arms above her head, enjoying the sensation of warmth spreading back through her bones and giving in to the sleepy state that was creeping through her body. It would have been nice to curl up and drift off with someone cuddling her. Irritatingly, she thought of Matt. Where was he in this spitting, hissing, crackling city? Was he out on the town? Or was he in his hotel room? Was he alone or with someone else? Had he picked up some other gullible floosie and was currently breaking her heart too? Or was he staring at the ceiling feeling lonely like she was? No, Josie Flynn, that mind set won't even be given house room! It was his bad luck that he'd missed out on the date of the century! She'd had enough doom, gloom and downright depression for today. It was cheer-yourself-up time in the time-honoured fashion!

Booze. Bath. Bed. And with those reviving thoughts in mind, Josie summoned what modicum of remaining energy she had and pushed herself upright. First things first, though.

Without ceremony, Josie yanked the lilac chiffon bridesmaid's dress over her head and threw it in the wastepaper bin without a backwards glance. Good riddance! She was never, ever again in her entire life going to wear lilac – it was clearly bad luck.

Availing herself of the hotel's complimentary cosy bathrobe in Demis Roussos size, Josie turned to the most pertinent of her requirements. She opened the mini-bar and rummaged through its contents, selecting two miniatures of vodka and the teeniest bottle of tonic she could find for swift and immediate consumption. The fizz of bubbles as she wafted a hint of tonic into the waiting tumbler made her sigh with relief. Now the bath.

A positive array of small containers filled with smelly things awaited her on the bathroom shelf. She could imagine herself floating in the fragrant water, closing her eyes and pretending the last two days had all been a bad, bad dream. Josie ran her fingers expectantly over them. Lily of the valley, jasmine, narcissus, carnation, rose. Heavenly scents which would transport her effortlessly to an English country garden. All she had to was pick one and pour. But as she turned the tap to fill the bath, the phone rang. It could be Martha! Looking longingly at the seductive shell-shaped soaps, she snapped the tap off again and rushed back into the bedroom.

'It's your mother,' the unmistakable voice said at the other end of the phone.

Josie sank to the bed. She'd forgotten, somewhere between bath and bed, to fit in the ear-bashing. Still, the booze would come in handy. She downed the vodka in one. 'Hi, Mum.'

'Well?'

'Fine, thank you.'

'I meant well, what about Martha's wedding well?'

'Mmm,' she said, wondering if the cord of the phone would reach to the mini-bar.

'What does mmm mean?' Lavinia said. 'I knew I should have been there.'

'I don't think it would have made any difference.'

'What wouldn't? And why are you back at your hotel so early?'

'Why are you ringing if you didn't think I'd be back?'

There was a weighty silent pause. 'On the off chance,' her mother said. 'Besides, your mobile phone doesn't work over there. Mrs Smithers told me it's decimal, not anal.'

'Digital, not analogue,' Josie corrected.

'So why are you being cagey about Martha's wedding? Why aren't you crying and saying it was lovely?'

'It's a long story, Mum. I'll tell you when I get back.' The cord was a foot too short. Damn! A dry conversation with her mother. Josie's heart sank.

'She did say yes, didn't she?'

'Sort of . . .'

'What sort of sort of?'

'I have to go, there's someone at the door.'

'Don't open it. What if it's a mugger pretending to be room service?'

'It's a risk I'll have to take.'

'Wait! Josephine! I have some bad news for you . . .'

Oh no! Abort Conversation Termination Sequence.

'Bad news?'

'Damien still loves you!'

'I know.' Josie smiled to herself. 'It's awful, isn't it?'

'I'm devastated for you. What do you mean, you know?'

'He came here.'

'To Martha's wedding! But he wasn't invited!'

'That doesn't usually deter Damien.'

'What a rogue!'

'That's exactly what I said. Damien, you rogue!' Josie lay back on the bed. It was soft and warm and the pillow nuzzled enticingly round her neck.

'Well, I know that you young ladies have a more expressive turn of phrase these days, but it amounts to the same thing,' her mother informed her huffily. 'He sounds as if he wants you back very badly, darling. I do hope you don't succumb to his charms.'

'I have never succumbed to anyone's charms in my life.'

Josie thought she heard her mother snort, but it could have been static. Well, she didn't *succumb* often.

'Promise me, darling.'

'Promise,' Josie said. 'Damien's more likely to f . . . f . . . fall in love with a duck than he is to want to be married to me again.'

'You don't know how reassuring that is.'

And you don't know how true, Mother!

'While I'm on the line, I might just as well tell you about Mrs Bottomley's in-growing toenail.'

Josie closed her eyes, the scent of lily of the valley, jasmine, narcissus, carnation and rose fading slowly but surely into the distance. 'This is costing you a fortune, Mum.'

'It won't take a minute.'

It usually took sixty.

'Did I tell you she'd had to go to Dr Pilkington and have it lanced?'

'No.'

'He said she was lucky not to lose it . . .'

'Really.'

'And Mrs Golding's no better. Do you remember Mrs Golding?'

'No.'

'You do. She had a sister who taught music at your primary school. It doesn't do to speak ill of the ill, but she was the woman who let you loose with a recorder. We had "Greensleeves" for break-fast, dinner and tea for three months until it was mysteriously broken.'

After weeks of searching, Josie had been bereft to find it in three shattered pieces in the back of her mother's lingerie drawer.

'You remember her.'

'Yes.' No!

'She's got bowel cancer. Not long to go, by all accounts,' her mother said gleefully. 'All those years of not being regular have finally caught up with her. That's why I'm such a fan of All-Bran . . .'

'Mmm.'

'Josephine, you are listening to me?'

'Yes, Mum,' she yawned, turning over on to her side and snuggling down.

Out there in this vibrant, exciting city, people were having fun. People were having lavish dinners in fancy restaurants. People were sharing exotic cocktails in sophisticated bars. People were falling in love. Other people, lucky sods, were making love.

Matt Jarvis could well be one of them.

And to think that instead of this long-awaited visit to New York, she could have spent her holiday on an educational school trip to Île de France with thirty-two hormonally challenged teenagers and several bearded, pipe-smoking teachers – and that was just the women.

Josie let sleep wash over her along with Lavinia's monologue about the ailments of her friends, neighbours, milkman and sundry other sick people with whose bodily functions she was intimate. For her, Josephine Flynn, it was the perfect end to a perfect day.

CHAPTER 45

'Come on, you little swine!' Damien was up to his knees in murky water and mud. 'Quack, quack,' quacked the little swine, and scuttled further away from Damien, who he clearly thought was an idiot.

Damien lifted his arms, poised in the style of Peter Cushing in an old Hammer House of Horror film, ready to pounce. 'I am going to have you come hell or cold water,' he seethed.

The other ducks were beginning to take an interest now and started swimming round Damien's legs. 'Look, fuck off,' Damien ordered. 'It's not you I want. It's Donald here.' He swashed the water, frightening them. 'There's no such thing as Duck Power. Just naff off and leave him to defend himself.'

The swashing of the water had also encouraged Donald to swim further away. 'Oh, for heaven's sake!' Damien lifted his hands to the clear, unconcerned moon. 'I could be here all night.'

Donald started to quack in a belligerent and frankly provocative manner.

'Right, that's it!' Damien stripped off his suit

jacket and loosened his tie. Aiming the jacket at the small ornamental jetty, he whirled it round his head and threw it with all his strength. The jacket landed in the water, mere inches away from its intended target.

'Bollocks,' Damien said, cursing his luck for the thousandth time tonight, and with a shudder of loathing dived head-long into the water.

Donald shot off with Damien in hot, or very cold, pursuit. 'I'll have you know,' Damien gasped breathlessly in the freezing lake, 'that I had my fifty-metres badge by the time I was five years old! How many can say that?'

Donald swam faster, and so did Damien.

'At thirteen I was Regent's Grammar School breaststroke champion – and not just behind the bike sheds! If that doesn't strike fear into you, I don't know what will.'

Donald had reached the other side. He padded out across the muddy bank, joining a milling group of fellow ducks, and stood shaking his feathers elegantly. Damien, hot on his tail, lurched out of the water and on to the mud, sinking to his knees with an anguished cry. The noise startled Donald, who scuttled forward, but not before Damien had launched himself in a dive across the mud and wrapped both arms tightly round the horrified duck.

'Got you!' Damien yelled triumphantly, resisting the urge to punch the air and, therefore, loose his grip on the duck.

Donald squawked with sheer terror.

Ominous black clouds rolled slowly across the moon and a chill breeze struck up, lifting the hairs on the back of Damien's neck and ruffling Donald's tail feathers. Damien sat in the mud, soaking wet, holding an upset duck with a diamond ring in its belly. If there had been any shred of relief provided by the fact that his investment was intact, it was quickly tempered by the thought that somehow he was going to have to get it out of him.

Damien held Donald firmly and gingerly slid his fingers into the duck's mouth, wondering if an investigative digit down the throat would make a duck sick up a diamond ring. Donald clamped his bill round Damien's fingers in a vice-like grip, squawking loudly. 'Ouch!' Damien yelled, withdrawing his fingers. 'You bastard!'

Damien and the duck eyeballed each other with loathing. It was true to say that Damien had done some low-life things in his time, things that he had subsequently come to regret, but he had never, to date, murdered in cold blood another living thing. He tried to assume a sufficiently menacing air. The duck, somehow sensing the change in atmosphere, quacked piteously.

'Fuck,' Damien said, the more erudite volumes of his vocabulary deserting him.

All it needed was one sharp tug and *snap*, it would be all over. He put his hands tentatively round Donald's neck and stretched. The duck flapped its wings in panic. 'Don't do that,' Damien pleaded. 'This will hardly hurt at all.'

Donald quaked and quacked with alarm and tried to fly away, while Damien tried to bring himself to squeeze. 'I promise you, you won't feel a thing. This is going to hurt me much more than it's going to hurt you.'

Donald's frantic flailings clearly said that he didn't agree. Damien looked away and stretched a bit more. The duck quacked as if its life depended upon it – which it did.

Eventually, when his lap was covered in duck shit and Donald was no closer to dying, Damien let go. Defeated, he sank back into the mud. He might be a lot of things, but he certainly wasn't a natural-born killer.

'Come on,' he said, tucking Donald under his arm and squelching out of the mud. 'You and I have to find a more humane way of doing this . . .'

And Damien, his ferociously expensive Paul Smith suit muddied beyond recognition and his head hung low, headed back towards Martha's wedding.

Matt was standing in reception, uncertain as to what his next move should be. But then he'd been very certain about his last few moves, they had been planned if not to the nth degree at least with some form of tortured logic, and they had got him nowhere but up shit creek with a totally inadequate paddle.

He had been joined by a small, swarthy man of Sicilian origin, who seemed to make up for his lack of stature by carrying an inscrutable air of respect around him. Alarmingly, he reminded Matt of Marlon Brando in *The Godfather* – but shorter, scrawnier and infinitely uglier.

The man eyed him with interest and nodded congenially. Matt nodded back with a cautious smile.

'The bridesmaids have great tits,' Uncle Nunzio said.

'Really,' Matt replied thoughtfully. 'I haven't yet had the pleasure. Although I am hoping to.'

Uncle Nunzio bared his largely toothless mouth in a grin, but before he could elucidate further on the anatomical merits of the female members of the wedding party, their attention was distracted by an extremely muddy man stomping from the hall into the reception carrying a wriggling holdall which appeared to be emitting a muffled quack.

The man was heading purposefully towards the main door of the hotel, chin set determinedly, eyes fixed on his target. Matt and Uncle Nunzio looked at each other and shrugged.

Damien wheeled towards them, his face dark and threatening. 'Do you have a problem?' he snapped.

Matt looked round to check that he was addressing them. There was no one else in sight. 'No, mate. But it looks like you do,' he said.

'Oh God,' Damien said, dropping the holdall containing Donald the Duck on the floor. 'It's you!'

'Oh God,' Matt echoed. 'It's you!'

'You're the bloke from the taxi!'

'So are you!' Matt cried. 'I didn't recognise you for the mud.'

Damien glowered at him. 'What are you doing here?'

'A lot less than you, apparently,' Matt said, pointedly eyeing the quacking holdall, which was attempting to scuttle across the floor.

'Are you a friend of Martha's?' Damien asked.

'Not exactly . . .' Matt answered.

'He's shagging the bridesmaid,' Uncle Nunzio supplied with a helpful smile.

'I am not!' Matt protested.

'Which one?' Damien's face had turned a delicate shade of black.

'None of them,' Matt insisted. 'Well, Josie.' He turned and glared at Uncle Nunzio. 'Thank you, ye old and wrinkled Sicilian shit-stirrer.'

'*Josie?*' Damien appeared to be slavering like a rabid dog.

'Well,' Matt explained reasonably, 'I haven't exactly *shagged* her.' He took time to fix Uncle Nunzio with another withering stare. 'I haven't *exactly* done anything, but I wouldn't mind.' Matt winked an all-boys-together wink.

'Oh, wouldn't you?'

'She has great tits,' Uncle Nunzio interjected.

Matt smiled. 'Who can argue with that?'

'I can,' Damien said in a menacingly low voice. 'I can, because Josie just happens to be my wife.'

'Wife,' Matt said, wondering why his lips had suddenly gone dry.

'Wife,' Damien repeated through teeth that were clenched in a way faintly reminiscent of a Rottweiler. A Rottweiler who'd just learned it was illegal to bite postmen.

'I'm sure she said she was divorced . . .'

'What am I then? Scotch mist?'

Words failed to form in Matt's brain just when he was sure he needed them most, but he was absolutely convinced that this apparently very angry person in front of him was a lot more solid and scary than a bit of Highland vapour.

'I can assure you, *my friend*, that she is definitely married.'

'Funny she didn't mention it,' Matt said with an attempt at bravado, even though his tongue seemed to be stuck to the roof of his mouth.

'Am I laughing?' Damien asked.

It had to be said, he didn't look as though he was about to split his sides. Though Matt thought he was potentially about to split his lip for him.

'She's a great shag.' Uncle Nunzio was clearly enjoying himself.

'Oh, for goodness' sake!' Matt pleaded. 'Where did you learn your English? Channel Four?'

'Wait a minute . . .' Damien narrowed his eyes to slits. 'You're not that Matt bloke, are you?'

'Er . . .' Matt momentarily considered the possibility of denying it. After all, there must be thousands of Matts wandering round New York who could claim to know Josie. Millions even.

'Matt Jarvis,' Damien said, dragging it from the convoluted recesses of his brain.

'Er . . .' Matt said.

'The rock musician,' Damien sneered.

'Er . . .' Matt said again. Rock musician? That sounded rather sexy, and who was he to contradict it?

'The one that my wife – Josie the shaggable bridesmaid – is in love with?'

'Really?' Matt's face brightened considerably.

'I don't know what you're looking so fucking cheerful for. I ought to kick your fucking teeth down your fucking throat.'

'Where is Josie?' Matt asked.

'What's it got to do with you?'

'I just wondered . . .'

'Well don't!'

'Is she here?'

'No,' Damien said. 'She's not.'

'Where is she then?'

'I thought you might be able to tell me,' Damien said.

'No.' Matt was very puzzled.

'Look,' Damien said with a weary sigh. 'Because of you, I've wasted thousands of pounds of my hard-earned cash in flying here, and made a complete arse of myself. Because of you, there is a cat without a father. Because of you, my wife's walked out. Because of you, there is a large and phenomenally expensive diamond ring inside a duck. Because of you, my Paul Smith suit is covered in nasty, smelly mud. Because of you, my favourite Patrick Cox loafers are ruined beyond redemption. Because of you, I know what duck shit tastes like. Because of you, I'm about to get sore knuckles. Because I have decided that I should have followed my initial instincts when we met during the regrettable taxi-pranging incident and I *am* going to kick your fucking teeth down your fucking throat.' Damien lifted his fist to Matt's face.

Matt pointed towards the holdall. 'Watch out, mate, your duck's escaping!'

Damien glanced towards the holdall, which was indeed waddling slowly and a little unsteadily across the floor.

Matt seized his opportunity and turned to run, only to be faced with Holly standing hands on hips, pert mouth pinched and pouting. 'You can't be left alone for five minutes without getting into trouble, can you?' she snarled. 'What's all this about?'

'I can explain,' Matt said, a fraction of a second before Damien's fist cannoned into his face, showering the inside of his brain with a thousand pretty fireworks, just like the ones that had lit up the Long Island skyline earlier, and thus rendering any explanations downright impossible.

Matt felt himself drop to the floor with a sickening thud. Physically and metaphorically. Why hadn't Josie told him she was married? He thought he remembered through a haze of abandoned alcohol consumption that she had told him she was separated. If she was, her husband didn't seem acutely aware of the fact. Hadn't they compared battle scars? Hadn't they compared solicitors' bills? Had she just been stringing him along for a bit of fun?

It was quite possible he had wasted his entire time in New York chasing a pretty lilac rainbow only to find that the pot of gold was already another man's. Cruel, cruel world! There was no way, after what had happened to him, that he would ever have become involved with a married woman. It was against all his morals. He didn't have many, but the ones that he did have, he stuck to like white cat hair to black trousers.

There was a maelstrom of confusion clogging his thinking processes. It was true, however, he thought through the swirling fog that floated before his eyes, that there was no pleasure to be had without pain. As he curled himself into a ball and drifted off to dreamless sleep, one clear thought stuck to his consciousness with all the tenacity of superglue. Josie might have failed to make mention of a lurking jealous husband, but there could be no doubt that she had told said husband that she was in love with him, Matt-the-rock-musician-Jarvis.

Now, more than ever, he needed to talk to her to get some answers. As the mist slowly closed over him, he realised for the third time in as many days that the only problem he had was finding her.

CHAPTER 46

In fact, Matt was mistaken in assuming that finding Josie was the only problem he had to contend with. He hadn't bargained on waking up with the prospect of facing Holly with a satisfactory explanation. There wasn't one, it appeared.

Holly had her own questions that she wanted answered, and Matt didn't know where to begin. He wished his head wasn't quite so full of cotton wool or he might have been able to think of some convincing lies. Mr Morality was clearly having a well-earned day off. Holly stood in front of him tapping her shoeless foot impatiently. Her hair was even more dishevelled due to the amount of tugging that was going on, and her face was flushed to the hue of tomato ketchup by a mixture of anger and booze. She did look very cross but at the same time unspeakably cute. If Matt hadn't been hurting quite so much, he might have risked a smile.

'And don't even think about smiling,' Holly ordered.

'I wathn't . . .' Matt muttered through chipolata lips.

'You need steak on that,' Holly said fiercely, pointing at the place where a black eye would very shortly be.

'I thought they only did that in cartoonth.'

'I don't know, Matt,' she spat. 'I'm not your freaking nursemaid, although I have to say it's starting to feel like it.'

Matt hung his head, which hurt in all sorts of places. He was propped half sitting, half lying against the reception desk and it made his back ache. The tendrils of a potted palm were making fast and loose with his hair, but he didn't feel he could contemplate moving just yet. 'Thorry,' he lisped. 'I've been thuch trouble to you . . .'

'Yes, you have.' Holly folded her arms, but softened her voice. 'Let's get you home. Everyone else has gone.'

On cue, the four chirpy members of Headstrong sauntered out of the dance hall. 'So long, Holly,' they said in unison. 'Catch you tomorrow?'

'Yeah,' she replied wearily. 'Nice set. You made a lot of elderly ladies very happy.'

Matt slunk lower, not acknowledging them as they failed to acknowledge him, although he could have sworn the one he had clonked yesterday – Barry, Larry, Gary or something – was smirking more than was necessary. With a wave to Holly they left, taking their unfeasibly large trousers, their puffy haircuts and their overactive hormones with them.

Matt rubbed his hand over his face. 'What happened to Duckula?'

'Gone,' Holly said. 'Him and the duck. He had a plane to catch.'

'Would it be too much to hope for a plane to catch him – preferably on the back of the head?'

'Probably,' Holly said.

'What about Martha?'

'Gone.'

'And the bridesmaids?'

'Gone.'

'All of them?'

'Yep.'

Matt looked at her questioningly.

'I have no idea what happened.' Holly shrugged. 'Maybe they had headaches. This is the weirdest wedding I've ever been to.'

'So,' Matt tried to lever himself up and failed, 'it's just the two of us.'

Holly twirled her toes into the floor. 'Looks like it.'

'I just want to say—'

At that moment Uncle Nunzio appeared, shadowed by a mountainous man wearing a black overcoat who looked as if he should be carrying a violin case but instead was lugging two teenage boys by the ears. He stood over Matt, legs splayed to support his huge frame, blocking out the brightness from the sunken reception spotlights and throwing Matt into semi-darkness.

'Uncle Nunzio wants to apologise,' the man said in a voice that sounded as though it had been born from a hundred Capstan Full Strength a day.

'I sorry,' Uncle Nunzio added, hand on heart.

'He feels this is his fault . . .'

'No, no . . .' Matt said.

Uncle Nunzio nodded. 'My fault.'

'No, no. It isn't,' Matt protested with a magnanimous wave of his hand. He paused. 'Well, yes, it is actually.'

'Uncle Nunzio's English isn't too good. It's been getting him into trouble.' The big man cuffed the two wriggling boys round the head without looking at them. 'He wants to make this right.'

'Right,' Uncle Nunzio echoed solemnly.

'In Sicily we are very big on honour.'

'So I've heard,' Matt said wryly.

'We believe in an eye for an eye, a tooth for a tooth. "Retribution without Remorse" is our family motto.'

'Ohhh-kay.' Matt sounded very hesitant.

'Where did the man with the duck go?' The big man addressed Holly.

'JFK,' Holly said.

'JFK,' the man said.

Uncle Nunzio nodded a barely perceptible nod.

'Don't worry, my friend.' The man bent down and took Matt's hand, crushing his fingers like soggy grapes. 'We will restore your honour.'

'Honour,' Uncle Nunzio said with a small bow.

And they left, hustling the boys into a car with blacked-out windows that would take up a whole block and a bit more.

The reception area was eerily silent, and Matt

and Holly stared blankly at each other. He thought it might take an awful lot more than the Sicilians had on offer to restore his battered honour. He pulled a face. 'Do you think we should have told them where he'd gone?'

'Hey, this is twenty-first-century America, not fourteenth-century Sicily. What are they going to do? Steal his frigging duck and eat it?'

'I don't know,' Matt said. 'But I wouldn't like to owe them money and then subsequently bump into them in a dark, deserted alley with only a fiver in my pocket.'

Holly scratched her chin. 'I think Martha might have told me once that her family had Mafia connections . . .'

Matt's mouth dropped open. 'No!'

Holly started to laugh.

'Oh yes, very funny, Ms Brinkman,' Matt said tartly. 'Kick a man when he's down.'

Holly stopped giggling. 'You should have seen your face,' she tutted. 'You watch too many movies.'

'I like gratuitous sex and violence.'

'So do I,' Holly said. 'Well, sex, anyway.'

Matt flushed.

'You do enough gratuitous violence for both of us.' Holly bent down and straightened his shirt. 'Let's get you cleaned up.'

Matt levered himself up from the floor, groaning as he did so. She put her arm round him and, with all the effort her hefty seven-stone frame could manage, hoisted him upright.

'Thanks,' Matt said, wincing. He looked down at her and attempted to move his mouth into an expression that read 'grateful'. For the millionth time he wondered why he was chasing an elusive flitting butterfly – a seemingly married elusive flitting butterfly to boot – when there was a perfectly gorgeous unattached one here on the cabbage leaf right next to him. Not that Holly would be stupid enough to have anything to do with him after the run-around he'd given her. It made Matt sick to his heart to think that, despite his best intentions, there were times when he couldn't help being a man.

'I can't believe I'm about to say this.' Holly raised her eyes to the ceiling. 'Before it's out of my mouth I know I'm going to live to regret it!' She looked at him and sighed heavily. 'Do you want to come back to my place for a nightcap?'

If Matt's lip hadn't been split, he might just have grinned.

CHAPTER 47

Everyone had gone except Jack. He was sitting in the darkened hall, perched on the edge of the raised podium sporting the bride and groom's lavish armchairs, which currently stood empty and abandoned. He was surrounded on all sides by dead party-poppers and wedding presents. The spangly 1960s ball rotated slowly, casting diamond sparkles of light round the room in a meandering forlorn sort of way.

Even Mr Rossani had left, and it had been hell to get him to go. Jack hadn't been able to bring himself to tell the father of the bride that his daughter had walked out of her own wedding and had disappeared into the night with the best man. How did you break that to someone without breaking their heart too? Jack had insisted Martha was upstairs resting with a headache, and after a little gentle persuasion her father was encouraged to go home and leave her to it.

Tomorrow would be soon enough to tell him the truth. Tomorrow, when he'd had time to sober up and wasn't likely to go after Glen with a sawn-off shotgun and several of the heavier-set Sicilian cousins.

Jack surveyed the tables littered with glasses of half-drunk champagne and plates of half-eaten canapés. Inside he felt as lifeless as the flat champagne, as cold and congealed as the discarded food. He hadn't been able to tell anyone. Only he and Josie knew what had really happened – apart from Martha and Glen. He snorted to himself without rancour. They all thought she had been overcome by the emotion of the day – which in some ways maybe she had. Now the guests had gone and so had the dream.

Putting his head in his hands, Jack bit his lip, stemming the tears that threatened to fall again. If this was being in touch with his emotions he really could do without it! What baloney he talked sometimes. This wasn't a time to explore your inner feelings. This was a time to get seriously, seriously drunk. Jack poured himself another glass of dead champagne and swallowed half without tasting it. How could he ever have imagined that someone like Martha would have wanted him in the first place? She was more suited to someone like Glen; someone richer, younger, more handsome. Glen would provide all the things that Martha needed in a more attractive package than Jack ever could. Yet Jack would have pulled down the moon and handed it to her on a platter if it had been within his power to do so.

He would move away, start again. There was no

way he could stand the talk in a small town like Katonah. Maybe they had all pointed at him beforehand and knew that his relationship with Martha was doomed to failure. He didn't want them knowing they were right. Perhaps if he hadn't tried to be so perfect for Martha, so in control . . . If she'd only known how much he needed her to add light and life to his world, maybe she wouldn't have run away.

The door clicked open and a figure came towards him in the gloom. It was late. The staff would want to clear up and go home. Home to their own lives, their own loved ones. They would want to sweep the debris of the wedding away. Jack wondered if he would ever be able to do the same.

Jack glanced up.

'Hi,' Martha said, hovering uncertainly in front of him.

The spangly lights drifted across her face, illuminating her pale skin. She looked tired and drawn and he guessed that he did too. The veil had gone, but she still wore her wedding dress and she still looked as beautiful.

'Hi,' Jack replied.

Martha let out a very weary breath.

Jack patted the podium next to him and Martha sat down heavily at his side. He lifted the only glass that looked unused from the tray next to him. 'Join me in some flat champagne?'

'You don't drink,' Martha said.

'I do now.'

He poured her a glass, noting the absence of bubbles, and handed it to her. Her hand was trembling and he wanted to take hold of it. Instead he clinked his glass against hers.

'What shall we toast?' Martha asked.

'I think I'm maybe the wrong person to ask, Martha.'

She sighed and put the glass to her lips, savouring the champagne, even though it tasted gross. Her eyes swept round the room. 'What a mess,' she said.

'It won't take them long to clear up.'

'I didn't mean this.' She picked up a shredded twirl of coloured paper and twisted it round her finger, and Jack noticed her wedding and engagement rings were still in place. 'I meant us.'

'I know.'

Martha's hands were tense, the knuckles white. She clutched her fragile glass so hard, Jack feared the stem might break. 'What did Daddy say?'

'Nothing.' Jack leaned back and looked at the ceiling. 'I didn't tell him. I didn't tell anyone,' he admitted.

'No one?'

'Not a soul. Only Josie knows.'

'Why?'

'I didn't know what to say without it sounding bad. It would have spoiled their day. I told them you had a headache.'

Martha laughed mirthlessly. 'Still thinking of me.'

'This isn't all your fault.'

Martha turned to him. 'Of course it is, Jack! I ran off with your best friend. At our wedding.'

'You must have had your reasons.'

'I'm not sure they were good enough.' She let out another weary breath.

'Would it help to share them with me?'

Martha smiled. 'I don't know if it will help, but I think maybe it's the least I owe you.'

'This isn't about "owing", Martha. It's about trying to find out what went wrong.'

'Nothing went wrong,' she said. 'Everything went wrong!' She blew down her nose. 'I panicked, Jack. Suddenly a lifetime seemed . . . like a lifetime. I'm only used to thinking for one. All my life it's been me, me, me. I've had everything I ever wanted handed to me on a plate, and I realised when I saw Josie with Glen that I couldn't have that any more. I wasn't one, I was two. Everything I would have to do from now on, for ever more, would have to take into account another person . . .' Martha looked up, 'maybe two . . . or more.' She rubbed her face. 'All our plans crowded in on me and I didn't know if I was ready and it was already too late . . . Oh, I don't know,' she said. 'I'm making excuses, when there are no excuses to be made.' Abruptly she stood up and kicked off her shoes. 'They've been agony all day,' she complained.

There was a weary limp in her step as she walked to where the wedding cake was displayed in all its ornate glory. 'We didn't even cut the cake,' she said, letting her fingers trail languidly over the intricate sugar flowers crafted in shades of lilac, blue and turquoise which made them appear like delicate bruises.

'We didn't really get the chance,' Jack reminded her.

'Want to now?' Martha asked, picking up the knife waiting patiently at the side of the pristine cake. 'I'm starving.'

'I don't think so.'

'I can't cut it alone, Jack. It's bad luck.'

'Do you think it matters? This wasn't exactly the start to married life I'd hoped for.'

Martha looked at him in the half-light. 'I've hurt you very badly,' she stated flatly. 'I never meant to. I don't know what to say.'

Jack poured himself more champagne.

'Come and cut the cake, Jack,' she urged. 'Please.'

He stood and walked to Martha with feet that felt encased in lead weights. His wife – strange to be calling her that – had the barely restrained air of an excited child, and he realised that as beautiful as she was, Martha still had a lot of growing-up to do. Maybe today had started that.

Martha held the knife poised above the cake, tip just piercing the crisp white frosting. 'Here,' she said, 'put your hand on top of mine.'

Jack did as she asked. Her hand was steady now, the tremble gone, although it was like marble to touch. 'You're cold,' he said, covering her fingers.

'And you're warm.' Martha looked into his eyes. 'Ready?' she asked.

'Ready.' Jack pressed down on her hand and the blade sank effortlessly through the icing. Martha manoeuvred the knife and together they cut a thin sliver of cake.

She withdrew the blade. 'That was painless, wasn't it?'

'I guess so.'

Holding the slice of cake in her hand, she offered it to Jack. 'I have no appetite,' he said.

'Eat it,' Martha instructed.

He leaned forward and took a bite. 'It's good,' he said, nodding. 'It's good cake. Our guests would have liked it.'

Martha put the cake down and leaned against the table. The glitter ball twinkled in the silence and Jack watched Martha's pulse beating in her throat. Her hand went to it and her fingers followed the line of her neck, and Jack thought he saw her swallow.

'I have made a terrible, terrible mistake,' she said, tears filling her eyes. 'I don't know how to make it right, Jack.'

He stood and watched the lights flicker over his new, uncomfortable, highly polished shoes.

'Can you ever forgive me?'

'I love you, Martha,' he said, looking back at his dishevelled bride. 'Nothing will ever change that. I gave you my solemn vow.'

'And I gave you mine and I broke it. I smashed it into little pieces right in front of you.'

Martha started to cry.

'Hush, hush,' Jack said. 'Don't cry. Not on your wedding day. It'll be all right.'

'How can I ever make it right?'

Jack lifted her face and held it in his hands. 'Martha, why did you come back?'

Martha sobbed. 'Because I couldn't stay away.'

'That's enough for me,' he said.

Martha sniffed wetly.

He pulled her towards him. 'Let's be a couple again, Martha. Husband and wife. We can put this behind us and just carry on as if nothing happened.'

'How can we do that?'

'With a little effort and a lot of love from both of us.'

'I've been unfaithful to you, Jack.'

'Infidelity doesn't have to be the most devastating thing that can happen in a marriage.'

'On our wedding day!'

'Maybe your timing could have been better.'

'What will people say?'

'No one else knows. They need never know,' Jack assured her.

Martha looked uncertain. Jack cupped her hands in his. 'If you say that Glen was a mistake, then I can live with that. What I couldn't live with is turning that into an irretrievable error.' His wife's mouth was still turned down at the corners and her lip was wobbling perilously.

'How can you be so goddamn forgiving, Jack Labati?'

'Martha,' he sighed, 'I have waited a long, long, lonely time to find someone I want to spend the rest of my life with. I don't want to throw that away lightly.'

'Even though I did,' Martha sniffed.

'What were the vows we made? For richer, for poorer, for better, for worse.' Jack brushed a tear from his wife's cheek. 'I think this might possibly count as an instance of "for worse".'

'Forsaking all others,' Martha said. 'For as long as you both shall live. This is my solemn vow.'

'To have and to hold . . .'

'Hold me, Jack.'

He wrapped his arms round her. 'I think this is the bit where I may now kiss the bride . . .'

Jack tasted Martha's lips with his; they were sweet and salty with tears. 'I love you, Mrs Labati,' he said. 'I always will.'

'I love you too, Jack,' Martha said.

Jack drew her on to the dance floor. 'Would my wife like to join me in our first dance as newly-weds?'

They both heard the music start, softly, just for the two of them. *Have I told you lately that I love you . . .*

'Do you think we'll get over this, Jack?'

'I hope that on our twenty-fifth wedding anniversary we can look back and smile at how young and foolish we were,' he said.

'How young and how foolish *I* was,' Martha corrected as she rested her head on his shoulder.

CHAPTER 48

Donald was struggling like a duck possessed. The holdall was bouncing around between Damien's knees, and he made a supreme effort to clamp his legs together tightly enough to stop Donald's bid for freedom, but not tightly enough to squeeze the living daylights out of him. Then again, it was a thought.

The check-in clerk eyed Damien suspiciously. 'Any hand baggage, sir?'

'Just the one.' Damien glanced down at his knees.

The frosty clerk followed his gaze, and in response to his obviously wriggling baggage and his muddy clothes, shifted her chewing gum to the other side of her mouth.

'I had an accident,' Damien explained. 'On the way here. I've got a change of clothes with me.' He patted his holdall.

Donald quacked.

'Did you pack your own bags, sir?'

'Yes.'

Damien scanned the other check-in desks nervously. He wondered how to stop perspiration appearing on one's top lip and how he could get rid of it without using his sleeve.

'Did you leave it unattended at any time?'

'No.' How could he, with a duck with a diamond and a death wish in it?

'Has anyone else asked you to carry items for you?'

'No.'

Damien's eyes travelled to the back of the next check-in. There appeared to be three very large, very sombre-looking gentlemen staring at him intently.

'Are you carrying any drugs, explosives or offensive weapons?'

Damien turned back to the desk and leaned on the counter.

'All three.'

The check-in clerk raised her eyebrows.

'Joke,' Damien said.

She didn't smile.

'No, I haven't any drugs, bombs, or guns.'

'Do you have any livestock?'

'Er . . . no.'

The clerk leaned on her side of the counter. 'Could I ask you why your luggage is apparently moving of its own volition, sir?'

'It's a toy,' Damien stated confidently. 'State of the art. The new Furby. It swims, it quacks, it goes great with orange sauce.'

She glared at him stonily.

'It's a robotic duck,' he said. 'It's for my

daughter . . . niece . . . friend's niece . . . a friend of my niece . . .' *Fuck!*

'We will require it to go through the usual security scanning procedures, sir.'

'That's fine.' *Double fuck!!*

Damien thought he could see the glimmer of a smile on the clerk's otherwise cheerless face. 'Here's your boarding card, sir. Please check the monitors for flight departure information.' It was definitely a smile. A supercilious one. 'Have a nice day.'

'Up your arse,' Damien said under his breath as he turned away.

'And you too, sir,' the clerk responded without looking up.

Damien found the nearest bar in the terminal and pulled up a stool. He dumped the holdall bearing Donald at his feet, and the duck emitted a protesting quack. Damien was seeing far too much of the inside of airports, and godforsaken places they were. And it was all Josie's fault. He had hours to kill before his flight. Hours to sit and ponder how on earth he had got into this flaming mess. Why hadn't he been content, if not with Josie, then at least with Melanie, instead of chasing grass that invariably turned out to be brown wherever you went? And even if the grass was luscious and green, it was usually because it was persistently pissing down with rain.

It was over now with Josie, he knew that. He'd always known it really. She was too down-to-earth and sensible for him. It had taken him a long time to realise he was a free spirit, a bubble of light, effervescent energy who needed someone who would allow him to float unfettered, not tie him to the sink of domesticity. He needed someone who would run naked through the fields of excess with him, not try to insist he went out in an anorak and woolly hat even in summer. Would he really have been able to commit himself totally to Josie if she had said yes for a second time? Would there have had to be a Melanie, or someone else on the side? Perhaps he would always need two women: one to provide a stable domestic underpinning to his life, the love, the nurturing, the ironed shirts; and one lurking permanently in the background to provide the fun and illicit jollity, the mild sado-masochism. And why not? Other men got away with it – pop stars, politicians, priests. It was as common as wearing blue socks. He looked down with an air of regret at his own muddied and ruined ones.

While the thought of illicit jollity was at the fore-front of his mind, he wondered where Melanie was now and felt a stab of fondness for the woman who he thought had been going to stab him only yesterday. She wasn't so bad – a bit frilly round the edges, but with a core that was pure steel and an iron will to match. She would have him back. A bit of the old Flynn-style flirting and he'd be back in her bed before you could say peep-hole bra. He smiled in what he deemed a mellow fashion and thought of the good times they'd had together, acknowledging that most of them had involved activities of a horizontal nature.

He might not have felt quite so cosy and smug if he'd been able to see what Melanie had been doing since his departure. He would soon find out that she had spent all morning in Debenhams forging Damien's signature on numerous credit-card slips for expensive costume jewellery, Jasper Conran clothes and small, but entirely unnecessary purchases of electrical goods. She had then returned home, untroubled by the exhaustion of shopping, to type out his resignation letter on his personal computer, taking time to call his boss a complete wanker – which he was – and, again, skilfully applying Damien's theatrical flourish of a signature to the bottom. She had then boxed up and given the computer, including colour ink-jet printer, scanner, digital camera and armfuls of brain-numbing games software, to her friend Valerie, who ran the playgroup, so that she could begin to warp the minds of the local four-year-olds. After that she rang the *Who Wants To Be a Millionaire?* question line from his office phone and left it off the hook – and at fifty pence per minute, she guessed that one person who wouldn't be was Damien. Finally, before retiring to bed with a bottle of Damien's favourite red wine, Stephen the leisure manager from their prestigious health club, and precious little remorse, Melanie had neatly pushed a small, unobtrusive North

Atlantic prawn into the CD connector of Damien's revered laptop.

Back at JFK, Damien heaved a sigh – as well he might. He had decided to let nature take its course and wait for Donald to have a crap, but time was running out and Donald had failed to produce one single little poo. Could terror give ducks constipation? What to do to extricate himself from his tangle? What to do to extricate his diamond from this duck? It was a subject too tricky to contemplate without recourse to strong alcohol.

'What can I get you, sir?' the barman asked on cue. He was a man who was clearly employing all his years of learned professionalism and appeared not even to notice Damien's filthy, bedraggled state.

'A brandy,' Damien said. 'A double.'

'Coming up.'

'Make it two doubles,' he added. 'And a beer.'

With a minimum of fuss and delay, the barman placed the drinks in front of Damien, who proceeded to swig the beer and the brandy in sequence. After another round, it was clear that Donald was becoming restless. Even though Damien was swaying slightly on his stool, he could tell that the duck was trying to waddle surreptitiously away.

Damien drained his two glasses, paid his tab and jumped down. 'Come on, duck,' he said. 'I need to think about what to do with you.'

As he picked up his bag, he noticed the burly

men again. They were huddled tightly in a group at one of the standing tables at the snack counter right next to the bar. Damien looked over his shoulder. They all swallowed their coffee and stuffed their croissants into their mouths, brushing errant crumbs from their matching dark overcoats. Damien moved swiftly away, clutching Donald to his chest. Who could they be? FBI? Customs officials? Perhaps they'd been tipped off by the surly check-in clerk, who clearly hadn't bought his robotic duck crap. He'd never have got a job on *Jackanory*.

Could you be arrested for smuggling a duck? Could you be arrested for smuggling a diamond in a duck? Perhaps because of his appearance they'd assumed he was a terrorist rather than a hapless romantic unlucky in love.

Damien hurried along the airport concourse as fast as he could given that it was swarming with blue-rinsed pensioners wearing straw hats who were clearly heading for warmer climes, and given that whenever he approached a decent pace Donald would quack with indignity. The men, Damien noticed anxiously, were striding purposefully after him.

He dodged inside one of the brightly lit airport shops selling last-minute things that everyone at some time forgot in their haste to get away on holiday. The men stopped outside, surveying the heads of the crowds of travellers. There was no doubt, it was him they were following. His mouth was dry, his heart beating fast, his duck leaping up and down inside its canvas prison. To quell his rising panic, Damien forced himself to walk steadily down the aisles, eyes flicking over the displays of cosmetics, condoms and chewing gum. He tried to concentrate on what his next move should be, his mind running too quickly for him to catch the jumbled thoughts that tumbled erratically through it like performers from Cirque du Soleil. Think, Damien! For fuck's sake, think!

The men were still outside the shop. One of them made a move towards him. Suddenly Damien stopped and stared at the shelf ahead of him. His feet rooted to the ground, everything else blurred into the background. His eyes focused on their target with pin-sharp clarity. He was so happy he could have wept with relief! Why on earth hadn't he considered it earlier?

'Shitshitshit,' he said and fumbled in his pocket for a few dollars of change. Keeping his eye on the advancing man, Damien reached out and grabbed the answers to his prayers.

'This will get you going, my bunged-up buddy!' he said with a grim smile, clutching the largest packet of Eezee-Go laxatives he could lay his hands on.

CHAPTER 49

The taxi had dropped Matt and Holly off outside her apartment block, and now they were both standing shivering in the sub-zero temperature, inadequately dressed for the cold wind that was slicing through them, while Holly fumbled with frozen fingers for her elusive key. Matt's new black eye was throbbing nicely, while his old one from his fight with Headstrong was clearly unhappy to be superseded so soon and had come out in sympathy. Stereo pain. Marvellous. First thing tomorrow he would have to go and get some Blues Brothers-style sunglasses to cover up the purple bruises and his humiliation. He didn't know whether this was anything to do with Josie, but he seemed to be turning into a rock musician by the minute, drinking, brawling and goodness knows what else. He was even considering looking out his old guitar and amplifier when he got home.

Realising he was about to freeze to the pave-ment and tired of Holly's fruitless searching, Matt scooped her up into his arms and carried her up the short flight of stone steps. She was as light as a feather and her hair tickled his nose as much.

Holly whacked him with her purse. 'Put me down, you big jerk!'

He held on to her as she wriggled. 'I thought your feet might be cold,' he said, eyeing her bare toes.

'They are,' she said through chattering teeth. 'I'll send you the bill for replacement shoes.'

He thought about pointing out that the broken heel her shoe had sustained in the taxi-bumping incident wasn't exactly his fault, but then if you examined the facts closely, all of it, the entire disastrous evening, was basically down to him.

'Be gentle with me,' he said. 'My credit card only has a three-thousand-pound limit.'

'Ha ha!' Holly said with a flourish of the wayward key, and Matt lowered her so that she could unlock the door. He pushed it open with his foot and carried her gratefully inside.

'Okay, you can put me down now,' Holly said as they crossed the lobby. 'I can manage.'

'You might stand on something sharp. And I wouldn't want to be responsible for causing you a fatal injury on top of everything else,' Matt puffed as he climbed the stairs. 'It's a long way up to your apartment, isn't it?'

'A very long way,' Holly said with a wicked glint in her eyes. She linked her arms round his neck and flicked her eyebrows with pleasure.

Matt pulled a face and pressed on.

'This could be seen as sufficient punishment for all your misdemeanours in the past few days,' Holly said.

'Thank you,' Matt breathed.

'Don't talk,' Holly instructed, placing a finger lightly across his lips. 'We don't want you to run out of steam too early.'

'You're all heart,' Matt said.

'This was your idea.' Holly examined her nails and swung her feet.

Matt staggered up the stairs, Holly's feather-weight frame turning steadily to lead with every step. They were nearing the top now and his legs had all the inherent strength of a half-set jelly.

'You need to lose weight,' Matt panted.

'You need to work out,' Holly crowed.

Thankfully, the door was in sight.

'Nearly there,' Holly pointed out needlessly and waved her door key in front of him.

Matt was seeing psychedelic whirly things in front of his eyes, which he thought was probably due to oxygen deficit. It had been a marathon sort of day in many ways and his body was clearly unaccustomed to staying the distance these days. All that 'Hava Nagila'-ing with Aunty Dolly had evidently taken its toll.

'Down,' Holly instructed as he swayed in front of her apartment door. Matt obeyed and gingerly lowered her to the height of her keyhole. His knees burned and his arms burned and his back had gone numb. 'Now let's see.' Holly pondered the keys in her hand.

'Get on with it, woman!' Matt shook her up and down, making her giggle, and as Holly unlocked the door, they swung into the room laughing like five-year-olds.

Matt staggered across the room and tipped Holly unceremoniously on to her couch. As he did so, his knees buckled beneath him and he tumbled on top of her. She lay beneath him, chuckling breathlessly as he panted with all the elegance of a spent racehorse.

Suddenly the laughing stopped and their breathing became heavier, more focused. The room was silent, the only noise their laboured breath and the relentless wailing punctuation of police sirens drifting up from the deserted city streets below. Matt was aware of her body, soft and small, fitting against the length of his. Her wild, proud mane of hair framed her face, making her look both wanton and vulnerable. His hands pinned her small white wrists to the cushion above her head, arching her body to his. Her lips were pink and moist, her tongue running tremulously across them. Matt saw a tiny, uncertain swallow travel the length of her exposed throat. A delicate flush spread over her chest and her uneven breath lifted her breasts, grazing her nipples against his shirt so that he could feel their heat on his chest. In the darkness, Matt looked into Holly's eyes. God, it would be so easy, so tempting.

'Ms Brinkman,' he said, 'I do believe I have you at a disadvantage.'

'Mr Jarvis,' Holly echoed, 'I'm sure you will respect my virtue. You are, after all, an Englishman and a gentleman.'

'Ms Brinkman, I feel you overestimate me.' Matt shifted his weight to his elbows.

'You have had, as you may well be aware, several opportunities to jump my bones,' Holly pointed out. 'And yet you have consistently resisted my not insubstantial charms.'

'I fear that may well change. In a few short moments I am about to behave like a cad and an absolute bounder.'

'A bounder, Mr Jarvis?' Holly looked puzzled. 'I'm an American, sir. I don't believe I know how an absolute bounder behaves.'

Matt brushed the hair from Holly's eyes. 'Then it will be my pleasure to show you, Ms Brinkman,' he said, brushing his lips against Holly's.

CHAPTER 50

The frightening-looking men were still waiting when Damien sidled out of the airport shop, clutching his Eezee-Go laxatives with an air of barely restrained glee. They had all closed round a Zippo lighter and were concentrating on drawing on their cigarettes sufficiently for Damien to sneak out unseen.

Stealthily he veered down a corridor and shot into the nearest men's room. This was ridiculous! It was like being in a bloody Harrison Ford film without the accompanying star status, fit tart and fat pay cheque.

He leaned back against the wall, breathing heavily in an unsuccessful effort to calm himself. Damien put the holdall on to the counter. From the noise Donald was making, it seemed his reluctant companion was getting very stressed too.

Damien looked round. It was a utilitarian establishment furnished with functional chrome and white tiles. Bill Medley and Jennifer Warnes sang 'I've Had the Time of My Life' over the sound system, which gave a surreal air to the proceedings that had not necessarily been lacking.

398

All the cubicles seemed to be empty. Damien checked carefully underneath the doors for feet. None apparent. Unless there was a very short midget taking a crap.

Damien zipped his holdall open slowly, employing extreme caution. He knew from bitter experience that this bugger could bite. One slip now and the whole shooting match could end in tears. Donald poked his head out from beneath the folds of canvas and a very unpleasant ducky smell wafted up from its depths. Damien zipped a bit more.

Given half a chance of escape, Donald flapped and made a valiant attempt to flee. He soared out of the holdall and into the wide-open space of the men's room, his voice heralding freedom.

Damien caught him mid-flight. 'Gotcha!' he cried. He winked at the duck. 'Sorry, but it's not that easy, mate!'

Donald struggled a bit and then collapsed into Damien's arms. 'All I want to do is give you a nice little tablet.' Damien unwrapped the laxatives. 'One teeny-weeny, ickle-wickle tablet. Or two.' He held it up to show Donald. 'Look, that won't hurt a bit, will it? It's hardly even the size of a diamond ring, is it? Eezee-Go!' He spelled it out. 'Says it all, doesn't it? Won't that slip down just a treat, eh?' Damien smiled encouragement at Donald. 'Yum, yum, yum!'

The duck did not look convinced.

'Open wide!' Damien prised Donald's beak

apart, taking care to keep his fingers out of harm's way.

Donald made enough noise to wake the dead.

'I'm not murdering you!' Damien insisted. 'Not yet!'

Even giving a worming pill to The Cat Formerly Known As Prince had been easier than this, and he'd turn into Brad Pitt in *Fight Club* the minute the words vet, tablet or flea powder were mentioned.

The duck opened his beak wider to produce the loudest quack ever, and in that moment, Damien tipped the entire packet of laxatives down his captive's throat and clamped his beak shut. Then he fixed the duck with an evil grin. 'Now all we have to do is wait.'

They had been waiting a long time. Damien checked his watch again. Fifteen minutes of nothing and his hand was starting to ache. He changed arms and closed his eyes against the agony. He was crouched down in a very cramped area, jammed up against the cold cubicle walls, and his knees were starting to know about it. Holding Donald down on the toilet seat wasn't exactly the most fun he'd ever had. In fact he'd had an in-growing toenail removed two years ago and that was a laugh a minute compared to this.

'Comeoncomeoncomeon,' Damien urged. 'Just one little poo. That's all it will take to end this misery and then we can both go home.'

Donald looked suspiciously as if he might be

falling asleep. 'Don't nod off.' Damien prodded him. 'We're in here to do the business.'

Donald's eyes rolled sleepily. 'Look, I'm going to sing to you, right?' Damien said. He searched his head for tunes suitable to facilitate ducks' toilet habits. Donald looked uninterested.

A light bulb pinged on in Damien's brain. 'I know!' He cleared his throat. Usually he needed considerably more of the amber nectar to even attempt to sing. His voice veered uncontrollably from the depths of Barry White to the heights of the Bee Gees without any clear direction from him. He coughed again. 'Old MacDonald had a farm, ee-I, ee-I, o. And on that farm, he had a *DUCK*, ee-I, ee-I, o. With a quack quack here and a quack quack there. Here a quack, there a quack, everywhere a quack quack. Old MacDonald had a farm, ee-I, ee-I, o!'

Damien sat back against the toilet door. 'Anything?' he asked hopefully.

'Quack,' Donald said.

'Again?' Damien offered.

'Quack.'

Damien huffed and then smiled encouragingly at Donald. His repertoire of duck songs was tragically limited. This little ditty always reminded him of that dreadful weekend he and Josie had spent supposedly having a romantic get-away break, when she had spent the entire night making farmyard noises through the wall to the couple in the next room, who were clearly having more rampant and uninhibited sex than they were. And it wasn't something, at this juncture, that he particularly wanted to be reminded of. Damien braced himself. 'Old MacDonald had a farm, ee-I, ee-I, o. And on that farm, he had a *DUCK*, ee-I, ee-I, o. With a quack quack here . . .'

'Quack,' added Donald.

'And a quack quack there . . .'

'Quack.'

'Here a quack . . .'

'Quack.'

'There a quack . . .'

'Quack.'

'Everywhere a quack quack . . .'

'Quack, quack, quack.'

'I don't want you to sit there fucking singing with me!' Damien shouted. 'Just shit, you stupid bird!'

'Quack.'

Damien slumped to the floor, defeated. 'This isn't working, is it?'

The quack that Donald gave in reply seemed, very definitely, to say no.

With a weary sigh, Damien settled Donald on the counter. 'Now look, my little feathered friend, on the one hand I do appreciate your predicament – you must view yourself as an innocent bystander in all this malarkey. You weren't to know that the tempting morsel that sploshed in front of you wasn't just another old bit of Hovis or Jacob's

Cream Cracker, were you? You just munched it in good faith, as ducks do, innocent of the fact that it was a girl's best friend you were swallowing.' Damien stared him straight in the eyes, man to duck. 'On the other hand, you are making this a bloody sight more difficult than it needs to be. I have tried as hard as I can to be reasonable, but the sands of time are against us. So unless you can shit within the next five seconds, old chum, this is where you and I have to say farewell.'

Damien clamped one hand round Donald's throat and with the other ran the tap, filling the men's room sink with warm water. Before he could consider the wisdom involved in trying to drown a duck, Damien snatched his quarry and pushed his head under the water. Donald fought with the strength of twenty ducks and flapped his wings maniacally, soaking Damien from head to toe.

'Die, you bastard duck from hell!' Damien shouted, struggling to hold Donald down. 'Die!'

At that moment, the door burst open and the three burly men blocked out the sun.

'I can explain,' Damien said, releasing his grip on Donald. The duck sat and spluttered on the counter.

The men advanced. Donald coughed. Damien retreated.

He held his hands up in front of his face. 'Don't hurt me,' he pleaded.

CHAPTER 51

Matt opened his eyes and tried to blink the sleep out of them. It was still dark. The curtains were open, but only a phantom wisp of grey light hinted at the impending dawn. Holly's bedroom looked as though a heavy metal thrash band rather than one solitary rock journalist had been staying the night. The floor was littered with clothes and bottles and various other unsavoury items. He lay back on the bed, arms above his head, exhausted. His body may have been unaccustomed to staying the distance these days, but it had come out with a sterling performance when the occasion required it, and Holly must surely be mentally awarding him ten out of ten for sheer effort, if not artistic interpretation.

They had made love on the sofa, over the sofa, on the hearth rug, in the shower, on the bathroom floor, on the bedroom floor, and finally on the bed. Oh, and in the kitchen against the cabinets somewhere en route. Matt was thankful that Holly didn't live in a mansion and had eventually run out of rooms. She hadn't, however, run out of condoms, and he had tried to put out of his mind that she had a wider selection than your average well-stocked Durex warehouse. If she put as much effort into public relations as she did her sexual encounters, then Headstrong would no doubt conquer America despite the fact that they couldn't sing for a Tootsie Roll.

Matt didn't like doing casual sex. Not really. The whole thing was a minefield. It was bad enough with someone you knew and loved, but with a stranger there were all sorts of disarming devices that could blow up in your face. First there were the physical elements to consider – were you big enough, too big (realms of fantasy), fast enough, slow enough, would you come too quickly, would you be able to come at all? Add to that all the emotional insecurities of being in bed naked with someone you didn't know, and Matt often wondered why people bothered at all. But bother they did, because invariably situations like last night had a habit of cropping up, if not often, then once in a blue moon, and that made them all the more alluring. Nights when there was too much flirting, too much drinking, too much build-up, too much opportunity, too much loneliness and too much of that ridiculously elusive and destructive random chaos element we glibly call chemistry.

Even when all these things came right, the pleasure was always short-lived, because it would trouble him for weeks afterwards that he hadn't been good enough. Even if he'd been left with a scribbled note of a phone number or a hasty departing promise to call there was always that nagging doubt. He never wanted his prowess between the sheets to be the topic of conversation at the local pub during the course of several Bacardi Breezers. His ego was far too fragile, and he knew all too well how women exaggerated when they'd had a few drinks. At least Holly was on another continent and, as such, her stories would never reach the ears of those at his local pub, the Slag & Handbag.

There was an added element to this too. He had been unfaithful to Josie. He had been unfaithful to Josie, and the thought made his stomach a cold mass of congealed porridge. Although he wasn't sure if you could technically be unfaithful to someone who was wholly and unconditionally unaware of your deep and abiding commitment to them. Someone who had, incidentally, forgotten to mention they might still be a tad married. Nevertheless, regret was writ large on his heart, which was unfair to Holly because, in his defence, he had shown no obvious lack of enthusiasm last night.

But that was last night and this was now, and with the passing of a few hours came the cold, clear light of dawn. As Matt was contemplating what to do, there was a fidget next to him in the bed. A slight movement of the sheet across his thighs.

He hated this moment. More than anything. More than someone else's body odour, more than

Lemon Puff biscuits, more than Metro City drivers and more than not understanding American football. It was fair to say that in his entire life he had never, ever been to bed with an ugly woman, but unfortunately he seemed to have woken up with quite a few. Would Holly suddenly have transformed with the sunrise to resemble the nice smiley monkey out of *Planet of the Apes?* Undoubtedly a nice monkey, but a monkey all the same. It had happened before. There was more than one occasion he could mention when he had gone to bed with Liz Hurley and got up with Les Dawson.

Matt turned and smiled uneasily at Holly's silhouette in the greyness, thankful to see that she was still quite lovely. She was sitting up in the bed, her hair sticking up all over the place, wistfully smoking a joint and watching the smoke rings she blew drift aimlessly towards the ceiling, curl up and fade to nothingness in the air. She smiled back, her teeth white in the surreal light. 'Hi.'

'Hi,' Matt said.

Holly blew another smoke ring.

'Okay?' he asked.

She nodded, but there was a cool tenseness to her manner and she had the sheet coiled coyly round her body, which seemed a bit pointless all things considered.

'I didn't mean to wake you,' Holly said between drags.

'I didn't mean to turn over and fall asleep,' Matt said sheepishly. 'It's a bloke thing . . .'

'I know. I've been here before.' Holly stubbed out her joint in an ashtray shaped like a shell that looked well used.

'I hate this bit,' Matt said. 'I never know what to say or do.' He propped himself up. 'It always sounds so corny to say "How was it for you?" or "Did the earth move, darling?"'

'Well,' Holly said, 'if you were to say that, I'd have to say it was nice, and although the earth didn't exactly move, it did rock a bit.'

'Really?'

'Really.' Holly let her mouth relax. 'And as for what you can do, you could just hold me.'

When he didn't object, Holly snuggled in next to him and it was Matt's turn to feel tense. How had he got himself into this? One minute it was all broken shoes and bridesmaids and the next they were enjoying bouncy cuddles and had added considerably to the world's waste-rubber mountain.

'Was it okay for you?' Holly asked.

'Yeah. Great. Fine. Fantastic. Yeah . . .' Matt's limited repertoire of superlatives petered out. 'Fab.' *Fab?*

'*Fab?*' Holly queried, and let her fingers wander over his chest and down towards his belly. 'Fab enough to want to do it again?'

'Now?'

'Why not?'

'Why not?' There were a thousand reasons why not and he could tell Holly none of them. Not least was that he had no idea where he might find the necessary energy.

'There's no time like the present,' Holly added.

Matt stayed her hand. 'What is the time? Oooh, my goodness me!' He peered in the half-light at the clock beyond Holly's shoulder.

Holly turned round and looked. 'It's not yet six o'clock.'

'Already? My, my, my.'

Holly pushed away from him. 'Don't tell me. You have to be going.'

'I have a plane to catch.'

'Not until this afternoon.'

'I have to pack.'

'You're avoiding this situation, aren't you?'

'Yes.'

'Why?' Holly said.

'I'm a bloke. I'm useless at this morning-after emotion stuff.'

Holly was not going to be that easily appeased.

'I'm an English bloke and we're even worse. We're known for it.'

'What have I done wrong?'

'Nothing,' Matt said. 'Nothing at all. Believe me.'

'Then why are you rushing out of here?'

'I'm not.' Matt shifted uncomfortably. He was desperate to go to the loo, but couldn't face getting out of the bed naked and limp and generally pathetic. 'Well, I am. But it's nothing to do with you.' He removed Holly's hand from his chest and squeezed it. 'This has been great fun . . .'

'Fun?' Holly said. 'Fun?'

Matt wasn't sure he liked the way 'fun' was sounding like a bad thing.

'Is that all this means to you?' Even with the lack of light, Matt could tell that Holly's face had darkened a few shades. 'Fun?'

'Er . . . yes,' Matt said. 'I thought that's what you wanted.'

'You think I do this for fun?'

'Er . . . yes.'

'I care about you, Matt. You must know that. I don't just jump into bed with every man I meet. What sort of woman do you take me for?'

'Er . . . a liberated, funky, feisty sort of woman,' Matt ventured. 'A native New Yorker . . .'

'I'm from Oregon.'

'Really? I've never been there . . .'

'So I'm a liberated, funky, feisty sort of woman who you can just walk out on the next morning because it suits you?'

'Holly, I do have a plane to catch. You knew this was a temporary thing.' Matt spread his hands, grasping for words. 'I knew I would handle it badly.'

'I don't see what the problem is.' Holly had her arms folded. 'We could have made love again. Shared some breakfast. We could have had some fresh fruit salad. I maybe could have whipped up some eggs. I might even have made you pancakes. And we could have both gone away feeling good. I don't understand the sudden change.'

'Pancakes would have been nice . . .'

'Stick your pancakes!'

Matt slumped back, resigned. 'It's me, Holly. Not you.'

'That usually means it's me and not you. If you see what I mean.'

'It's good old-fashioned guilt. I can't make love to you again because I feel so guilty about everything.'

'Guilty?' Holly sat back. 'What about?'

'This. That. More particularly, the other.'

'Why? We're both free and single, aren't we?'

'Er . . . yes. It's just that things look different in the morning, don't they?'

'I don't know, Matt. You tell me. Last night I was single when I went to bed with you and . . .' Holly checked her ring finger, 'and I still seem to be at this moment. That just leaves you . . .'

'Errrmmm . . .'

'Are you in a committed relationship, Matt?'

'It depends *exactly* what you mean by committed.'

'I mean a wife, two children, a house in the country committed.'

'Then no, I'm not in a committed relationship.'

'But there is someone else?'

'Errr . . .' Matt was beginning to wish he was up and dressed and out in the street, and not in bed and naked and in direct line of Holly's laser-beam stare.

'All along I've felt there's something you're not

411

telling me.' She screwed her nose up as she said it.

Women can scent deceit, like cats can scent cooking chicken a mile off. The difference is, Matt had come to realise, women sometimes prefer to ignore it. By instinct, cats find the innocent chicken and gnaw its legs off straight away, no messing. Women can choose to ignore even the strongest, most tempting aroma until it suits them. Through years of conditioning they wait and wait and wait to begin leg-gnawing until the time is right for maximum impact.

Holly's nose twitched some more. 'Is this to do with Martha's wedding?'

'Yes.'

'And that bridesmaid business?'

'Yes.'

'So there is someone else?'

'Yes.'

'And that's why that guy hit you?'

'Yes.'

'Are you in love with her?'

'Yes.'

'And she's in love with you?'

'I have absolutely no idea.'

'So what are you doing in bed with me?'

'Messing up what could have been a perfectly good friendship.'

Holly slid down in the bed and pulled the sheets up round her neck. 'I think you'd better leave, Matt.'

'Right,' Matt said, and wondered how he was going to get from the bed to his clothes and, subsequently, to the front door without looking like a complete prat.

CHAPTER 52

Damien had one man on either side of him. They were holding him under the elbows and his feet were barely touching the ground as they escorted him briskly through the terminal building. The other man was carrying Donald, now firmly ensconced back in his holdall.

The blue-rinsed and Panama-hatted crowds parted as they approached, and Damien wondered if they could see the terror on his face, and if they could, why no one was doing anything about it. Damien briefly considered screaming, but even in his petrified state he still had his street credibility to consider.

'Who are you guys?' he asked as he was rushed out of the building and across the road, the men risking his life and limbs amid the screeching taxis. They squeezed his elbows harder. 'FBI?' he ventured. 'Customs?'

'Quit talking,' the man at his right elbow rasped. 'We brought someone to see you.'

'See me?' Damien said as they hurried him into the car park and towards a waiting black limo with blacked-out windows and menace written all over it. 'You must have the wrong person.'

The man wrenched open the door and pushed Damien inside, banging his head on the door frame. 'Ouch,' Damien complained, fingering his skull. The man squeezed in next to him, sandwiching Damien firmly between him and Uncle Nunzio.

Relief swept over Damien. 'Oh, thank the Lord! It's you! From Martha's wedding!' Damien held his chest dramatically. 'You had me going for a minute.'

'Uncle Nunzio is here to see honour restored,' the man next to him intoned solemnly. Damien noticed that Donald was sitting quite happily on his knee, head poking inquisitively out of the holdall.

'Honour.' Uncle Nunzio nodded.

'Honour?' Damien said. 'Whose honour?'

'You did a disservice to our friend back at the wedding, and now you must find a way to make amends.'

'What friend?' Realisation dawned on Damien. 'Not that Matt Jarvis wanker! Oh, for heaven's sake!'

'You must make good what you have put wrong,' the man insisted.

'Make good! That man has single-handedly destroyed my marriage! The very least I could do was give him a knuckle butty!'

'We have decided,' the man continued undeterred, 'to take your duck as compensation.'

'My duck!' Damien was incensed. 'Not on your nelly!'

'Nelly?' queried Uncle Nunzio.

'No way, José!' Damien clarified. 'That duck has been in my family for years. He's like a brother to me. And no one messes with my family.' Damien wished he could look more intimidating and a little less terrified.

'We want the duck,' the man repeated.

'No one fucks with my duck,' Damien said emphatically.

They all stared stonily at each other, and then the heavy flexed his knuckles, cracking them like the sound of gunshot.

'Wait, wait, wait!' Damien held up his hand. 'This is all because you overheard that diamond ring bullshit, isn't it?'

No one spoke.

'Isn't it?' Damien repeated. 'You think this duck has a diamond ring inside it. Am I right?'

Uncle Nunzio and the heavy eyeballed each other.

'Well, you are very much mistaken. How do you think I'm going to get it through customs? Don't you think they'll X-ray it? I can't believe you fell for that!' Damien slapped his thigh in true panto-mime style.

Uncle Nunzio and the heavy looked less certain.

'It's a Diamond Ring duck,' Damien said with a tut. 'That's the make . . . the model . . . the type . . . breed . . .'

The heavy looked to Uncle Nunzio, who remained impassive.

'You are making this situation very difficult for us, my friend,' the heavy said. 'Either you have to lose face or we lose face.'

'Oh look,' Damien sighed. 'I am sick of all this. I want my face to stay exactly the way it is. I'm tired. I'm weary. I have a plane to catch. And I really want to be on it because I just want to go home. You can have the duck.' He pushed Donald away from him. 'Go on, take it. Take it. Take it. Can I get out now, please?'

The heavy looked puzzled. Uncle Nunzio shrugged. The heavy got out of the car, leaving Damien considerably less squashed.

'I can't say it's been a pleasure meeting you,' Damien said to Uncle Nunzio. 'Martha has some very interesting relations. I hope you and my duck will be very happy.'

The heavy stood by the car door and Damien got out straightening himself up with as much dignity as he could muster, given that his legs were wobblier than a pair of Slinkies. 'Look after him.' Damien reached out and patted Donald's head. 'He's called Donald.'

Donald quacked miserably. The heavy looked moved to tears. Damien bit his trembling lip. He leaned towards the holdall. 'Goodbye, old son . . .'

With a lightning swiftness of movement that Will Carling would have been proud of, Damien snatched the bag from the grip of the perplexed heavy and raced off, swerving through the honking traffic. Donald honked back, loudly. Damien glanced back, laughing as the men attempted to follow but were cut off by a mercifully long stream of yellow cabs. Who said there was never one around when you needed one!

All he had to do now was work out how he was going to get Donald through customs, and at the moment, that seemed a bit of a tricky one.

CHAPTER 53

Josie had the mother, sister, daughter, father, brother, cousin, uncle and any other close relative you cared to name of all hangovers. She had lain in bed for a full thirty minutes, trying to will the room stationary and summoning the necessary courage to venture towards the upright.

Now she stood in the shower, letting hot water stream over her body, eyes closed, swaying slightly, portraying accurately the epitome of all that advertising executives rely on to sell surefire hangover remedies.

The full horror of the events of yesterday had not diminished now that she was rapidly becoming sober. She wondered where Martha was now and how long it was going to take her father to find her and kill her. As a sure sign of how thoroughly traumatised she was, she longed to ring Lavinia. Josie felt so alone in this big city that only a mother's love would do to comfort her – and then she remembered that it would involve a fifteen-minute continuation of 'I'll name that medical condition' and decided to sweat it out alone.

Turning off the shower, she wrapped herself in

a warm, fluffy towel, cleared the steam from the mirror and took a long, hard look at herself. Not since Tom Cruise in *Interview With a Vampire* had she seen eyes so red and bloodshot. Suitably horrified, Josie padded back into the bedroom. The air-conditioning and the central heating were locked in deadly battle for supremacy and were producing a sort of freezing fug laden with dust. It was a stifling, airless combination, and as always in New York hotels, the bedroom windows were locked, nailed and barricaded shut.

Below her the city was stirring, sleepy Sunday-morning movements that nudged rather than bustled the Big Apple back into life. Below her somewhere Matt would be stirring too. She drew back the curtain and looked out. Should she search for him? If she tried really, really hard could she remember where his hotel was? Was it two blocks away or was it ten? Heaven only knows. It was information that had probably fallen off the back of her brain as irrelevant to make room for all that her grey matter had been forced to take in over the last forty-eight hours. Was he worth it anyway? Maybe he had finished his interviewing and had already gone back to London. She would never know.

A soft pink tinge of sun made a valiant attempt at warming the harsh grey light of the cool dawn. There was no point sitting here being a maudlin wimp on her last day in the USA. Tomorrow, too soon, it would be back to the depths of Camden and the jolly old grindstone of Information Technology. She had to get out into the city and the comparatively fresh air, make the most of the time she had left.

Josie picked up the hotel's copy of *Where in New York* and flicked through the packed entertainment pages. Sunday Gospel service in Harlem – too much singing, too much noise, too much cheerfulness. Brunch at Lola's – food, stomach churn, never going to eat again. Take a lift to the Top of the World – heights no good, need feet to be near earth. Browse, browse, browse. Stop. Her red, sand-papered eyes tried to light up. *Bike Hire*, the advert said. Josie smiled to herself and it made her face hurt. Where better to head to chase a hangover away than Central Park, the green and vibrant lungs of the city, armed with pedal power.

Holly had thrown fruit on his head. Matt had done his best to leave on good terms, be jocular, consoling, complimentary, placating, light-hearted, concerned. In fact he had run through the entire range of his 'embarrassing situation' emotions while he hurriedly dressed, but none had succeeded in tempting Holly from beneath the bed covers to where she had silently retired. Which, in some ways, he didn't mind, because there was just no cool way to put socks on.

When he had left and was out in the street it was a different matter. She had thrown open her apartment window and assaulted him with a battery of apricots, kiwi fruit, oranges and sweet tiny apple bananas, which were totally delicious and something you just couldn't get back home. All accompanied by the words 'fucking bastard' at full volume. When she had offered him fresh fruit salad for breakfast, he hadn't quite envisaged this. As he had tried to dodge the barrage of Vitamin C missiles, it struck him – as did the fruit – that no one else in the street was turning a hair. Perhaps they were used to Holly pelting hastily retreating men with exotic produce, or maybe this was just your average Sunday morning in New York. Finally he had moved out of Holly's range and she had slammed the window shut with a parting 'fuck off'. It seemed she had not taken his premature departure well.

So what now? Matt had breakfasted on pancakes at a steamy diner – alone – and was now standing on the sidewalk wondering how best to fill the empty void that represented his last morning in the Big Apple. He could take a circuitous route to his hotel and check out before deciding what to do. His body was aching all over from the various skirmishes he'd had over the weekend, and all he really wanted to do was lie down and sleep. Preferably unaccompanied.

The breeze ruffled his hair and made his scalp throb, and Matt realised he probably looked like shit – it was certainly what he felt like. Running his hand over his chin, he massaged the sore dark shadow of his beard which, no doubt, protruded out of the pasty pallor of overindulged and dehydrated skin. Nice. No wonder Holly had taken to hiding under the sheets.

It would do him good to take a walk; the fresh air would help to clear the last vestiges of champagne and tequila from his weary brain. He needed time to think about Holly and how he had managed to get that so wrong, and he needed time to think about Josie and how he had managed to get that so wrong too.

He could make it up to Holly when he returned to England. He would send her flowers, chocolates, maybe some replacement Jimmy Choo shoes and maybe some replacement fruit, which he hoped she might find amusing enough to class as a joke and forgive him. And he would write a glowing article comparing the up-and-coming boy band Headstrong extremely favourably against the late great John Lennon, even though it was against every fibre in his body to do so. He would rather be stuck in a lift for five hours with Des O'Connor than ever clap eyes on the collective anathema of Justin, Tyrone, Bobbie and Stig, a.k.a. Headstrong, again. With Josie, it would be infinitely more difficult.

Matt looked up at the vast expanse of sky above him. The weak winter sun had succeeded in burning away the greyness, leaving a clear azure canvas. She was out there somewhere, underneath the same sky, and he would find her. Some way. Somehow. If it was the last thing he did.

It was turning into a beautiful morning. A hard

white frost sprinkled the tips of the skeleton trees, making them shimmer in the light and adding crispness to the air that nipped at exposed ears and noses. Matt pulled his coat around him and set off, walking at a pace that said he knew where he was going, when in actual fact he hadn't the slightest idea.

CHAPTER 54

Damien was in a quandary. Behind him were the three heavies, who had weaved with the effortless grace of prima ballerinas through the stationary traffic and were now jogging purposefully across the terminal building, sights set squarely on the target of Damien Lewis Flynn. In front of him were three customs officers, who looked equally mean and bulky. At least, rather than chasing him, the customs men were leaning uninterestedly on their counter.

Donald was wriggling in his bag, and not for the first time, Damien wished he'd had the nerve to strangle the blessed thing while he had the opportunity. There was no time to do anything about it now. He would rather take his chances with the customs men than find himself swimming with the fish in the murky depths of New York harbour, or adding bulk to the concrete foundations of a new skyscraper. With a backward glance, Damien passed through Passport Control and into the customs hall. The men had come to a halt; a wall of black overcoats that had been foiled in their dastardly plan to relieve him of his feathered friend. Damien risked a sneering smile. For a brief and liberating minute, all seemed to be going well.

He approached the customs men and Donald gave them a welcoming quack. The three men ignored it.

'Please put your baggage on the conveyor, sir,' the biggest and burliest of them said.

Damien swallowed hard. What should he do? Come clean now? His hands were sweating and he felt as though he had twenty-two kilos of Class A heroin in his bag rather than a belligerent duck that was more indestructible than Captain Scarlet. Was it a crime to carry livestock out of the country? Quite probably. Or, when they discovered the diamond, would they think that he was an international jewel thief and that Donald was merely a ruse to cover his diamond-smuggling exploits? God, he could murder Josie for getting him into this situation!

'Your baggage, sir,' the customs officer repeated. There was a queue forming behind him now, and people were starting to stare.

Damien put the bag down gingerly and watched Donald as he was swallowed, quacking, into the black metal tunnel of the X-ray machine.

'Sir.' One of the officers was beckoning him through the security gate.

As Damien passed through it, an alarm bell rang, nearly inducing a cardiac arrest in his frantically beating heart. Perhaps this would all be too much for Donald and he would die of heart failure in the confines of the X-ray tunnel, and all this would have been for nothing. The security guard ran a metal detector over him.

'Keys,' he said.

Damien's lips had cemented themselves together. 'What?'

'Your keys are in your pocket, sir.'

'Oh, right,' Damien said. Plonking them on to a tray, he passed through the security gate again without incident. He walked to the end of the conveyor belt, where the three customs men had now gathered behind the operator of the X-ray machine.

'Did you know that you were carrying livestock, sir?'

'Er . . . yes.'

'Did you know that was in direct contravention of the laws of the Federal Drugs Administration?'

'Really? I had no idea.'

'Would you please accompany us, sir?' the officers said in unison, and for the second time today Damien was taken by the elbows and frog-marched away.

'I am afraid that we will have to take this livestock into custody,' the officer insisted, hugging the holdall with Donald in protectively to his side. Donald's head peeped out, monitoring the proceedings with interest. 'It is a federal offence to attempt to smuggle livestock out of the United States of America.'

Damien was sitting in a sparse little room, clinically threatening and claustrophobically small. It was hot and he was dirty and smelly and tired and increasingly bad-tempered. He tugged at the neck of his shirt, loosening his already loosened tie. The customs officers were standing, and from this angle they all looked very tall. Damien dropped his head into his hands. 'I've told you,' he said wearily, feeling as though he was speaking a foreign language, 'there is a reason why I wanted to take this duck back to England. And I wasn't trying to smuggle him.'

The last time he had seen faces so lacking in expression, they had been carved into a cliff.

'My wife and I have been over here attending her cousin Martha's wedding. And unfortunately, through no fault of my own, we had a little tiff . . .'

'You and your wife?'

'Yes,' Damien reiterated. 'A tiny little lovers' tiff. You know what it's like when you've been married for a while . . .' If they did, they didn't show any overt sympathy for his plight. 'And,' he continued only slightly daunted, 'unfortunately, my wife threw her engagement ring into the lake, where it was swallowed by this duck . . . livestock.' Bastard animal.

'And where is the ring now?'

Damien gestured at Donald. 'Inside the duck.'

The three customs officers looked blankly at each other.

'You can do what you like with the duck,' Damien

said magnanimously. 'I just want the ring back. My wife will be so upset if she thinks she's lost it.'

'And where is your wife now, sir?'

That one was a little trickier. 'She's following me on a later flight. She wanted to spend the day in New York, shopping.'

The customs officers regarded each other again.

'It sounds very far-fetched, doesn't it?' Damien laughed weakly.

'We would like to believe your story, sir,' said one of the men. 'It has a very cosy *ring* to it.' The other officers sniggered in agreement. 'But,' he paused for effect, 'no trace of a ring, diamond or otherwise, showed up on our X-ray.'

What little blood was left in Damien's face drained. 'There has to be.'

'I'm sorry, sir. But your duck is full of . . . duck shit.'

'It must be in there!' Damien stood up, snatched Donald out of the holdall and shook him vigorously. 'Where's my fucking ring?' he shouted.

Donald quacked loudly in a pained fashion.

'Can we X-ray him again?' Damien asked. 'Maybe your equipment's faulty.'

All three of them looked very unhappy at this suggested slur.

'Your X-ray machine,' Damien stressed.

'Come this way, sir.' Damien followed meekly, Donald under his arm as they all strode back towards the machine.

* * *

'Perhaps if he just sat on it rather than going through in the holdall,' Damien ventured. 'That might give a clearer picture.' And without waiting for approval, he plonked Donald on to the conveyor belt. The four of them huddled round the scanned picture. There were all sorts of ducky things to be seen. Ducky ribs, ducky heart, ducky lungs and all manner of ducky detritus in Donald's ducky stomach, but, as the customs officers had originally said, no sign whatsoever of a diamond ring.

'It can't be working properly!' Damien kicked the machine.

One of the officers held his arm. 'Please, sir, don't abuse the technology.'

Donald chugged out of the X-ray machine. Damien wanted to wail with pain; instead he fell to his knees on the airport floor. 'It can't be,' he said, massaging his eyes. 'It can't be. It must be the wrong duck. In the darkness, I must have grabbed the wrong duck!'

The customs officers regarded each other and then shrugged. 'Sir . . .' one ventured.

'Have it!' Damien said. 'It's no good to me. Shoot it, gas it, eat it. I don't care. I tried to do my best by it and this is how it's repaid me.' Damien covered his eyes. 'Take it from me.'

One of the officers carried Donald carefully away.

Damien looked up from the floor. 'Can I go now?'

'In good time. Would you accompany us, sir? We have one or two routine procedures we'd like to carry out.'

Listlessly, Damien plodded behind them back to the little white room and his hard, uncompromising chair.

'Please wait here, sir.'

'Can I make a phone call?' Damien asked.

'You'll be read your rights in a moment, sir,' one of the officers replied as he shut the door on Damien.

Rights, my arse, Damien thought. He was going to ring Melanie. There had to be something he could salvage out of this mess, and it might as well be her. With a bit of luck and a bit of Flynn Flannel, she might be waiting with open arms for him when he landed at Heathrow Airport. Damien pulled his mobile phone from his pocket and a stream of murky pond water flowed steadily out of it.

'Fuck,' Damien said as he threw it on to the table.

The customs officers were having a well-earned cigarette in the rest room. Donald was watching them intently.

'So what are we going to do with him?'

They all took the last drags of their respective cigarettes and ground them out in the ashtray.

'Let him go. He might as well take his chances above the skies of New York. There's no need for us to keep him.'

They all laughed together. 'Diamond ring!'

431

One of the officers wandered to the emergency exit and pushed the bar to open it. 'Okay, buddy,' he said, lifting Donald and carrying him to the door. 'You're free to go, little duck. You be careful out there. So long.'

With a brief look round at his surroundings, Donald quacked a last goodbye and waddled amenably out of the door and on to the grassy verge that bounded the airport.

'Now, shall we go back in and sort this guy out?'

'I think he needs the full treatment.'

'He's definitely hiding something. Guys like him always are. And I want to find out what.'

'Will you do the full body search, or will I?'

The biggest, burliest, meanest, cussedest customs officer smiled and rubbed his hands together. His colleague handed him a box of surgical gloves marked 'Extra Large' and he selected a pair, pulling the cream-coloured latex over his sturdy fingers with a resounding snap. 'It will be my pleasure,' he said.

CHAPTER 55

Matt had wandered around aimlessly for over an hour, and now his feet were hurting and his body needed a caffeine or chocolate injection. A group of Japanese tourists bustled past him, bowing with apologies for having disturbed his peace. Their petite guide, wrapped against the cold in a yellow duffle coat, was yabbering loudly in their native tongue and holding up an umbrella, which she waved enthusiastically in a vain attempt to keep them all herded together. Matt looked up, wondering what was causing them to click their cameras so eagerly. He was at the end of West Seventy-second street, opposite the Dakota building, the place where John Lennon was brutally shot down by a nutter who called himself a fan.

'Oh, Yoko Ono,' the guide said, and pointed at the building.

'Oh, Yoko Ono,' they echoed with broad smiles and much nodding.

Matt smiled to himself. It was said that she still lived there, and the Japanese clearly excited by this, clicked their cameras some more.

Matt pushed his hands deep into his pockets. Life after John goes on. One of the biggest pop icons of our times dies and life continues, crap bands do crap cover versions of his songs and world-weary journalists on little-known rock magazines write uninspired pieces about the impact he had on other people's lives and music, but nothing much else is changed. The songs plummet out of the charts to make way for the next equally unoriginal tune, the articles line waste-paper bins, and the people that really knew and loved John Lennon carry on as best they can.

He crossed the street, ambling between the cars as they sped along Central Park West. Life after Josie would go on too. After all, she wasn't even dead, just misplaced. And there would be other Josies. Blonde ones, brunette ones, stroppy ones, nice ones. Ones who might even like him back. And he might be less careless about losing them. Perhaps they might not all be as cutely packaged, but there would be other women in his life and, given time and a few self-help books, he might not make such a cock-up of things as he had with Holly.

He strolled into Central Park, which spread enticingly before him like a beautiful green carpet in the midst of a cluttered junk shop. Sunday morning in the park. The dog-walkers were out, and the cyclists and the rollerbladers, all making use of this small green space that wasn't choked with carbon monoxide. The frost was still hard and he could see his breath as he walked. He was in Strawberry Fields, the small hillside garden planted in John's memory. It was a place of quiet solitude in a city where that precious commodity was hard to find. Matt stopped to clear his mind.

There were red-nosed couples wrapped up against the cold, walking hand in hand, laughing, giggling, oblivious to the world. It was sickening. Why was it that everyone else was in happy lovey-dovey coupledom when you weren't? Why was it that some people could do the couple thing more easily than others? How did some people slip seamlessly from one relationship to another, flowing into someone else's life without sharp edges and pointy corners to negotiate. Why did some people manage to fit their relationships together like a neat little jigsaw, making fine adjustments until they had a flat, smooth, pretty picture, while others (e.g. him) clicked continuously round each other like an unfathomable Rubik's Cube until they either lost interest or gave up, defeated and exhausted by the effort involved. And why were some people who thought they might just have found a person to make a jigsaw with stupid enough to lose the address of the fucking restaurant they were supposed to meet them in? It was too cruel to contemplate, and Matt headed for the nearest unoccupied bench and sat down, alone, to do just that.

Josie found the bike rental garage easily enough, and armed with a typically American paranoid list of dos and don'ts, she headed off to Central Park with a cronky bike, the obligatory cycle helmet that she wouldn't be seen dead in slung over her handlebars, the wind in her hair and no desire to remember exactly how long it had been since she was last on a bike.

Risking life and limb to cross Columbus Circle, she entered the park, wobbling through a deadly mixture of lack of practice and alcohol-locked muscles. Entering the park was like going into a different world. The rush of traffic noise retreated, to be replaced by the sound of children laughing, the dull clonk of leather ball against baseball bat and the airy swoosh of rollerblades. The crush of buildings peeped longingly over the tips of the bare trees, crowding round the outside to get a better and, therefore, higher-value view of the slender rectangle of prized greenery. The chill air rushing past her was blowing the cobwebs away and clearing her head. Grief, what had happened yesterday was awful. First all the business with Martha and Glen doing their vanishing act, and then Damien turning up out of the blue – it was more like a Magic Circle convention than a wedding.

She felt terrible about Damien, now that there was some space between him and her anger. Supposing he was trying in Damien's own parti- cularly showy way to be sincere. Supposing the diamond ring had been a ferociously expen- sive love token and not some cheap stunt. Maybe she shouldn't have behaved so badly. Damien might have been a lying, cheating, philandering pig, but he wasn't all bad.

Her legs were finding a long-forgotten rhythm and she pushed on into the park, determined to revitalise her battered constitution even though she felt like death and not even death warmed up. She passed the lazy tourists in brightly painted carriages being plodded round the park by bored horses who had done their route a thousand times before. The ice rink was crowded with families swathed in woollen scarves and mittens, tottering children trusting that their equally tottering parents would somehow get them round the slippery surface without harm. Josie felt a sudden pang of loneliness. Being alone and self-sufficient was all well and good, but wasn't one of the major joys of life sharing all these little pleasures with someone else? Somehow she was going to have to let the barriers down again, otherwise no one would ever get inside her protective shell to find the real Josie hiding inside. Wasn't it better to love openly and freely and take a chance on getting hurt than never to risk those emotions again and deny herself so much? She looked at the trees around her. After the harsh bareness of winter, there was the fresh start of spring, the opening, the blossoming, the renewing. It was nature's order; all you had to do was accept it. Oh, but it was so much easier said than done!

Pushing her thoughts to one side, Josie pedalled on into the park, the exercise pumping the blood round her body, warming her from the inside and making her feel glad that she'd come. Central Park might be an oasis of relative calm in this striving city, but New Yorkers still managed to make every inch of its scrubby grass and expos-ed bedrock alive with activity. She cycled down The Mall, a straight avenue guarded by American elm trees and lined with statues of great literary figures, and then wheeled left and along the borders of Sheep Meadow, a place where anything noisier than picnicking was banned.

Her face was glowing now, her veins zinging with pulsating energy and her lungs burning with their unaccustomed exertion. Normally Sunday morning was a lie-in with tea, toast, the *Mail on Sunday* and The Cat Formerly Known As Prince – but no more! She was going to get up and cycle every Sunday morning from now on. Well, *nearly* every Sunday.

Josie slowed down, giving her legs some respite. There was a small hillside garden in front of her, and she stopped by the low railings, thinking she might rest for a few minutes before exploring the rest of the park. She jumped off the bike and, pulling off the restraining scrunchie, shook her hair loose, letting it fall round her shoulders. She leaned the bike against the railings and set off up the slight incline, hoping that her rented trans-port would still be waiting for her when she got back.

The plants were sparse in their winter garb, spreading out their white-tipped fingers to best effect. A sparkle of frost glittered on the breeze, giving the place a hint of magic. The brave winter sun was starting to warm her frozen cheeks. Josie let out a sigh and felt some of the tension leave her body. It was a good place to be. It was good to be alive. It was good to be young, fit and healthy. It was good to abuse your body on occasions to remind yourself to appreciate it more.

At the top of the hill there was a huge grey and white plaque set into the floor, marked in a star design with the word IMAGINE in the middle. There was an air of peace and tranquillity to the space and now she knew why. Josie hugged her arms to her and glanced around. There was no one else in sight except a scruffy, unshaven man sitting alone on a bench opposite her. His head was bowed down, almost resting on his chest, and he looked lost in thought. She moved closer to the plaque and the man looked up.

'Josie?' he said.

Josie peered closer, but she couldn't believe her eyes. 'Matt?'

Standing up, he came hesitantly towards her. 'Josie.'

Her nose was running with the cold and now her eyes started to prickle with hot tears and a laugh started in her throat. 'Matt!'

He stood in front of her, amazed. 'I can't believe it's you!'

They stared at each other, neither of them moving.

Matt shook his head 'I have been all over this godforsaken city searching for you!'

'You have?'

'I thought I'd lost you!'

Josie sniffed her tears away. 'I thought you'd stood me up.'

'You would not believe the things I have done to find you.' He laughed in disbelief. 'I have been to two Marthas' weddings, I have been used as a punch-bag by an unbelievably bad boy band and your husband—'

'Ex-husband,' she corrected.

Matt gave a relieved laugh. 'You don't know how pleased I am to hear you say that.'

'You've gone through all this looking for me?' Josie asked.

'And you would not believe what else . . .' He tailed off. 'And you're here.'

'Yes,' Josie said.

He came and put his arms round her, sweeping her from the ground and lifting her into the air, twirling her round.

'I thought you didn't care,' Josie gasped.

Lowering her back to the ground, he took her face in his hands. 'Of course I care! I have been to hell and back, *and* to Long Island, trying to put this right.'

Matt pulled Josie to his chest, crushing her in the folds of his tatty rock-journalist coat. 'I don't want to lose you again. Not ever.' He bit his lip. 'I can't believe I'm going to say this,' he tutted.

'You might want to shout or kick me in the shins or do something unpleasant to my testicles . . .' He took a deep breath. 'I love you!'

Josie didn't know whether to laugh or cry. 'I love you too.'

They hugged each other tightly in an unspoken promise to have and to hold from this day forward. For better, for worse, for richer, for poorer, in sickness and in health.

In their joy they failed to notice the small, insignificant duck who waddled serenely into Strawberry Fields behind them. With a little straining and a great sense of relief, he managed to rid himself of something that had been upsetting his tummy for hours. Then, with a happy quack, Donald set off to find a convenient pond, leaving in his wake a rather mucky and rather large diamond ring.

Matt held Josie away from him and with a damp-eyed smile said: 'Imagine meeting you here.'

Josie laughed through her tears and ran her fingers over Matt's cheek. 'Imagine,' she said.

And somewhere, somehow, in the skies above Central Park, John Lennon started to sing . . .